# THEY CALL ME ANGEL

OTHER BOOKS BY
ALEXIA MUELLE-RUSHBROOK

**THE MINORITY RULE**

THE MINORITY RULE:
**BEYOND THE FENCE**

THE MINORITY RULE:
**INTO THE FOG**

# THEY CALL ME ANGEL

ALEXIA MUELLE-RUSHBROOK

This is a work of fiction. Names, characters, places, and incidents either are the product of the author's imagination or are used fictitiously. Any resemblance to actual persons, living or dead, events, or localities is entirely coincidental.

Copyright © 2023 by Alexia Muelle-Rushbrook

Alexia Muelle-Rushbrook asserts the right under the Copyright, Designs and Patents Act 1988 to be identified as the author of this work.

All rights reserved. No part of this book may be sold, transmitted, published, stored, resold, adapted, or translated in any form or by any means, without the prior written permission of the copyright owner except for the use of quotations in a book review. For more information, address: alexia.muelle.rushbrook@gmail.com

First paperback edition 2023

Book design by Richell B

978-1-7392662-4-0 paperback
978-1-7392662-5-7 ebook
978-17392662-6-4 hardcover

www.alexiamuellerushbrook.co.uk

*They Call Me Angel* contains incidences referring to and dealing with domestic abuse, murder, drugs, death, miscarriage, and depression. Ultimately, the author hopes to shine light through the darkness, but readers who might be affected by these themes may wish to reconsider reading this novel.

*For all angels, may you shine.*

# 1

My death was no surprise to me. I'd thought about it a lot in the days and months, maybe even years, before it happened. One way or another, I knew Hayden would be the death of me. I was just too afraid and too stupid to do anything about it. Having buckled myself onto the ride, come rain or sunshine, loose bolts or not, I wasn't getting off until death us do part. My father grimaced the day I made that vow for all to hear. There was no pride, no beaming adoration for the adult he had nurtured from a babe. I'd defied all logic and married my boyfriend on a childish, naive whim that I, through marriage, through claiming him once and for all, could make him into a decent, loyal, loving person.

I couldn't. I didn't. I died.

Except I didn't die, not fully anyway. Unless this is what is 'next' for us all? I hope not. I watch the living. I watch life. But I am nothing. Nothing in life, now nothing in death. Hayden would laugh if he knew. He laughed when I died. As I laid in a heap against a tree—dazed and silently weeping, trying to piece together what had just happened, not yet realising I was neither lost nor found—he looked over the cliff edge, smiling, chuckling, without an ounce of remorse. Not in public of course. The moment he called 999 and the paramedics arrived, from my muted, invisible front row seat, I witnessed his charade of woe as he flawlessly played the distressed, grieving husband. Desperately, I tried to communicate with someone, anyone; however, no doctor assessed me for injuries or offered me reassurance, no policeman listened to my screams to arrest the man they sought to comfort—in fact, no one acknowledged my presence at all.

As they searched extensively for me, I called and pleaded like a child vying for attention at a grown-up's party, but my hope that this was some elaborate joke diminished with every passing second, and slowly my new reality sunk in.

Days later, cold irony hit me when I heard Hayden lament the loss of his 'childhood sweetheart' and 'beautiful soul mate' to the local reporter. In life I was 'a shadow of my former beauty,' 'an embarrassment trying to flirt with his friends,' 'cheating on him with customers,' 'disrespecting our vows,' 'angry,' 'grumpy,' 'miserable.' You name it, I was accused of it, but I rolled with the punches—literally.

And why? Why? Good question. In my solitary afterlife, I still question my choices. A life wasted. Wasted in the belief I could help, that we loved each other and that was enough. He didn't mean what he said. I could take it. I had to take it.

Maybe he was right, it was all my fault…and so I had to fix it.

Now I think you cannot fix that which is fundamentally not right. You cannot polish a turd and Hayden is the biggest shit going. He got away with murder. *My* murder. And now I live in between Earth and Heaven—the latter I cannot see, I just hope for, the former I see and wish to either die for real or live and make a change.

But you cannot make a change when no one sees nor hears you. So instead, I watch this little town called Adtoft bustle all around me—observing the rhythm of time via the waves as they crash against the shore, marking the transition of day to night, summer to winter, and round again. Tourists come and go, squealing on the amusement rides, threading their pennies into the slot machines, licking ice cream, and losing their chips to the gulls that I am now convinced are significantly more intelligent than those they steal from.

As I came to terms with my status I wondered if I could haunt people. Hayden was obviously my first target and I spent longer than healthy—if the dead have such a scale?—following him around, trying my hardest to throw objects large and small at him. I tried screaming in his ears and spitting in his face, calling him every rude, foul, or defamatory word I could think of. He heard nothing, not even a whisper in the breeze. My eyes are open, my time is finally my own, yet I have zero to show for it. If I am here to even the score before I depart, I fail to see how.

The only amusement I have is Hayden doesn't have my money. He clearly thought he would. His anger when he realised he doesn't was one of the few pleasures I have felt in life or death. He was so red I thought he was going to attack the solicitor, but sadly he is brighter than that. Hayden is a clever bully—not so clever he doesn't eat his fish and chips in front of angry seagulls, but intelligent enough to know how to play his part, be the charmer that everyone except me, and maybe my dad, thinks he is.

When Gran died, Dad begged me to keep my inheritance a secret and place it in an account far away from Hayden's reach. Dad was so solemn I agreed and set it up to sit unspent, unseen, accumulating interest. Part of me thought it was my 'get away' fund, but I never had the courage to get away. My wages went directly into our joint account which Hayden would immediately drain into his own, leaving me my allowance—which was to cover the household bills and my 'attempt at beautification.'

A few weeks before my death, Hayden came home late, half-drunk, and smelling of cheap perfume. Again. The raging pit of disgust in my stomach had erupted out of my mouth and I screamed that I was leaving, had my own money (though thankfully, not how much), and wouldn't take his crap anymore. That was my window of escape, my last chance—I know that now. Yet my resolve was weak, my self-esteem non-existent, and I crumbled in floods of pathetic, insecure tears at his feet the second Hayden turned on the charm.

Later, I was still beaten for my half confession of financial stability and then beaten again when I refused to give details, but he was careful to leave my face unmarked and my chain to him intact enough so he felt in control and free from any suspicion.

As my spouse, Hayden obviously thought that upon my death he would automatically receive my hidden treasure chest. His arrogance didn't allow him to consider an alternative scenario before he acted. However, to maintain secrecy, I used Dad's address and made him joint account holder, meaning he inherited it all—and made damn sure my husband saw none of it.

My one 'fuck you' to my murderer.

With no way of causing further harm or insult, tired of following the man I once loved, but now loath, seeing him as nothing more than a reminder of my own stupidity, I finally stopped watching him and his pathetic life of drink, lust, and abuse masked by charm and selfish enthusiasm.

People watching, taking in snippets of different daily lives as they strut around town, has proved diverting. I have a few regulars, ones I observe like favourite characters in a weekday evening soap opera. The majority laugh and chatter about people they know and love, yet there are still plenty who moan and berate those they know but wish they didn't. Listening to phone calls has become a habit. I get up close so I can hear the voice on the other end and amuse myself by imagining what they look like, what scenes and scenery they can see. This is my only way to travel, for in my purgatory I seem to be stuck in this town, my childhood town, like in death some comedian gave me a new umbilical cord.

No fresh start for me. *Thanks.*

So, I follow my characters, waiting for them to walk the promenade and give me an idea of what joys and sorrows befell them since the last time they visited the seafront. I could follow them around town—I do occasionally if the weather is poor and the walkers are few, but I find peace in the rumbling waters and don't like to leave them for long.

During my darkest time, I tried finding eternal peace in the rolling waves, but even that option is taken from me. You cannot drown that which does not breathe. The current simply scoops me up and throws me back onto the sandy shore. Sometimes I do it to feel wanted—just to prove that I am here by some design, not some freakish accident. I choose not to see it as a blip or bug in eternity's system.

I need the glitch to be on purpose—to *have* purpose.

*If only I knew what it is!*

I am certainly open to suggestions.

# 2

After I died, I moved back in with my dad. He doesn't know it obviously, but despite the time lapse since we lived together, he has left my old room largely untouched, so it felt like the only place worth calling home. Another irony. For in life, this was no more home than Hayden's thanks to my stepmother. Sally wasn't cruel as such—ignorant, indifferent, disinterested, certainly, but not actively cruel. However, it was enough to see me look for an alternative place to live as soon as I could, and Dad, wanting to keep his wife happy, let me go, telling himself it 'was what teenagers do and all would be well.' I think he realised his major error when he met Hayden, but then it was too late, my heart was set, and reason went flying like a leaf in a gale.

I wish Dad were happy, but he doesn't seem to be, not at home anyway. Sometimes, I go to work with him and marvel at the change in his face, at the jokes he tells, and the stories he listens to as he cares for people with disabilities and the elderly in their own homes. It is obvious that they enjoy his company as much as he does theirs, yet when he leaves a solemn cover seizes his face that nothing at home can shake.

Despite our differences, I always loved my dad, and I knew he loved me.

Love. Not loved.

I still love, and so does he. Although I rarely hear him speak of me, I know because he planted a magnolia tree in the back garden with an engraved plaque in my memory. Sometimes I see him staring at it and want to cry for the relationship we could have rescued, had time allowed.

Dad organised a family gathering-cum-funeral after my murder. A few school friends came out of past loyalty, but as Hayden had crushed all friendships that were not directly from his circle, I had few people to genuinely mourn me. Aunts and uncles consoled my dad and told him that they were sure my mum and I were together in heaven, looking down on him and smiling peacefully.

If only.

Mum had a head start and died with multiple witnesses when I was eight after a lengthy and cruel battle with cancer. As I see no other 'invisibles' (I am aware of the oxymoron in that statement), I choose to believe she is in eternal peace as expected. Dad still visits her grave and lays flowers once a month for her and my gran—respecting the dead, continuing to love them as he did in life.

Besides the magnolia tree, I don't have a grave or memorial anywhere because I am yet to be formerly declared dead. Everyone refers to me that way, but officially I am listed as missing and until seven years pass or they find my body I cannot officially be upgraded to deceased.

Gone, largely forgotten, but not dead.

The police dredged the seabed below the cliffs I supposedly met my maker from. They also posted my picture all around town and on the TV, appealing for information whilst warning dog walkers they might find me on the beach. However, my bloated corpse has never turned up and three years later I am still invisible.

I couldn't tell you if my body has substance anywhere or to anyone but me. All I know is if I pinch myself, I feel it. If I stub my toe on the corner of the bed, like I did for the hundredth time this morning, I feel it, but I do not feel pain, not really. It is more the idea of pain, a phantom ideal, a memory of what was, not actual physical pain.

I do not bruise, I do not get ill, I do not bleed.

I just am.

Dad ate semi burnt toast this morning—grumbling he took it out too late and he should replace the toaster—to which Sally just laughed. Ignoring her, Dad left for work with little more than a 'see you later,' and Sally waited all of thirty seconds before she pulled out her phone and started texting.

Sally starts work an hour later than Dad and I don't normally hang around to see her leave. Today I waited because I now know she is having an affair with Rob, a decorator who lives three doors down. I had my suspicions she was cheating but hadn't wanted to waste my day watching her—and truthfully, didn't want to verify her infidelity if I could do nothing about it.

My clarification came yesterday after a particularly wet, and non-eventful day observing people on the pier. In search of a plate of phantom chips, I walked into the local pub, *The Boatman,* only to be put off my food. Wrapped around Rob—who seemed to have fallen into a paint palate and decided to call it fashion—Sally could easily have been described as mutton dressed as lamb. Together they looked akin to something the Divine Comedy would sing about. I felt sick, but on reflection, I wish she would leave my dad for Rob. I don't think it would break his heart; I think it would be a relief. However, I don't think Dad is brave enough to rip off the band-aid himself—and Sally is too selfish to make the call.

They don't fight, not really, not like Hayden and I used to. They simmer and pout, grumble and grunt, but mostly they just co-exist in silence, in routine that once had some affection, some spark of romance and interest. Maybe more truthfully, of convenience. He was grieving and wanted comfort, she was recently divorced and wanted stability. What was convenient then, is barely tolerable now. Officially dead or not, Dad could spend my inheritance, but to my knowledge, he hasn't touched it. I haven't even heard him mention it to Sally, but I wonder if she is waiting around for payday to materialise. Probably. After all, money seems to be the root of most evils. Power and money—neither of which I have ever had much luck with.

Disillusioned with people and not wanting to see the particulars of Sally and Rob's morning 'meeting,' I told myself I didn't want to people watch today, yet I find myself sitting on the edge of the pier anyway, wiggling my legs as I stare out to sea.

A mother and child walk past me, giggling into the warm summer breeze, and I am relieved that someone is happy. The fact that the child skips through me is neither here nor there. It is not the first time, nor I daresay, will it be the last. Almost daily someone walks through me, into me, or even occasionally, sits on me.

I have seen movies which depict the dead and show the living feeling chills as they are touched by the spirits of those not quite gone. That doesn't happen to me. No one shudders or sighs at my presence. No one says someone walked over their grave, or that Jack Frost touched their cheek with an icy finger. All pass me carefree. The advantage is that I, as a now serial observer, get to watch unabashed and can listen without censorship.

It is not only my stepmother who cheats on her husband, I see and hear all kinds of intrigues. If I were a detective, my position would be pure gold, but it is not only the negative I witness. I have observed love stories, promotions, friendships, and joy. The broad spectrum of humanity flows through this town as much as the water in the sea. I yearn to join it. To appreciate it. Not to be the cameraman of my own silent movie. I am Laurel and Hardy, only without the humour, desperately waiting for the director to call 'cut!'

A group of teenagers are hanging out nearby. They are regulars, especially when the weather is nice like it is today. The pier is full of extra amusements for the holidays and the boys are trying to impress a group of four girls who are sitting near the Big Wheel.

Thanks to Hayden, I hate that bloody thing. Pretending to want to enjoy a romantic ride, he once took me on there, yet the moment our carriage was at the top, Hayden, along with his friends in the next seat, soon revealed this was a premeditated adventure as sweets and stones were pelted back and forth with forceful delight. They were nothing if not prepared. The enthusiasm with which Hayden threw swung our seat horribly, and before long I thought he was going to fall out of the stupid thing and take me with him.

In hindsight, Hayden never did display much interest in preserving my life nor limbs—though half crashing the car into rock and propelling me into a tree, was a new level of abhorrence, even for him. Past grievances aside, I can see history repeats itself as the group of teenage boys are now screaming and shouting at each other as they bounce around on the Big Wheel, much to the onlooking girls delight below.

Only this time, seconds before the ride is frozen by the angry owner, a boy does fall. Shouts of glee turn to horror, and red blushes turn to white despair. Running to the fallen boy, I stride through the crowd, and kneel by his side. I don't know why I do it. Maybe I just want another front row seat to misery, maybe a part of me wants to help, even if I know I physically can't.

All around us voices rage, calls for an ambulance are repeated, and his friends cry out from the wheel above, pleading for safe release and their friend to be okay. Time seems to slow, even though I don't think it is long before a more coherent adult arrives and tries to assess the damage.

The boy is barely conscious, and his colour is dangerously pale. The sound of sirens approaches, and I sigh with relief. Without realising what I am doing, I take his shaking hand, squeeze it, and tell him to hold on, help is coming. It has been months, maybe years, since I tried talking to anyone, so I have no idea why I do it now, but suddenly the boy opens his eyes and looks into mine. He pulls a weak smile as his eyes focus, then almost beams, as though he is feeling or seeing something of real serenity. My body quakes as I return his smile, repeating my earlier ideal that he will be all right, and he nods before passing out.

Stumbling, I sit backwards as the paramedics arrive, but do not leave his side. He saw me. I am sure he saw me. Heard me even. As the paramedics prepare him for a stretcher, I listen to their desire for a speedy arrival at A&E, and when they carry him away, I follow.

\* \* \*

Adi, as I soon learn is his name, has test upon test plus emergency surgery for internal bleeding. When his parents arrive in floods of tears I try to comfort them, yet they do not hear me—none of them hear me.

All night I silently wait by his side, but Adi remains dormant until the following afternoon. The lines on his heart monitor are so etched into my retinas that I am surprised I am capable of seeing the pattern change, but my heart skips with his as consciousness returns to him. Taking his hand, I squeeze—gently at first, then a little harder, waiting for recognition to grasp us once again.

Holding my phantom breath, I tell myself I will breathe again when Adi sees me. But he doesn't, he looks through me, like everyone else looks through me. His hand, though in mine, is not. The glitch and glimmer of what I feel and others experience, much like my so-called ability to eat, once again leaves me wanting. I am alone. My brief connection to the living, again lost.

I wail.

I disturb no one but myself, but I wail.

Having only popped out to speak to the doctor, Adi's parents rush to his side, calling out with relief and love at the sight of their conscious son. The father, happily oblivious to my presence, sits on me. Standing to leave, I stop in the doorway to take one last look at Adi, hoping he will notice me.

He doesn't.

That brief moment has rattled my tender acceptance of my existence. So much so, I walk straight to the sea and keep walking—hoping the waves will at last take me out, not in.

They don't.

Instead, they roll me onto the shore, screaming and spluttering like a violent, tantruming toddler.

Finally, out of tears, I lay motionlessly facing the sky, watching the seagulls as they circle above. Feeling hollow, I focus on their dance, waiting for slumber to find me if death will not.

Eventually I drift off—but not until long after the tide has turned.

# 3

Reluctantly, I dragged myself off the sand this morning after three joggers, four dogs, seven seagulls, a stray plastic bag, and a persistent piece of seaweed finally convinced me I should move.

The weather isn't bad, but I cannot really be bothered to walk—even if walking is generally my only option. Two days ago, I was so overwhelmed by the feeling of connection that I perched myself in the ambulance with Adi without considering whether I could. It wasn't until this morning that I realised my oversight and appreciated that I was able to be driven by someone other than my dad for the first time in three years.

Hoping I might have retained one new ability at least, I walked into the car park, spotted someone who was about to leave, and tried getting into their car. After failing to even grasp the handle of a dozen such cars, I have concluded my completely hollow norm has returned.

I am disappointed, but not surprised. On a typical day, my phantom status is pretty limiting and the most I can do is open doors, windows, and cupboards. I cannot walk through walls—although I can walk through traffic.

Yes, I have tried both.

Cars, buses, trains—none stop me or for me. I don't like the sensation of being passed through though, so, even if I don't need to, I still stop for moving vehicles.

To be refused transport by all, in any realm, is pretty annoying. I cannot sit in or on them—not even on a bloody bicycle. Dad's car is the only real exception, but even then only if he is driving locally—otherwise I am left behind and must walk everywhere. I will not get fat in my death. Ironically, the kiddy helicopter on the pier will take me for a ride. I suppose it goes nowhere, so it doesn't count. The teacup ride, however, will not.

Go figure. I don't make the rules.

I'm sitting on the bright orange, smiling helicopter now. I don't think it is doing anything for my mental status, nor, unfortunately, is the bag of sugary doughnuts I took from one of the promenade stands. Before I drive myself mad, I need a plan for the day. Going to work with Dad would have been a good idea—perhaps I can catch up with him now. I have learnt the addresses of most of his clients and one is close by—thankfully, otherwise I'll still be walking to the first person when he clocks off.

Hopping off the helicopter, I pass two teenage girls as they giggle whilst munching on their newly purchased candyfloss and turn away from the sea front. In the distance I can hear the call from the ever-increasing number of amusement rides and confectionary stalls—although the Big Wheel remains eerily silent as the owner has yet to resume using it. Instead of walking into the heart of town, I head left to a quiet little cul-de-sac that's close to everything, but somehow hidden from the hustle and bustle of shoppers and tourists. Adtoft has a few of these treasure troves. It has its poorer side, like any town, but it is certainly not short of its expensive, picturesque houses—nor its matching quaint and quirky inhabitants.

One such lady lives in this cul-de-sac—in fact, she always has. "My lungs breathed sea-air the moment I was born, and shall breathe nothin' else till I die," she told my dad last week when he tenderly suggested she needed more care than he was able to give. Dad wasn't suggesting moving town, just house, but to Mrs Crook a move to anywhere is a move too far. Dad has been caring for her for as long as I can remember—although at times I don't think he charged because I stayed with her during Mum's numerous hospital appointments as well as in the school holidays while he worked.

I didn't mind, her cottage is beautiful, and her pantry proved to be the perfect setting for my childish imagination to flourish. Somehow that one room has more shelves and cupboards than the nearest corner shop, and Mrs Crook has an amazing selection of jars, tins, and pots, all filled with goodies that I commandeered each visit. I cannot have been more than five or six when I found her collection of old coins from around the world. Mr Crook, who was then alive, but all too often absent on a boat, collected coins on his travels. Some were new, some extremely old, but I was allowed to play with them all—and I did, simultaneously turning them into currency that Mrs Crook needed in order to claim anything from the pantry. This was a win-win situation for me. I got to play shopkeeper, banker, and chief bakery assistant all in one day.

After Mum died and I started high school, babysitting was neither necessary nor possible due to Mrs Crook's ill health. She was, however, by then regarded as family, so I still visited on weekends, but as Sally never truly appreciated Dad 'taking his work home with him' as she called it and Hayden had no time for 'old ladies,' my visits declined rapidly. In my death I have come to lament this. I loved my time with Mrs Crook and am ashamed I let Hayden persuade me I didn't need to visit her more—especially after her husband died, just a year before I did.

Dad is right, an independent, but fulltime care home would be better for her; however, she has invisible, permanent roots growing into the walls of her cottage and only death will see her seek refuge anywhere but here. Dad knows this too; I just think he needed to voice his concern for his friend. I could see from her grin and his light sigh that they understood each other.

My steps feel lighter as I think of their friendship and turn the corner with a smile on my face. However, all lightness evaporates the moment I look at the white cottage and see an ambulance outside—it's blue light silently twirling as two people dressed in green walk inside.

Running to the cottage, I enter through the front door and instantly hear voices coming from the living room—which is adorned like the 1950's, adding to its old-fashioned charm. A man and woman are crouched on the floor by Mrs Crook's body while Dad gently strokes her hand.

"Mrs Crook?" says the male paramedic. "Mrs Crook—Gladys—can you hear me?" I never called her by her first name. To me it was like calling Grandma by anything other than 'grandma'—you just don't do it. Dad calls her Gladys, the only exception used to be when he spoke to me about her, then he would revert to the unspoken Mrs (X), Mum, Grandma title rule that adults seem to have with their children.

"How long has she been unresponsive?" the female paramedic sorrowfully asks my dad.

"She wasn't conscious when I arrived—I called you straight away—but that was…erm, thirty minutes ago?" As a home carer Dad has called countless ambulances over the years and has inevitably lost some clients. I know he feels for them all, yet Dad is usually so cool in an emergency—I have never seen him this rattled.

Turning my attention to Mrs Crook, despite being laid out on the floor, I think she seems peaceful—pale, but peaceful. Her breathing is a little heavy, but the paramedic reaches into his bag and places an oxygen mask on her as his colleague goes to collect the stretcher.

Kneeling by her side, I take her lukewarm hand and startle as she squeezes it and looks me straight in the eyes. My alarm turns to gentle, rhythmic serenity as we breathe in unison, smiling at one another.

"Ah, my beautiful angel," says Mrs Crook, in a sweet whisper as the hairs stand up on the back of my neck. "I should have known you'd guide me to safe harbour, thank you." With that she closes her eyes and stops breathing.

The warmth leaves her hand as a gentle breeze tickles my ear and disappears into the realm that is closed to me. I feel peace for Mrs Crook. Peace for the end of a life of quiet happiness and contented love—yet I also feel envious.

Envious, not only for being unable to say the same about my life, but also because I, just for a second, felt the joy and tenderness that enveloped that breeze. I would love to follow her into it. Why do I not have that welcome from either side of life?

Tears flow down my cheeks and I ignore the fact the paramedics are now trampling over me as they and Dad realise their efforts are in vain. The man, handsome and probably in his early thirties, looks focused as he attempts CPR. I want to tell him it is of no use, but the words will not form in my mouth—not that it matters, he will not hear me anyway.

Eventually the woman calls a time of death and both men just nod sadly. The officialness seems odd—odd as in its finality, but also odd because I want to correct their paperwork and tell them she died minutes earlier.

I don't know if they heard Mrs Crook's final words. If they did, they didn't react—or I didn't notice. Perhaps the words were just for me, maybe they were just *with me*—a brief, but poignant moment together in between times.

Maybe that is all I am now: the welcome mat for weary souls. But Adi didn't die…so maybe I unwittingly admit or deny entry to 'next'? Did I kill Mrs Crook by not trying to stop her? Oh, shit, no, I cannot cope with that possibility. I had no choice: I can do nothing. And she sounded…I don't know, happy—*grateful* even—to see me. Not reproachful or afraid. Certainly not murdered.

Not like me.

# 4

I stayed in the cottage until they zipped Mrs Crook into a body bag and then left. With no interest in watching jovial children, listening to trivial family dramas, or even witnessing the local wildlife outwit tourists, I have walked to the quietest end of the beach. It is the furthest southern point from town before the sand gives way to the largest cliff edge in Adtoft. I rarely come here because it is painfully close to the point Hayden attempted to launch me from—in fact if I carry on and go into the water, I will be directly below the rock that bears the scars of our crash.

The police should have used their brains a little more that day. At the very least, they could have questioned Hayden on his skill set—and examined the bloody car better. Someone who works so extensively with cars in a garage and breakers yard—who fixes and reports on insurance claims for motoring companies—is going to have a particular knowledge of where, how, and how fast to take out a car without killing himself. Not to mention that Hayden and his mates love the local racetrack and regularly take old cars and trash them if there is no monetary value in fixing them. In hindsight he was literally practicing 'how to remove your wife from a speeding car without dying' months in advance of doing it.

Hoping the police were suspicious, I went to the station and read their report. To say I was disappointed is an understatement: 'An unfortunate combination of inclement weather and a mechanical failure on a cliff turning resulted in the vehicle impacting rock and the propulsion of the passenger into the ocean.'

It's not raining now, but in my mind, it will always be raining on top of that cliff. The road will always be a sandy, slippery rink of terror, and the car, although long-ago crushed and cubed, will forever be a torture scene of domestic abuse. There was no angel as Mrs Crook called me. I circle around the question: 'Why not?' For three years I have asked the question, but today, more than ever I can focus on very little else.

Apparently, I am not the only one seeking a solitary walk along the shore as a dog walker suddenly appears on the path from the cliffs above. You'd never walk down the front or sides of the main cliff but winding through a few small trees at the back of the beach there is a path where people and canines alike can safely wander. If you turn right, it will take you away from the sheer cliff face, through the edge of the grassy dunes and ascends into a pretty wooded area which has always been popular with walkers. There is a secluded road—ironically called 'Lovers Lane'—which leads to a beautiful lookout point and picnic site. Whilst pretending the forecast was a surprise to him, declaring it romantic, Lovers Lane is where Hayden picked our final fight.

Ugh.

I am too trapped by memories.

Seeking a distraction, I try to focus on the dog. It is big, brown, hairy, and gives a loud, exuberant bark as his owner throws a ball across the sand. Suddenly a small white and tan terrier comes flying down the path (presumably encouraged by his companion's call) and I cannot help chuckling as it throws itself in the face of the big dog, stealing the ball in one swoop.

As the dog walker makes his way towards town, he pauses, noticing an artist near the shoreline. She is almost always somewhere around the beach. During the peak holiday season, in the hope of attracting tourists, she is more frequently on or near the pier. Sometimes she quietly paints with a few completed pieces for sale surrounding her, but mostly she displays a sign offering portraits. It is amazing what she can do in a very short period of time, but today she seems to be in no rush as she delicately strokes the canvas with colour, capturing the horizon in paint. Wandering over to her, I sit down, silently absorbing the sound of rolling waves and brush strokes. It feels a little rude sharing her tranquillity, but suddenly I do not want to be alone—and besides, it's not like she knows I am here.

Long after the dogs have probably reached home and their owner has given them tea, the artist's phone bleeps. She startles, grasps her mobile, groans, and packs up her things in a matter of minutes. As we walk towards civilisation in silent, semi-unaware companionship, I feel a pang—a longing—to walk home to someone. To have someone call me, to call *to* me, to want *me*. I thought I had achieved a sort of acceptance regarding my existence—I have never not mourned or questioned what the point is, but I was resigned to being unseen. Having two people see me, however fleetingly, has stirred and renewed pain.

When I get home, I expect to find Dad in front of the TV. Normally if one of his clients' dies or is particularly poorly, he puts on an action film. It is never a new one—it has to be one he knows he loves, as though he is visiting an old friend who will not let him down with an inconsistent plot, poor acting, or dubious prop continuity. But he is not in the living room, nor is he anywhere in the house. Sally is watching some reality TV programme with half naked girls bouncing their fake breasts in their would-be partners faces in the hope of a cash prize—so maybe it is no surprise Dad isn't with her, but I cannot imagine he has walked to the pub tonight either. Tired, I am about to give up my search and go to bed when the neighbour's cat triggers our security light in the garden. Suddenly the green leaves of my magnolia tree hold colour and a shadowed figure by her trunk becomes apparent.

"What are you doing?" shouts Sally out of the window. I didn't notice her go to the fridge, but apparently the light caught her attention too. Sighing, Sally walks outside, placing a hand on my dad's shoulder as she reaches him. "I know it's sad she died, but she was old, and you'll get a new client."

Wow, Sally really missed her calling as a therapist.

"Right," says Dad.

"You know what I mean—don't roll your eyes at me. It ain't that dark, I can see you."

"Gladys was like fami—"

"I know that. I'm just sayin' d—"

"Okay," says Dad, getting up. "It's been a long day. Good night."

They walk indoors in stale silence. As soon as Dad has shut the bathroom door, Sally starts texting Rob—quietly chuckling as they comment on the programme they are obviously watching together, just a few hundred feet apart.

Something needs to change here. I just wish I knew how.

# 5

Sally was right, Dad did quickly get a new client. I'd be surprised if he were remotely concerned about that though because I've often heard him lamenting the lack of care staff, and—when she is in a more caring mood—Sally has been known to moan at him for trying to take on too much.

The new lady, Sophia, is paralysed from the waist down and lives with Flossy, the old guy who runs the candyfloss stall on the pier. I doubt that is his real name, I'm not even sure if he is anyone's actual uncle, but when I was little he was called 'Uncle Flossy' by all the kids at school and so he is still called that now.

Although fit for his age, Flossy is over eighty years old and not capable of lifting his forty-year-old granddaughter. Sophia is as independent as she can be, but a car accident five years ago left her in need of assistance, and four years ago her husband left her with Flossy for the day while he 'went to an important meeting'—and never came back.

I'd like to say I can't imagine someone being such an arsehole, but, sadly, I can. *Obviously.*

Dad likes her, I can see he does because they chuckle at the stupidest jokes, despite only having met a week ago. I am glad Mrs Crook's replacement makes him smile, heaven knows he needs to. Dad and I went to her funeral this morning. I was pleased to see a decent number of her friends from the local WI came, but the recurring song of 'we're all dying off fast now' was not easy to hear.

"I thought I'd go first," said one old lady.

"Nah, Old-Joe over there will go before you," replied her friend. "Even his son thinks so, he told me this mornin' on the way over 'ere. He wants Joe to move in with him, says he doesn't want him to die alone. No one should die alone," she said sadly.

And that's when a thought came to me: What if more people can see me—maybe even find comfort in seeing me—during their final moments? It sounds like a pretty melancholy epiphany, I know, but despite the frustration and emptiness I have been left with since being briefly seen, I find myself clinging to the hope of being useful—*of being peaceful and giving peace.*

These thoughts have led me to the hospital to see if my purpose lays at the foot of a death bed. Upon arrival, I felt strangely positive, however, after three hours of aimlessly wandering wards and corridors that tender optimism is ebbing. I try to block out self-deprecating thoughts, but by the time I have visited A&E and unsuccessfully attempted to hold the hands of twenty or more patients, the wisdom of this excursion seems to have all but gone.

Maybe it is for the best. Surely, there is nothing heroic about looking for people who might be severely injured or likely to die in the near future. Am I attempting this because I want the thrill of being seen or do I genuinely want to help people?

The voice in my head—the only one I can have a conversation with—whispers, *it is okay to want both.*

A hospital chaplain walks past me and enters a room. With nothing better to go on, I follow him and listen as he gently greets an elderly gentleman who is laying on a bed. The chaplain's voice is calm and gentle, while the patient's is hoarse and weak, though clearly comforted by the words of his visitor. I feel like I am intruding on a serenity that isn't mine to share in because this man is at peace and is not alone—yet maybe I have been sent here to watch him until he passes? I wish I knew.

After an hour, the old man rests his eyes and the chaplain leaves, satisfied he has done his best, yet I remain standing in the corner by the window, watching sparrows bop from branch to branch in a tree. Regardless of the cars in the street, the trolleys going up and down the hall, or the endless beeping from the nurses' station, in here there is a tranquillity. The longer I stand here, the more I feel it and it sings to me like a lullaby—almost like the music comes *from* me—and I become lost in it.

"That's beautiful," says the elderly gentleman lying a metre from me.

I turn, wide-eyed, to face him as he looks straight at me and smiles—the same serene smile Mrs Crook did moments before she passed.

"If that is the song of heaven, then I am ready to go," he says calmly.

"You hear it too?" I gently ask.

"I hear the voice of an angel guiding me on," he replies. I feel myself beaming. "And with a smile like that, who needs doubt?"

"Then go in peace, good sir." The words come out of my mouth like a song that someone else is singing, but as I do, a warm breeze floats by and I know I have seen another soul safely onwards.

Mesmerised by what just happened, I stand statuesque, even after a nurse comes into the room. Slowly my senses return and, deciding I have no further part to play, I turn to leave. Passing the desk, I hear a doctor call the man's relatives, and cannot miss their lament at not arriving in time to be with him. Other than these all-too-brief moments, my tormented soul may feel a lack of love, yet I wish I could tell them he knew he was loved and went onwards feeling love—and will continue to feel it.

Walking outside, I stand on the pavement by the main entrance, watching people come and go. The mixture of relief that injury or illness is not too severe, combined with the concern of others when it is, is hard to balance. If only I could help in some way.

When I was alive, I wanted to be a nurse. I suppose I grew up seeing my dad care for people and wanted to copy him. Helping people, even if difficult sometimes, seemed like a noble way to spend the day. I think I would have made a good nurse. I hope so anyway.

Hayden didn't like the idea of me being exposed to disease—I think he was more concerned with me passing any disease to him rather than me getting sick, but instead of standing up for what I wanted, I did what he wanted: I studied to be an accountant. There is nothing wrong with that—I like numbers, but I didn't love it and never would have. It paid well, and Hayden knew exactly where I was at all times because I ended up working for him—which I suppose was the point. I tried working in other offices to begin with, but that is when the jealous, violent beast within became too much. Any colleague I mentioned resulted in me being called 'a dirty, money-grabbing, cheating whore' or something to that effect. If I told him he was stupid, I got hit. If I ignored him, I got hit. After a while doing his accounts seemed like the best way to go…although I still got hit.

An ambulance pulls up in a bay nearby and a paramedic jumps out of the driver's seat. It takes me a second, but I realise it is the same man who attended Mrs Crook. He looks worn out as he calls to his colleague in the back—in fact, they both do as I hear them muttering about how long they are going to have to wait to unload their patient. Walking to the back of the ambulance, I am surprised to see the artist from the beach laying uncomfortably on the stretcher.

"I just fainted," says the artist to the paramedics. "I'll be okay. If everyone is so busy, I had better just go home. My girlfriend will be worried about me—"

"I'd imagine she'd be more concerned about us letting you wander the streets with a possible concussion," replies the female paramedic kindly. "We are happy to call her for you, if you'd like?"

"No, that's okay, I'll text," the artist says quietly, pulling her phone out of her pocket, nearly dropping it in the process.

"Here, Oki, let me," says the male paramedic, holding out his hand. It's the first time I've ever heard the artist's name.

"I can do it—but thank you," she says tapping on her phone, trying to focus on the screen.

Within seconds of her putting her phone away, Oki's phone rings and she weakly answers. Being nosy, I lean in.

"Oki?" says the voice.

Oki gulps. "Hi, Hun, err, you got my message?"

"Yes! What the hell? Fuck. Is it bad? Why didn't you call? Are you there now?"

"It's all right, Nina, I'm sure I'll be home soon. I'm outside the hospital in the ambulance waiting to go in."

"Why the hell aren't they taking you in now?" screams Nina. "Let me talk to them. I'm coming now. Let me talk to them."

"No, no, they're busy…"

"Fuck that, put one on the phone NOW!"

The paramedics don't need to be leaning in to hear Nina's demands and the male paramedic doesn't wait for an invitation as he gently takes the phone from Oki's shaking, paint-stained hand and takes a deep breath.

"Hello, is this Nina? Oki's partner?" Nina barks an affirmative. "Okay, great, this is Daniel Hudson, I am one of the paramedics looking after Oki. She fainted on the promenade and hit her head pretty hard. She needs to be seen, she should be seen quickly, but please be calm with her in the meantime. If you'd like to come down and give her reassurance, that would be brilliant."

"*Like to?* Of course I am fucking coming. I'll see you in a few minutes—she better be with a bloody doctor by the time I get there!" Nina must have hung up because the phone bleeps.

Daniel raises his eyebrows to his colleague—they have obviously dealt with this sort of situation before—and returns the phone to Oki.

"She is on her way," says Daniel calmly. "Try to relax."

Oki looks anything but relaxed. Tentatively, I try taking her hand and am relieved I cannot. Hopefully, this means all is well—or soon will be.

As Oki is finally taken into the hospital, a family of three comes out, smiling and chuckling to one another. I recognise the son immediately: Adi.

My heart fills with joy to see him walk out of hospital after his fall, and I am glad my first encounter was one of calm in the face of danger, not death; however, seeing him and not being seen again leaves me feeling empty. My encounters are too tantalisingly brief.

I run up to him—I cannot help it—painful or not, I need to test my connection with him.

If he feels anything, he doesn't react. He just smiles as the salty, summer breeze whips down the road, ruffling his hair while he walks to the carpark with his overjoyed parents who cannot wait to take him home.

# 6

This town has too many ghosts for me. Of course, they are still living, breathing ghosts, but they haunt the streets and make my general amble about town pretty frustrating. Today, I find myself walking past a giant advert for 'Lennox Motoring Group.' This sounds benign enough—to most it is—but to me it is just another reminder of my past. 'Lennox' was my married name: a name I will neither claim nor utter ever again. It is a poison on this land as far as I am concerned.

The advert is referring to my ex-father-in-law, Maddox, who is a well-respected, well-liked member of the community. He is a man who knows exactly when to say something and how to say it—he has a silver tongue, but, just like his son, can also be razor sharp. The apple did not fall far from that tree.

Thank goodness I had no children—although I came perilously close once. I had an early miscarriage, which in itself was traumatic enough, yet the thought of trying to protect a child when I couldn't protect myself petrified me so much that I had a coil fitted. I was a nervous wreck hiding it from Hayden, but thankfully he just thought I had a heavy period and cramps. He wanted children, he probably still does, but I could not watch him raise our daughters in fear or our sons in misogynistic fury.

Why did I let myself get trapped there?

How could I have been so blind?

Although only Hayden carries the Lennox surname, Maddox has three sons, with three different women—none of which he married or particularly cared for, but in hindsight I think they had a lucky escape. His current wife is somewhat of a trophy piece to perfect his all-round, nice guy image. I very much doubt if it is a happy union, but for the last ten years they have remained under one roof—much to Hayden's disgust. To him she has always been an object to scorn: I think this is largely for no greater reason than because she's a woman, but I also believe he resents the possibility of an extra sibling competing with his father's already lacking paternal interest. Undeterred, Hayden has spent his entire life trying to win his father's approval and built a business to compliment Lennox Motoring Group without really questioning why his father didn't just invite him to join in a family business.

Leo, Maddox's eldest son, is a focused, dangerous mix of his parents and even Hayden fears him—not that he'll ever bloody admit it. Thankfully, I have spent very little time with Leo because he grew up with, and still works for his mother; however, I am certain he has inherited the Lennox double façade that I have grown to despise. Hayden and Leo have always been firm rivals, not real brothers, and although his younger brother, Rufus, came to our wedding, I think Hayden truly prefers to think of himself as an only child.

Scuttling past the advert, I wish I had a sensor that would alert me to their proximity so I could avoid unpleasant reflections on the past. I'm heading back to the beach. That should be a safer place as ironically in my latter years I didn't get to visit as much as I'd like—I doubt I need to say why.

The seafront isn't busy yet, though it looks set to be a nice day. The seagulls are in full swing, the pier is playing its ridiculous blend of music, and Flossy, the candyfloss guy, has a line of teenagers waiting to fill their faces with sugary goodness.

Recognising Flossy's helper, a groan slips passed my lips—Rufus. He is nine years younger than Hayden and although nearly twenty-one, he is very baby-faced. The girls in the queue clearly think he is cute as they are giggling and pointing in his direction. Grinning broadly, Rufus seems to enjoy playing the part of attractive mascot—which is possibly the only useful part of him being on the stall as Flossy is doing all the actual work.

A new hotdog stand has opened on the front of the pier with the questionable name of *Grab A Hottie-Dog*. Flossy scowls as a large, heavy-set man steps out of the new stall and casually swings his arms as he lollops in his direction.

"A'right old boy," says the man to Flossy.

"Hello," replies Rufus while Flossy serves the girls, ignoring them both.

"I was talking to Grandpa," sneers the man.

Rufus swallows hard, obviously deciding to keep his cool, and blanks the man, turning back to his admirers. He smiles and winks, telling the smitten girls he hopes to see them soon as they happily set off along the promenade.

Flossy watches them go, waiting until they are out of ear shot before he returns the man's sneer and says: "You can fuck off to your hot dogs and stick one up your—"

"Now, now, that isn't very becoming for an old boy," chuckles the man. "I come in peace Grandpa Floss—you know that, you've been told." He scoffs. "Besides, your wet-faced side kick here ain't exactly gonna protect you, is he?"

Flossy firmly grasps Rufus' arm as he turns red with anger and clenches his fists, ready to swing. He may be the youngest of Maddox Lennox's children and uses a different surname, but he is still a Lennox. Calm until not. Reasonable until not. "You can—"

"Oh, calm down," the man smirks, waving his hand to dismiss whatever Rufus was going to say. "We've a reputation to uphold—your shit can wait. Your time is numbered here."

"'Come in peace,' my arse." Flossy spits on the floor by the man's feet. "You've a fuckin' cheek. I may not scare you, but you should be scared. I ain't held this spot all these years to be pushed off by anyone, especially not a snivellin' shit like you."

"All reigns fall in the end," the man says walking to his stand, smiling to his young, female colleague who has been silently watching. As the man catches her gaze, she matches his self-important smirk.

I feel like I am missing something here. Why would hotdog and candyfloss sellers hate each other? Surely the burger van 200 yards away would have more financial concerns regarding the newcomer than Flossy?

"You want me to call it in?" says Rufus, once they are alone.

"No, lad, not yet," replies Flossy.

"You sure, Uncle Flossy?" he says upholding the old man's life long, honorary title.

"Sure," he nods. "They want to spark a reaction. Now ain't the time. Wait, my boy, just wait."

Another group of teens arrives seeking their sugar fix and Flossy immediately reverts to his normal, friendly persona. It takes Rufus a moment to follow suit, but I suspect the arrival of a half-naked group of girls in their late teens helps to distract his fiery mood.

A scream for help suddenly rings out across the promenade, frosting any thoughts of flirting as all eyes search for the identity of the screamer.

"There!" shouts a girl, pointing at a café.

"Where?" asks her friend.

"At the table. Look!" she says running over, forgetting about her candyfloss.

"HELP!" screams a woman in her fifties. "She's choking, my daughter is choking!"

She's not wrong.

A woman who (if her skin were its normal tone) could easily be a twenty-year-younger version of the one yelling, is grasping at her throat, trying to breathe. The waiter runs indoors, declaring she will call 999, but no one seems to be physically helping. If the mother knows how to do the Heimlich manoeuvre, her panic has frozen everything but her lungs, and no one else is stepping forward. Some basic first aid was one of the few things Dad taught me before my desire to be a nurse was squashed by Hayden. My rational side tells me I'm just setting myself up for disappointment and failure, however, another part of me—a part I really do not understand—tells me to grab this lady and do my best.

So I do.

Grabbing her from behind, I place one foot slightly in front of the other for balance, make a fist with one hand, grasping it with my other in front of her abdomen, and press hard and upward—whilst hoping and praying the quick thrusts are felt by more than just me.

On the fourth go I feel her splutter and spit. As I hear gasps from the surrounding people as well as the woman herself, I let go and she turns around. Her eyes are watering, her face is a mix of pale and hot flushes as her blood races to recover normal function, but again I feel the serene haze of recognition. She sees me. I know she does.

"Are you okay?" I ask, quietly.

"Yes…thank you," she wheezes.

"Elana?" her mum grabs her arm. "Oh! My baby! My baby!" she declares pulling her daughter into her arms. "I thought I was going to lose you! We are never going to eat peanuts again!"

Still coughing, Elana pulls away from her mother, but keeps hold of her hand. Her mum begins to weep and cries out: "I am useless! I stood like a useless statue! What good am I?"

"It's all right, Mum," Elana replies, wiping her own tears away. "This lady saved me."

"What lady?" replies her mum, confused.

Elana looks at her mother blankly and turns to me, this time looking past me as though I might have gone into the café. "Oh? Where did she go?"

"Who, my love?"

"The woman that grabbed me and made me cough up the nut?"

"What woman? You coughed it up yourself—only I and these teens were here."

Elana glances between her mum, Rufus, the teen girls, and the apparently invisible space in which I stand. She silently appeals to them for clarification and the teens nod in agreement just as the waiter returns, mobile in hand, talking to the emergency 999 call operator. "Oh, she's all right!" she sighs in relief. "You're okay, right, madam?"

"Yes, thanks to my guardian angel," Elana says softly.

Ignoring any potential meaning beyond being thankful to be alive, the waiter passes the phone to Elana's mum, and I can hear her being given instructions to ensure Elana is seen by a doctor. Her mum immediately agrees and collects her bag without hesitation, declaring they are heading straight to the car.

Drama over, the teenage girls disperse, and Rufus returns to Flossy. Elana doesn't protest as her mum leads her away; however, she does pause to take one last look backwards. For a brief second our eyes lock, she smiles, gives a little wave, and then disappears out of sight.

# 7

Being seen is becoming a bit like an addictive drug. I could compare it to the dangers of teenage experimentation: the more you try, the more you want. However, just like a drug, the all-too brief, momentary high, is followed by a head-splitting ache of depression as I return to my solitary, lonely state. Years ago, I wanted to pass unseen—I thought I deserved to pass unseen. Loneliness has all too often been the safe, reassuring, less painful option. Maybe I don't deserve anything else.

No. That is Hayden's wife talking.

*I am Hayden's wife.*

No. I am not. Not now.

*Am I?*

Ugh.

The high: I will concentrate on the high. The joy of being helpful...useful...seen. I can save as well as give peace to onward travellers. That is a gift. I *must* see it as a gift. As a calling perhaps.

It is a relief to see Oki, the artist, back on the beach today. She has her easel set up and is busy sketching a charcoal portrait of a couple who are lovingly posed in front of her. Oki has dark rings around her normally bright eyes and looks like she needs a good night or three's sleep, but otherwise she seems all right. Beside her on a deck chair is a woman reading—or rather pretending to read, because she looks up every few minutes to check on Oki's progress.

Once the portrait is finished and the happy couple take their new keepsake away, the woman closes her book and sighs: "Damn, I thought they'd never leave!"

"What do you mean, Nina?" says Oki nervously. "I thought they were nice."

Nina snorts. "What would be nice is if they tipped you."

Oki doesn't reply, instead she shakes her head and stares out to sea.

I suppose it is kind that Nina has chosen to spend her day with Oki at work, especially as she was ill so recently, but I think painting holds considerably more charm for Oki than it does for Nina.

"I'm thinking of cutting my hair short," says Nina, pulling her free-flowing dark brown hair together in her hands. "What do you think?"

"How short?" asks Oki, raising an eyebrow.

"My chin?" Nina replies, demonstrating the length she means. "Or a bit shorter, maybe?"

"Oh, no, I like it long…and the curls, they need length I th—"

"You mean I'm too ugly for short hair?" Nina looks offended.

"What! No, I didn't say that at all—you know that. Hun, please," Oki pleads. "You know you're beautiful."

Nina sits back, satisfied, then suddenly chuckles. "Maybe I'll dye it though, just for the wedding on Saturday—

bright bloody green, just to piss off Nadia and her colour coordinated picture-perfect bridesmaid crap."

"Oh, don't! Not for that—Dewi would be so upset, you know they just agree to Nadia's demands to make life simple, it's not their fault—"

"Of course it is. Dewi could have fallen for a less dramatic girl or at least not agree to such stupid wedding plans—don't raise your eyebrows at me! Hey, you've a customer, I'll leave you to it." Nina gets up, kisses the top of Oki's head, and walks off muttering, "Maybe I'll find something green on the way home—bright pink theme my arse. Do I look like I wear bright pink?"

Oki greets her customer, totally ignoring any possibility she might have heard Nina rambling. The woman is probably in her mid-twenties, with a perfect, beach-ready body, and long, blonde hair which is tied into a ponytail. As she props herself on the provided seat, she unties her hair, letting it tumble past her shoulders while her eyes scan the promenade.

"He'll be here in a minute," she says, impatiently.

"Who will?" Oki replies, looking around for the mystery 'he.'

"My boyfriend. He told me to go ahead and book you before someone else got here first again. We were going to come earlier, but you were busy...he *was* supposed to just answer the phone quickly." She suddenly stares Oki in the eyes and says, "You can do two people, right? You just did two—"

"Yes, yes, for a little more," replies Oki. "I am happy to do doubles, I—"

"Oh, whatever, I am not worried about cost. I just want quality."

If I could throw sand in this girl's face on Oki's behalf, I would.

"Ah, here he is!" The woman jumps up, waving her arms. "Here! Where have you been?" She doesn't wait for an answer, but semi-pushes the man into the chair and sits on his lap.

Oki looks up. "There is another chair, if you—"

"No, no, we want a portrait like this, don't we Daniel?"

Never has a question, been less of a question. Turning to the man, I realise it is the paramedic I keep bumping into, minus the green uniform—maybe Nina just stole it. He just shrugs his shoulders before saying: "If you say so."

"Exactly," she replies triumphantly, as though the finer detail of her portrait holds power over the rotation of the planet. "Oh, we should have brushed your hair." She runs her hand over Daniel's head and beard, correcting any daring wayward strands—not that his beard is long enough to have any. "You can smooth out any *issues*, right?"

"What Raquel means is: can you please use your artistic licence to remove any spots she might have?" says Daniel, laughing, paying zero attention to the indignant look on Raquel's face.

Oki's face changes from weary to amused in an instant.

"Are you feeling better?" Daniel asks Oki kindly.

Oki stares at him for a second, then smiles, but Raquel jumps in before she can answer: "What? I'm fine—oh, do you mean her? Do you know her? Why didn't you say so?"

"I fainted the other day," explains Oki. "Daniel was one of the ambulance drivers. Sorry, I didn't recognise you at first."

Daniel chuckles. "No worries, I get that a lot. But how are you?"

"Better, much better. Thank you."

"Good, I am glad," smiles Daniel. "I hope you don't mind painting us?"

"Not at all, I'd be glad to."

"Excellent," jumps in Raquel. "I'm going to put it on our wall."

The following tone of conversation is light and friendly, and I thoroughly enjoy watching the skilful, yet almost carefree way in which Oki commits her subjects to canvas.

When she has finished and Daniel and Raquel get up to leave, Oki checks her phone and sighs. Apparently, she has somewhere to be as she collects her things, but before heading towards town she looks wistfully down the southern length of beach—Adtoft's quietest, least trodden beach. She doesn't attempt to walk that way though, and neither do I as I want to check in with Dad and see if Sally has come home—or if she is in fact embarking on some painter-decorator time of her own.

# 8

Dad is home alone when I get in, watching a movie and eating a tub of cookie ice cream. When I was little, he and mum would let me share a tub with them and we'd all take turns dunking our spoons in, but they would always leave me the last bit and I loved it. Grabbing a spoon from the kitchen, I weightlessly curl up on the sofa next to him, dipping my spoon in when he isn't looking. I don't need to, of course—I could scoop out the whole pot while he digs for cookie chunks and the glitch would let my phantom thieving go unnoticed. However, clinging to happy memories, I like to pretend that we are both aware we are watching a movie together.

Sally returns, shopping bags in hand, acting like she has had a long day at work. Maybe she has, but somehow, I doubt it. She doesn't ask Dad for help unpacking and he doesn't offer. He carries on watching the telly, but the rhythm of his breathing is continuously interrupted by sighs, and he keeps wobbling his jaw, forcing the bones to click and pop horribly.

He needs to get a stress ball…

No, he needs to vocalise whatever words he is chewing on.

Holding another pot of ice cream, Sally enters the living room. Apparently, that is their mutual answer to their marital issues—who needs words or therapy when Ben and Jerry's will do? Her phone pings, and I glance over to see her attempt to hide an amused grin. Dad notices, I can tell because he raises an eyebrow, but he won't let himself ask who is messaging her. He won't let himself be *that* kind of husband—the jealous, suspicious kind of husband, who needs to know and control everything. That, in a way, sounds wonderful. I had nothing but 'who's that?' and 'what do they want?' or even 'give it here, I want to see' from Hayden, yet I have to believe there is a happy medium out there. An acceptable, trusting, *balanced* level of interest in your spouse's correspondence—because as damaging as too much is, too little is just as catastrophic.

"*Shit!*" cries Sally, discarding her pot of ice cream, sending the spoon flying into a hairball on the unvacuumed carpet. Any amusement in her messages has definitely ebbed.

"What is it?" Dad asks, as Sally heads for the front door.

"Fire! Quick, there's a fire!"

"Where? Nearby?" Dad says jumping up, following her out the front door.

He doesn't need her to reply—the billowing smoke coming from down the street answers both questions. The houses here are all detached, so although the immediate threat is limited to one home, the speed in which the flames are licking through the building doesn't give me enough confidence to say it will not spread.

The house is owned by a family who moved in after my death, so I've never really met them, but the wife is outside, clutching her two weeping children, screaming out her husband's name.

"Where is he?" asks Rob, who is already by her side. "The fire brigade is coming, but where is Jaiden?"

"In there!" she screams. "He went back for the dog! JAIDEN! *JAI-DEN*!"

I cannot bear to hear her wails. Dad runs to her side, immediately trying to assess any injuries they might have sustained. Sally and other neighbours mutter words of sorrow and despair, but no one moves towards the house in search of Jaiden. Only a fool would—the ground floor is now completely alight.

As I am already dead, does it matter if I am that foolish?

It is possibly one of the few methods I have not tried, but I have not tested fire as a means of escape from my current status. There's no time like the present, so without further thought, I run in through the front door—what is left of it. I feel hot and sweaty, and breathing is like being locked in a car with an inconsiderate chain-smoker, but I am not burning.

Running upstairs, I hope Jaiden is here, because if he is downstairs, he is already dead. I shout out his name, but there is no reply. Opening the door to a bedroom, I quickly realise it is empty of life, as is the bathroom, but when I get to a child's bedroom, with a doll literally melting in front of me on the blazing floor, I call again and hear a whimper.

Dropping to the floor, the smell of melting plastic hits the back of my throat, but I push the desire to gag aside and look under the bed. It takes a second for me to focus, but I see a dog—thankfully a small, easy to carry Cairn Terrier—huddled in the corner.

As I call to him, he throws himself into my arms. Relieved, I give the dog an affectionate squeeze before checking for any sign of Jaiden. The air is a churning mess of fire and smoke, yet I suddenly realise there is a man laying prostrate, semi hidden by the open wardrobe door, on the other side of the bed.

Clinging to the dog, I crawl around to Jaiden, pull him clear of the wardrobe and bed, and try to shake him into consciousness. He doesn't move. If I don't get him out of here in a minute, he and his dog are going to die. The entire house is increasingly like an inferno and although somewhere in the distance I can sense the approaching siren of a fire engine, I know it will be too late.

I feel useless.

What is the point of me not burning to death if I cannot help? *Breathe* a voice says to me from within—from the part of me I do not understand. I do not question. Grasping Jaiden's face, I breathe into his mouth and instantly feel his lungs inflate. He splutters into consciousness and continues spluttering.

Of course, he cannot breathe this air. I breathe into his mouth again and the warmth that I have become so addicted to envelops us and he smiles. I stand and he stands, picking up his dog. Taking him firmly by the hand, I lead them down the stairs. The fire should be burning them, but it doesn't.

Somehow the warmth that we—*I*—have created is holding off the furnace, and we calmly walk to the now non-existent front door.

Screams and wails from Jaiden's waiting family fill my ears as my eyes are startled by the mix of black, dense smoke, bright red from the glowing fire, and swirling blues from the newly arrived ambulance and fire engine.

Stepping out onto the doorstep, I let go of Jaiden's hand and he stumbles to the ground, coughing and gagging for air. A fireman grabs him, immediately carrying him to the waiting paramedics—none of whom I recognise this time. The dog runs towards his calling family, but like Jaiden, collapses on the grass. Rob runs forward and scoops him up, and I am relieved to see both man and dog receive oxygen within seconds.

"It's a miracle! How on earth did he walk out of that?" A neighbour cries out as they watch in disbelief.

Equally baffled, no one answers her, instead they simply repeat the question—hoping repetition alone will solve the riddle.

Exhausted, I sit on the grass of the neighbouring lawn while the emergency services tackle the fire. The united family rejoice at their lucky escape—all too thankful to question the details yet or consider the hard days ahead as they rebuild their lives.

Satisfied the house is empty, the paramedics pack the family into ambulances. Before they leave, Jaiden peers out the back door, his eyes searching the gathered crowd as though he has lost someone. When his eyes rest on me, he stops and his face fills with gratitude—too great, too overwhelming to be put into words—and his eyes well with tears. As if he is about to say a prayer, he puts his hands together and humbly nods his head. Smiling meekly, I return the gesture. The doors close and I lay back on the grass, thankful, but too tired to move.

# 9

I haven't visited the hospital for a few days. It seemed wise to stop myself from going because I don't want to set myself up for disappointment. Continuing to search for connections with people after each event just ruins the joy *of* the event.

I have helped: that must be enough.

Remembering that Oki and Nina mentioned a wedding, I have decided to look for joy in other places today. There is no need to look hard because yesterday a marquee appeared on the beach and the surrounding area has transformed ready for the happy occasion. Bright pink ribbons and flowers adorn every spare inch of the giant tent—much to Nina's disapproval—and there is an excited atmosphere that I wish to soak up.

Beach weddings in Adtoft are not unheard of, especially in the summer, but people tend to rent out one of the churches or halls and then use a smaller marquee on the beach or hire a bar later. Listening to the people setting up the decorations, I learn the bride, Nadia, is the daughter of Adtoft's mayor—so commandeering most of the seafront suddenly seems less of an expensive push and more of a parental perk of the job.

The marquee has been set up next to the permanent bandstand, which is normally run by *The Swinging Anchor*, a local bar-restaurant. It is on the more affluent end of the seafront—away from the noise of the slightly northern-set pier, but before the quiet grassy dunes to the south—and it is not uncommon for the bar to host music nights with varying genres playing. If you want pop and disco, one of the clubs in town is probably more your thing, but otherwise this is a good place to sit on a warm evening—or an August Saturday when there is a wedding.

Not wanting to be rude, I have dressed for the wedding. I do not need to be told this is unnecessary. I have absolutely no false illusions about being seen or heard and am very much hoping the only 'hitch' today is of the planned variety—but for once I want to dress up and think about what I am wearing rather than blowing around town like some sort of unkept tumble weed.

The sea air was never a friend to my hair, and although I shower, I don't think I ever really smell—well, that, or I am just really used to my own odour. Mostly, I wash and change to maintain routine—each day trying to remind myself what it was to be alive, clean, and tidy. To feel human. That said, all I have smelled for the last few days is burning fibres, melted children's toys, and singed dog hair. The fragrance of rose petals and sand is positively heavenly in comparison.

However, there is a definitive complication, a lack of incentive, when it comes to me changing wardrobe: I cannot keep anything in this realm—nor pay for it. Repeatably, I apologise to shop staff as I walk out of their stores with a new item. I am (again) being ridiculous, the item is still on their rack and I, like bloody Cinderella, return all items of clothing each night.

Only the clothes I died in stay with me—the glitch happily replaces them on my body along with my wedding ring as I sleep, so I wake each day with a memento of how I got here. I've considered nudity for this very reason—hey, until recently no one saw me, so what is a little bare flesh between me and the pixels of never-never? But regardless of how I sleep, the clothes still return each morning and the idea of walking about with nothing on just feels weird. Heck, I don't even like undressing in clothes shops and always seek the changing rooms, making sure I shut the curtain—which is fine until someone tries to join me, and it gets weird again.

Today, I have chosen a long, flowing summer dress—not quite full, formal wedding attire, but perfectly suitable for a seaside, summer wedding. It is white with subtle yellow flowers (there wasn't a pink version), and I've let my hair flow down my back freely with the exception of two selections from the front which I have twisted into plaits and tied at the back. To complete my outfit and match my dress, I stole small yellow roses from the florist and have poked them into my plaits. They'll probably die in the sunshine—but then again maybe not, perhaps phantom sunshine rays are different?

As the guests arrive, I sit at the back of the marquee and watch the beautiful scene of love unfold. The bride is adorned in white, but as foretold by Nina, the bridesmaids are all in bright pink. Despite Nina's protests, both she and Oki are amongst the five bridesmaids and three best persons, and Dewi, the groom, looks so handsome as they stand proudly waiting for Nadia to float down the aisle.

The ceremony is performed to perfection and there's nothing but smiles all around as the photographer captures the day in digital form. I feel like a thief again as I later tuck into the buffet and wedding cake, but as no one in this realm seems to be rushing forward to stop me, I carry on.

The speeches become more interesting as the level of alcohol consumed increases, but thankfully the parents of the happy couple manage to deliver their soppy speeches before the head bridesmaid makes a more questionable toast and it is declared time for dancing.

I love dancing. I really miss it—particularly slow dancing, being tenderly held by someone you love and who loves you. I guess in hindsight—the only reliable sight I now have—I have never really done it. If Hayden truly loved me, he would not have treated me the way he did, let alone have murdered me. I would not have miscarried after being thrown down the stairs; I would not have needed a medical implant to ensure I didn't become pregnant again; and I might now be a mother to a happy, healthy child in a loving, stable relationship, slow dancing as I join in the celebration of another couple's union.

But I am not. He did not.

Instead, I must enjoy watching. I cannot bring myself to slow dance—or any kind of dance—next to someone who cannot see me. My pride stops me, it compels me.

I must observe.

After all, I should be good at it by now.

Oki and Nina look happy as they sway in each other's arms. Nina hasn't fulfilled her threat and dyed her hair green, but she has one, tiny green flower in amongst the pink at the back of her head. I have to laugh. It will not ruin any photographs, but I suppose it helps her feel like she hasn't submitted entirely to the whims of another.

As they turn on the dance floor, Oki suddenly exclaims and greets the neighbouring couple with genuine, but unexpected pleasure. It takes me a second to identify them in their formal wear, but I chuckle as Oki bashfully introduces Daniel and Raquel.

"This is Nina—remember, you briefly met as you left me in the hospital?"

Daniel grins, extending his right hand. "Ah, yes, pleasure to meet you on a happier occasion."

"Likewise." Accepting his hand, Nina smiles, but makes no attempt to apologise for what I am guessing wasn't her best behaviour.

"We love the beautiful painting you did of us," says Raquel. "It's hanging on our living room wall."

"Lovely." Blushing, Oki smiles coyly before quickly changing the subject. "How do you know the happy couple?"

"I am Nadia's solicitor."

"And college friend."

Tapping Daniel's arm, Raquel lightly tuts. "Yes, of course, we go way back. What about you—how do you know them?"

"We're childhood friends of Dewi's—we grew up as neighbours." Oki nudges Nina. "Didn't we, Hun?"

"Indeed. We've been in this town together since the year dot." I detect a slightly disgruntled tone, but if Daniel or Raquel do too, they ignore it.

"I wouldn't want to be anywhere else." Daniel's genuine love for Adtoft radiates from both his tone and expression.

Oki must sense it too because she lights up as she answers: "Nor I. Painting on the beach here is what sets my soul free."

"This is a beautiful setting for a wedding, that's for sure," says Raquel taking in the numerous decorations before gazing out the doorway towards the sea. "We'll have to remember this."

"Oooh, are you getting married?" Oki's enthusiasm is instant.

Daniel fidgets with his cufflinks. "Err, well—"

"In time, yes, of course."

"Fabulous! I do love a good wedding." Nina squeezes Oki's hand. "It's something we've discussed, isn't it, O?"

Oki curls her fingers around her partner's, smiling sweetly. "It is."

Glancing around the marquee, Nina releases a noise that's somewhere between a snort and a chortle. "Though, another beach would be good—somewhere where the weather is a little less iffy."

"It is beautiful now!"

"By chance." Nina rolls her eyes, ignoring any offence Oki might have taken.

"Life is a string of chance and luck, don't you think?" Daniel smiles playfully, yet thoughtfully. "But true love can weather any storm."

Raquel links her arm around his, smiling: "Absolutely."

Pfft, *any storm*. Sure, if you choose wisely—and *if* the love is true.

"But it helps to have a marquee at least." Oki winks.

I laugh. No one hears me, but I like this girl. In another life, I am sure we would be friends. Real friends, not just phantom friends where I follow her about, sharing her news and marvelling at her artistic skills. Daniel laughs too, but I cannot describe Raquel's, or indeed Nina's reaction without using the word 'scowling.'

Leaving them to their dancing, I select a stool at the edge of the long bar; however, after being sat on too many times, I decide to revert to my more usual position on the beach. As the evening progresses and the music is designed for faster dancing, the party spills out onto the shoreline. A few couples, Daniel and Raquel included, go for a romantic stroll away from the noisy hubbub of the more drunken partygoers, but I remain on my spot in the sand, watching.

I don't know when exactly someone got a dinghy out—I also don't know when someone decided a four-man boat can take six people—however, four men and two women, all drunk, get into the inflated boat and clumsily float themselves out into the water.

I cannot help thinking this is literally a recipe for disaster and suddenly wish my connection with people in danger has a pre-emptive function—a 'hey, you, don't be a twat!' warning sign at the very least. Wading into the water, I tell myself I should at least try to stop them, but as I reach the merry crew, my hands go through the rope and miss the oars, resulting in me just waving in mid-air.

Sighing, I go back to the beach and sit down, feeling like a grandparent trying to educate wild, spoilt toddlers. After a while I lose sight of the group, but I can hear them singing and laughing in the dark as they row down the shoreline. Deciding I am a poor guardian if I do not watch, I get up and follow just as a group arrive looking for the drunken sailors.

"For fuck's sake, Manni, is that you out there?" shouts a woman from the beach.

"Pen?" replies a slurred voice. "Hey, Pen! I'm out 'er! It's bootiful!"

"Fuckin' idiot," shouts another voice.

"Sis? Oh, don't be mad! Jezzer's out here too!"

"Jeremy? Oh, you've gotta be kiddin' me! Get here. I wanna go home—the babysitter should have left an hour ago!"

The exchange continues for some time. In frustration, the people on the beach sober up, but I am sure the people in the dinghy are continuing to drink as I can hear cans as well as renewed singing.

Frustrated by the angry people on the beach dampening their spirits, one of the sailors declares: "Oh, for fuck's sake, have him. Come on! Come get him!"

Suddenly the people on the dinghy start arguing.

"What the fuck, man? Stop it!"

Someone laughs.

"No, piss off, I don't wanna hear it no more!"

"Hey, it ain't my fault!"

More laughter.

"Leave off, you twat!"

Someone squeals.

"What? What are you doing out there?" shouts one of the women on the beach.

No answer, just the sound of jostling drunkards.

"Are you out there?" calls a voice, slurring. I think it is the one they called Manni. "Come on, come get him before he drowns!"

The sound of a brief struggle is followed by one almighty splash, shouting, then repetitive, frantic splashing.

"Shit! Did they just fall in?"

The people on the beach rush into the water, ruining their formal clothes as they desperately search for their drunken loved ones.

Sodden people soon start crawling out of the sea—some coughing, some laughing, most exclaiming with varying degrees of amusement, anger, and relief.

As the ill-suited dinghy is dragged onto the beach, expletive laden curses turn to panicked cries when one woman realises her husband has not been found. More people react to the anxious calls, including Daniel and Raquel as they reappear from their walk.

Much to Raquel's dismay, Daniel doesn't hesitate longer than it takes him to remove his jacket, and my heart sinks as I too throw myself into the water. I knew this would happen. Another two men dive in, and I do my best to track the movements of all parties, hoping that I am not needed in either capacity as guardian or guide to anyone's *next*.

Within a minute, a voice calls out across the water that he has found his friend, and a cluster of people dart to assist him. Relieved, I watch as both men are safely pulled to shore, yet I only breathe again properly when I see the lost man splutter back into his realm.

"Daniel?" screams Raquel. "Where's Daniel?"

In my joy of seeing the man saved, I didn't think to check if Daniel had heard the good news and returned. Racing back into the waters, I head in the direction that I saw him last. The current is much stronger here and if it were daylight, or even better moonlit, I think I would see a darker strip of water, for I am sure this is a rip current.

Beginning to panic, looking all around me, I finally spot a lump in the water. He is much further out than I expected. Swimming to the floating body as fast as I can, I manage to grasp a hold of his arm just as the current tries to redirect me. The warmth I normally love envelops us and instead of feeling a high, I fear it, for I fear it being the path to another world, not a safe passage back to Daniel's own time.

Looping my arm under his, keeping his back against my chest, I swim with every ounce of my power back to the beach. In life, I was a good swimmer and thankfully death has added to my skills, yet even so it still feels like an eternity until I get to the shore.

A warm breeze hits my face as I pull Daniel onto the sand and I want to cry, but I focus my efforts on the task at hand. I think back to Dad's training—even to the days of watching reruns of Baywatch with David Hasselhoff—and I tilt Daniel's chin and head backwards and lean in, checking for any sign that he is breathing.

Nothing. Dammit, dammit, dammit.

Pinching his nose, I breathe into his mouth, once, twice, three times...*come on*...four, five...nope.

I move to CPR—how come the drunken idiot didn't need CPR but this poor guy does? Pushing my hands together down on his chest, I start singing that Bee Gees song 'Stayin'

Alive.' I must have stored that memory somewhere in my brain from when Dad taught me because I have a vague, happy feeling as I remember—just sadly not happy enough to override the feeling of uselessness as Daniel doesn't respond.

Do a minute of compressions...then breathe twice, compress thirty, repeat...is that right?

Why is no one else seeing us? Or at least Daniel?

They are too far up the beach—I shout for help but no one responds.

It's me or nothing and that damn warm breeze is still swirling in my face.

Suddenly, water bubbles out of Daniel's mouth and he rolls on his side, coughing and throwing up water onto the sand. I want to sing the hallelujah chorus, never mind the bloody Bee Gees. I rub his back—I don't know if it helps, but he doesn't bat me away as he stays on his side in the recovery position until he finally begins to breathe more evenly.

The warm, hazy breeze is still very much present, and I begin to think back to my death—was the breeze there then? Maybe. I was so out of breath, so dazed, so angry, so hurt and confused, I didn't pay attention. Either way, I've never known it to last this long with someone I've helped before.

Is he okay? Is he staying with me? Is that even possible? Do I want that? I'd be less lonely...but to wish this half-life/half-death on someone seems cruel.

Daniel turns to me, and I stop rubbing his back, suddenly feeling self-conscious as I realise he is indeed looking *at* me. A calm, sweet serenity wraps around us, and I feel as light as a feather. He smiles and I am certain he feels it too.

Two souls are meeting—truly meeting one another.

Slowly, he lifts his hand to my cheek, and I lean into it, internally glowing as my skin tingles at the touch of his fingers. I am about to open my mouth to speak, hoping to add to, not break the beautiful spell, when a woman screams Daniel's name. As he turns to view his girlfriend running towards him, the warm breeze passes. Instantly, I feel the chill of the night and I know that I am once again alone.

# 10

Sitting back, I numbly watch as people tumble down the beach towards Daniel. Raquel half smothers him in kisses before the lifeguards get to him. Everyone declares how lucky he is, simultaneously praising and chastising him for his actions. Daniel doesn't say much beyond reassuring everyone he feels okay and makes no attempt to explain what happened—and certainly doesn't mention me.

Possibly he doesn't remember—whatever ripple through the realms joined us may have already stilled for him. It hasn't for me though: I feel it keenly. Now, I feel like something is missing inside and no number of momentary encounters will fill the void that has just been made.

I could howl.

Some may agree with Lord Tennyson's *it is better to have loved and lost than never loved at all* theory, but if that warmth was true love—if that was possibly the meeting of soulmates—yet all our allotted time together has been already spent, then I do not feel better for having known it.

I want to follow as Daniel is taken off the beach, but my legs will not take me. Instead, I watch, desperately hoping he will look back for me as others have, telling myself I will go to him if he signals that he still feels my presence, but he does not. He focuses on each footstep, allowing himself to be guided away and gradually the beach empties. Turning back to the rumble of the rolling sea, I stare as wave upon wave crashes onto the shore and when the sun eventually rises, I quickly lose count of the seagulls as they again start to fill the sky. Above, there isn't a cloud to be seen—I think I have swallowed them all, for inside my heart is raining.

Behind me, early morning walkers exercise their dogs and people start dismantling the marquee, returning the beach to its normal state. Normal. Everything is back to normal. No one else died. I am happy for that, of course I am. It is selfish to want anyone else to join me. This status, this hollow, this…this calling, is mine alone.

Alone.

That word once sparked a decision to seek those who may be about to embark on this life's end and ensure they are not alone. I must return to that ideal. I cannot stay in this state, grasping at sand as though I will not sink into it.

Getting up, I dust myself off. As the grains of sand scatter to the ground, I realise I am still wearing the summer dress from yesterday. I haven't slept, so maybe that is why my normal attire of golden ring, pale pink long-sleeve blouse, and black trousers hasn't returned? Yet the dress is clean without a salty tide mark in sight—which is weird because that normally only happens after I've slept.

Whatever, it is still better than my death clothes.

Walking towards town, I pass Flossy as he heads towards the pier. Rufus isn't with him today although two, large guys in their late twenties are. I don't think I know either of them, but they are scanning the promenade as though they are pre-empting trouble.

Curious, I watch at a distance as they reach the candyfloss stall. Flossy immediately begins his morning routine, while the two men circulate around the pier. One stops in front of the hotdog stand and says something to the young woman who is sat there. Unlike the first time I saw her, she does not have a smug expression, instead her face is a mixture of fear and anger—that awkward spot between self-preservation and courage—but whatever she replies makes the man laugh and return to Flossy.

This time Flossy looks smug as he turns to the woman and waves. She scowls and immediately picks up her mobile phone, causing the younger man to roar with laughter to the point that I can hear him. As my curiosity peaks, I regret not following them and consider changing my plans when Flossy's first customers walk up to his stall. He reverts to his normal 'Uncle Flossy' persona, taking the boys' order, and in that instant the stale ambiance calms.

I'm not sorry. I listen to enough promenade drama. Today I can take no more. The lives and loves, the quibbles and squabbles of the living is too much. Turning on my heels, I set off to the hospital, looking for an onward soul.

\* \* \*

Walking around the back of the hospital, I decide that A&E is not the place I want to start today. I do not want to see Daniel again if he cannot see me and I do not want to risk seeing people's lives cut short due to accident or injury. I nearly saw that last night and that was enough for a lifetime. If I touch anyone, I want to give the elderly their final farewell.

Someone who has lived long and happy; someone already fulfilled, who sadly, but naturally, has run their course on this earth. Is that still too morbid? I don't know, but it seems fitting—it seems noble in a surprisingly logical way in my illogical state.

Suddenly I see Rob, neatly dressed and hand in hand with Sally. What are they doing here? As if my insides weren't groaning enough! Navigating the hallways with purpose, they do not stop until they enter a ward of six elderly ladies.

"Mum?" says Rob as he sits down next to a bed. "Mum, it's me. How are you?"

"Robert?" says the lady trying to sit up. "Ah, how good to see you—and you, Sally. It's so lovely you've come."

"Of course, we've come," replies Sally, gently stroking the lady's hand. "How do you feel?"

"Oh, you know...like I'm dyin', but the staff are lovely, and I've met some new friends," she says, trying to sound cheerful.

Walking to the window, I gaze out. I am angry at Sally on Dad's behalf, but I feel like an intruder when it is plain to see that the lady is glad of her visit. It is obviously not a first visit—and nor is it a secret that Sally and Rob are an item. If they are wandering around so blatantly, why not just tell Dad? Or are they still testing the waters to see if their boat will float? I suppose Dad might be sunk, but he is anchored at least.

"It's my time, is it?" a lady next to me says suddenly.

Turning, I expect to see someone has entered the room without me noticing, but the lady is looking directly at me. She pats the edge of her bed and I sit down as directed, taking her outstretched hand when it is offered to me. The window is closed, but a warm air twirls around us and although it isn't as fierce as last night, it is no less beautiful in its own way.

"I've been waiting for you," says the lady. I feel bad I don't even know her name. Maybe I don't need to. I feel the warmth of spirit and that no longer needs an earthly name—just a safe passage of love. "I hope my George awaits on the other side."

"I don't doubt it," I reply softly.

"Oh," she says as tears well up in her eyes, "it's been too long!"

"It'll be as but a blink—for true love is patient. It always waits." The voice is mine, but the words come from the other voice within.

The lady nods and I feel the gesture ripple through her body and into my hand as I continue to hold hers. The warm breeze whips around us one last time before disappearing and I know my work, for now, is done.

# 11

I've spent a lot of time in the hospital over the last couple of weeks. Sometimes I forget to go home and suddenly find myself asleep on hospital gurney's—sometimes alone, sometimes not. This morning, I woke up next to a naked man in his sixties and decided it is time I returned to a more balanced routine—one that includes sleeping in my own bed and doing more than wandering hospital corridors looking for anyone who might be dying.

Walking home I pass by the burnt out remains of Jaiden's house. There is still a lingering smell of ash and ruin, but the site is completely dormant as it waits for the demolishers to arrive. A gate clicks and I turn to see Jaiden and his little wheaten Cairn Terrier coming out of the back garden carrying a bike and a few dog toys. I can only assume they were safely tucked in a garden shed as I cannot believe they came out of the house.

While Jaiden pauses behind his car to search for his keys, the dog suddenly runs up the road towards me. Instinctively, I check for someone beyond me that might have caught his attention, but instead of darting past me, the dog stops at my feet with his tongue hanging out and tail wagging in an excited circular motion.

Amazed, I stare at the dog, and he stares at me.

"Yip!" says the dog.

Well, who can ignore such an invite? Not me, that is for sure—it is the most any healthy, living creature has said to me in years! Bending down, I pat his head, but he immediately lifts his chin, indicating I should scratch there. This is a dog who knows what he wants! Laughing, I instantly comply with my hairy little friend's request, losing my fingers into his beautiful, coarse coat.

Too quickly, Jaiden finishes loading his car and calls out: "Dougal! Come boy, it's time to go!"

Looking up, beaming from the joy of Dougal's affection, I hope that Jaiden can see me too, but he gazes through me. Maybe he just sees his dog sniffing a flowerpot or a bit of the neighbour's fence. Who knows? I hope it is many, many years before Jaiden needs passage to his *next* and I can ask. Maybe even then I'll never know—because why would he remember?

Giving a second yip, Dougal runs and jumps into the car. As the vehicle passes me, the surrounding trees rustle with a gentle warm current that I am sure wasn't there a minute ago.

\* \* \*

Once home, I shower and eat which helps me begin to feel human(ish). Dad is at work, so I wander to the beach in search of some familiar human 'TV.' It might sound a little sad or sarcastic, but I have missed watching my regulars on the sea front. I enjoy the variety from the tourists, and like tapping into extracts of their lives in further away places, but I really do love seeing the familiar faces of Adtoft residents. To me, they are homely, and I find it reassuring to see life rolling on in a continuum that only they can provide. Thinking about it, it is the only way I can be sure time *is* rolling on.

To my surprise—I cannot say horror or pleasure because I really do not know—Daniel is here. I avoided the ambulance bay at the hospital, telling myself I cannot let myself chase that connection. I badly want to, but the pain, the emptiness of being left alone was so great I have not dared pursue it and risk increasing the chasm inside me. Yet here he is anyway, sat away from the busier areas of the beach, but not where I saved him, looking out to sea. Three friends are with him, yet he seems a little lost, or maybe like he is daydreaming—either way he is certainly not paying attention to whatever they are talking about.

A familiar voice speaks behind me, and I turn to see Raquel. Four women are perched around a picnic bench licking ice creams—except Raquel, who I think is regretting her abstinence as she is watching her friends eat with decidedly green eyes (hers are blue).

"Is he okay?" says one friend after she has run her tongue around the top of the dripping cone.

"Who? Daniel? Yes, he is fine," replies Raquel. Sighing, she rolls her eyes adding: "He works too much for too little and takes unnecessary risks trying to save drunken idiots, but he is fine."

"Yeah, I heard about that."

"Everyone we know heard about that—I made sure of it just in case he didn't realise how stupid it was. I love him, but damn, that kind of heroic action is not what I want to see."

"You can't change who he is," replies her friend. "You have to—"

"Smooth the edges." Raquel cuts in.

"Well, okay, that wasn't what I was going for." She laughs. "But okay."

"You know what I mean." Raquel shrugs.

"Sure," chuckles her friend.

"I saw him go into the library yesterday," says another friend. "Is he starting his studies again?"

"Oh, no, sadly not. He doesn't want to be a doctor apparently. He likes the ambulance work."

"That's good, isn't it?"

"Of course, I'm proud of him. Doing what you love is so important." Raquel beams with pride, backing up her words, but something tells me this is a mantra she tells herself rather than an absolute belief. Her friends all dutifully agree, then start talking about dinner plans.

I walk away. I cannot help these people, and this is not the kind of seaside drama I find relaxing or satisfying. Oki is in her usual 'open for portraits' spot, sketching a mother and child. The mum is bouncing her toddler, singing a little ditty in the hope she can appease him long enough for Oki to finish. They have a parasol protecting them from the sun's rays, but Oki has sweat beads pouring down the sides of her face and I am sure if I could touch her back she'd be soaked with sweat. It's no wonder really because she is seriously over dressed in a long sleeve t-shirt and dungarees. I have seen her wearing this kind of outfit before—she seems to like to alternate between wearing a more stereotypical artist outfit and wearing light, girly dresses with flamboyant colours.

She is beautiful and either works for her, but sometimes I wonder if she is still trying to find her fit.

I'm one to talk. At least she has the courage to experiment—in life I wore the same, safe clothes. This was mostly because I knew what Hayden would accept, but also, I was too afraid to branch out. Now, ironically, I can branch out, but just not keep—although the summer dress has stayed since the wedding, so maybe I have paid my dues to the blouse and trousers. Each morning, I still wake up expecting to see them remoulded to my frame and prepare to pull them off and throw my ring into the sea, but for now I will enjoy the change—even if that also holds a separate pang of regret.

Continuing my walk, I pass by numerous bodies as they stretch out across the sand on little chairs and towels—each one hoping to top up their tan on what could be one of the last truly hot days of summer. I am blessed with a naturally dark skin—not that Hayden ever left me believing it was a blessing for long. Sometimes, especially in our early days, I was his 'gorgeous Grecian beauty,' but they were just words because I don't think I am beautiful and am certainly not Grecian. Hayden used to say that when it suited him—always turning on the charm at the right moment to show off or get his own way. In private...well, let's just say he wasn't always so complementary.

His father is no better. At our wedding reception, when he thought I was out of earshot, Maddox congratulated Hayden on his 'coffee-cream wife.' I don't know what was more frightening: Maddox's words or Hayden's beaming smile.

I really should have heeded the warnings earlier, shouldn't I?

Ignorant bastards.

With everyone I see or hear annoying me, I head north on the beach and do not stop until I find myself on the edge of where the glitch allows me to walk. I have no particular interest in watching a shipping yard and should remember that if I go so far on foot, I also have to return that far on foot. It is a simple equation but one I all too easily forget.

In the distance, a container ship sails by with 'L.G. LOGISTICS' plastered across the boat. For fuck's sake, there really is no escape in this town, is there? This could be seen as an overreaction by some. Maybe it is—Lianna Garvey hasn't done anything to me. I could be fair and say she is just another victim of the Lennox curse—she was the first to spawn a Lennox child after all. However, she is also now a multi-millionaire, so I don't think I'll cry for her for too long.

Fed up and needing the friendly ghost of family to rock me to sleep, I head home.

# 12

The glitch doesn't give me shoes and to be honest, I don't need them because nothing I stand on particularly hurts and I like to feel the sand between my toes. However, yesterday I think I walked too much, so today I decide to go to work with Dad. I hop onto his passenger seat and do up my seatbelt, readjusting myself like an excited child who has finally been given front seat privileges. Dad turns on the radio, listening to the local early morning breakfast show, humming along to the catchier tunes as he heads to his first client's home.

I love the good-natured banter that Dad has with all of his clients. There is no doubt that some of them endure a lot of hardship, but I know his visits provide not only an essential physical service, but a mental one as well.

Watching, I wish that I could help or take part in their conversation, but as the day goes on, I am also thankful that none of them can see me—meaning no one is close to death. Normally I am looking for a connection, but I really want Dad to have something stable and good—I want his clients, his friends, to have something stable and good. After all, I may be able to find peace in my role, but that does not mean I wish to blow the life out of people just so I can briefly feel like I belong.

Dad is with Davie, his fourth client of the day. He is an elderly man with multiple ailments, but none so strong that he will concede his independence. All the houses on this street are close to the road and Davie is recounting how many people have peaked through his living room window today: "Eleven! Would you believe it? Eleven! Nosy bast'rds! Well, they saw more of me than they bargained for, that I can tell ye!"

"Why?" asks Dad anxiously. "What did you do?"

Davie heartily chuckles. "It d'pends…"

"On what?" Dad raises an eyebrow suspiciously.

"How long they looked and how quick I could pull down me pants."

Dad's eyes widen and he tries not to smile. "Oh." He gulps. "Maybe I should get you a new net curtain?"

"Why?" snorts Davie. "I just threw one out!"

"Precisely."

Dad proceeds to reason with Davie, but I can see one isn't listening and the other is losing the will. As the topic eventually changes and time ticks by, I begin to think Dad is clock-watching. It is weird, I know Dad has to be conscious of time in order to get to everyone, yet I have never seen him look like…I don't know…like he is *wishing* time away.

When Dad gets back into his old car, he pulls down the mirror and readjusts his hair. He doesn't need to, there was nothing wrong with it, but he fidgets and straightens himself like he is going on a date. And then it hits me: the reason he is watching the time so closely is not because of where he needs to be, but *who* he is going to see. Sophia.

Parking his car in Flossy's driveway, Dad wastes no time approaching the front door, letting himself in after a cursory knock. Sophia is in the living room reading a book, but she immediately puts it to one side as Dad approaches. He is professional, yet friendly, so maybe most people would not notice anything, but I know my dad, I know what is normal for him—the twinkle in his eye when he looks at her is not normal. The casual, easy ambience I felt the last time I was here has gone: he *really* likes her, and I think she feels the same as she bashfully, yet playfully laughs at his jokes. My heart flutters at the possibility of romance flourishing.

Flossy isn't home—I shouldn't be surprised, there is rarely a day when he isn't on the pier—but I doubt it would matter if he were. These two are so wrapped in those early days of attraction that no one else needs to be around. Yet they do not speak of it or truly act on it. Even in my phantom state I can feel the tension of restraint in the air. Surely his ghost of a marriage isn't holding him back? I am sad to say Sally deserves no such courtesy.

Once Dad has finished bathing and tending to Sophia, he walks to the front door and she wheels her chair behind him, but instead of saying goodbye, she mentions a new film coming out at the local cinema. She tries to sound casual, like the thought has just come to her, but I am sure she has practised this conversation as I see a spark of hope in her eye.

Silently, I urge Dad not to hold onto misplaced loyalty and take Sophia up on her thinly veiled hint that they go together. He grabs the doorknob and casually says, "Yeah, I should go see it sometime. Okay, see ya, soon!"—and then grimaces as he walks down the path.

I want to shake Dad's shoulders and spin him around, but he calmly gets into the car. Jumping onto the passenger seat, I stare, willing him to answer for his inaction, but Dad just slowly turns the ignition key, reverses down the drive, and gently steers the car away. It isn't until he is three streets away that he swears. At least I know I am right—he does like her. Not that it will do any good if he will not say anything.

\* \* \*

When Dad has finished his rounds, he stops outside *Off The Hook,* his favourite fish and chip shop. He asks for takeaway, but one of his neighbours spots him and invites him to join them on the benches outside. He seems relieved to be asked and although I sit and listen to their light conversation for a while, chuckling at the antics of their wayward children and groaning at their ideals for the government, I decide I have heard enough for one day. The only sound I now want is that of the sea—my old, unstoppable, ever changing, but reliable companion.

It is a dry, grey day and there are fewer people than normal on the beach—probably because it is a weekday, and the children are back at school—although Flossy and the pier entertainers still have a steady stream of clientele. Oki has just packed up for the day and is walking away with Nina. She doesn't normally paint too late on autumn evenings, but they were possibly encouraged to leave by the fact a group of teens have just started a volleyball match next to where she was set up.

In search of my typical quiet reflections, I walk south—not so far I cannot hear the faint thud of the pier, but far enough so it does not bother me. Sitting on the sand, lulled by the water, I feel myself drift off to sleep. I haven't dreamt since I died—that privilege has been revoked, but at least sleep gives me the opportunity to switch off.

I don't know how long I have been asleep when I become aware of a presence around me. This is strange within itself because unless just dozing, I am not normally irritated or disturbed by anyone. The sensation gently confuses me until I begin to feel heat—springing my limbs into action as I bolt upright and stare.

It takes a minute for my eyes to focus. If dreaming is an impossible explanation, then Daniel is sitting next to me, alone, and reading a book. My heart skips and my cheeks flush, but my breathing remains steady. Why is he here? What are the chances of him 'just' sitting next to me?—The same as the chances of me 'just' bumping into him on emergency calls and pulling him out of the sea I suppose.

Maybe we are destined to help humanity from our different states of reality together. Part of me says that sounds nice…but the other, really lonely part says it would be nicer if we were both aware. I still feel the strength of that connection we shared—but here, right now, he sits happily oblivious to me ever having existed.

I should go.

Yes, I should really go. This is tortuous…but it is also so calm and quiet here. Remaining seated, the thoughts in my head slow down to the point that all I am focused on is the water rolling and the occasional turning of a page. It's blissful.

The peace is rudely broken by a mobile phone going off centimetres from my ear.

"Daniel? Daniel!" calls Raquel down the phone when he eventually pulls it out of his pocket and answers. "I'm so sorry, I am late home again. Have you eaten?"

"Hi, oh, don't worry. I've eaten takeaway, sorry."

"Oh, no worries…I'll grab something with Olivia and be home later."

"Okay, I'll see you in a bit. I'm on the beach reading at the moment."

"Really? Why? It's almost dark."

"I just wanted to be outside."

"We have a garden…"

"That square of concrete is not a—"

"I have pot plants!" Raquel protests. "And what is the point of grass neither of us wants to mow?"

"Yeah, okay, but that doesn't change the fact I love the beach. It's been a long day and—"

"Yes, fine," Raquel cuts him off. If in person, I can imagine she would be dismissing him by waving her hand in his face. "Though," she says, lightening her tone, "when we have children, a garden might be good…"

Daniel rolls his eyes, but chuckles down the phone. Raquel takes this as a win and moves onto telling him about her day and he patiently listens to her complain about an inconsistent client.

"Oh!" Raquel says abruptly. "Before I go, Olivia wants to know if you know any good child therapists?"

"What?"

"I know that's not what you do, but I wondered if you might know of one or could ask at the hospital about someone who is good?"

"Yes, sure, I can, but what's up? Can you say? Don't give me private info if you're not—"

"Oh, Olivia doesn't mind. She has tried the school councillor, but apparently, they are useless and pretty much says they should just wait and in the meantime be glad their son wants to help at the homeless shelter. Can you imagine that? A therapist saying that a traumatised boy suddenly half ignoring his mates in favour of giving out soup to the homeless on lord knows what street corner is 'something to be glad' about?"

"You just said it was in a shelter."

"What?"

"Not the street—you said he is helping in the shelter..."

"So?" I can hear Raquel sneering in confusion.

"*So*, it sounds like the boy is being overseen, plus the vast majority of the homeless are decent, honest people who have had really crappy luck. Too many people are one step from real, unavoidable poverty. You're fortunate to have been born into privilege—you shouldn't be so judgemental." Daniel pauses and Raquel grunts in quiet recognition of his admonition. "Anyway, it *is* nice to hear of youth caring for more than football, drink, and sex."

"That's a gross minimization of teen interests," retorts Raquel, obviously deciding she can't let Daniel be wholly right. "Olivia's older son is a keen climate activist, and she couldn't be prouder. In fact, he has helped implement changes in the office and the charity budget is—"

"Then what is wrong with the younger son helping out in another way?" Daniel looks frustrated.

"Adi is only sixteen, had a nasty accident pretty recently, and has school and exams to focus on—not wandering around talking about angels and raiding Olivia's cupboards for food, spare bedding, blankets, and whatever else he can get his hands on. There is 'passing on the peace and giving back to society,' as he calls it, and just being weird!"

"Angels?" asks Daniel, as the hairs on the back of my neck stand on end.

"Yes, ever since he fell off that stupid wheel, he has muttered about angels. Anyway, can you text me someone's number? Or do it tomorrow when you've asked at work?"

"Yes—yes, of course," stutters Daniel.

"Great! Well, I'll see you soon, though you'll probably be in bed by then. Love you!" Raquel, impatient to carry on with her plans, doesn't wait for Daniel's muttered answer.

Daniel stares at his phone as the light goes out and slowly puts it back into his pocket. He looks out to sea, wobbling his tongue in his mouth and then shakes his head. I'd love to know what he is thinking. Suddenly he turns back to his book and my heart pounds as I read the title for the first time: *Do Angels Walk Amongst Us?*

# 13

My insides have been dancing since I heard that phone call. Sometimes in a happy dance, sometimes not. It is hard to say which emotion is stronger. On one hand I am overjoyed to discover that my encounters might have left some sort of echo, but on the other hand, I am distraught to be no more than an echo—a curiosity to move past.

That is what Adi's school councillor described our encounter as during their session. I know because I went to his school and read his file—yes, that is low, but it is not like I have many options, is it? Shivers shot all over me as I read: 'Adi vaguely describes the trauma of falling from the Big Wheel before being comforted and saved by a guardian angel. He will give no more information and says he requires no further help from therapy although I suggest extra sessions may be beneficial. Adi has been told it is perfectly normal for the brain to process a nasty, potentially fatal, trauma this way and although it is also wonderful (and to be encouraged) that he feels the desire to help humanity (passing on the baton as it were), he must also enjoy being a teenager—as well as focusing on his homework. Regardless of details being factual or part of a coping mechanism, it is my belief that he has experienced a curious and unsettling event, but it is not one he cannot move past with routine, love, and time.'

After searching for what seemed like an eternity, I found Adi in an English lesson, and then followed him to the sports field with his mates. I don't know what he was like before his accident, but he isn't the loudest of the teens by a long way now. He declines an invitation to play football, lamenting that his doctor said not to because his bones are still healing. I'm not sure that is true—they should be healed by now and I saw no medical warning in his file—but either way one girl has hung back with him, and they are quietly sitting on the swings while the others play.

The girl fidgets with her hair, twisting the red locks around her fingers, chewing the corner of her mouth. Every now and again she glances at Adi and sighs but doesn't speak until he finally looks at her.

"Are you all right?" she asks.

"Sure," Adi replies. "Why?"

"You just seem distant…like you're either not here, or you are, but aren't."

"Sorry," he says, shrugging. "I don't mean to be like that. It's just—" He shrugs again.

The girl leans forward, her eyes widening, hoping he will finish the sentence. He doesn't, but emboldened, she asks: "*It's just*, what? You can tell me; I won't repeat anything. You know that, right?"

Adi hesitates. "I do, but…"

"So, you do doubt me?" She looks hurt.

"No! Not you, Ammi…but—but, you'll think me nuts and not want to be with me," he says scuffing his feet in the dirt.

"No, I won't, and yes, I will," Ammi says reaching out, curling her fingers around his.

Adi looks her in the eyes and gulps as his cheeks blush. She smiles and he returns it but seems no less nervous about sharing.

"Everyone I tell thinks I'm a freak," he says, eventually.

"Fuck 'em," says Ammi.

"They might be right."

"Still fuck 'em," she says squeezing his hand.

"So, you don't think me wanting to help at the homeless shelter is weird?"

"No, why would I? It's a good thing, surely?"

"Mum will only let me do it once a week now. She wanted none, but thankfully Dad spoke up for me. She thinks it's dangerous and I won't do my homework."

"That's daft. And you do your work, right?"

"Yes, all of it—on time," grumbles Adi.

Ammi shrugs, appearing to weigh up her thoughts before she asks: "Is that it? I thought it was maybe something to do with the wheel…Liam says his mum said—"

"I'm a freak," Adi cuts in, rolling his eyes.

"No! No one used that word!" declares Ammi. "She said 'you have had a unique, but relatable experience'—"

"Psycho-babble code name for 'freaky.'" Adi chuckles dryly. "I shouldn't have told Mum about the angel. I knew she wouldn't get it and would blab." He shakes his head. "She's booking a full-on therapist now."

"Tell me," Ammi says. "I promise to just listen. No judgement, no analysis shit. If you want to tell me, do."

Adi pauses as he looks into his friend's eyes. I hope he can tell her. I hope whatever echo I have left on him is a positive one, not something that haunts him and makes him into a loner.

I do not wish that on anyone.

Suddenly, I feel like an intruder. I've spent so long almost feeding off the conversations of others I sometimes forget to feel bad for listening. It is easy to forget I am not watching actors or reality TV stars who have chosen to be recorded and played to the nation. Instead, I am the silent, uncensored, viewer to anyone whom I happen to find.

The novelty here is this boy is talking about me. Does that give me the right to listen in? I don't know, but I am sorry-not-sorry to say that I am not turning off now.

"When I fell—off the wheel I mean," says Adi, gazing at Ammi, waiting for further encouragement. She nods, he hesitates, then continues: "When I fell off, I felt like crap...I felt like my organs were bleeding and collapsing into each other. I felt cold—" he again stops, grimacing as he relives those moments and Ammi stifles a shudder. "I felt really cold, like that was it, I was dying...but then I didn't, it—it was like being wrapped in a warm hug or a bubble of air. I don't know, but I felt *calm* somehow...and I saw her."

"Her?"

"The angel. She told me I would be all right—and I believed her. I felt it..." Adi drifts off into his own thoughts and Ammi stares across the field, watching their friends play, her eyebrows twitching as she attempts to reconcile what Adi has said.

"So..." Ammi finally says whilst sucking in her bottom lip. "Then what?"

"Then—then, I passed out and woke up the next day in hospital, feeling groggy, but happy to be alive."

Ammi gently rocks her head in acknowledgment. "What did she look like? How do you know she was an angel?"

"I felt it rather than saw it. She looks human, but she feels *extra*."

"Huh. Have you seen her since?" I find myself leaning in although I do not need to.

"No," Adi says quietly. "But—"

"Yes?" Ammi asks.

He shakes his head. "You think I'm nuts, don't you?"

"No," she says lightly, but firmly. "Not at all. This kind of thing isn't new to me. My gran is into spirits and otherworldly stuff. She's not well at the moment, but she'd probably love to talk to you about it—if you want to. She'd be far better than your mum or the school councillor anyway."

Adi's face lights up. "Really?"

"Yes, *really*. And you can always talk to me. That's what girlfriends are for. I am your girlfriend, right? We never... but I..." She pauses, waiting for Adi to respond.

"I was hoping so..." he says coyly, "but wasn't—"

Ammi jumps off the swing, pulling Adi off his at the same time. She takes a deep, theatrical breath, pulls him in, and gives him the cutest kiss I've ever seen.

Stepping back, beaming, while keeping a hold of his hand, Ammi pulls Adi into a walk.

"Where are we going?" Adi asks, still half blown away by the kiss.

"To get dinner, *we're* hungry!" She chuckles.

# 14

Deciding it might be useful to learn where he lives, I followed Adi home last night. He had a sweet skip to his step that made my phantom mouth smile as he bid Ammi good night and I was excited to hear him ask her to arrange a visit to her gran's today. Not wanting to miss this meeting I have spent the day following Adi around school, listening to lectures on subjects I didn't think that I would ever hear again, and chastising myself for not remembering more.

As soon as the final bell sounds Adi looks for Ammi. He finds her propped up by the bicycle shed, grinning. I laugh—neither of them came on a bike, but for some reason these sheds continue to be the meeting spot for each generation of children that study here. It was certainly no different in my day.

Good grief, I feel old saying that.

Ammi and Adi casually wander out of the school gates, ignoring their friends invites, and walk into town until they turn down a little side street—one that would be very easy to miss if you didn't know it was there.

"Your gran lives here?" questions Adi as he peers up the steep staircase.

"Yeah, I know, it's not where you'd think you'd find an eighty-year-old woman," chuckles Ammi. "There's a night club in the basement now. Mum wants her to move in with us, but Gran won't have it."

"But there's no lift. Surely she doesn't walk up these steps?"

"Until recently she did. Now she just stays up on the top floor, watching the world from her balcony. She can see the sea and the promenade, so she says she's okay. She's—"

"The cat's mother!" cuts in a stern, but shaky voice.

"Oh, hey, Gran. I was just—"

"I heard. Pfft, never mind that," says the voice from above. "Is this Adi?"

"I am, madam. It is a pleasure to meet you."

"Well, aren't you well brought up?" smiles Ammi's gran as they reach her. Her teeth are amazingly white, and her hair is dyed silver. "Call me Omi. Come in, come in."

They make small talk as they walk through the flat which is basically a library. The walls are filled with books on spirits, ghosts, angels, herbs, auras, and white magic—and there are more fragranced candles and hanging crystals here than any shop in town.

"Wow, you have so many books on so many subjects!" says Adi in awe.

"Ah, yes—I don't like to limit myself," Omi replies, opening the balcony door.

They seat themselves around a little table which has a swirling purple patterned cloth covering it, but despite the chairs all looking comfortable and it being warm for an evening in late September, the old lady only settles once she has wrapped herself in a thick winter blanket.

"So...you wanted to talk to me about spirits?" Omi asks.

"Yes," says Ammi. "Or Adi does. He is shy, like I said on the phone, but he is worried—"

"Let the lad speak, my dear. I can see he is shy. There's no need to fear me. I've seen my share of odd things—and I do not believe we are as alone on this planet as others think." She smiles warmly. "Who or what did you see?"

"I don't know her name—do angels have names?" replies Adi.

"An angel, huh?" The lady rubs her pale chin. "Tell me more."

Adi hesitates at first, but then sighs and again recounts his story.

"Intriguing...yes, very intriguing. But this is good, isn't it?" says Omi. "You've been saved, so why do you seem so troubled?"

"Because now I cannot forget her or the peace I felt when she saved me. It has to have been for a reason—it has to *mean* something. I cannot just take her gift and not do something with it."

I wish I had answers to that myself.

"If this is the result of being saved from the brink—the focusing of a better, more thoughtful human—then it is a pity this angel doesn't come for us all." Omi chuckles. "Certainly, the little shits from number three could do with a little of the *peace* you are describing."

"It's not funny," says Ammi, looking a little disappointed in her grandmother's reaction.

"No, no, it ain't. But Adi here understands, and I understand him. I commend him, actually. I can tell he is a good soul. He has a good aura—I sensed that the moment you walked up the stairs. Even now the air is full of purple, gold...and white." Omi stops and closes her eyes as though that will help her see better, then smiles broadly. "I wish I had the answers of why and what for. I reckon that is for you to decide, but spirit guides and guardian angels are a blessing we should not ignore. I wait for one now. Maybe she or he or they are present..." She pauses, smiling again. "But maybe it ain't for me to know until I know; any more than it was for you to see more than what you saw, while you saw it."

\* \* \*

They chatted for some time, and I listened with amusement as well as interest, yet as I leave the flat, I cannot help feeling a little disappointed. I don't have any right to be—I am happy Adi has people to talk to and my effect has been largely positive, if not a tad confusing. However, if I am honest, I think I was hoping for answers.

After I had just died (well, after I stopped trying to attack Hayden), I visited the library and researched afterlives. There were some fascinating theories, tales of meetings, and potentially plausible sightings, but none matched my exact experience, gave solidity to my circumstances, or definitively answered anything. My conclusion was that I am alone and if anyone, either past or present, is like me then they cannot write either—not that I'd have anything useful to impart if I could.

I suppose it was unfair to expect anyone to give me answers now, yet I still found myself clinging to hope that Omi might be the missing link. She is wise enough to know to be appreciative and undoubting of life's how's and why's, even without explanations. Perhaps that is my lesson; however, my cynical side says that is a whole lot easier to accept if you are not so wholly alone as I am.

Adi and Ammi walk hand in hand, quietly chatting. Passing the library, something suddenly catches Adi's attention on the noticeboard, and he stops in his tracks, glaring.

"What the fuck?"

"What?" says Ammi, innocently.

"Is this your idea of being funny?" he sneers, dropping Ammi's hand.

"What?" Confusion washes over her face.

"The poster. Look at the bloody poster!"

Over his shoulder, I see the poster and gasp—not that anyone hears. Pinned in the centre of the board is an A4 sheet with a blue background. The drawing in the middle is pretty crude, but it is obviously meant to be an angel in a white dress with dark hair, surrounded by a yellow light. If it weren't for the dark hair colour (which I've seen is often blonde in books), it would be fair to say the artist has gone for the stereotypical image of an angel—whether for simplicity, belief, or lack of ability, I couldn't say.

In black block capitals the heading reads: HAVE YOU BEEN TOUCHED BY AN ANGEL?

*"Have you had an experience you cannot explain? Maybe a near-death or just chance encounter? Meet by the bandstand on the promenade at 19:00 on Wednesdays to chat to a non-judgemental kindred spirit (pun-intended)."* Ammi turns, chuckling to Adi. "Seriously? Who wrote this?"

"You?" spits Adi.

"What?" Ammi looks hurt. "Why would I?"

"I trusted you with—with whatever this is. I told you how my mum and family think I'm nuts and want me to go to therapy—and twenty-four hours later *this* appears. Am I supposed to think that is just a coincidence?" Water wells in his eyes.

"I didn't, I promise!" Ammi cries as tears tumble down her cheeks, and her breathing quickens as she panics. "I would never. My gran, she's the only one I told—and you said I could...."

Adi's face drops and crumbles as he sees the hurt in Ammi's expression.

They stare at each other and neither speaks for a minute or more. Maybe she is encouraged by Adi's silence, but Ammi turns back to the poster and says: "We could go? Just to see who is behind it?"

"What? No way! This is private. I'm not telling some random whoever on the promenade."

"Just think about it," she says, wiping her face before reaching for his hand.

Adi shrugs but doesn't pull away. "It really wasn't you?" Ammi turns to him with her mouth open and eyes wide, again filling with tears. "No—no, it wasn't. I know that. Sorry...I'm really, really sorry." Adi reaches for her other hand, and she lets him take it. "Don't hate me. It just surprised me. And the timing—"

Ammi swallows a residual sob and takes a deep breath. "Yeah, I know, I get it. But don't accuse me like that without talking first."

"I'm sorry," repeats Adi, with genuine remorse.

Ammi twists her mouth as she thinks, then smiles kindly. "Let's go," she says, pulling him away. "Besides, I could draw better than that when I was six!"

They both laugh.

I am pleased their disagreements can be so easily brushed aside. I have never personally experienced an argument that blew up and dispersed as easily—so decidedly *non*-violently. Surprise, disappointment, and confusion do not have to be resolved with fists. Words can be used without venom—it is possible to learn to rearrange them into stronger, healing sentences and not cause heartache and insult. If at sixteen they are already starting to figure this out, maybe there is hope for humanity after all.

# 15

There are ten posters around town. Most are on random posts or poles, but one is by the main bus stop and three are on the pier. I wasn't sure if they were Daniel's handiwork until I saw the three so close together, but it is too much of a coincidence that the posters appeared quickly after he learnt Adi believes he saw an angel. I suppose he figures that if Adi saw me here and he saw me on the beach, this is as good a place as any to appeal for other sightings—and hopefully catch Adi's attention.

Of course, my curiosity has compelled me to attend Daniel's meeting. It is a grey, dusky evening and the sea is rougher than it has lately been. A few hardcore walkers are out despite the imminent threat of rain and although Flossy is on his stall with Rufus and the hotdog-heavies are in place, staring at each other across the pier, very few other people are around. Certainly, no one is hanging about looking to attend a spiritual meeting.

The bandstand is a beautiful structure with solid, old oak posts forming a square, with ornate beams and a thatch roof. Years ago, someone on the council was petitioning to buy it and the surrounding grassy patch, proposing to replace it with a larger, circular, metal frame that was 'better suited to a modern, forward-thinking enterprise.' Thankfully, the local residents objected, and *The Swinging Anchor* purchased the rights, promising to preserve it as a historical feature as well as continue to use it as part of their music nights. Only the councillor who wanted to buy it objected and the promenade now proudly displays elements of the old and new, depending on where you look.

Spits of rain become persistent and suddenly a familiar sandy-blond man darts past me under the cover of the bandstand. Daniel glances around the semi-circle of fixed empty seats and sighs. He checks his phone for the time—18:55—before proceeding to pace, sporadically pausing to stick his head into the rain to get a better view of the promenade.

By 19:30 I think he is ready to give up and go home; however, to my surprise he instead pulls a book out of his jacket pocket and sits down to read under the central light of the bandstand. I cannot help questioning why he didn't do this for the last thirty-five minutes, but with nothing better to do, I sit behind him and read over his shoulder.

*My Walk with Angels* is the book's title—I suppose he must have finished the previous one. The library has lots of books with similar, if not matching titles on the subject, but I cannot remember reading this one.

"Hey," says a voice.

Daniel and I look up to see Ammi and Adi, hand in hand, standing awkwardly by the conductor's podium.

"Hi!" says Daniel, quickly putting his book away and standing up. "I'm Daniel. Did you see my poster?" He sounds uncharacteristically anxious, and I think he is forcing himself to look them in the eyes.

"Yeah," says Ammi. "I haven't seen an angel or anything, but he—" she swings Adi's left arm forward, trying to encourage him to speak. He doesn't.

Daniel waits for a moment—possibly a second too long, as Adi shakes his head and turns to leave, but thankfully Daniel overcomes his nerves long enough to find voice: "I have," he says, and Adi stops. "I have seen, I have *felt*, an angel—here, in Adtoft, on this very beach." Daniel points to the southern beach for added effect.

Gazing cautiously, Adi silently considers his options. Ammi patiently waits, but the corner of her mouth curls into a smile when he makes a move towards the chairs. Once both men are seated, she places herself by Adi's side.

"I was on the pier," Adi says. "I was half dead and she saved me. Do you think I am nuts? Is that even possible? Can you be saved by a spirit?"

Daniel smiles. "It must be, for I should have drowned."

They start comparing notes. At first in short sentences, testing out the others reaction, but after a while they become more open, more honest with one another. Ammi has barely spoken, but she has wiped a tear away more than once as she listens to the men talking. This is a therapy session worth attending—although I feel guilty leaving people so marked that they need therapy.

"Do you think it is just us?" asks Adi after a moment's silence. "Do you think the angel guards all of the Adtoft residents or just us two?"

"I have no idea. I put up the posters in the hope I wasn't alone in this experience. That I wasn't—"

"Crazy? Seeing things?" fills in Adi.

"Exactly."

"My mum thinks I'm nuts. What does yours think?"

"I've not told her. She's not well, I don't want to worry her," replies Daniel. "I've not told anyone."

"Not even your partner?" asks Ammi.

"Especially not her." He pauses, then chuckles. "She'd either think I've lost it or be jealous that I'm thinking of another 'woman' so much."

"You should tell someone," says Adi. "Maybe not your partner if she's—well, you know, but your mum or a friend. The knot in my gut got so much better when I told Ammi."

"I just told you, didn't I?" smiles Daniel.

Adi laughs. "Good point."

"Thank you so much for coming. Really, I—"

"Nah, likewise. It's just a shame you aren't a therapist. If you were, you could sign me off and keep my mum at bay." Adi rolls his eyes, then turns to Ammi. "We better go, I promised your mum I'd have you home by 9:30 and I don't want her on my back too."

"Okay," she says, standing up.

"Will you come again?" says Daniel. "Maybe someone else will join us?"

"I dunno. Maybe," says Adi. "I'm glad we chatted…even if it answered nothing, it helped." Adi starts to walk away and stops, laughing. "By the way, you may want to improve your artwork."

Daniel smirks. "I know, it isn't her at all. I searched in books for inspiration or to copy someone else's image, but in the end all I got right was the colour of her hair."

"Yeah, you got that right, but her skin is darker, and you didn't put her in the right clothes."

"Oh? She was wearing white with—" Daniel stops and fidgets in his top pocket, pulling something out in his closed fist while Adi cuts in.

"Huh, she was wearing pale pink when I saw her. I wonder why the different clothes? Do guardian angels change clothes?"

"As long as she is your guardian angel and keeps you safe, I don't care what colour her skin or clothes are!" interjects Ammi, linking her arm with Adi's.

Daniel looks at them quizzically, as though he is attempting to balance and make sense of what they just said. "Agreed," he says eventually. "She—no, I can't say just *she*, *it*, or plain *angel* like I'm describing a thing. *Angel*. Angel kept us safe in our hour of need, but I cannot deny she has also left me wanting to know more—to have more."

Adi nods thoughtfully in recognition. "I'm not sure if 'more' is what we are supposed to have, but I do sometimes feel like Angel is still with me."

"Do you feel that now?" asks Ammi.

Adi flushes crimson and so does Daniel. Do they feel my presence? Or could it be they just feel that way now because they are recounting their stories together?

"Wow," says Ammi, wide-eyed, as she interprets their blushes. She looks at Daniel's still closed hand and says: "What were you going to show us?"

Daniel sucks in his bottom lip and sighs as he stares at his fist. "When I saw her, Angel had flowers—small yellow roses—on her dress and in her hair. I was so peaceful, so happily overwhelmed as I held her cheek that I never wanted to let go. Then my girlfriend called me—almost like I was being dragged back to Earth—and I felt my hand fall through Angel's hair to the sand and the sudden lack of her warmth left me totally numb. I knew people were around me, checking me, talking to me, but it wasn't until I got in the ambulance that I realised I was holding something in my hand." Daniel opens his palm to reveal one of my roses in perfect, unwilted condition and my heart skips a beat.

"Is that the same one?" asks Ammi. "It can't be…?"

"It is," says Daniel calmly. "And I haven't been able to let it go ever since."

# 16

I am trying to tell myself this means nothing. I am still nothing. I help in brief, life threatening, life altering moments, but that is it. Being remembered, being named, means nothing—certainly no more than the joy of being appreciated. Why Daniel was able to pluck a rose from my hair and why it has not died, I do not know, but he is alive, I am dead—a shadow at best. I cannot and will not fall in love with the living, no matter how strong the connection I felt with him. To pursue it into present and future tense will only bring me more pain. I must be satisfied with the momentary.

That is my role. *That is my role.* THAT IS MY ROLE.

I cannot chase that which is not mine.

But it's interesting though, right?

I have split my schedule between the hospital, following Dad, and the beach. I think the balance is working for me and I sleep soundly in my own bed each night—except on Wednesday's when I crash in one of the beach huts after I have sat with Daniel on the bandstand. He arrives like clockwork five minutes early each week with a different book to read and I sit behind him, reading over his shoulder. I shouldn't, I know, and I silently repeat that I am only going to hurt myself—but I turn up every week anyway.

Adi didn't return the next week, nor the following three weeks after that. Maybe he thinks he has said all he needs to and has his life to lead. I decided if that's the case, great, but to be sure he is all right, I waited for him after school yesterday. He appeared from class, laughing, and joking with Ammi, and when I followed him home later that evening, I detected no great stress or strain beyond being a teen. Relieved, and not wanting to intrude anymore, I went on my way.

Nobody else has appeared in answer to the posters claiming to have seen me, but random people have come out of curiosity. One chatted with Daniel for a while, however, it soon became clear their take on guardian angels was very different and, as the stranger didn't relish the potential of being wrong, the conversation soon dried up. Another was hoping for free tea and cake (something Daniel has never thought to provide, even for himself) and quickly left disappointed; while another stayed far longer than either Daniel or I wanted, telling him that angels were just demons playing tricks. If that were true, I would have happily played a trick on him there and then.

Today, a pair of women who study mystics have spent an hour chatting with Daniel. Their philosophies are interesting: one believes each person has a specific angel sent by God, the other believes they are generic, neutral beings that are neither good nor bad and just take or save souls according to the whim of the moment. The second woman slips her jacket off her shoulders, revealing winged tattoos on either shoulder, stating that is her way of paying homage to all winged guardians. Staring at the wings—one white, one black—I feel confused. I have been referred to as an angel many times now. That could just be a collective term, a way to be inclusive when true understanding is limited, but if that is the case, why do people always assume spirits and angels have wings? I definitely cannot fly nor appear at will, although I wish I could.

Caught up in their conversation, I don't immediately register that the women are gradually leaning their bodies closer and closer to Daniel—like they are forming a pincher manoeuvre in order to capture him in their lusty web. At first, I laugh because I can see Daniel isn't responding. Maybe he is used to it, I wouldn't be surprised if people flirt with him at work—especially drunks on nights out who decide the whole 'I'm a damsel in distress, the handsome paramedic has come to save me' scenario is worth pursuing.

Daniel continues to adopt a 'carry on talking seriously and hope they take the hint' method of deflection, opening the book he is referencing with the intention of reading them a passage which debunks the fallen angel theory they are discussing. As he turns the page, searching for the exact paragraph he is looking for, the tattooed woman gently grabs his leg and starts stroking him.

"Oh, sorry, I'm taken," Daniel says, calmly brushing the woman's hand aside.

"Oh, really?" she replies softly, returning her hand to his leg slightly higher than before.

Panic shoots across his face and anger flashes across mine. Not stopping to consider the logistics, I grab the woman by the arm and tug.

"Ahhh! Who was that?" screams the woman, jumping up and brushing her arm.

Daniel takes the opportunity to get up and step away from both women.

"Who was what?" asks the friend, checking behind her. "Is there a spider, Carla? I hate spiders."

Carla scowls. "No, it wasn't a fucking spider! Spiders can't hold you, for starters!"

"What then?"

"What kind of fucked up prank is this? Are we on camera?" Daniel stares blankly at her. "Don't give me that—you did something, didn't you? You invite people here to talk about supposedly real things, then scare the shit out of them with your tricks! Well, I ain't laughing. Fuck you and fuck your 'guardian angel.'" She looks around again. "Where are they?"

"Who?" asks Daniel innocently. "I didn't do anything."

"Whatever. I know what I know. Come on Kel, let's go. This guy is just a dick."

As the woman walks away, I try to touch her again. I feel mean intentionally trying to scare her, but the need to know if I can deliberately, willingly, touch someone spurs me into action.

I shouldn't have bothered.

My hand glides through her like rain through a cloud and I feel flat as the fleeting feeling of potential slips by.

The women both walk off muttering curses and I hear Daniel release a deep sigh of relief before glancing around the seats, reassuring himself that no one is there. Obviously, he cannot know it was me—why would he? To him I am a past encounter, a rose-carrying phenomena maybe, but not an all-too-frequent spirit companion.

I have never touched anyone like this before—in life or death come to think of it. I want to have physical form and abilities, yet I am now freaking out as I consider a new possibility: Was I protecting Daniel against unwanted hands or was I jealous? Was he in danger? He was probably quite capable of stopping their advances, I just didn't give him the chance. Daniel isn't mine to defend from women. He has a partner for that—a living one.

"Daniel?" says a voice.

Turning, I see Rufus leaning against the bandstand entrance. I didn't know they knew each other—and cannot say the discovery is a happy one.

"Hey, what are you doing here?" Daniel says, still looking flushed.

"I just finished for the day helping Uncle Flossy. You?"

Daniel sighs. "Does Mum know?"

"What?"

"That you're still helping Flossy? She did ask—"

"Don't start that again. I'm getting paid. You should be happy."

Daniel shakes his head and gazes out to sea.

Rufus continues: "Look, Leo is looking out for me—he got me work. I ain't about to turn that down."

"I got you that interview—"

"I know, I know. But it was part time and—"

"It was supposed to fit in with you going back to college."

"That isn't for me, I am a doer." Daniel opens his mouth, but Rufus waves a hand, saying: "Yeah, yeah, I could do an apprenticeship. It's cool. *I'm okay.*"

Daniel sighs again. "Just be careful. In the ambulance, I hear...you know...bits and pieces," he says carefully.

"Well, close your ears." Rufus snorts. "There's nothing to hear you need worry about."

Daniel scratches his forehead and scuffs the floor with his foot but doesn't answer.

"Anyway, I came over 'coz I heard two women moaning about some weird guy. What the hell did you do? You aren't cheating on Raquel, surely?"

"Of course not!" Daniel declares as my irrational heart sinks. "I was reading a book on angels, and they started chatting about them, then got, erm, *too friendly*, and—"

"Bloody Casanova. Woman always were after you," laughs Rufus.

"You have your fair share, I've seen you," chuckles Daniel.

Rufus giggles and nods happily. I've already observed he enjoys flirting as he watches Flossy work—I cannot describe what he does as working because I have yet to see him do more than carry Flossy's cooler box across the promenade.

"How is Mum today?" Daniel asks.

Hang on... Are they referring to the same 'Mum'?

"OK, a bit green round the edges. Are you still taking her to her appointment tomorrow?"

"Yes, of course. 9 a.m."

"Good, you're much better at that sort of thing."

Daniel just nods.

I feel sick. I knew Rufus had a half-brother, I knew his name, but it's not an uncommon name and I didn't consider the possibility of a connection. Plus, Hayden and Rufus were on strained terms, so I never met the brother...*in life*.

If Daniel and Rufus share a mother, and Rufus and Hayden share a father…

Then blood related or not, Daniel is a mile too close to a family I want to forget.

Disappointment and anguish hit me like a brick from a great height.

It is too much. I cannot cope.

I must walk away.

# 17

Whilst continuing my rounds at the hospital, I am avoiding the ambulance bay, the bandstand, and anywhere else in town that I might bump into Daniel, Rufus, or any other Lennox. Although determined not to get dragged back into that family, the sea calls to me, so I cannot give up the beach; I just will not look for Daniel—or rather, I will not go to him, for he is currently sat three hundred yards from me on the edge of the promenade.

No, I must leave the living to live and keep to my role—remind myself of my calling. I have not been given a mandate to protect one being. I am for Adtoft, not the Lennox's—or whatever surname each individual might adopt.

October half term has filled the pier with children of all ages dressed in Halloween costumes. As some of them comically run around town seeking various forms of candy, I laugh, but I am also thankful that no one seems to be falling off the Big Wheel as it is now back in action.

On the first 31$^{st}$ of October after I died, I wandered around the graves in the cemetery, wondering if I was about to get a special audience or insight into this curious festivity, but there was nothing—only a large number of sugar-high children dressed in plastic outfits. I commend those who at least reuse or recycle their costumes, but I have seen too many tossed into the bin, adding to the already colossal household waste issues. Maybe I am over cynical—but the 'trick and treats' I received each year courtesy of Hayden lasted longer than any witch outfit and more than once involved a broom stick, so it is probably unsurprising that I am not keen on this festivity.

Walking south, I skirt around a few groups of youths, reminding myself everyone is only young once as they giggle and shout with their candyfloss, toffee apples, cheap alcohol, and cigarettes—the latter two items half of them are too young to have. In no rush, I sit at the base of the cliff by the grass dunes, watching the gleaming water in the beautiful moonlight until way past midnight and the pier has silenced.

A light appears in the distance. At first, I think it is just the moon reflecting in the ever-changing currents further out in the water, then maybe a small boat as it passes by, yet as I watch, the light grows stronger and comes slowly towards the shore before turning out entirely.

Confused, and even beginning to question what realm I am watching, I stand up. As the white horses crash in perfect motion on the shore, the dark form of a large, but not particularly stable dinghy comes into my view. Twelve people tumble off the inflatable boat and drag it onto the beach. I cannot understand the language they are speaking; however, it is clear that they are expressing their relief to be on dry land—despite being wet from walking in the sea. Their journey would be dangerous on any day, but they're lucky their vessel made it to shore because the shimmering waves might be pretty, but they are particularly volatile at this time of year.

Shivering, they collect their things and make their way towards town. I am about to follow them when I see a second light approaching, only this one is not as steady as the first and rather than making a beeline for the beach, it seems to be pointed towards the rocks.

The light again clicks off, however, they quickly lose their nerve and put it back on, turning it out to sea, switching it on and off, then back to the shore—presumably in the attempt to signal assistance from whomever might be more likely to help. No one from the first boat turns back and if anyone at sea is watching them, no one cares enough to come to their aid. The fear and persecution someone must have faced in another country for *this* to be the better option is unbearable to comprehend.

Cries for help echo off the rocks and I know I cannot just stand here. I have never tried helping more than one person at a time before: I hope I am given strength to pull a boat that size—but there is only one way to find out.

Wading out into the water, I trace myself along the rocks. The current is strong, and I am too slow as a wave thumps the boat into the cliff edge. Trying my best to swim, I carry on, but quickly approach the edge of my pixelated tether. With the imminent threat of a tug backwards, I fear all I have achieved is a closer view of a horrible death for these poor, petrified immigrants. Legal or not, no one deserves to die like this.

The boat smashes again as the waves increase. It capsizes, emptying the majority of its cargo before righting itself and springing away. Still, cold, and lifeless, a child floats to me. Grabbing her arm, I swim into my boundary and hold on tight as the glitch pulls me in. She coughs the moment I get her onto the shore. Relieved, but anxious to help more people, I pause just long enough to be sure she is breathing without water in her lungs, before dashing back into the sea.

Just shy of the glitches limit, I find a woman who is probably in her twenties, and I throw my arm around her, swimming backwards as fast as I can. Unlike the child, she doesn't immediately breathe, so I tilt her chin and start mouth-to-mouth. On the third breath she splutters back to life and the child wails with relief. It takes a minute for the coughing to subside, but as soon as she can, she calls the child to her and salt tears of joy and sorrow mix in a chilling scene that will stay with me forever.

Running back into the sea, I cannot see anybody. The boat has disappeared along the rocks, but the sound of it crashing into them as it searches for the shore rattles in my ears. No voices call out in any language and the waste of life hits me—how many souls were on that boat?

I swim out as far as I can, smacking and bruising into the cliff as I go, taking one last look for any life. Finally, resigned and frustrated that there is no one else to help, I wait for the glitch's embrace as it escorts me back to safety.

\* \* \*

Rescue crews eventually came for the mother and child—who is no more than a toddler, with dark grey, wide, soulful eyes. It may have been insufficient to soothe their inner turmoil, but while they waited I was thankful to be able to provide warmth by wrapping myself around them.

Solemnly, I watched as the search and rescue teams scoured the coastline the next morning and cried as they dragged in the remains of the boat and corpses of those I failed.

Having wandered aimlessly, I now find myself sitting in a café in the middle of town, listening to the waiter telling one of the regulars what they know—which isn't much. The fascination in which they recount their story could easily lead the listener to believe it was no more than a fairy tale. Possibly to them it is, for who wants to believe that anyone dies in this town or that weary, desperate illegal immigrants come here? All the bad things happen somewhere else—to someone else.

Is empathy not possible without symmetry? Can we not simply care and act *just because*?

And what sick, selfish bastard put them in that ill-fated boat in the first place—and for how much?

Pouring myself another cup of coffee from the pot, I startle as a new voice joins in the conversation. "Too many drugs, too many illegal imports—human and otherwise," says the familiar voice. Dad. I didn't see him come in.

"Drugs?" asks the waiter. "Do you think there is a problem in Adtoft with drugs?"

"Of course, there is," grunts the other customer. "My grandson came home high as a kite last night. I told my daughter it would happen if she gave him such a free rein, but did she listen? Huh? Did she? No!"

Dad buys two coffees and two cakes to go. As he exits the café, I expect him to find his car in the nearby street, but he takes off on foot, walking up the street, through a little green, and turns into a cul-de-sac—only stopping once he is outside Mrs Crook's old house where his car is snuggly parked. I haven't been here since she died and other than a sold sign being hammered into the front lawn, nothing seems to have changed.

Dad walks up the path, cuts across the lawn, briefly looks around the flowerpots, before opening the rear garden gate and disappearing out of view. Surely Dad hasn't got another new client who lives here? I am about to follow him when a car pulls up and a smartly dressed woman gets out with a clipboard in her hand.

Approaching the front door, she extends her arm to knock, but Dad opens it first.

"Hi," he says. "Come in, come in. Are you thirsty? I just got fresh coffee. How are you?"

By the familiar way they are chatting and laughing, it is obvious they know each other well. They wander into the kitchen and Dad unwraps two moist slices of carrot cake.

"So, all the paperwork is in order," says the woman, sipping on her coffee. "You just need to let me know what you want done and where."

"Fabulous," says Dad. "I have all the plans and colour charts you gave me here. I've marked my favourites with a red star."

Dad pulls a brown, A5 envelope from his pocket and passes it to the lady. She opens it and looks over the designs. "Okay," she says when she has finished. "Well, I'll draw these up formally and send them to you one last time, but we should be all sorted for a pretty quick start."

"By email, right?" Dad says cautiously. "You'll send all by email?"

"Yes, yes—the one you gave me."

"Excellent." Dad's face relaxes. "Oh, there is just one more thing."

"Yes?"

"How difficult is it to move an adult tree without killing it?"

"Some are harder than others—but with the right skills and timing, it can normally be done."

"Wonderful."

"Which tree do you want to move?"

"It's not here. It's in my current home—house. Is that still doable?"

"Sure. What kind of tree is it?"

"A magnolia."

# 18

To my surprise, Dad has not mentioned moving to Sally and neither has he brought a single cardboard box into the house. Everything is exactly as it was—except it isn't, because if he has bought Mrs Crook's house with the intention of doing it up and selling it, why would he want to move my memorial tree there?

Hoping to find an answer, I have been following Dad on all of his rounds, paying particular attention to Sophia. I felt sure I would find some kind of breakthrough in their relationship, yet all I can see is the same tense, unspoken love that you see in films and really want to shake the actors for—only this is my dad, not some Hollywood heartthrob.

In fact, Dad seems so tense today that he actually looks relieved when Flossy comes home early, complaining about stormy weather and fickle punters.

"Oh, I'm sure you'll have sun another day soon." Dad says, trying to sound casual. "No one can resist your goods, I'm sure."

Sophia gazes at him with a raised eyebrow, like she is unsure whether to laugh or not, but Flossy just chuckles and kicks off his shoes. "Yeah, well, if I don't, the young'uns can do the selling *another day.*"

"Very wise," says Dad, "you're always too busy."

"Huh." Flossy snorts. "I thought about retirin' until 'em hotdog twats turned up. Little Miss Mae and her mister fuckin' men aren't what we had planned."

Dad stares at Flossy and Sophia stares at my dad. Flossy pulls his legs onto his footstool, groans, and picks up the newspaper—he clearly has no intention of expanding and I don't think the others dare ask.

My ignorance is frustrating. With no way of asking questions, I really wish I had a crystal ball to look into—some kind of wisdom of foresight—so I understood the present as well as the future. Perhaps then I could try to guide people to a safer, more tranquil path.

Thinking of crystals reminds me of Omi, Ammi's gran. Her flat felt homely, and I had intended on visiting again to read some of her books. As I feel lost and clueless here at Flossy's, I welcome the idea of quiet reflection, so set out for Omi's, reaching it as the sun is setting.

Standing on the balcony, Omi is wrapped in a blanket, wearing a thick woollen, rainbow coloured hat that hides most of her silver hair. The air seems to still as we leisurely admire the view and neither of us return inside until the last dregs of light disappear over the horizon. Once she has taken off her blanket and hat, Omi slowly hobbles into the kitchen to make herself a cup of tea while the numerous shelves of books welcome me.

Vaguely aware of the gentle jangle of hanging crystals as a light draught wisps through the ailing balcony doorframe, I tuck myself into a cosy chair by the unlit fireplace and lose myself in the joy of reading.

"You better drink it before it gets cold," says Omi.

Startled, I turn to the old lady and realise she is looking straight at me. She nods towards the little coffee table that separates us where two bone china mugs are filled with steaming black tea.

"It's green tea, so I didn't give you milk or sugar—but both are in the kitchen, if you'd like?"

I feel myself blinking, as though I am trying to wake from a dream.

"Thank you," I whisper.

Omi bobs her head and turns to her book, slipping on a different pair of glasses as she does.

Every hair on my body feels like it is electrified with indescribable emotion: *I am talking to someone, and not only do they* hear, *but they* also see me...

Am I dreaming? I must be...

"Excuse me," I say, doubting my sanity.

"Yes?" Omi says, quietly.

"You—you, can see me?"

"I see white and gold...and black," replies Omi calmly.

"Pardon?"

"Your aura, my dear—I sensed it when you visited before. I wasn't sure at first. The boy, Adi, has a colour, like a lingering scent, surrounding him, yet I now know the true, vibrant colour comes from you."

"What do the colours mean? Black doesn't sound good—is it death?" I ask, hesitantly.

"While gold can suggest divine protection or even enlightenment, and white is pure and can signal an angel—or in this case, *does* signal an angel, black is not always bad. Black signals protection as much as it can be the draw of energy from unreleased grief." Omi pauses to take a sip of tea. "You are a plethora of colour within, you must banish negative energy and shine, my angel, shine."

"I do not know how," I barely whisper. I feel silly. Isn't it normally the living seeking answers from the dead, not the other way around?

"None of us do. Self-doubt all too often restrains us. If you believed in yourself more, you could do more, see more—and though now gone, be seen more."

"I only rattle and echo for those who see me."

"Pfft, you give me peace," smiles Omi. "To be brought peace so close to my end, to know those here, in this town, might have hope in your peace: it is a blessing—a blessing, you hear? Never doubt it. *Shine.*" Omi falls silent for a moment. "Now, drink your tea—not everyone can say an angel drank their tea, you know."

Chuckling softly, I reach for the mug. It is warm and smells amazing. It smells real—is that possible? Looking back at the table, the mug is there, but as I drink from the mug in my hand, the liquid on the table reduces. "See?" says Omi. "It's good, isn't it?"

"The best."

# 19

After two days of quite companionship with Omi, I feel a pang coming from the hospital—like the glitch is telling me I am needed—so, despite worrying I might lose our connection, I leave late in the evening, promising to return the next day.

I don't normally visit the hospital at night, and I spend most of the walk over there rebuking myself for ruining anything that makes me happy for more than a minute. However, as I walk into A&E it is as though the glitch wants to slap me with an 'I told you so' as a man with a stab wound is rushed past me.

At first the man is conscious, and a policeman tries to get some sort of statement as the doctors and nurses work, yet he quickly begins to slur his words and the policeman is shown out as everyone else battles to keep him alive. The colour drains from his face like an emptying ink cartridge, telling me which of my services is required. There will be no statement and justice will have to be served another way, for as the man grasps my hand and looks me in the eyes, the breeze whips in and flies out, and it is all over.

The emergency services talk to one another, trying to piece together what happened on the promenade to cause this sorry waste of life. They know very little and certainly nothing makes sense to me, so feeling my job is done, I head towards the exit. However, before I can step out into the night I am distracted by a screaming mother and another emergency team bringing in an unconscious teenager.

One paramedic is already performing CPR, while the other explains the patient has had a suspected overdose. The mother declares this is impossible—there must be another reason her daughter is unconscious and foaming at the mouth—while a nurse calmly pulls her aside so the team can work.

Reaching for the girl's hand, I immediately shudder.

We are all too late.

I cannot even help her in her final moments—they have already passed.

As a doctor finally calls time, the mother wails. My heart breaks for her—no parent should have to bury their child—and I am sorry not to be of use. Hopefully, another angel was present for the girl.

Surely other angels exist, somehow?

Maybe I am an apprentice and there is a realm where other angels dwell together? Who knows. But as I am alone, and this poor, devastated woman has people to attempt to comfort her where I cannot, I leave, slowly making my way back to Omi's flat, were I fall asleep in one of her armchairs.

\* \* \*

"You've almost got a shape," says Omi, greeting me the next morning.

"Oh?"

"I think the nearer my end I get, the clearer you become. Is that normal in your experience?"

"You're the first to see my colours, Omi," I reply. "But yes, I believe I am seen clearly at the end—or in times of danger. Perhaps you are in some kind of danger, not dying?"

"Pfft, no," says Omi lightly. "I'm old. Danger and death are one of the same—and I've known I've cancer for a while now."

"I'm sorry," I say, heartfeltly.

"Tis what it is, but thank you." Omi shrugs. "So, did someone die last night?"

"Yes, at the hospital."

"Young or old?"

"Young. Too young."

"Oh, dear. Was there foul play? Do you do policework too?"

"Not to date—unless you want to be my voice? So far, my findings have fallen on deaf ears."

"And where would I say my info came from? If I tell them the truth I will be dying in a padded cell, not my own bed." Omi pauses. "*So far...?* So, you have seen things?"

My mind flashes to my murder. To Hayden pretending we had had an accident and I had been propelled over the cliff. To the police being totally oblivious to the truth, despite me screaming in their ears. Yes, I have seen things—too many things.

But Omi doesn't need to hear this. She is right, as a housebound, elderly lady she cannot report on crimes she could never possibly know any details of. She is dying—I can sense it now. I didn't want too, I told myself I couldn't, because selfishly I didn't want to face losing my only friend, but as she sees the air around me, so I now begin to focus on the air around her. Her aura moves differently in time with the other particles in the air, vibrating with excitement as her next prepares to claim her. Being with her, in this flat, I have learnt so much in such a short period of time, and I feel she has truly helped to centre my senses. My gift to this lady will be peace and hope—not news of drugs, murder, and betrayal.

"No," I lie, "I don't look for such things." Suddenly the hanging crystals swing a little harder from their ropes and chains. "You need a new door on the balcony—you'll catch a cold from that draught."

"My husband built that door. I'll not change it now," Omi replies. "Plus, it's not cold at all when you are here, is it?"

"Really? I didn't know. Om—" I pause. "Do you want me to call you *Omi*? You were not born with that name, surely?"

"It is as good a name as any and has served me well for many years." She pauses. "Hmph, a bit like *Angel* is not your name, it describes who and what you are. It is up to you to keep it or not."

I am not sure this is true. I have no control over what others call me. They call me that because it is the closest to what they understand—but if Omi finds identity in her title, which after all is just German for 'grandma,' then who am I to judge?

We spend the day quietly reading and drinking tea, occasionally pausing to share a thought on a passage we have just read. I don't seek larger answers from Omi and nor does she from me. For now, it is all right that I have none, because serenity has absorbed us both.

When Felicity, Omi's daughter visits for an hour, I step onto the balcony, leaving them to enjoy family time together. Her daughter offers to stay instead of returning to work, but Omi calmly insists she is fine. As they affectionately hug, worry clouds Felicity's eyes, but she reluctantly leaves, telling her mother she loves her and promises to be back late evening after her shift. Omi smiles sweetly, repeating the declaration of love and desire to see each other soon, yet when the front door clicks shut, she solemnly turns to me. We both know in this life they will not meet again.

Later, watching Omi slowly shuffle between the bathroom and her easy chair, I feel impotent. She doesn't once complain, even when I tell her it is okay to express pain—instead, she just mutters a rebuke and chuckles.

As night-time falls, the music from the nightclub below begins again and I ask Omi if it bothers her.

"No, not at all. Sometimes I don't notice it, it has been there so many years. Anyway, I like some of the stuff they play."

"Really?" I say, staring.

"You might be surprised to know old people were once young." Omi grins. "It isn't just teens who like to dance—and not everything has to be strictly ballroom, no matter how much I like that, too."

I laugh at Omi's gentle reprimand, and she chuckles with me. We fall into pleasant, companionable conversation, but after a while Omi grows tired, so I offer to let her rest.

"No, read to me, if you will. Pick anything that interests you," she softly replies.

Scanning my eyes over the nearest bookshelves, I am spoilt for choice. I could literally sit here for a month and not run out of 'anything that interests me.'

"Do you have a favourite—or one you'd like to suggest?"

Omi smirks. "Try, *My Magical Memoir*. It is the one with the purple cover on the third shelf, nearest to you." I act as directed. "My dear husband wrote it before he died. He shared my love of spiritual studies and being in harmony with all the elements of Earth. He'd have loved to have met you."

Smiling coyly, I open the book. As I read, I quietly hope her family are aware of this book and treasure it once Omi has gone. It is full of strange and wonderful happenings mixed in with family history that is probably unknown to most. Omi faintly smiles as I read aloud, reliving tales of her and her husband's adventures together. Not all the chapters are happy, but there is always hope hidden in between—hope and unfaltering affection perfectly blended with mutual fascination of life's idiosyncrasies.

Giggling, I read chapter sixteen which recounts early attempts to understand white magic via the 'guidance' of a less than wise mystic, yet my mirth is quickly squashed as I glance up and see the air around Omi coloured more brightly than before.

She weakly reaches for my hand, and I kneel in front of her, cupping both her hands tenderly in mine. I don't need to look into her eyes to know the timer is about to run out, but I hold her serene gaze anyway, whispering words of love, and wait while an unseasonably warm sea breeze races through the cracks in the door, gently swaying the crystals all around the room.

The final peace befalls Omi as she crosses over, but rather than totally sharing in that peace as she breathes her last, the first of many tears roll down my cheeks and I mourn the passing of a friend.

# 20

Felicity, Omi's daughter, arrives and I sorrowfully watch as she calls for help. Knowing her mother was near the end of a loved life doesn't change the fact the family will now keenly mourn their loss, and I am sorry for their pain.

Going downstairs into the little side street, it feels wrong to see people laughing and joking as they spill out of the nightclub in various degrees of excitement and inebriation. A group of seven or eight are huddled in front of where I want to walk. Obviously, I can go through them, but I am stopped in my tracks when one mentions last night's stabbing.

"That was pretty fucked up, you know," he says, pausing to release a breath of tobacco infused air. "Phil was all right—a bit dim sometimes, but all right."

"I know," says another, "I can't believe it. They'll pay for this. The Boss won't let it slip—"

"Fuck that, *I* won't let it slip! None of us will. This is our turf, we warned them, and they just fucked us well and truly—"

"Yeah, well, tonight we wait. We celebrate the kid's birthday and drink one for Phil. Let the cops sniff about for a day or two, it don't matter 'cause the Boss has plans—we won't let Phil down."

They stamp out their cigarettes and walk inside the club towards the back of the room where a larger group of people are gathered. I recognise a few faces from my beach front observations, but I don't think I know anyone by name until I see a head of familiar sandy-blond hair. As the head turns, I realise the profile is different, with no beard, but I immediately scold myself for not seeing the familial resemblance between Daniel and Rufus earlier.

Rufus and many of his companions are pretty drunk and, as their returning friends approach, the group starts to sing happy birthday—I am guessing not for the first time tonight. One plonks a hat on Rufus with '21 and ready to have some fun' written on it, and Rufus immediately plays the jovial, celebratory part they are clearly expecting of him.

One of the men clocks someone sitting at the bar, and he gruffly pulls Rufus to one side: "What the fuck is she doing here?" he sneers as though it is Rufus' fault who the club does or does not let in.

Rufus begins to ask who, but as he turns, he also pales. "Oh, you've got to be jok—"

"Is that your fuckin' brother? Has that twat no family loyalty?"

"Shit. He can't be that stupid, can he? I know he and Leo aren't exactly best—"

The man grabs Rufus by the front of his shirt. "Birthday or not, I, or Leo—or both—will kick the shit out of you if you invited *her*."

"I—I didn't bloody invite her! I didn't even invite *him*! He just text askin' what I was doing for my twenty-first. If he is with her, that's news to me!"

The man grunts and releases Rufus. "Well, I suggest you go find out before I do." He spits on the floor. "I just said we ain't gonna spill more blood tonight, but if the guys get wind of this—"

"I'm going, I'm going. She has her back turned—hopefully, no one else will notice who she is." Rufus takes off his hat, passing it to his friend and walks towards the bar.

Only now do I dare look at the bar. At first, I just see a row of backs with the odd hand on a drink or mobile phone as people perch along the metallic front, but then, as the crowd moves, a girl with beautiful black hair in red catches my eye. I have no doubt the very tight, short dress was selected for that very purpose, but other than her notable attire, I do not understand the hate she has invoked—until I pay closer attention to her face. The makeup is heavier now, her hair is curled to precision, but it is undoubtably the girl who regularly sits on the new hotdog stand. She is sitting with a leg crossed seductively in front of a man…a man whose name I know only too well: Hayden.

My stomach churns, and I stand in a statuesque stupor, watching as they tenderly link fingers and she smiles at him, silently telling him exactly what she wants to do when they are alone. I feel sick on so many levels, but what makes me the most nauseous is the realisation that part of me is jealous.

Not just angry, disgusted, afraid, enraged, violent, murderous, spiteful, venomous, or any other of the multiple feelings that also hit me.

*Jealous.*

Jealous of a girl who is sitting with my murderer—my husband. The man that swore to our forever and then took a hammer to it. I was loyal, I played my doting part, but I was thrown to the rocks. No metaphor required. My first thought should be to shout and tell her to run—to run and never look back. He is lying, deceitful, and abusive in every fashion of the word. Yet my initial thought is: why not me? Why was I not enough?

How pathetic am I?

"Hey, Hayden," says Rufus the second he is next to him. "What are you doing here?"

"Hey, to you too, little brother!" says Hayden, grinning. "Happy birthday!"

"Thanks, but—"

"Well, that's a welcome! What, do you think I'm going to cramp your style?" Hayden laughs carelessly. "I mentioned to Mae it was your birthday, and we thought we'd just pop in for a pint and maybe a quick dance."

For the first time, Rufus looks at Mae and she grins broadly.

"Sorry, this is Mae. Mae, this is my little brother, Rufus."

"We've met," says Rufus coldly.

"Oh?" says Hayden, obviously surprised and immediately suspicious.

"Hey, Rufus, good to meet you off the pier," Mae says innocently, extending a hand.

Rufus freezes, but Mae giggles and places her hand on Hayden's knee, immediately distracting his attention.

"Where is your other brother?" Mae softly asks Hayden. "You have two, correct?"

"Half, yes, but—"

"Keep the fuck away from him—even better, away from *all* my brothers," snaps Rufus, but Mae doesn't react. "Do you know who she is?" he asks Hayden.

"Don't be a twat, Rufus, I thought you'd be cool. Shit, how possessive can you be about some bloody candyfloss?" Hayden chuckles, sarcastically. If he doesn't understand Rufus, his pride won't let him show it. He has only one interest today: to show off his pretty new girlfriend.

"We're here for your birthday, that's all." Mae winks. "No need for business talk, *today*."

Impatient for news, Rufus' friend walks over. He is tall—well over 6'—and extremely well-muscled, with a very stern expression. "Well?" he demands as Rufus turns to him.

"They have come to wish me a happy birthday," says Rufus, unconvincingly.

"Evenin', Kev, not seen you in a while," says Hayden.

"If this is your idea of good company, it's a pity you didn't keep it that way," sneers Kev. "Leo is coming."

"So?" says Hayden defiantly. He'll die before ever expressing concern verbally, but his eyes dilate at the mention of his rival's name. Unlike Hayden, Leo never particularly sought his father's approval, instead favouring the significant boost his mother provided in her logistics business. Maddox Lennox, however, sees greatness in his eldest son's financial concerns and openly praises him for them—which only adds to the brothers' hostility.

"It's fine, H," says Mae sweetly. "I am ready to go—if you are, of course?"

"We were going to dance," says Hayden, rubbing his hand up her thigh.

"We still can," she winks.

I am going to vomit. Everything in my body is telling me this is not my party, not my fight—not my family. It has been a long, emotional day and I actively want to leave this crap behind. Whatever these idiots have got themselves into, whoever this bastard is into, I really, really, do not want to know.

But the tie, the connection—whatever the heck it is that pulls me to Daniel, tells me to watch his brother for him. It almost commands me to observe, but I do not know why. I have no means of acting, even if I see! I promised myself I would not be sucked into Hayden's affairs—literal or otherwise.

I am dead, that kind of damage cannot be undone.

But what if I could see *him* undone? If there was a way, would I—*could I*—take it?

Probably, yet I fear the energy that would require. Not physically—mentally. I am a delicate balance and seeing Hayden is not helpful or conducive to any sort of happiness—*he* is the black I carry. Omi told me to banish negative energy and shine.

So, I am sorry, I will not accept this mission.

# 21

No, no, no, no!

I have woken up with my wedding ring back on my finger. Why? Why be so cruel? I had just begun to wake up without that feeling of dread—without wanting to rip off my clothes and throw my ring into whatever sea or crevice I first encountered.

Is this the glitch's idea of an early Christmas present?

Well, it's still November, and I want the bloody receipt.

At least I have woken up in my white dress with little yellow roses—although I have obviously been tossing and turning in it as there are creases everywhere. Pulling the ring off my finger, I roll it in between my thumb and first finger. A perfect symbol of stupidity with my wedding date engraved on the inside. I'd scratch it out if I thought the glitch wouldn't replace it in the morning. It did the last time I bothered, although it didn't heal the cut I gave myself with Dad's drill as quickly—not that I bled anything other than tears for my efforts.

I flushed the ring down the toilet once. That was a lesson in 'what will flush and what will not.' Not: in case you are wondering, but when I woke the next day, it was back on my finger, and I am sure it smelt of toilet water as a punishment.

Despite that incident, I still prefer the act of throwing my ring rather than just leaving it somewhere. I like the sensation of violently, disrespectfully, discarding it and all it signifies. My most frequently used ring rejection site is the sea, but because I plan to walk inland and may not get there today, I drop it down a sandy storm drain and hope it finds a permanent grave.

Realistically, much like that yellow cat in the 1980's anime film, it'll probably be back to haunt me tomorrow—but at least for now it is gone, and I can try to forget it.

Today, I am going to Adtoft's main hospice. On my way home last night, I pondered on the fact that Omi knew she was dying for some time, which led me to consider the possibility of others who might be in a similar situation but may not be living at home or be in hospital. These people are just as deserving of a warm hand as they reach their last tunnel, so I am walking inland, hoping the glitch will allow me into the hospice despite it being very close to my sanctioned perimeter.

It is a cold, windy day and everyone I see are wrapped in thick, winter jackets, not light summer dresses like me, but as I am not cold—underdressed or not—I don't bother getting changed.

The journey should have taken me one hour, not two, but I took several wrong turns thanks to relying on my memory of a map I saw on a leaflet in the hospital. In hindsight, I should have tried to find the leaflet again because I wrongly assumed there would be signs directing the way. I suppose most people have cars and satnavs these days—and are not dead—but either way, I finally walk down a driveway labelled, *Quiet Acres Home of Rest,* and feel it is well named.

The hospice is a relatively newly built building, but it is done in harmony with its semi-wooded surroundings, and I cannot help thinking there are much worse places to die. If the sea were in view, it would be perfect, but as Adtoft's more familiar settings hold too many ghosts for me now, possibly even that change of scenery is welcome.

At first, I think the glitch is warning me I am too close to the boundary and is about to stop me—which, unlike being at sea, simply involves me being bounced backwards a metre—but then I realise I am feeling a *pull*, not a *push*.

Following the sensation, I find myself walking the halls of the hospice and am surprised to be led to the resident's day room, not a private bedroom. Scanning the room for inspiration or acknowledgement, all I see is quiet contemplation of a game of chess while others read or watch the TV. I try to focus on the air around each individual; however, the colours and vibrations that I have begun to be able to sense are all embracing one another in sympathetic, unified preparation for what is soon to come for the residents.

A nurse enters, and I am struck by her pale face. She is wearing a light blue uniform and—despite the fact she looks like someone should be caring for her—she diligently wanders between patients, checking on whatever needs they might have.

Surely, I have not been sent for this lady?

I tell myself off: why do I think I have the right to say who is the kinder, more caring—less deserving of death— person compared to the others?

It is not my place to decide. I have no right to judge.

The nurse, regardless of her sickly colour, has a warm smile and it is clear the patients are fond of her. If not working like my dad, I think this is the kind of nursing I would have liked to have done. Even if I find the brevity of my connections painful, and I knew I was going to lose Omi—whose loss I doubly feel as it was the longest respite I've had from my solitude—it has not dulled my desire to help others. The idea of working in a small, consistent team of like-minded people, helping others through their toughest moments appeals to me. There's no doubt it is extremely draining, but giving as much dignity and comfort to people as possible is something to be proud of.

Possibly I should be proud of what I can do; however, I am just not sure I can take true pride in something I have no control over.

I need to stop wasting time putting myself down and focus on why the glitch brought me in here. Sometimes I wonder if I should come up with another name for it. 'Glitch' suggests an accident or malfunction of order (which, is exactly what I used to tell myself all this is). Yet, the longer I am here, like this, the more I have to admit the glitch is organised—even if I cannot profess to understand it.

Perhaps I need to focus better? More feeling, less fight?

Closing my eyes, I let the air guide me.

For a moment, I don't feel anything, but then a warmth tugs me towards a large chair in the corner where a gentleman is reading a spy novel.

He looks up as I approach and sighs. "I don't suppose I'll find out who dun it, hey?"

"It was the vicar's wife," I say with authority, although I've never read the book.

"Huh," he replies. "I thought it was the vicar." He smiles. "Never mind, ay?"

"No, you've a new chapter of your own," my voice says, without me thinking to speak. Maybe the glitch is me and I am the glitch...or just its minion.

"I'm ready." He smiles, taking my outstretched hand, simultaneously dropping his book.

"Jimmy?" calls the nurse as she sees the man's physical arms fall while his spirit whisps away. "Jimmy, are you okay?" She takes his pulse and sighs deeply. There is no resus cart here: trying to revive him would be a cruelty, not a kindness.

"Kath?" calls another nurse as he walks into the room. "Oh, has he—"

Kath nods as her colleague approaches. She strokes Jimmy's cooling hand and stands up, brushing aside a tear from her cheek. "I'll get a gurney."

I follow the staff around all day, humbly watching them work. On top of all their other duties, they talk to the bereaved family with genuine empathy; somehow managing to shoulder the responsibility whilst enjoying companionship with each other. I envy that.

Kath and three colleagues stop for a tea break, and I listen to them talking about their lives. One man's wife has just had a baby, another is considering adoption with his husband, while the lady has joined the local amateur dramatics group in the theatre.

"You're welcome to come with me tomorrow," she says to Kath.

Kath laughs. "I'm not an actor. I'd be too nervous and would never remember my lines!"

"I'd not be so sure, but you could just watch, if you like? Then we could have dinner after?"

"I'd love to," Kath replies, "but my son is taking me out tomorrow."

"Ooh, that'll be nice. Wait, which son? Not Rufus? The last time he took you out, it wasn't exactly—"

"Ha-ha, no, not Rufus." Kath shakes her head. "Bless him, he meant well, but I could have cried as we drove up to the racetrack."

"Idiot. Who takes someone who has just had chemo to a bumper car race?"

"He is young, Layla, he can't help it half the time. He is led too much by his mates. I'd love to see him settled—or at least on a better path before I go."

"Don't say that Kath, you'll—"

Kath gently grabs her friend's arm. "It's true. We see enough end of life to know what it looks like. I may not be moving in here yet, but I am just claiming extra time, not a cure with my chemo."

Layla stares at Kath, but I doubt her vision is clear as she wipes tears away.

"You're too young…it's not fair." Layla's voice wobbles as she speaks.

"Fair is as fair does." Kath shrugs. "I want my boys to be happy. With them, I am blessed. Sure, I have known love and lost it with two utter wastes of space, but I have real love from my family and friends—"

"And that you always will," Layla says, pulling Kath into a hug.

As I witness their tender embrace, I awaken from my frozen state of observer. Words and names replay as though I pressed rewind on a film I daydreamed through.

Has the glitch brought me to Daniel's mother?

I am seriously questioning if any thoughts I have are really my own. Is the glitch just teasing me as it guides me through Adtoft? —I cannot say *through life*, for I cannot call this *living*. Why is it so determined that I do not forget this family that it drags me all the way out here? I had hoped to have found a new path, only to have the glitch laugh in my face and show me another connection to my past.

Only it is not the past, is it?

These people are alive.

The story carries on.

But what am I to do with it?

# 22

The day is still but very cold—or at least I think it is, as any brave walkers are thoroughly wrapped up, and the old ladies who normally have Thursday breakfast on the promenade whilst gossiping about their neighbours' affairs, are inside a café today instead.

Oki is set up down the beach away from the few people who are around. I suppose she has decided the chances of someone wanting to sit for her today are slim, so she may as well work on a private piece to sell. She is well clothed and only her fingertips, nose, and eyes are open to the elements, but even so I think it is a miracle she is holding, let alone using her brush as her fingers are a funny colour.

Sitting on the sand beside her, I gaze between the canvas and the horizon and am awestruck by her ability, like I have been so many times before. She must have completed numerous variations of this coastline, yet I doubt if any two will ever be the same.

Seagulls dance and call above us. Following their performance with simple pleasure, I catch sight of a figure approaching. My heart skips as I recognise Daniel—ignoring the reality that he is, of course, heading for Oki. Smiling, he greets her, and she replies with a warm, friendly tone, even if it is muffled behind her pulled-up scarf. If judging by sound alone, all would seem well, yet her eyes don't truly register any pleasure in being seen. I want him to ask what is wrong and focus hard on the question, but he doesn't ask, and she doesn't answer.

Although frustrated by my inability to add to the discussion, I do enjoy listening to them. They chat about their mutual friends who married in the summer, the weather, her painting, Nina and Raquel—nothing beyond standard polite, friendly conversation, but I easily become lost in the sound of their voices.

When Daniel says he should go Oki doesn't protest and quickly returns to her painting, but I find myself watching him leave, wishing he would come back.

Presumably he still has his angel meetings—certainly, his posters are still up—however, I cannot bring myself to attend. I look down at my dress—my totally inappropriate for winter dress. I really should change, but I know he had—*has?*—one of my roses from that day and subconsciously I think I see the dress as a piece of that connection which I can hold onto.

I am ridiculous.

I am just torturing myself with thoughts and memories. With feelings that connection sparked.

Wasn't I supposed to be letting go? I certainly keep moaning that the glitch pulls me in his direction.

Enough.

I *am* letting him go—

Then why have I followed him across the sand and sat next to him on a bench?

Shaking my head, I rise and walk down the promenade, telling myself this is an act of self-preservation, but suddenly a thought disrupts my resolve and I gaze backwards: what if the glitch is trying to tell me something?

I can't see how...or, possibly more specifically, *what.* Yet I suppose I have time to observe him for a while.

All I seem to have is time—even if it passes for others, not me.

Resigned, I sigh and return to Daniel. He has a book in his hand, and I peer at the title: I am relieved to see it is a crime novel, not a spiritual guide to angels this time. As the bench silently takes my ethereal weight, Daniel smiles like he is reacting to a private joke with the author. I'd like to read the book with him, but he is already halfway through, so the characters will mean nothing to me.

Instead, I peacefully watch the water.

"Danny?" says a female voice. Kath.

Daniel immediately looks up and beams. "Hey, Mum, how are you?" He stands and kisses his mother's cheek.

"Ooh, how are you sat out here and still that warm?" Kath says, sitting down on top of me. "It's freezing out, we should have met indoors rather than you waiting out here. I hope we're going for lunch somewhere warm?"

"Yes," Daniel replies, chuckling. "I'm taking you for a proper, three course meal."

Kath's smile diminishes a little. "It might only be two, I'm afraid."

"Why?" Daniel seems concerned. "Ah, are you still feeling sick?"

"A bit."

"Are you okay to go—"

"Yes, yes, I've been looking forward to this all week. I told Layla all about it yesterday."

"Well," Daniel says, linking arms with his mother, "we better get going then."

This is normally the kind of promenade meeting that I love to tag along to. In the early days it was awkward—not for them, of course, but I equally imagined, hoped, and feared the embarrassment of being 'unmuted' and caught listening intently to a stranger's conversation. That was fantasy, I know that now. There will be no reintroduction into the realm of the living—embarrassing or otherwise—so although I usually enjoy human TV without any guilt, I am battling my growing desire to be near Daniel, telling myself to listen and not listen simultaneously.

"Rufus?" calls Kath.

Following her gaze, I see Rufus waiting outside of *The Swinging Anchor*.

Kath smiles as her eyes dart back and forth between her sons. "What's this?"

"We thought we'd surprise you." Rufus says, smiling as he hugs his mother.

"As I was working on Rufus' birthday, and we never eat as a family these days, I thought—" Daniel stops and embraces his mother as he sees her happy tears. "I thought you'd be pleased," he says, into her shoulder.

"What more can a mother want?" Kath says with a wobbly voice.

Continuing to ignore the part of my brain that sounds a self-preservation alarm, I follow inside and sit at the table with them. The music is set to provide a pleasant, subtle atmosphere, the smell from the kitchen is amazing, and I enjoy listening to their easy, affectionate banter. Instantly, I can see why Kath told her friend she knows love from her sons.

There are obvious concerns for Rufus' future as Kath gently nudges him during the main course to reconsider his career choice. However, Rufus has apparently decided today isn't the day to challenge this topic because he instead opts for deflection, turning the focus onto his older brother's pursuit of angels.

Kath's blank expression makes it clear she is unaware of her son's posters, and he blushes heavily. Rufus is triumphant for a moment, but Kath, to everyone's surprise, quickly shrugs and starts talking about her own fascination with spirits and guardian angels. Rufus seems mildly disappointed not to have prompted maternal disapproval on someone other than himself, but he has the sense to enjoy the change of focus and Daniel seems happy to share his own thoughts now his mother is encouraging him.

"Is that why you're reading that book?" Kath says after a brief pause.

"Which?" Daniel asks, putting his hand in his coat pocket. "This one?"

"That's a thriller, isn't it?" says Rufus, half sneering as he reads the cover upside down.

"Yes," says Kath, "but the crime is solved by a spirit…or was it done by the spirit? I forget—"

Daniel groans. "Thanks, Mum, I think you've just given me a massive spoiler."

"No, no, no I haven't—you meet the spirit early on!" Kath flaps her hand. "Don't look at me like that! You know I haven't ruined it."

Daniel shakes his head, chuckling. If he is annoyed, he isn't going to tell her.

Kath sighs. "You didn't answer my question: is that why you are reading it?"

"Maybe. I've read a lot about angels and spirits—both fictional and otherwise—since my incident on the beach." Daniel exhales deeply.

"It's all fictional, if you ask me," says Rufus.

"I'd not be so sure." Kath turns to Daniel. "Do you ever feel like they are with you? I do. It could be my way of coping with the job, but I like the thought that we're all watched over."

"I've often wondered if we are," says Daniel, smiling. "Sometimes I think I am crazy, but…"

He doesn't try to finish his sentence. I wish he would, but I am left guessing because Rufus simply shrugs, and Kath is too busy having a silent conversation with herself to probe her son.

Suddenly, Kath reaches for Daniel's hand across the table before gesturing to Rufus to take the other. She clears her throat quietly and chews on her lip, then says: "While we are together, I need to say some things. I've told you about my results, what Dr—"

"Don't talk like that, Mum," Rufus says. "You don't know they're right—"

"I do, Rufus, I do..." Kath pauses, notably gripping her sons' hands tighter as she swallows hard. "I need to know you'll both be all right without me when I'm gone."

It is impossible to say which of the three chokes up more at this point—make that four—but the ensuing conversation bizarrely gives me hope that not all of Hayden's bloodline is as rotten as him. Rufus is young and impressionable, I can see that, but under that hard shell, he is also sweet, like Daniel.

I don't know how they feel about their absent fathers, but as Maddox had very little to do with Rufus' day to day upbringing, I cannot help questioning if Hayden would have been a much better person if his father had been restricted to a sperm donor. Nature might still have caught up with him, but Maddox's version of nurture made sure Hayden had the groundworks to flourish and excel as a first-class shit. I can't say his mother helped the situation though. She tries, I know she does, but she doesn't realise the scale of monster she has raised with her inconsistent, self-indulgent methods of parenting. It is a shame Kath didn't raise all of Maddox's offspring.

An idea hits me: maybe Kath could be a potential older version of me?

No, that sounds really arrogant—I should say, a *better* version of me.

Sure, she is not physically well now, but even though—like me—she made some terrible choices with her men, she has broken free and found a more fulfilling life.

I wish I had something to show for my angst. I wish I could sit around a table with people who loved me and say, 'I made mistakes, but I came out the other side.'

...*Although*, if Hayden were locked up or dead for his crimes, that would be even better.

Alas! Here is why Kath is the better person all round. I am not fit to compare our situations. She isn't sitting here spouting desires of vengeance—she is peaceful. Maybe justice was in the breakup. Perhaps she has peace because she learnt life's lessons without being consumed by anger and self-loathing. Or maybe Maddox is an idiot, but even he doesn't realise the extent of evil his spawn has achieved?

I need to leave. I am just going round and round the same painful points. This isn't healthy and these people do not need me.

The crisp sea breeze whooshes around my cheeks as I walk outside. For a split second the glitch forgets to keep me lukewarm, and I feel the cold snap—it is wonderful. If I could chase it, I would, but as I stroll down the street, I return to my 'just right' setting, furthering my lonely reminder of being neither alive nor truly dead.

Seeing Kath and her sons has made me anxious for family though. I could walk to Dad's, but as Mrs Crook's house is closer I make my way in that direction, wondering if I will find any further clue to what Dad is doing there.

\* \* \*

Two white box vans and a massive yellow skip are parked outside Mrs Crook's house. The front door is wide open, and I can hear a radio playing. I would prefer if it were one of the national stations rather than the local one—there's nothing wrong with the local one, except it plays adverts and as I walk in, one about Lennox Motoring Group booms into my ears.

I am beginning to wonder if the glitch is run by the devil.

Blocking out the radio, I check the rooms and barely recognise the building I have walked into. I used to feel like I had time warped coming here, but now all the old décor, the ancient furniture, and quaint tea pots are gone. The carpets have been ripped out and thrown into the belly of the steel beast outside, the wallpaper has been scratched off to nothing so the numerous tins of smooth, matte, magnolia paint can soon be applied, and the kitchen has been gutted.

In fact, the entire house has been disembowelled. It makes me sad—possibly it shouldn't, I know Gladys is in a better place and has no need of her earthly possessions, but I cannot help being sorry to see every trace of her removed this way.

Walking into the pantry, I close my eyes and allow my memory to replace what has gone. I see pots, jars, and the little tray of money just as they used to be. The baking tins line the shelves, each containing the glorious smell of love and home cooking that were always ready to greet me.

Gone, but not forgotten.

A decorator walks behind me and I remind myself why I came: I was supposed to be looking for signs of what Dad is doing here—or was I just searching for a memory of home? If that is true, then I have already found it.

If I concentrate harder, it in fact never needs to leave me.

Upstairs is just as bare as downstairs. Everything is a long way from being finished and there is nothing individual, nothing private, to suggest who will live here, but these workers are moving fast. I get the impression some of the doorways are about to change, possibly the odd wall—even the staircase is being altered. The only thing that undeniably remains from before is the gorgeous sea view from the bedroom window. How I would love to wake up to a view like this every morning!

Returning downstairs, one of the decorators has opened the second reception room door into Mr Crook's office. I rarely entered the room when I was little; I wasn't banned, yet it became one of those places that I just didn't go—except on the odd occasion when my childish fancy told me I should *just check*. Although what I was just checking *for*, I could not say.

From my sporadic inspections, I knew the office was large and had books and files lining two walls, with a dark blue easy chair and lamp positioned beside the sizeable old bureau. Even when curiosity compelled me, I had little incentive to make use of any of Mr Crook's books because historical records and sea charts didn't interest me anywhere near as much as Mrs Crook's fantasy novels—all of which were kept in the living room.

Looking inside now, I marvel. This room has not been touched—or rather, it has not had anything *removed*, for many of my favourite items are stacked carefully within.

My time capsule has been reduced, but it is still very much present. I giggle out loud when I see the pot of old, foreign coins on the bureau, and immediately sink my fingers into them.

If time were money, or better, money was quicksand in time, I would happily slip through it now to a simpler age.

# 23

I have spent a few days at the Crook's house, reading books on subjects I once thought dull as well as revisiting old favourites. After the builders left each day, I considered making some sort of bed upstairs so I could watch the sunrise over the ocean, but instead I opted for Mr Crook's old easy chair and tucking myself in amongst the stacks of old furniture. I don't know if the items within are simply in holding until everything else is done or if Dad intends on having them all collected at some point, but at least they do not seem to be destined for the skip.

After a particularly rowdy few hours, I have heard enough knocking and banging from the builders, so venture onto the beach. The brisk sea air is rattling every flag, sign, or person that is in its way, meaning most people are tucked up inside or moving at speed as they try to avoid being frozen. In preparation for the Christmas holidays, the pier is covered in decorations, and although I am not close enough to hear, I am sure extra merry music is playing to attract any stray, chilly punters.

Despite the weather's best efforts, the atmosphere in festive Adtoft is always warm and inviting. Each year, all the shops along the promenade make a big effort and people enjoy strolling through the colourful lights and the special market that pops up too.

It is lovely, yet sometimes, when in a foul mood, I wonder if humanity doesn't just set itself up for depression come January 1$^{st}$. We spend December building up to one day where we celebrate each other in body and spirit, then turn the fairy lights out, go back to work with no friends or loved ones around, and stumble alone through the long dark nights.

Or maybe that was just me?

*Is me.*

Ugh.

Not feeling particularly festive, the pier does not appeal to me today, yet the grassy sand dunes in their cold, wild state, seem strangely inviting. Wandering down the winding path, focusing on the sand as it grinds between my bare toes, I try to clear my mind.

It almost works until I make the mistake of looking ahead to a dog walker and my negative thoughts swiftly return alongside a few expletives. Of course, she doesn't hear me—that privilege has been well and truly revoked—and maybe I shouldn't be surprised, I see people litter more often than I care to admit, but I still cannot contain my disgust.

The woman goes to the effort of removing her woollen gloves, pulls a bright blue plastic bag out of her pocket and bends down to scoop up her dog's turd—that's great, but then she ties the bag onto the wobbly dunes picket fence.

Waiting, I tell myself she is just putting her gloves back on, she will take the bag with her—but no, I am giving her too much credit. She grimaces as though she has been duped into ownership of a creature that dares to defecate and walks away.

I want to fling the steaming bag at her. Even the dog looks confused at his mistress' actions. Why bother putting it in a plastic, non-biodegradable bag, and tie it to a fence? She would have been better off flicking it into a grassy lump off the path—or even better, carry it to the shit bin that is five hundred yards away!

Maybe I am just a grumpy, resentful ghost, but I grab the bag and throw it. It pixelates in time—one in hers, where it remains on the fence, and one in mine, where it slumps into her left shoulder.

To my surprise, she turns around.

Suddenly I am unsure whether she can see me, and I blush. Then I remember why I threw the bag—my point remains, her act was vile, *but* it was also a pretty disgusting thing for me to do.

Dead or alive, I am old enough to do better.

The woman glances around wearily whilst trying to check if anything is on her shoulder. Confused, yet satisfied there is no one around, she stares at her dog. Perhaps she thinks the German Shepherd tapped her on the shoulder? Or maybe she thinks he might sniff out the perpetrator? With neither woman or beast noticing me, she shrugs, deciding she was imagining things, and walks away.

The woman's lack of admonition replaces my remorse with renewed disgust, so I pick up the bag and throw again. This time it lands in front of her feet, and she slips on it.

I feel like I could be participating in a comedy sketch, but the woman isn't laughing. I'd love to know what she is seeing, although I am pretty sure I am not included because she keeps glancing between where I threw the bag, the bag she left on the fence, and her dog who is sat two metres in front of her, panting lightly.

As my confidence in anonymity restores, I laugh. Before my bitter amusement goes too far, I should leave, but I walk to her side, and gently nudge the bag in front of her with my big toe.

Turning green, she takes the hint and attempts to pick up the phantom bag. Her hand floats through nothing, causing her to let out a little squeal as her petrified tongue grasps oxygen. Dilated, her eyes dart to the fence where the bag still hangs. Immediately she runs over, untying the bag with a shaking hand, and scurries away with her dog jogging in blissful pursuit behind her.

I should feel bad: I have probably just ruined this spot for her for life, but then again, why should she and others like her ruin this area of natural beauty because they are too lazy to use a bin?

Hmm, if my abilities are improving, maybe I have found a new calling?

*Litter angel.*

...We'll see. It could be a hobby at least.

A shout from the beach distracts me. In the distance I can see that Nina has joined Oki, but I don't think she is enjoying her time in the cold because she is flapping her arms whilst shouting something. Oki isn't saying anything, or certainly nothing I can hear as she quickly packs her things away.

As they walk towards town, something tells me to follow them. They have a big head start, so even running they are a long way down the promenade by the time I catch up. With only a few metres left, a couple approaches them, and everyone stops in unison. The man, who is the taller of the two and dressed in police uniform, looks at Oki and Nina blankly, but the woman is enthusiastic with her reply as Nina greets her.

"Hey! How are you both?" says Raquel warmly. "This is my dad. Dad this is Nina and Oki—I don't know if you met them at Dewi and Nadia's wedding, but you have definitely seen Oki's portrait of Daniel and me at home."

"Ah," says Raquel's dad, smiling. "Indeed, it is a beautiful piece. You are very talented."

Oki blushes. "Thank you."

"I take it you are police?" Nina bluntly says with a cheeky smile.

"Chief Constable Rogers," Raquel says proudly, linking her arm around her father's.

He smiles and pats his daughter's hand. "No need for the title now, we're just off for a late lunch—so, *Sean* will do!"

Nina and Oki politely giggle.

"I've not bumped into you recently," says Raquel, shivering. "Probably because it's been so friggin' cold! Have you been painting out here, Oki? Aren't your fingers like icicles?"

Nina rolls her eyes. "That's what I keep saying to her. I want her to set up a little studio in my office, but—"

"I like the beach," says Oki, defensively.

"There's no customers on the beach!" Nina declares. "You *need* a studio..."

"Your office is already small; I can't keep using it—I need my own space. There's a little shop for rent in town, but it's too much..." Oki shrugs and stares out to sea.

Suddenly I find Oki's behaviour unsettling. She turns away from her companions looking downcast, but quickly looks back with a decidedly cheerful demeanour—like the sea has somehow repainted her face with feelings that are not her own. "Anyway," Oki says with a bubbly voice, "what's new with you? I saw Daniel recently, but—"

"Out here?" Raquel groans. "He spends so much time out here now."

"Doing what?" Sean asks.

"Reading, mostly, I think. He says he just loves the air, but I don't know."

"Does he still have his weekly angel meetings?" Nina asks, casually. "One of my mates went once. I think he was searching for an old grey guru or something like that—he has a thing about spiritual guides, and apparently has a stereotypical idea of what they look like—so Daniel, with his green eyes, sandy-blond hair, and well-trimmed beard wasn't exactly what he was hoping for!"

Oki laughs with Nina, but Raquel seems confused.

"Angel meetings?" Sean says, thoughtfully. "Do you mean those posters? What does it say...?"

"*Have you been touched by an angel?* or something to that effect." Nina chuckles.

Raquel blinks. "They're Daniel's? *My Daniel?*"

The term 'my' stings. It shouldn't—I know it shouldn't, but I would be lying if I said it doesn't.

Oki nods, then glances awkwardly at Nina. There wasn't any reason to suspect Raquel didn't know. I confess I am surprised she doesn't by now because Daniel seemed fairly relaxed speaking about it to Kath. I assumed he hadn't said anything to her before as she is ill and has other things to consider—but why hasn't he shared with Raquel? Of course, she might not share his interest or want to attend a meeting, but to omit the subject for so long seems...well, unexpected.

"Huh," Raquel says, "I suppose that explains all the angel books he keeps reading."

"You didn't ask?" Oki says—I believe without thinking because she looks apologetic immediately afterwards.

Raquel laughs. "Why would I? Do you have to ask Nina before you choose a novel or whatever?" She doesn't wait for an answer. "Of course not. Sure, the meetings are a bit weird, but if that's what he wants to do while I work late, so be it."

Everyone looks a little awkward for a moment.

Sean laughs. "Hell, I've heard a lot worse!"

"Me, too! Oh, the stories I hear at work!" Raquel shakes her head. "Anyway, Dan's mum is really ill, so I've no doubt this angel thing is a way of coping with that."

"He must see death all the time at work," says Nina, half to herself.

"But your mum is always different," Oki says, carefully.

"Indeed," says Sean, glancing cautiously between Oki and Nina.

"Well, on that happy note, we best get off," says Raquel. "Your break will be over if we don't get on." She gazes at her father, willing him to get the (not-at-all) subtle hint.

"Hmm? Yes, yes, of course," Sean replies. "It was lovely to meet you both."

The four repeat their civil goodbyes and walk away, but Sean pauses, watching Nina tug on Oki's arm as she directs their path.

"Erm, excuse me, Oki?" he says, and she turns back to him. "Your art studio—how big do you need?"

Oki's eyes boggle. "Ha, well, anything from a shed to a mansion would be lovely—though the latter I really have no money for!"

"What about a beach hut?"

"W—what? Seriously? Is one available? Nah, no, they are more expensive than some houses." Oki splutters.

"I own two—sorry, I don't say that as any form of boast, but my wife bought a second one on a terrace up on the northern beach and has more or less abandoned the one nearer the pier. It was my father's, so I don't really want to sell it, nor loan it to some family member that might—well, never mind that. I think it could be well placed for you if you wanted to get a permit to have a little shop-cum-studio?"

"Really? Oh, my, that would be amazing!" squeals Oki.

"Mmm," mumbles Nina. "What's the catch? I dunno…"

"No catch," Sean says, reaching into his top pocket. "Forgive the formal card, it's all I have. Give me a call or email. I'd love to see the old shed used."

Oki takes the card, beaming, and the two pairs walk away from each other.

Doubly intrigued, I am not sure who to follow. Raquel's face is questioning but not unhappy as she and her dad stride away. Oki looks delighted, but Nina worried.

As I struggle to decide, an elderly man walks past and I see the air around him frantically vibrating with multiple colours—instantly, I know my choice.

Duty calls.

# 24

This year's Christmas Fayre in Adtoft is bigger than ever and the whole town is alive with activity. Every weekend in December has an extra-large Saturday market, but this weekend there are three days of street stalls, music, and family entertainment. The promenade is jammed with people and the pier is as busy today as it is on a warm summer's day—only the people are significantly more layered with scarfs, hats, gloves, and coats to tackle the North Sea breeze.

I wish she weren't here or that I had chosen a better place to people-watch, but amongst the general flow of human activity, I can see Mae, dressed in a red Santa's helper costume, serving her customers hotdogs. The costume isn't unique, many of the market stallers are wearing bauble earrings, festive head pieces, red suits, or tinsel, but as Flossy is dressed as Santa anyone walking past would be forgiven for thinking there is harmony amongst the stallholders. However, the longer I observe, the more cold glances, sneers, and grimaces I detect—leaving me in no doubt that the mood here is anything but festive.

A young girl says something to Mae and in response she beams, raises her voice, and calls out to the crowd, inviting them to enjoy Santa's goods as well as his helpers. She turns back to the child, smiling sweetly and says, "If you're a very good little girl, Santa might give you a freebie." Mae looks up to the girl's big sister and winks. "Just remember, his helper is the best one to buy from."

"Oh, I know," the older girl chuckles, returning the wink. "Shall we go see Flossy—Santa Flossy?" She says to her sister, walking away.

"Santa Flossy!" declares Mae. "There's a name that should stick all year!"

Hearing Mae, Rufus repeatedly scowls and mutters under his breath to Kev who has been awkwardly standing with him for the last half an hour. Maintaining his cheerful persona, Flossy has largely ignored anyone who isn't interested in purchasing candyfloss, but Mae's determination to wind him up finally hits home and he sneers at her the moment the two girls have walked away—with a free stick of candyfloss. Seeing Flossy's mask crack, Rufus unleashes his disgust and mouths 'fuck you' at Mae.

Laughing, she puts every muscle available into action to show her mirth, causing her previously stern-faced bodyguard-cum-co-worker to join in. If it weren't for the abundance of witnesses—living ones, who can actually report crimes—I think Rufus would cheerfully punch them both.

Flossy nods into the crowd and suddenly two men approach. In a strange, silent dance, Mae does the same, and the pier begins to fill with more muscle than a night club entrance, let alone a hotdog stand and candyfloss stall could ever possibly want in a lifetime. Neither side engages with the other and no one else seems to notice what is going on as they enjoy the rides, the food, and endless opportunities to buy Christmas gifts.

Mae looks triumphant—like a true queen of the promenade—as she calls out, "Oh, come on Rufus, we might be family soon!"

"Unlikely." Rufus sneers again.

"I'd not be so sure." The expression on Mae's face is hard to describe. It is beyond confidence or arrogance, but the glare she receives from Rufus can certainly be summed up by 'raging contempt.'

Flossy nods to Kev, who in turn grabs Rufus' arm.

Rufus shrugs him off but doesn't move his feet. "I know," he grumbles to Kev. "You ain't gotta say. I know."

"If your brother has chosen that side, so be it. None of us will—"

"*I know,*" Rufus says through gritted teeth. "I tried. I told him—but fuck knows what she has said because the dipshit has swallowed it. He thinks she is sweet!"

"Twat." Kev scoffs.

As if summoned by mere mention, Hayden appears, striding towards the front of Mae's stand like an overconfident peacock. My stomach knots and revolts as she immediately skips out the side of her booth to greet him with an affectionate kiss for all to see.

Mae lets Hayden dictate the length of the embrace, but masterfully turns their bodies as they step back so she can smile sweetly to Rufus while Hayden is watching—much to his obvious approval when he follows her gaze. However, the second Hayden looks away, any sweetness morphs into a scornful grin.

She is good—really, I mean it. She perfectly balances her portrayal of an innocent, gentle, but sexy little girl and Hayden is too arrogant to see her smirks when his head is turned.

I wish I had it in me to stick to my convictions and walk away, to leave this drama well alone—especially now Hayden himself has been thrown into the mix—but I cannot. Whether it is me or the glitch that insists on me adding to my inner turmoil, I do not know, yet I do know that I wish I could shake the need to compare myself to Mae. The fact is this feisty, self-assured woman is the complete opposite of me—of anyone that Hayden would normally look at twice. Originally, I thought she seemed meek, minus the odd grin towards her co-worker. Sure, she was obviously complicit in whatever was going on between the two stalls, but she left him to antagonise Flossy, yet now that impression has completely melted away. She is enjoying Rufus and Flossy's anger and is actively seeking it.

Can Hayden really not see her true personality?

Is it possible that the moron has finally bitten off more than he can chew?

I hope so.

I really, really, hope so.

I hope she eats you alive, you absolute fuckwit.

"Morgan, I am taking a break," declares Mae, already starting to walk off down the promenade, hand in hand with Hayden.

Morgan nods to one of the guards that appeared earlier and without a word he walks into the booth, puts on an apron that has 'Nathan' printed on the name tag, and smiles to the next customer in line, asking to take her order. The surrounding men on both sides readjust themselves and filter back into the crowd. None of them disappear, I can see them all, yet if I hadn't been observing so closely, I doubt I would realise their purpose now.

I don't understand. For years I have thought of myself as a silent detective—or at least in the position to be one if I wanted. I almost prided myself on 'being in the know' on the lives and dramas of the frequent visitors to these sandy shores, but now I have to confess that I fear I have been as blind in death as I was in life.

Maybe people only want to see the things that do not need challenging or changing?

Maybe life is easier that way?

Or maybe that attitude is what will—one way or another—ultimately kill us all?

"Can I have two hotdogs, ketchup, and two extra napkins, please?" says a teenage boy to Morgan's new helper.

"Certainly," Nathan says, smiling.

The air around me is swirling, like the sea is whipping up a brisk wind that is finally capable of clearing my ignorance. I walk over to the hotdog stall, no longer willing to be the stationary observer, hoping, if not believing, that there is no code in the boy's order.

Morgan grills two hotdogs and unceremoniously stuffs them into finger buns with ketchup dripping out of the sides. Nathan reaches under the counter and immediately comes up with a fist full of napkins—totally uninteresting, white napkins—and says, "Here, have a few extras."

"Cheers," says the boy, raising his hand with a twenty-pound note in his hand.

"Merry Christmas," Nathan says, winking, handing over the small wad of napkins in a semi-cupped hand.

"Merry Christmas," the boy says, walking away.

Morgan grills more hotdogs for the next people in line, and Nathan puts the money away, ready for the next payment. No one bats an eyelid.

The boy returns to his friends. Three of them are already eating hotdogs, the fourth reaches out to his friend, relieving him of one of his purchases.

"We good?" he asks, taking a bite.

"Yep, all good." The first boy lifts the napkins out of his pocket enough to be seen before shoving them back into the depths of his coat.

"Cool," says one of the girls. "I've beer at mine and Chelsea is bringing more later. We can crash in the loft. Mum and Dad are going to the panto, they won't know we're there 'til late."

Leaving the bustle of the town behind, I follow the teens to the girl's house and into her converted loft bedroom. It is huge and yet snug at the same time. I can see why they were so keen to retreat up here, I would have loved a space like this when I was growing up—or now, for that matter.

"Come on then! Let's start this party!" declares the boy I first followed, retrieving the napkins from his pocket. As he carefully unfolds the layers, a small, plastic zip bag with white, powdered contents emerges. The group giggles, and a girl drops to her knees and pulls out a cooler box from under the bed, revealing a stash of alcoholic drink, while another girl fiddles with the radio.

Teenagers playing with drink and drugs is hardly a ground-breaking revelation. I know Adtoft has its supply of drugs like any other town. I have known that for a long time—long before I had that poor mother's wail engrained into my soul as she realised her overdosed daughter wasn't coming back—but I am still shocked that I am daft enough to not have seen this particular reality earlier.

I only see what I want to—and what I wanted was quiet, harmless, household dramas. Not real issues, pain, or anything that darkens the idyllic atmosphere of a peaceful, sleepy seaside town. *I* was miserable darkness enough for everyone.

*Shine*—that's what Omi said. Rid myself of Hayden's curse of self-doubt and be a beacon of peace. That would be easier if I knew how, but I do feel the glitch guiding me more than restricting me these days. Am I finally learning to listen or is it finally trying to speak?

My vision has glazed over while I think, but the pop of the cooler box lid snaps my attention back into the room. The box reminds me of Flossy's, the one he gets Rufus or whoever is with him to carry across the promenade each day. The one that is dipped into at random points—oh, right, of course—I know, *I know*.

Realising I will not gain anything else by watching teens misspend their youth, I leave the loft, slowly walking down the steep staircase that is lined with a lush, soft carpet, and silently let myself out the front door. Almost marching, I pass the festivities, blocking out the endless repeats of Christmas songs until my feet stomp to a halt in front of Flossy's stand.

Flossy is chatting jovially to a father as he prepares two sticks of pink, fluffy candy while Rufus fiddles with his mobile phone. Walking around the back of the stand, I let myself into the booth where Flossy has his chair perfectly positioned to reach the candyfloss machine, the money, and the all-important navy-blue cooler box. His legs are straddling it, so if I want to look, I will have to reach between them. I'd rather not, even if he won't know. Grimacing, I tell myself no one else will ever know and sometimes needs must. I want to see—I *have* to see.

Reaching over his lap, I effectively glide through his legs. I hate the sensation of traffic passing through me, but right now, I would prefer that. The box lid rattles in my realm but remains motionless in Flossy's. As I open the lid, I feel a little flat. All I see are ingredients for a perfectly legitimate candyfloss stall.

Flat or relieved?

*Both.*

"Hey Uncle Flossy, do you have extra sticks today?" asks a man in his mid-twenties with an enormous grin as he confidently approaches.

"Sure do, Craig, sure do." Flossy chuckles as he reaches down to the cooler box.

Delicately, but swiftly he moves items, expertly slipping a little plastic bag into his fingers. From my close proximity I see the flash of tiny pills, but no one else would ever see such a masterful sleight of hand as the candyfloss and bag is exchanged for money.

For a lightning-fast moment, the glitch hits me with an icy wind. It is obvious it is showing me this for a reason, but my heart sinks as I doubt what I can do about a drug-laced turf-war.

All I currently know is, no good will come from this.

# 25

Feeling absolutely lost, I am not going to be labelled the angel, phantom, ghost, or spirit of Christmas cheer at the moment. Having shown me the pier's secrets, the glitch has not guided me for days, so I have returned to my previous tasks visiting the hospice and hospital, but I made the mistake of lingering with one gentleman. His smile, along with the warmth of spirit that surrounded him left me momentarily happy and I didn't want to burst that bubble by moving. What I didn't count on was his imminently visiting family nor the effect their loss would have on me. I desperately wish I could comfort the living as well as the traveller—and being close to Christmas just makes it worse.

Wanting to avoid sad scenes, I have seated myself outside one of the high street coffee shops and am focusing on the happy, bubbly shoppers as they bustle past. That doesn't mean I cannot see stressed shoppers too—the ones that cannot afford this overindulgent holiday, or those who cannot find the perfect present for the loved one they are hoping to surprise—but today I choose not to observe them. My channel must be set to only the joyful, otherwise I will sink into woeful tidings and be lost to yet more self-pity.

Adi and Ammi suddenly walk by arm in arm. They definitely make me happy, especially because I know where they are going. I am not saying there would be anything wrong with them going to the beach, a party, the park, or any other perfectly good place, but it pleases me to see them continuing to volunteer at the homeless shelter. I'd be even happier if there were no homeless people *to* shelter, but until society as a whole sorts that out, I am relieved to see people caring for one another on their own accord.

My musings are interrupted by a couple sitting down at my table and I startle when I realise it is Sally and Rob. Neither of them is dressed in their usual attire, in fact they both look very smart, if not rather downcast.

As they slowly sip on their coffee, I wait for one to speak, but as the beverages disappear, the only communication comes from Sally as she reaches across the table for Rob's hand. Sucking in his bottom lip, he gently rocks their hands, then continues to absent-mindedly gaze into his empty coffee cup.

It suddenly dawns on me that Rob's mother has probably died. I should have recognised the ashen expression faster. Sorry as I am, the overriding feeling I have is astonishment that they are sitting here so openly as a couple. Has Sally's regard for my father really plummeted so badly?

Probably.

They didn't even perform their typical grunts whilst eating breakfast today because Dad left early without a word. As it is Christmas Eve, I had half planned on riding with him, but I woke up to the sound of the front door closing and Sally simultaneously rolling out of bed.

I had hoped Dad's regard for Sophia would have gotten the better of his reserve by now, yet now I know about

Flossy's true enterprise, I am not sure how safe a relationship with her is. One member of Flossy's crew is already dead, how long is it going to be before that spills over to home calls?

Only this morning, on my way to throw my wedding ring into the sea, I heard three old ladies lamenting a grandson's hospitalisation following a night out. None of them seemed to know the details, but given the man was found near Hayden's garage in a pool of blood, I am guessing he was one of Mae's men.

Happy thoughts.

Happy thoughts.

*Today I promised myself happy thoughts.*

As though the sun has suddenly risen behind me, a warmth radiates across my back. Searching for the source, my eyes find Daniel and I shake my head.

Is this the glitch's idea of a joke or an apparition of a happy thought?

A voice calls and Daniel instantly looks across the street to a parallel coffee shop where Raquel is waving—*cue an unhappy thought.* He waves back, checks the traffic, crosses, and kisses Raquel before they enter the café and sit in the window seat, smiling and laughing as he bites into an enviably large piece of red velvet cake.

"What would I do without you?" Rob suddenly says to Sally. I had almost forgotten they were there.

"You don't need to find out," she whispers back, squeezing his hand tighter.

Rob uses his free hand to brush a tear away, but his emotions get the better of him and he has to reach for a tissue when the flow doesn't stop.

"Oh, honey, honey," Sally softly says. I don't think I have ever heard her use such a caring tone before. "I am so sorry. Your mum was a wonderful woman, but you're not alone, you hear me?" Sally moves her chair closer and grasps Rob's face with both hands. "Are you listening?"

Rob, with—what can only be—bleary vision, looks Sally straight in the eyes.

Sally smiles. "You want this, right?"

"Undoubtedly."

"Then that's all that matters," she says firmly.

"You'll leave him? Finally?"

"In the new year, yes. We'll find a—"

Rob sighs heavily. "It's always *in a while*, *sometime soon*, or *just after…* I can't keep doing it. Not like this."

"I can't tell him on Christmas Eve!" Sally says in a more familiar tone, sitting back.

"Why? He won't even be with you tomorrow!"

"He will in the evening at the pub…"

Rob gets up to leave. "I can't do this right now. Let's go, okay?"

"Fine, of course, sorry." Sally reaches for Rob's hand, and he doesn't reject her. Remaining seated, I watch as they silently walk down the long high street, pausing aimlessly to look in windows as they go.

*So much for happy thoughts.*

Searching for happier faces, I settle on a young family as they come out of a shop. The father is holding his toddler with one arm and the hand of a child of six or seven with the other, while his wife clutches multiple well-filled shopping bags. Behind them is a distracted girl, possibly aged ten or twelve. She has obviously been to see Santa in the shopping mall—the council employed one, not Uncle Flossy, the part-time drug baron—as her face is painted and she is holding a neatly wrapped gift that I know Santa's elves were giving out earlier.

The parents check that they are all out of the shop, confer with one another about their next destination, and point across the street. They look left and right and call to their daughter, glancing to check she has heard them, but neither adult notice her attention waning as they step onto the opposite pavement and walk up to a window display without a care in the world.

Playing with the shiny gold ribbon of her present, something drops out of the girl's pocket—from where I am sitting, it looks like a white and yellow figurine of some description—and she pauses in the middle of the road to pick it up.

The traffic in town is unpredictable at best and today is no exception. As the girl delays in the road, an equally distracted driver pulls around the corner. I don't know if it is their phone, the radio, a recently opened sweet packet, or what, but to my horror the road and any unexpected occupants are not what they are considering as they manoeuvre around a parked van.

Needing no direction from the glitch, I run, forcing every one of my phantom muscles into action—simultaneously pixelating my chair as it flies away from the table. Wings would be really bloody handy right now.

Pumping my arms for all they are worth; I hear a gasp from across the street as the mother finally turns around and sees where her daughter is. Following his wife's gaze, the father shouts and the girl looks up just as the driver looks ahead properly. Brakes screech and rubber burns seconds before impact—milliseconds after I reach the girl, encasing her in my arms and rolling her away from the path of the car.

Feeling all four wheels grind over my legs, I want to be sick, but I know that I am not harmed because I simultaneously feel warm air flush and billow around us as though we are caught in a protective bubble.

Sitting up, I release the girl. She unfolds herself and sits, staring at me with the biggest smile—almost illuminating the painted stars that are all over her face—and I return the gesture with true pleasure.

"That was close," says the girl quietly, but confidently, as if we were sat alone sharing a harmless joke, not recovering from a life-threatening event with a gathering crowd.

"It was," I reply, calmly. "I suggest not stopping in the road in the future."

"Yeah, good point," she replies. "That could have been bad."

"Very bad," I say, softly. "And what would Santa have done with all your presents tonight? Not to mention your family, who love you very much."

The little girl turns towards her parents as they rush towards her in slow motion with panic-stricken faces. I feel bad for the delay in their relief, but grateful for this unexpected moment of reflection. Why the glitch has done it, I couldn't say—maybe we are caught in a pixelated time bubble that is just waiting to burst—but it is calm and peaceful. I like it here and am in no rush to leave, but I am also comforted in the inexplicable knowledge that is temporary. This girl belongs to the living and *will* return there.

"Here," says the girl, extending her left hand. "Is she yours?"

I reach out and she drops her little figurine into my hand. It is an exquisitely carved, hand painted angel.

"She's beautiful," I say with a wobbly voice. "Where did you get her?"

"Dad makes them. He made one for the nativity scene at church and now sells them. This one is mine—or was. Maybe she is meant for you?"

"Oh, no," I say, returning the figure to the girl's hand. "I couldn't. This is yours and shall always be. You must take care of her—"

"Like you do me?" the girl says, tilting her head.

My heart is so full it could burst. My eyes fill as I reply, "Exactly. We'll look out for each other."

The girl pauses for a moment as determination spreads across her face. "Okay, it's a deal." Getting up, she turns apologetically to her family. "I should go, they look worried."

"They do. Go in peace, and live in love and happiness, my angel." I feel myself and the voice within speaking in harmony.

She giggles happily. "You too, Angel, you too."

The air whooshes and whips down the street as time restores itself. Voices scream, shout, rejoice, and lament.

The driver jumps out of her car in fits of tears; the girl's mother, having dropped her bags outside the window she was so nonchalantly perusing, embraces her daughter whilst sobbing.

A familiar voice rings in my ears and I turn to see Daniel dropping to his knees, declaring he is a paramedic and offering any assistance. The mother reluctantly, but gratefully releases her beloved child as she seeks reassurance that all is well while the father clutches their younger children, stuttering thanks for Daniel's swift response.

"Hi, I'm Daniel. What's your name?" he says professionally, but so caringly.

"Faye," the girl replies. "I'm okay, honestly."

"I'm glad to hear it, but that was a very near miss, Faye." Daniel replies. "And I think your parents would be happier if I just make sure, is that all right?"

"Sure," Faye says, shrugging before lifting her chin, signalling she is ready.

Daniel looks into Faye's eyes, checks her ears and reflexes whilst asking her a few questions. Her parents anxiously watch while her siblings look mildly bored until the flashing lights of the arriving police distracts them.

Satisfied that Daniel is helping, an officer asks to speak to Faye's parents while another interviews the driver of the car. Her voice shakes as she says, "The sun was in my eyes. I was sure the road was clear. I'd never put anyone at risk..."

Her words are genuine, I have no doubt about that, however serious the potential implications of her lack of judgement could have been. Really, I feel sorry for her, but had she hit Faye, the blame and misery would have undeniably landed squarely on her shoulders—accident or not.

Daniel chuckles as he declares: "Well, I think you are possibly the luckiest girl I know! I am going to recommend to your parents that you are double checked at the hospital because that was a hard, speedy roll—but it seems like Santa saved you!"

"It wasn't Santa," Faye says, smiling. "Everyone thinks I don't know, but he is the church elder dressed up. I just pretend for my brothers' sake." Surprised, Daniel raises his eyebrows and laughs. Faye pauses, then casually adds: "It was Angel. She saved me."

Daniel's face freezes for a moment, but Faye's dad overhears and says, "Do you mean your figurine?"

Faye pulls the wooden angel out of her coat pocket, twiddling it between her hands thoughtfully, but diverted by the police asking him a question, the father doesn't wait for an answer.

Understanding her dad, Daniel replies, "Ah, no, sweetie, your angel nearly got you seriously injured. I saw you pick her up—"

"No, not *this* angel," Faye says gazing straight into Daniel's eyes, "...though I must look after her now more than ever. She is my lucky guardian angel charm, I think."

Daniel either looks baffled or like he has just heard a revelation—I'm not sure which.

Faye steps to stand closer to her parents, but Daniel gently touches her shoulder, pausing her instantly. "Sorry, Faye, erm, before I go…"

"Yes?" she says with interest.

"Sorry, I have to just ask. Did you see *her* then?"

"Who?"

"Angel. You saw her, didn't you?"

Faye beams. "You've met her too?"

"I have. She saved me, once."

"Really? Wow, that's great!" I feel like I am glowing as I take in Faye's smile and then blush as she adds: "She's beautiful, right?"

"She is, definitely she is," Daniel replies.

"I wish I had black hair. I doubt Mum will let me dye it until I'm *at least* thirteen." Faye gazes at Daniel with concern. "Do you think in two years I'll be allowed?"

"Maybe," chuckles Daniel. "But brown hair is lovely too."

"You think?" Faye runs her hand over her hair, smiling.

"Absolutely."

Faye beams, but their conversation is interrupted as her mother gently pulls her into a hug.

"We can go. The police have our details if they need us," Faye's mother says, slowly regaining some colour, despite the tears in her eyes. "Is she—is Faye okay?" she asks Daniel.

"She seems absolutely fine, but should be double checked in A&E, just to be sure," Daniel says, only half looking away from the child.

"Of course, we'll get her checked straight away. Thank you so much—*so, so* much."

"I didn't do a lot," Daniel says humbly.

"You came forward immediately to help. That means the world to me."

The mother's heartfelt gratitude is hard to ignore and Daniel gulps as he replies, "Of course. My pleasure."

Behind them I can hear the police warning the driver again about the seriousness of her actions. Tears flow and tempers rage as a few members of the public add their thoughts, so the police urge Faye and her family to leave.

Faye walks one way, and Daniel goes another, presumably to catch up with Raquel.

Deciding I've done all I can, I step to walk away just as Faye turns, calling: "Hey, Daniel?"

"Yes?" he replies, instantly retracting a step.

"I feel better knowing you and Angel are here. Thank you."

Daniel smiles softly. "Any time."

Faye's face lights up. "She's just there—you should say hello!"

I don't know who is more shocked, but Faye waves to me, runs up, gives me a hug, and skips back to her baffled parents. They'll probably just peg this action as their daughter coping with a traumatic event in the best way a young girl can, but as they walk away, Daniel hesitantly walks towards me. Stopping where Faye stood, he gazes carefully as though he is studying each molecule of air in front of him—presumably searching for a sign that I am here.

It is painfully obvious that he cannot see me—that our realms remain split—yet we are so close we could kiss, and I can feel the warmth of his breath as his heart races in time with mine.

"Are you there?" he whispers.

Gulping, I reply: "I am."

I am desperate for him to hear me, but the look of disappointment on his face is all I need to know. Maybe subconsciously he feels me? I certainly feel his presence as well as see him, but the glitch refuses to give us a moment—audible or tangible—like it granted with Faye.

Why does it connect us, but not?

It is cruel.

So close...yet so very, very far.

Closing my eyes, a tear tumbles down my cheek.

The isolation in this moment is too much.

My eyelids jolt open as Daniel whispers again. "I sense your warmth, you know?"

Rather than looking for me, Daniel is gazing at the palm of his left hand. My heart stills as I realise that he is holding my yellow rose—still unwilted and as fresh as the day I put it in my hair. Without deciding to, I lift my right hand to the rose and gently pinch the base of the flower with my fingers, but do not attempt to remove it from his palm.

Immediately the rose turns red, and we gasp in unison.

Neither moves. I'm not sure if we are even breathing.

"Daniel?"

Not again. *Please, not again.*

Raquel calls a second time and we both turn to her, absorbing the confusion in her face as she wonders what Daniel is doing standing in the street with a red rose in his hand. Raquel examines the shop we are standing in front of, and confusion turns to gleeful assumption. I understand before Daniel and want to die all over again. Devoid of hope, my hand drops to my side and tears stream down my face while Daniel stutters some gibberish.

"Is that for me?" Raquel asks, still smiling and seemingly encouraged by his inarticulation.

"Is what?" Daniel follows her gaze to the rose. "Ah, no, sorry, I just picked it up and then daydreamed. Sorry, ah, but I thought I'd get you a better one—more than one—you know…"

Daniel shoves the rose in his coat pocket as Raquel wraps her arms around him.

"Can I not have that one anyway?" She winks, nodding at the jewellers. *"For a starter."*

Daniel stumbles, twisting his ankle a little. "Ah, nah, come on, let's go. Mum just called."

"When? I just watched you check that girl while I finished my coffee!" Raquel seems indignant. "I went to the toilet briefly, but I doubt I was gone long enough to have missed that—she doesn't do quick phone calls normally."

Daniel looks flustered. "Sorry, you caught me. I was going to go in there, as a surprise." He tilts his head towards the jewellers, much to Raquel's pleasure.

I can't listen to this anymore.

The morgue would be less depressing.

Self-preservation tells me to walk away—again.

Turning away, with a wobbly voice, I mutter, "Merry Christmas."

The timing is probably no more than a coincidence, an added kick when I am already down, but I manage no more than five steps when time stops still as Daniel's whispered voice reaches me. "Merry Christmas, Angel," he says—shutting the jewellers' door.

# 26

Walking away with tears streaming down my face, I am only vaguely aware of the slowly disbursing crowd and am certainly ill prepared to navigate a stationary man in the middle of the pavement. Too preoccupied to care, I decide to just walk through him when an unusual vibration of colours catches my attention.

Stopping to wipe my eyes and focus beyond the conflicted colours, I realise the man is my father. Dad is dressed as though he is going to work, but he is wearing his best winter jacket, not the one he generally wears. I don't know if he has stopped in town for a gift, an item for a client, or for something to eat, but right now he is standing statuesque, staring across the street.

I follow his gaze in time to see Sally spot him. She turns white, squeezes Rob's hand, muttering under her breath. Rob looks confused, however, as he follows her line of vision his face flushes red and his eyes bulge as he sees my dad. Dad is neither white nor red, in fact his expression isn't giving anything away at all, while shock on the other side of the road continues to mix with embarrassment as both guilty parties mouths' gape like fish out of water.

I wish I knew what Dad was thinking. He cannot be entirely surprised, but only a very cold person wouldn't feel the pain of betrayal in such circumstances. I hate Hayden, but that didn't stop me feeling rejected when I saw him with Mae for the first time—or the second.

Sally and Rob confer with one another without turning away from my dad. I can only lip read a little bit, but they seem to be trying to decide whether to cross the road. Rob gives a quick nod, checks left then right, but then hesitates as the traffic is suddenly released by the police as they conclude their immediate inquiries following the incident with Faye.

Realising his wife and her lover are preparing to confront him, Dad gives them a gentle sideways nod like he is wearing an old-fashioned hat and continues on his way. He waits until his face is undeniably out of their vision, but as I scuttle down the street after him, I see the corners of his mouth pull upwards into a smile.

Is it possible that, unlike me, my father is glad? I suppose it isn't such a leap, not really. They have been like miserable strangers, housemates without the mate part—in any sense of the word—lodgers that tolerate each other. He too loyal to convention to separate, she too cowardly to confess. But not now, now fate has handed them a pass and Dad, I think, is relieved.

Sally and Rob look bemused, talking to each other in split, unsteady sentences. Sally pulls her phone out of her pocket and obviously dials Dad's number as his phone immediately rings. He glances at the screen, reads 'Sal' and wipes the red receiver left and stuffs his phone back into his trouser pocket.

Putting her phone away, Sally shrugs, then walks down the street in the opposite direction, still holding Rob's hand.

Dad must be ordering his thoughts as the agitated colours that originally caught my attention begin to slow and steady into a traceable stream around him. I rebuke myself for envying his ability to process bad news. We all have our different ways of tackling events, it doesn't make one better or less feeling than another, but I wish I could balance my feelings and find true happiness for my father.

Reaching his car, Dad takes off his coat, removes a brown A4 envelope from the inner pocket, and neatly lays both on the back seat before getting in. As he steers out of the car park, I wonder what he is thinking and where he is taking us. My romantic side envisions him driving to Sophia's house and declaring his love; while my pessimistic side sees him driving to the nearest pub to drown his sorrows as the reality of his broken marriage at Christmas sinks in. I should, however, know my father better, because he does exactly what he always does—remains loyal to his work and goes straight to his next client.

After travelling with him to three different clients—all of whom heartily wish him merry Christmas and do not suspect anything is wrong—Dad drives home. He pauses for a moment as he lifts his hand to the front door and holds the key in position without twisting the lock. Suddenly he shakes his head, abruptly opens the door, and sighs with relief when he is greeted by cold silence.

Casually checking the cupboards for food, Dad settles on baked beans on toast, a vanilla yoghurt, and a bottle of cider—which is possibly not a gourmet selection, but it seems to satisfy his hunger while he watches the news.

Pushing his plate aside, he pulls his phone out of his pocket and loads up a home shopping site. To my surprise, he takes all of a few minutes to select what he wants, ordering cardboard boxes and packing tape before texting his sister. All the message says is 'Are you and Joel able to help moving boxes after Xmas?' but my aunt immediately calls him.

"Hi," says Dad, casually.

"Hi, yourself," my aunt replies. "You're moving? Are you okay?"

"Yeah, yeah, just time for a change. This house is not a home now—it's time I moved on."

"I know, I know," my aunt says sadly. There's a pause before she continues. "What about Sally? Is she—"

"She is moving in with our neighbour." Dad replies calmly, but my aunt instantly understands.

"Oh! Oh, no, no. What a f—"

"Don't. It's okay, Keeley, it's—"

"It's not okay! How can you—"

"Fine," Dad says, waving his arm as though my aunt can see him admit defeat. "It's *not* okay, but it *is*—no, let me finish. We aren't happy. *I* am not happy. I didn't want to say, but—"

"Where are you?"

"At home. Why?"

"I'm coming over."

"No, no, you've the fami—"

"Don't be a twat, *you are family*."

"Aren't the kids over? You can't just—"

My aunt sighs sharply. "Get your arse here then, but one way or another, you're spending Christmas with us."

"I've got to work..."

"So? Fucking come and go from here! Forty minutes. If you ain't here in forty minutes, we're all coming over."

My aunt hangs up and Dad laughs.

I miss my aunt. I am very glad Dad contacted her. My cousins are grown up now and one has two children already, while the other got married last year. We were all fairly close when I was little, but life—including a second wife and control-freak husband—got in the way too much. If this is the start of Dad bridging a gap and being with family, it can only be a good thing.

Dad wastes very little time packing a few essentials into a carrier bag—including whatever wine bottles and mince pies he can find—before locking the house and sliding into his car.

My aunt and uncle live just outside of Adtoft, surrounded by rolling fields in a beautiful, converted barn. Despite knowing the boundary rules, I would love to spend Christmas with them, so I try to get in the car. The glitch isn't granting Christmas wishes though because the car door handle vaporises in my hand, leaving me standing on the driveway as my father turns on the engine and disappears down the street.

Puffing out my cheeks, I cross my arms, hug myself sadly and return into the house.

If Dad is moving out, I'll have to find a new place to sleep. Hopefully, he is going to stay in Adtoft. I can't see him leaving, not really, and Mrs Crook's house would seem like the obvious choice—that would explain him wanting to move my tree—but it is probably a bit much to hope that he will rebuild my bedroom wherever he is going.

Wandering into the kitchen, I look out the window. In the dark, I can see the shadow of my magnolia tree. I hope it doesn't die when it is moved, I like the idea of Dad taking it—*me*—with him rather than just buying a new one.

Tired, I make my way upstairs to my room, but feel myself pulled into Dad's bedroom. I don't know why, I never usually go in here, yet something has me like a fish on a hook.

The room is as cold and still as any other here. Dad is right, it is a house, not a home. Objects sit in every room, but the absence of love and laughter strips each item of its value. A chill draws me to the dressing table where Sally has apparently left a few pieces of makeup, a pen, and a brush—nothing of interest, until I realise that a brown envelope is laying underneath the pen with a document poking out of the top.

Sliding the pen aside, I read the title: *Petition of Divorce*.

Has Sally been sitting on this?

Maybe, but then why would she not have mentioned it to Rob earlier when he was begging for a commitment from her?

I read on.

It's not Sally's. The petitioner is Dad—and he has already signed it.

Did he collect this from a lawyer today? Either way, he must have signed it this evening, but already had it in motion, waiting for such time that he or Sally gave a push.

So, he knew, he knew he wanted out—he was acting, but in a really slow, cowardly way.

I grimace. Who am I to judge? I waited for my husband to murder me before I left. I wanted out but made no grand announcement. I sought no help. I did too little, too late.

Life has been kinder to my father.

Good.

Walking into my bedroom, I curl under the duvet, whispering, *'Merry Christmas, Dad. May you use your time much more wisely than I did.'*

\* \* \*

Aiming to pass Christmas quietly, but not be totally left to my own thoughts, I decided to take advantage of the town hall committee and church combining their resources to put on a lunch for anyone who found themselves alone.

For a few hours, I placed myself in the corner of the room, absorbing the atmosphere as well as a phantom version of their turkey roast. In the absence of my own family, I found the scene soothing as the genuine warmth of their fellowship was impossible not to enjoy until one of the volunteers got down on one knee, proposing his undying love to his girlfriend—now fiancée. Of course, this just added to the general light mood of the many, but my cruel minds-eye replaced the couples faces with Daniel and Raquel's, dashing my peace, forcing me to take myself for a walk along the beach.

Some families are out with their dogs, either walking off or preparing for the indulgence of their festive meal, but no one is stopping today—they have better, warmer places to be. Reaching the southern edge of the sand, I cannot help pausing and bowing my head in memory of the immigrants who lost their lives here. Another boat was found further up the shore last week. I didn't see it, but I saw it on the news. No one died that time, but it doesn't mean they won't on the next boat—or the next, for they will keep coming.

Sitting on the beach might be too cold for the living, but it suits me. Sinking my fingers into the sand, I sigh, trying not to question if Daniel and Raquel are now engaged. It shouldn't matter either way, it's not like Daniel and I have a future together. But why am I so pulled to him? Why did the rose turn red? Red signals—

*Enough!*

Red, yellow, purple—it doesn't matter. I am a phantom. Call me Angel if you want, try to assist those in peril I might, but I cannot claim the living any more than I can control my own death.

I stare out to sea.

It has been a while since I have felt so low that I want to test the glitch's determination to keep me 'alive.' In general, I now feel like I have purpose—I *do* have purpose, even if it leaves me lonely more often than not. I will not give into these moments of sorrow.

Getting up, I walk inland.

Let's see where the glitch takes me.

# 27

The Accident and Emergency room has been really busy this week. My slightly dark side has taken to guessing what stupid thing each new patient has done. Eating a balloon, stuffing things in holes that are exits, jumping off and or swinging from fixtures that are not meant to take a human's weight (or their 'festive weight' as one guy tried explaining was the issue), all makes for mildly comical, if not ridiculous entertainment for me—as well as hard work for the hospital staff.

I prefer the ridiculous though. The presence of the ridiculous indicates that humanity is bubbling along without any great cares. I would rather believe that Adtoft has no great concerns, however, as my ears are now filled by angry, drunken threats and police wandering hallways, I cannot pretend Adtoft is exempt from its share of woes.

The simmering gang war has escalated—not that either side are remotely interested in talking to the authorities. Had they reorganised themselves before a neighbour followed their screams and found his shed on fire I don't think any of the current casualties would be here. However, the emergency services cornered the burnt and bloodied assailants, so now they are laid out in a grumpy mess in adjacent rooms.

Wandering between wards, I have watched their angry auras race, but despite their hatred, they are united in their story—much to the obvious frustration of the police. "It was a rogue firework," they all explain with nearly identical wording. "It went off at the wrong time, hit another, and then another, then they started bouncing off the shed walls into people."

It's New Year's Eve. Three people had already been brought in with firework related injuries, but when these guys came in the atmosphere noticeably changed. Not all of them regularly frequent the pier but I've no doubt that they are associates of Flossy and Mae because Kev is one of the injured.

Having been called to speak to the notably louder, more intoxicated patients who have just arrived, the police step out of the room. The second the door closes, Kev turns to his friend, sneering as he holds his burnt wrist. "Keep it together, Stu, all right?"

"I am," replies Stu, who is younger and more significantly injured than Kev.

"You heard what Flossy said. Don't fuck up now. We get patched up and get—"

"I heard, okay. *I heard.*"

Kev scoffs but doesn't answer.

"You should have let me stuff some weed in that bastard's pocket at least," mutters Stu.

"Are you fuckin' dim?" spits Kev.

"No. I was just sayin' th—"

"Idiot."

Stu pauses, looking genuinely confused, then says, "Why?"

"*Why? Why? Shit.* I should have let them stick that rocket up your arse and kept walkin'." Kev closes his eyes, rubbing his forehead with his good hand before suddenly staring straight into Stu's eyes. As he slowly speaks, he only uses the quietest whisper, but is enough to send chills down my spine and silence any further questions. "Because, if the cops find *goods* on one member of a suspicious party, they are highly likely to roast everyone. But, *if* they can only pin stupidity on us, they will ultimately let us go and we live to resolve this war another day. *If*, on the other hand, we get stuffed by another one of your dumb as fuck comments, then get out of here or not, the boss *will* mince you up and feed you to the fuckin' gulls."

Stu audibly gulps but neither man speaks again until a nurse enters a few minutes later. Kev immediately turns on the charm. He is tall, dark, and very muscled, and clearly the nurse is attracted to him as her checks take longer than necessary. I hope this performance is purely a distraction for both parties and that this young woman will run a mile away from any serious notion of dating Kev. Kev reminds me of Hayden—beautiful on the outside and capable of appearing to emanate beauty from the inside but is ultimately rotten to the core. Anyone who is happy to threaten to mince someone else, is *definitely* rotten.

The nurse releases a girly giggle in response to Kev's silvery tongue and he takes the plunge and asks for her number. I scream '*DON'T DO IT!*' but of course no one hears me. The nurse reaches for a pen from her uniform pocket and chooses the corner of a spare hospital lunch order sheet to write her number on.

Grabbing her pen, I don't let go, hoping sheer willpower will propel the pen into my realm.

It doesn't.

Instead, the pen remains firmly placed between her fingers and she is totally unaware of my failed restraint. Frustration hits me, yet as she attempts to write the pen refuses to make even a cursory mark on the page.

"Huh," says the nurse, staring at her pen. "This pen is new."

"How annoying, I hate it when you get a dud," replies Kev, lightly.

"Yeah, but it worked five minutes ago..."

Undeterred, Kev grins at her. "Can't you get another?"

Whether sense has just hit the nurse or what, I do not know, but she suddenly shivers and loses the light, flirty tone she had only seconds before. "Yeah, yes, of course, but I better finish my rounds first."

"All right, but don't be long," Kev says, winking.

She leaves the room, walking straight to the nurse's station where a male colleague is typing on a computer. Without speaking, she selects a notepad and scribbles on the corner with the dead pen and immediately the black ink flows. The nurse stares for a moment, then retrieves the sheet she tried writing on a moment ago, gently fingering the clean paper—presumably testing it for any ink resistant properties. Leaning the paper on the counter, she writes 0-7-7 and then stops, releasing a semi-stifled gasp.

"Juan, could you do me a favour?"

Her colleague immediately turns to her. "What's up, Meena?"

"Can we switch rooms? I know I said I wasn't bothered, but you're right, a man might suit those two better—but you'll need someone else with you, too, I think."

"Sure, no worries—is everything okay though?" he asks, looking concerned.

"Mmm-hmm, I just, erm, got a feeling, you know—like when someone is whispering a warning in your ear?"

"Like a guardian angel?"

Meena smiles coyly. "Yes, exactly."

"Cool. I always listen to mine. I call him Angelo. Angelo has gotten me out of so many silly situations with men—and women, come to think of it." They chuckle, but I cannot help circling them both for signs of another angel.

Sensing nothing, I walk away rebuking myself. I have told myself a thousand times that other angels must exist, but, for whatever reason, this gig—my frequency—is not the same as theirs.

It is understandable that I look for companionship though, right? Surely even the most resigned, beaten soul still searches for their own sometimes? *Surely,* me pining for a paramedic who probably just proposed to his warm blooded, breathing girlfriend is not healthier than looking for Angelo the spirit guide of Juan the Adtoft nurse?

Whatever.

Well, that's just put me into a lovely, depressed mood.

Happy fucking New Year to you too, glitch.

Needing air, I walk outside the A&E into the dimly lit carpark. Fireworks are still popping in various directions, and I pause to appreciate the colours, even if I am less enamoured by what they stand for. A puff of smoke catches the corner of my eye as it trails out of a cracked car window, and I squint to see Rufus sitting in the driver's seat of a shiny, new 4x4 truck. How the hell has Rufus got enough money to buy—or rent—a vehicle like that?

In my heart I know the answer. I know who and what funds his new lifestyle—and why Kath and Daniel were both trying to persuade Rufus to take a different path. As an added reminder, Kev's mincemeat threat replays in my head…so, I guess, I also know why the glitch keeps throwing me into his path.

I am to protect Rufus from himself.

I just don't yet know how.

Walking to the passenger door, I try to get into the truck, but nothing happens. I would scream if I thought it would help, but as the glitch seems determined to play with me—and in case me screaming amuses it—I remain silent and hoist myself onto the truck bonnet instead. If Rufus drives away, I'll likely be left sitting on my arse on the damp, dirty carpark, but until such time, I will wait to see what happens next.

Patience, after all, is apparently a virtue.

\* \* \*

Three hours and a very numb bottom later, Kev strolls out of the hospital propping up his friend, giving a knowing nod in Rufus's direction. Distracted, I don't get up, so as Rufus starts the engine my prediction comes true, and I glide through the engine to earth. While I pick myself up, both men climb in, and Rufus drives away without anyone uttering a word.

It would seem that the 'no questions in public' policy is already well understood by Rufus. Oddly, I find that reassuring as I think I am therefore less likely to have to scrape Rufus out of a sausage machine in any near-future attempt to guide him to his *next*. Shuddering at the thought, I really hope my primary purpose is to maintain life and promote peace in Adtoft—not clear up after thugs.

It might be worth finding out where they live though—maybe I will find some clues if I do. But without being able to follow them by car, that could be difficult.

Or maybe not? I could read their medical files and look for Kath's address in her file at the hospice. Also, I'm pretty sure I know where that truck was bought, but I really, *really* don't want to go there.

A breeze whips around me, making me take a step forward.

Oh, wonderful, *now* the glitch gives me hints.

Well, I am not doing that right now. I can't. I won't. I am not ready.

I'll find the addresses and decide another day if I need to visit them, but afterwards I am going home—while it is still home—because I need to see if Dad has started packing.

# 28

Like every day since Christmas Eve, Dad wasn't in when I got home, however, in my absence cardboard boxes have sprouted everywhere, filling with items from around the house. No room is exempt, including my own, and I had to move boxes before I could crash into bed.

Before long, I won't even have a bed.

Lazing under the duvet, I know it is time that I left all of these things behind, but I still feel sad seeing 'charity shop' scribbled on the side of all of the boxes. I am being daft, I know that. Anything I seemingly move will pixelate back into position the second I release it. No object will come with me unless I am wearing it—and even that is on a timer if I attempt an unsanctioned wardrobe change.

Despite the dress being totally inappropriate for winter, I like what I am wearing—possibly a little too much, if I am honest. Although not as often as I should, I have changed clothes since the wedding in the summer, but part of me is afraid some random event will come along and either return me to my death clothes each morning or take away the only memento I have from the day I saved Daniel.

*Ugh*—my words replay in my head.

I need to get changed, don't I?

Like Dad, I need to shed the past and all that clings to me. I will—soon, there's no rush.

While I mull over my clothing, my wedding ring suddenly feels like it is burning me. The sensation is entirely in my head, but I panic and fumble as I hastily pull the ring off my finger. Sneering at the offending item, I roll it between my fingers—like I have so many times before. I know it cannot really hurt me, but this is one reminder I do not need.

Sighing, I drop the ring into one of the charity boxes. It seems applicable—both metaphorically and literally. I can only continue to hope that it might one day grant me peace and stop reappearing.

The bathroom door opens, and I peer into the hallway expecting to see my dad, but instead find Rob. Somehow, he has snuck in without me noticing.

"Sal?" he calls out, sticking his head out of Dad's bedroom doorway.

"Yeah?" Sally appears at the bottom of the stairs.

"There are boxes everywhere—even your clothes are packed up."

Sally doesn't answer, instead she climbs the stairs and walks into her room, inspecting each box. She pauses as she reads the side of a box.

"He has had help," Sally says.

"What do you mean?"

"The handwriting on this box isn't his—someone else helped him pack."

"Yeah, me." We all turn to see my aunt and I want to hug her. She has one hand on her hip and an eyebrow raised. "Morning, Sally. I assume this is who you've left my brother for." There is no sense of a question in her speech, just a cold statement.

Rob steps forward awkwardly. "I'm Rob. Are you—"

"Uninterested? Yes. My brother has charged me with boxing up his clothes. Can I assume you are capable of removing your own clothing?"

"Where is he, Keeley?" Sally asks.

"At work," my aunt replies. "Why?"

"Well, we need to discuss things, we—"

"I believe you have the divorce settlement in writing—you've certainly managed to sign it."

"Can you stop with the sarcasm?" Sally sighs. "I'm a shit. I get it. But we haven't been a couple, not really, for such a long time. This—"

"Sally," my Aunt Keeley says, rolling her eyes, "I don't need your excuses. You both let yourselves drift apart—you, apparently, didn't bother drifting very far—"

"Hey!" interjects Rob.

"*Really?*" my aunt stops Rob's protest with one dry, word. Shaking her head, she continues, "The papers are with the lawyers now. There is no reason this shouldn't go through swiftly as long as you stick to what you've signed. You gain much more than you deserve, that's for sure."

"I didn't ask to keep adultery off the declaration—or for half the house." Sally pouts.

"Well, aren't you just the regular ray of innocence!" my aunt laughs sarcastically. "My brother wants a clean break. That is the only reason he has offered you so much—I certainly didn't advise such generosity."

Sally hangs her head for a moment, but then asks, "Does he have someone else too?"

My aunt glares. "You'd love that, wouldn't you? That would vindicate your little dalliance and lessen your guilt." Aunt Keeley sneers, twisting her whole face. "Well, you neither get nor deserve any such—"

"Okay, I get it," Sally says sadly. "But I cannot help falling in love." Rob smiles and my aunt scoffs. "We need to finish—"

"You are finished. Where he moves to next is none of your concern. Any correspondence in the future can be directed via lawyers and any stray post to my house. You have my address?"

"I do."

"Good. Select what you want out of the house by Monday. I'll finish on Tuesday; the cleaners and estate agent will be here after that."

My aunt doesn't wait for any further recognition, instead she walks past me, into my room, grabs a box marked 'SAVE' and leaves the house.

I wish I had looked through that box. Truthfully, I hadn't even realised any of the boxes in my room said anything other than 'charity shop' until it was in my aunt's arms. If Aunt Keeley takes it to her house, I'll never see the contents again. If Dad claims it for his new home, I might—if I work out where that is.

Mrs Crook's house seems like the logical answer. The more I think about it, the more I realise Dad was preparing to leave Sally. He had the divorce papers, the new house—he just hadn't dared actually do anything directly with either until Sally and Rob unceremoniously presented themselves on the High Street on Christmas Eve. I always thought that Sally must know about Dad inheriting my money, but as she has made no mention of it, nor the new house, she must be in total ignorance of both. The new house is less surprising, but I hadn't realised their marriage was so rocky three—nearly four—years ago when I died.

I feel guilty. I should have seen that Dad was unhappy, but instead I was too busy being unhappy myself. Two peas from a crumbling pod.

As a thought hits me, a chuckle bubbles out of my mouth. Sally told my aunt she didn't ask for half the house. She obviously realises that Dad could try to walk away with everything, so considers the deal she has been offered a good one—yet she has actually lost out on the chance of far, far more than she realises.

Well done, Dad, I am proud of you.

Gran's money should go towards one of us having a future and moving past our mistakes. If I could just ask for a spare room to be laid out with a pillow and duvet, that would be wonderful. I don't really want to sofa surf or start sleeping in random hospital beds again.

# 29

Deciding to investigate Mrs Crook's house, I leave Sally and Rob going through boxes and walk out into the damp, misty day. The majority of people seem to have found their way to work already as everywhere seems particularly quiet. Perhaps the thick fog rolling in off the sea isn't encouraging exercise, plus children are now back in school after their winter break, but instead of a vibrant, inviting town, Adtoft feels like somewhere a ghost should reside today. There's something oddly romantic about the eerie atmosphere, but if that is supposed to make me feel more at home, it doesn't.

Taking a small detour, I walk along the seafront, noticing that both the candyfloss and hotdog stands are closed today. Either both parties have hospitalised each other again, decided to have a day off because footfall is so low, or they have another, warmer, outlet around town. Thinking about it, it is quite likely that all three options are correct—especially the last one. There is no way they only sell from one point in town, that wouldn't make sense.

I doubt I want to know where the others are.

Carrying on my walk, I briefly glance away from the sea when someone hurriedly joins the promenade to my right: Oki. Although I haven't seen her for a few weeks and she is wrapped up like an Eskimo, I'd recognise her hazel eyes anywhere—even if they are not currently giving any emotion away.

She quickly walks past me, heading in the opposite direction, but being nosy, I immediately turn on my heels and follow. Ahead, a woman is waiting outside the bandstand. Like Oki, she is well wrapped up, but under the woollen hat, gloves, and expensive coat, I can identify Raquel's long blonde hair and beaming smile.

If it weren't for a self-deprecating sense of wanting to hear Raquel's news, I would turn around again and leave. But I must force myself to be the fly on their wall. If there is wedding news, I need to hear it. Holding onto a notion of spirits uniting across the realms and hoping for a lasting connection will only cause me pain.

Yes, a reminder of reality—*my reality*—will do me good. I can be an angel without losing my heart and mind. Romantic ideals are not for me. My peace comes from watching others' happiness.

*That* is my blessing.

"Hi! Thanks so much for coming," says Raquel enthusiastically.

"Of course," replies Oki. "Is everything okay? Your message was a little cryptic."

Raquel giggles. "Sorry, that was deliberate. I was afraid if I was obvious you wouldn't want to come."

"Oh?"

"It's nothing bad! It's just when we bumped into each other last week you didn't sound as keen as before, so I thought I'd lure you down here and then..." Raquel waves her arm backwards. "Tada! Your very own beach hut awaits!"

"What?" Oki's eyes boggle. "What do you mean? I didn't—"

"I know. Dad said you still haven't contacted him, but he really would like to see the hut used and thinks you'll be the perfect tenant!"

Oki shuffles her feet awkwardly. "I can't. Things are tight, plus I would need a licence and—"

"That's what I'm here for! Between Dad and I, we have all the contacts you need. I have the council form here for you." Raquel opens her bag, producing a folder labelled 'Beach Hut.' Oki's face has turned as pale as the fog that surrounds us. Looking up, Raquel notices. "Are you angry? I'm so sorry, I—"

Oki extends her right hand, gently clutching Raquel's as she holds the paperwork. "I'm not angry—how could I be? I'm just surprised, that's all. I thought we'd said no to you last week, that's all. Nina and I—"

"Will you come and look at least?" Raquel says sweetly. "Just see it before you say more?"

Sighing softly, Oki shrugs her shoulders. "Sure, why not?"

"Excellent!" Raquel puts the folder away and links her arm with Oki's, guiding her towards the beach huts.

There are a lot of beach huts in Adtoft and, if for sale, they usually fetch a high price. A few have been turned into kiosk's selling ice cream, fish, or local gifts, but the majority remain as intended, providing shelter for people wishing to relax by the sea. Raquel leads Oki to one on the end of a terrace near to the pier—a perfect location for someone wanting to set up a miniature art studio.

"Dad is happy for you to decorate as you see fit," Raquel says, releasing the padlock, revealing a surprisingly spacious interior. "Mum has claimed our other hut further up the beach and has moved all of her things into it, so there's nothing here that cannot be moved. There is a solar panel on the roof linked to batteries in the cabinet, so electricity isn't an issue, and there's a little sink that you can plug a water bottle to quite easily. It's not huge, I know, but from what I've heard you say, you are pretty cramped at home—"

"Yeah, that's an understatement." Oki scoffs—without thinking, judging by the guilty look on her face afterwards. Panicked, she continues, "Well, you know, I manage, but I hate being on top of Nina."

Raquel senses Oki's reluctance to continue, so smiles encouragingly as she adds on Oki's behalf, "Of course, and trying to paint undisturbed when Nina's working must be difficult—not to mention if you get a commission for a portrait, you probably can't have people sit for you while she's there."

"No, definitely not."

"Well, here is the perfect solution! And you love the beach, I remember you telling Daniel and me there's nowhere you'd rather be."

"True. This would give me so many more options, even if I would like to continue setting up on the sand sometimes."

Clearly Oki is beginning to allow herself to dream of possibilities and it's wonderful to see the creative spark ignite in her eyes. Heartened by Oki's reaction, Raquel exclaims, "Exactly—you have the choice at your fingertips! Won't you say yes?"

Suddenly the brightness in Oki's expression drops like someone has smacked her across the face. "I'm not sure. I'm not sure I can justify it. Can I have a think and let you know?"

For a brief moment, while Oki awkwardly gazes around the hut, the disappointment on Raquel's face is almost tangible. However, her quick, determined spirit—which I'd imagine makes her an excellent solicitor—clicks into gear as a smile flashes across her face. "Sure, no rush. Let's go for lunch, I'm starving. It'll be my treat—I insist."

Relieved, Oki doesn't protest as Raquel closes the hut doors and leads her down the promenade. Their quiet chatter pauses when Oki abruptly halts by a post to read one of Daniel's *'Have you been touched by an angel?'* posters. Having spent several months being attacked by the North Sea winds, the posters around town are all rather worse-for-wear and the image of me honestly looks more tragic than angelic; however, even in their faded state, I have avoided the posters whenever possible—and have certainly kept away from the bandstand on Wednesday evenings.

"Does Daniel still have his meetings?" Oki asks, pointing at the poster.

"Huh? Oh, right, yes, I think so." Raquel shrugs. "We've chatted about it a little, but it's not something I really believe in, if you know what I mean. It's a coping mechanism as far as I'm concerned—but if it helps Daniel..." She shrugs again.

"You don't believe in spirits or an afterlife?"

"No, I can't say I do. I think we have enough to contend with in this life. Do you?"

Oki smiles. "Yeah, actually, I do. Nature and all Earth's beauty, it's order—that's no mistake or coincidence. And I *feel* energy, here and now, in town, in people, in the air." She chuckles. "Nina would probably agree with you, but I wonder if Daniel is onto something."

"Why not go to one of his meetings then?" Raquel suggests. "He'd be glad of a friendly, sympathetic face. No one went before Christmas, so he had a week or two off, but last time I heard he was going this week."

"Hmm, maybe."

I keep waiting for Raquel to pull off her glove and reveal an engagement ring. Perhaps she is waiting for the grand reveal once they reach the warmth of a restaurant, yet Raquel seems pensive—sad even—as they continue walking.

"Is he okay?" asks Oki, suddenly reading Raquel's expression too.

Raquel tries to brush her thoughts aside with a smile, but whatever is troubling her obviously creeps back as the smile fades.

Concerned, Oki stops and faces her. "What's wrong?"

Raquel chews on her bottom lip before answering. "He—Daniel—is just a bit lost at the moment...*we're* a bit lost, if I'm honest."

"Oh. Sorry. Do you want to talk about it?"

Raquel smiles again, attempting to chuckle. "I'm being silly. We're fine, it's just, well, before Christmas I thought he was going to propose, but instead he bought me a necklace—a beautiful one, but—"

"Yeah, I can see how that'd be an anti-climax," Oki says sympathetically.

"It was. I know it will come, we've talked about it a few times over the last year or more. It's just I'm ready to go forward, you know?" Oki nods. "But then yesterday—" Raquel rolls her eyes. "Yesterday, he announced that he is moving back in with his mum. It came as a bit of a shock."

"What? Did you fight?"

"No, no, not at all—well, maybe a little when he told me. He wants to care for his mum. She's not got long left, so I understand, of course I do. It just feels like a step backwards. Does that make sense?"

Oki takes Raquel's hand kindly and pulls her into a hug. "It does, it really does," she says into her shoulder. Pulling back, staring straight into Raquel's eyes she adds, "But I agree, it makes sense he wants to be with his mother now, when she needs him most. My dad has already gone, and believe me, there isn't a day that goes by when I don't wish I had spent longer with him and cancelled that 'important meeting' or not seen whatever new film I thought was necessary at the time." She scoffs. "*Time*—time is as cruel as it is precious."

Chewing on her lip, Raquel nods in recognition and I realise I am doing the same. I think all three of us understand the truth in that sentence, even if it's for vastly different reasons.

After a long silence, Raquel wipes away a tear and sighs. "That sentiment could also apply to doing what is important to us individually, you know?" Oki tilts her head in a wordless question, so Raquel continues. "Time *is* precious. We should be with the ones we love and who truly love us—but not make the mistake of being hung up by those who don't or by living a muted existence under the expectations of others."

Oki wrinkles her nose as she thinks. "What do you mean?"

Raquel gazes into the distance for a moment before turning to her companion. "You wish you'd spent more time with your dad. Daniel wants to spend more with his mum while he can—*which he should*—but we also need to balance that by taking time to be ourselves and not allow others to forge who we become." Raquel softly scoffs. "I wish I had realised that earlier, but I'm trying, truly I am."

"That's good," Oki says quietly.

"I envy you and Daniel in a way, actually."

"Oh?" Raising her eyebrows, Oki doesn't hide her surprised curiosity.

"You both followed your dreams. Daniel became a paramedic instead of a doctor like his dad and a few others said he should be, and you are a fulltime artist—which, I'd imagine, someone told you wouldn't happen."

Oki laughs. "For a long time, Mum wanted me to do something else—almost anything else—and just paint as a hobby."

"Mine too—not that I wanted to be an artist, I can't draw for toffee, but as a teen, my mum felt I was drifting, so she and dad pushed me towards studying law. Mum owns her own law firm and always wanted me to join her, so I had a guaranteed job and good money waiting for me once I jumped through her harsh and narrow hoops—"

"Did you resist?"

"Nah, not for long. It was easier to do as I was told." Reading pity in Oki's face, Raquel forces a light chuckle. "It's okay, really it is. My parents—well, mostly my dad—have mellowed with age. He helped me tame Mum and she's been nothing but supportive since I chose my major. I would have liked to have travelled first, but I genuinely love what I do now, so I wouldn't change career—but my point is, don't live for others at the expense of yourself. Follow your dreams. Those who truly love you will support you, not hold you back."

Oki nods but doesn't answer and they continue walking in contemplative silence until they approach the restaurant that Raquel has chosen.

Pausing outside the door, Oki says, "You said you wanted to travel—you still could, you know? You can take holidays—"

"Of course, I know that. I can. I will." Raquel sighs. "I meant that I might have tried living elsewhere once upon a time, before settling in one place. But Mum wanted me here and then I met Daniel and his roots have always been firmly embedded in Adtoft—like yours, I guess."

"I can't speak for Daniel, but yes, this place is home for me and always will be. Nina isn't sure, she would like to travel or expand her…"

As Oki trails off into her own thoughts without finishing her sentence, I see a flicker of satisfaction in Raquel's expression. Either she has made or confirmed the point she was after, or a new idea has just hit her. Speaking firmly, yet warmly she says, "Adtoft is my home. I don't see that changing now—I'm not sure I want it to, but that's *my* choice, *my* path, *my* happiness. It's not always plain sailing, but I want us to be a couple, yet that means choosing some things individually. I wouldn't dream of trying to make

Daniel be someone he is not or stopping him from doing something that makes him happy."

"Like…renting a beach hut, you mean?" Oki coyly grins.

"Precisely." Raquel beams. "You'll never have a better landlord or more supportive friend in me. *You deserve this.* Your work is outstanding, but you need space and I just know that—"

"Okay!" Oki laughs, blushing. "Okay, I get the point!"

"You'll take the hut?"

Oki's smile lights up. "I will."

"*Fabulous!*" Raquel opens the restaurant door. "Let's celebrate!"

# 30

Sitting with Raquel and Oki, I listened to them agree to terms for leasing the beach hut while they shared a meal. I soaked up their excitement and felt a warm, fuzzy happiness as I witnessed a blossoming friendship. It's a shame my part in their friendship is so one sided—it would be lovely to share in others' highs and lows as an equal, not a shadow—but I cannot hang on to the shoulda, woulda, couldas that are left behind me.

I'd be lying if I said I wasn't hanging on to Raquel's every word regarding Daniel or that my heart didn't skip when she said they were not yet engaged—or that I didn't check her left hand when she finally took her glove off to be sure. If it helps, I told myself off each time, but honestly, the only one I am hurting is me.

Visiting Daniel's mother isn't going to make it any better or worse, right?

Meh, well, it's too late. The glitch took me to the hospice originally anyway, so I'm going to blame the glitch. Of course, I don't know if the glitch intends for me to keep visiting or if it even actually wants anything—yet some days it seems to. Maybe I am just one of its angels and it has no further interest in me beyond overseeing those in-need, injured, and dying in Adtoft. Perhaps I am a fun pawn to torment.

Maybe I am both. But like it or not, I have a connection with some more than others and I cannot ignore or avoid it—so I have come to the hospice looking for Kath.

During my search, the vibrating colours and warm draw of an onward soul distracts me, so I pause my quest until the breeze peacefully takes them. Walking out of the now-soulless bedroom, it occurs to me that Kath may not be working anymore if her health has declined to the point that Daniel wants to live with her. Now might be the time to do a home call, but for that I need her address—hopefully, I can find that in the office.

Approaching the end of a corridor, I feel the glitch tug on my left hand. There is only one door to my immediate left, so ignoring the confused feeling that comes with being guided, I open the door and find Kath patiently bathing a resident, chatting away in her calm, relaxed voice as though there is nothing wrong with her at all.

For the next hour or more, I watch Kath pause outside doorways for a breather, but push away any fatigue the second she opens a door. I don't think Kath wears much makeup on a normal day, yet today she has put on extra in the hope of hiding her illness and exhaustion. For those not in the know it might work, but when her break time finally arrives, she melts into an armchair, making it painfully clear that her struggles today have been immense.

Layla, her colleague and friend, enters the room as Kath lets out a long groan.

"Oh Hun, what can I do to help you?" Layla asks kneeling by her side.

"You can't, unfortunately. I've had my quota of drugs for today," Kath half whispers. Shaking her head, she continues, "I can't go on. I know it's my last day, but I'm going to have to quit early—do you have my replacement lined up like I asked?"

Layla voice crackles as she replies, "I do."

"I wanted to finish—"

"You've already worked longer than you should. You give so much to others, it's time to take time for yourself, Kath."

Kath just smiles and Layla watches her with worried lines crinkling her brow.

"It's funny," says Kath after a moment, "I didn't think I'd be able to do today at all when I woke up, but despite the pain, I have felt a warm, strengthening, protective presence with me."

"Like a guardian angel?"

"Yeah, I think so."

"Well, I hope they are telling you to rest now." Layla smiles, but the concern hasn't left her face.

Kath weakly smirks. "I know it's time to rest and take however long I have left with my boys, but I don't regret a single day here."

A tear rolls down my cheek. The colours around Kath are beginning to dance to a new, next-worldly rhythm, but it is not her time yet. Her aura is one of love and kindness—being in her presence soothes me, so if she feels some kind of strength from me, then I am honoured.

Sitting opposite the two friends, I feel the pang of forthcoming loss, but the blessing of true friendship. These women have dedicated their lives to helping people, to caring for people in their most difficult hours. My role is the same, just minus the friendship. I envy that, but I also suddenly realise that I like my calling—odd as it might be. I always felt that this work would be fulfilling for me, just not quite in this form.

Alive would be better.

Or dead, but not murdered.

I always go around the same points, but maybe I should just focus on the possibility that death has given me a second chance at a meaningful, content life.

The break room door opens, and Daniel's face pops around the edge. Layla smiles, Kath quietly exclaims her pleasure, and my heart thumps so loudly that I can hear it.

The three chat until Layla's breaktime is over and Daniel declares he should take his mother home. Promising to visit her soon, Layla walks with Kath and Daniel to his car. Silently I follow, telling myself that I, too, will endeavour to find their house.

"Hold onto that extra strength," Layla says, squeezing Kath's hand once she is settled in the passenger seat. "If anyone deserves a guardian angel's strength, it's you."

Hearing her words, Daniel looks over the top of the car quizzically at Layla, but then grins like someone has told a joke when Kath replies: "Oh, I will. She's coming home with us."

Hoping this is a tangible invite, I reach for the rear passenger side door. As it opens in my hand, I swallow hard on the lump that immediately forms in my throat. Fearing this is just a pixelation that will leave me disappointed—

whilst equally afraid I will miss my chance, or the glitch might change its rules again—I waste no time in getting in.

Shuffling myself into the central position of the car, I can see Daniel's eyes in his rear-view mirror. For a second, I think we lock eyes in the glass, but he quickly looks away, puts on his seatbelt, starts the engine, and navigates down the driveway, taking us all home.

# 31

Riding in Daniel's car, I question if I am really here. Nothing about my reality is explainable by conventional methods and having failed at every attempt to ground myself, I pinch my arm, hoping for proof of existence. At best it is distracting, but it reaps no conclusions, so the riddles rage on in my mind. Could there be a purpose to my new-found chauffeur or is the glitch just finding new ways to play with me? Is it thanks to Kath? Or could the connection with Daniel truly be lasting—increasing even? The possibility that I have always been able to get in Daniel's car hits me. Having never tried before, I cannot really claim that this is new.

It might be worth trying other people's cars again. Other than my dad's, the ones that I've tested have rejected me, yet I was able to ride in the ambulance with Adi. Have I been trying the wrong vehicles all this time?

Perhaps I should stop asking questions for a moment and just enjoy this ride…

Absorbed by gazing out of the window, I watch hedges and gardens flash by to the point anything inside the car fades into the background. The vehicle edges around a sharp bend and something moving on the seat reclaims my attention. The car is pretty tidy, definitely tidier than Dad's, but laying on the backseat is a heavy winter jacket, a small ball of reusable shopping bags, and an umbrella that I doubt has ever been used. Placing a hand on the jacket, I feel something hard underneath. Curious, I gently lift one side of the navy jacket and cannot help smiling when I reveal three non-fiction books on angels. I do not understand our connection, and part of me fears that Daniel only regards me as a spiritual phenomenon to research like an astronomer does the stars, but I continue to take heart at being remembered at all.

My stomach jolts as we go over a speed bump a little too quickly, but Daniel's iffy driving just acts as a reminder of my initial joy of being in a new car. It's funny what becomes a treat. When I was alive I thought next to nothing about vehicles. They were Hayden's source of income, figures on endless spreadsheets for me, and objects which could be manoeuvred around forecourts or transport me from A to B. The size, model, et cetera was of little interest, no matter how much Hayden tried to impress me with his knowledge. I cannot say I have much more interest in the brand now, even if I know it and could probably order spare parts with very little trouble, but suddenly the joy of a simple journey is enough to make me feel giddy.

Checking out of the window again, I look to see if I recognise where we are when Kath suddenly thanks Daniel for volunteering to care for her but expresses concern for his relationship with Raquel.

In the mirror, I watch Daniel's eyebrows rise and fall briefly, but as he reaches for his mother's hand, he simply replies: "There is nowhere else I want to be right now, and Raquel understands perfectly."

Seemingly satisfied, Kath gently nods her head and changes the subject to Rufus and whether he might be home to cook tonight. Daniel laughs, sparking a lighter tone of conversation and I lose myself listening to their gentle mother and son banter.

When Daniel pulls his car onto the small driveway of a terrace house, regardless of it not being a richly adorned area, I feel at home. There are very few places in Adtoft I do not know, yet over the last few years, I have often chosen to stick to certain sectors. This is an area that I have frequented less, however, I quickly realise that Kath's house is only three streets away from Flossy and Sophia's. How strange that I have been so close to Daniel's family home without knowing it!

Daniel puts a reassuring arm around his mother as she gets out of the car, but she softly says she can manage. Stepping back, he watches Kath walk into the house before collecting the jacket and books from the back seat along with a sports bag from the boot.

Kath laughs, saying she knows that Daniel has already been here as the floor has been vacuumed. As it's my first visit, I wouldn't have noticed, but I do instantly inhale the glorious, welcoming smell of a slow-cooking stew coming from the modest kitchen.

While they settle in, I take a tour. Kath's home is relatively small, but cosy. There are three bedrooms—the smallest of which must be Daniel's as a suitcase is laid at the bottom of the bed. The garden consists of a small green square with some bushes, shrubs, and flowers bordering it with a sizeable bird feeder hanging at the far end. Kath is obviously a keen gardener and bird watcher because she has neatly positioned an armchair in the living room window with a bookcase full of gardening, wildlife, and bird books—complete with a pair of binoculars resting on top of the window ledge. The binoculars would be more useful on a walk, but I suppose Kath feeds enough birds to make observations from home pleasurable.

Settling myself into the armchair, I notice that Daniel has laid the books from his car on the window ledge. Picking up the top book, I begin flicking through: *Guided by Angels: Encounters of a Spiritual Kind.* It is obvious that Daniel has spent a long time reading it as he has dog-eared multiple pages and highlighted different passages. One chapter, headed *Revelation,* has been circled repeatedly and I read with eager curiosity as the author recounts an experience she and her girlfriend had one foggy evening whilst lost on the Scottish moors:

> *'The light was fast fading, and we were panicking. Our hike had taken us much further than we had planned, leaving us far from our B&B without a mobile signal, anything useful to protect us for the night, or any hope of finding another settlement by nightfall. While we lamented our stupidity, a middle-aged man dressed in green hiking gear appeared on the path ahead of us. Rather than fearing that we were about to fall victim to some violent act that has since been suggested to us, we both*

*instantly felt at peace, like a warm, white haze had hugged us.*

*Wasting no time, we called to him and asked for directions. Smiling, he pointed us north, saying we'd find exactly what we needed there. We thanked him but, sensing our reluctance to walk alone, he offered to accompany us until we were certain of our path. For ten minutes this man walked with us, listening to our anxious, yet somehow-calmed, prattle. We climbed a grassy hill, crossed a relatively flat field, and then reached a road marked as leading to the very village we were staying in. Reading the sign, we giggled with glee and turned to thank the man, but he was gone. There were no trees, no ditches, no buildings which he could have suddenly disappeared behind. No vehicle past and no human could have run out of sight so fast. But we felt him—the warmth, the unquestionable presence of one who cared, protected, and guided, as he sought to see us safely home.'*

The testimony of this author has moved me to tears. She goes on to describe her lasting sense of gratitude towards the stranger and how both she and her partner desire to spread the feeling of reassurance to others who might feel physically, mentally, or spiritually lost. The rest of the book is filled with a mixture of positivity for individual growth and appreciation of the power of walking with a spiritual guide.

All of it is interesting, but the chapters that fascinate me the most are the ones where the author recounts conversations with others she has found who have also had experiences that cannot be explained by known logic. I say *known* because I am proof of humanity's logic being defy-able.

What humanity *knows* and what *is* or *can be*, are not necessarily the same thing.

As I reach the last chapter, I sigh. This book is possibly one of the closest I've read, but none of the stories truly mirror my own. They describe people, beings, or angels, appearing and guiding in varying forms during moments of trouble; some describe repeat encounters or feelings of a supportive presence, but no more. Certainly, none have answers to the origins or longevity of these angels—only theories at best.

Having read so many volumes on the subject, I should not be surprised—nor disappointed, but I admit that I am. Part of me likes being unique, yet the majority of me would like a guide, a manual—something that says, '*Ah, yes, this happens, then that, then...*' What exactly I am hoping the blank will be filled in by, I do not know, but a clue would be nice.

Of course, it is possible that there is no '*and then...*' Maybe *this* is my next, my *eternal* next.

Eternal loneliness.

Eternally watching—helping.

Eternally searching.

Eternally an angel.

If that is the case, I hope my abilities strengthen. Recently I have felt like my connections are less pixelated, yet I do not feel in control. Each time I have a connection I am as surprised as the person I am trying to touch. In this book the author describes multiple accounts of angels seemingly choosing who to help and when to appear or disappear.

I do not choose anything.

Does the glitch guide and tease them? Did they have easier transitions from their living selves?

"Worry less about others' paths and more about the lessons of your own."

My eyes bolt across the room to where Kath is laying on the sofa with her feet up, facing away from me towards the TV. Is she talking to me? If she is, she can read my mind because I haven't uttered a word.

"Mum?" says Daniel, walking in from the kitchen.

"Huh? Oh, no, I was talking to the telly. I've been waiting for this girl to tell her friend she loves him, but she keeps getting distracted by everyone else, worrying what they are doing or how they will react—it's quite infuriating!"

Daniel leans on the back of the sofa, chuckling. "Do you still watch this crap? I thought you gave it up!"

Kath mock hits him with a cushion. "It's not crap—it's romantic!"

Daniel walks back to the kitchen, laughing.

Shuddering, I try to dispel the freaked-out sensation that has hit me. She is watching a soap—a drama. Fiction. Perfectly timed fiction.

"Dinner!" calls Daniel.

Kath groans as she rolls herself off the sofa and makes her way towards the kitchen.

Putting the book down, I start to follow, yet my whole-body freezes as Kath replies, "We're coming."

# 32

Daniel didn't notably react to Kath's use of 'we' as she responded to his summons and although I have hung off every word she has said all evening, she has made no further references that could possibly acknowledge my presence. I'm imagining things. I want longer, more meaningful conversations—friendships—so I am fabricating meaning in throw away comments, private musings, and mispronunciations that are simply not there.

I would be lying if I said that I wasn't hoping for a repeat of my connection with Omi because those few days gave me more hope than the last three years combined. Perhaps it was her unique appreciation of spirits and auras that allowed her to see me days before her death instead of minutes. Thanks to her, my focus on auras is better, stronger. Seeing hers fuzz and dance, I monitor Kath's colours with sadness, but I also find peace in the kind, loving, warm serenity of her natural character. Turning my eyes to Daniel, it is plain to see that his warmth of spirit has both been inherited from and nurtured by his mother. I hope living me had colours from both of my parents—before I squandered them.

As Kath checks the time on her phone, she sighs and her colours vibrate, turn a muddy red, and seemingly hang heavily around her as worries flood her mind.

"Where's Rufus?" she asks Daniel. "He should have been back by now."

Daniel shrugs. "I don't suppose he has set hours in his line of work, does he?"

"I begged him to do something else—again. He just rolled his eyes and laughed at me. I should have moved years ago. If I could've afforded to, I would—"

"Mum." Daniel says, reaching out for her arm. "Rufus is responsible for his own actions. It is nothing to do with—"

"But it is. I should have taken him out of his father and half-brothers' radar. I sensed Leo was trouble, even as a young man. He commands attention whenever he is present, and Rufus sees that strength as an unquestionable positive. So yes, it is my fault." Kath pauses, running her fingers through her chin-length, sandy-blonde hair—the trademark colour for the Hudson family. Sighing again, she continues, "I hope you will be able to guide him, and the angel will watch over you both. I am so sorry to ask."

"Mum, we've been through this. He will be okay. I will be okay. We love you; we thank you for—" Daniel's voice cracks and breaks. "—*for everything*. You are the best mother, guide, friend, and example that either of us could ever ask for. I am proud to call you Mother."

"And I you, son." Kath hugs her son as tears flow.

A lump cements in my throat. I have had so many reminders of my mission and it is not to just sit here and selfishly soak up a tender family moment. I am to guide, watch over, and care. Kath didn't name me this time, but I, Adtoft's angel, heard her request: Watch over her sons. Plural.

Standing up, I take one last glance at them before walking out into the night. I don't know where I am going to find Rufus, but as Flossy's house is so close, I am going to check there first.

Of course, it is raining—not heavily, but just enough to be a nuisance to anyone who wants to get home dry. I shouldn't really complain because I don't get cold and the glitch will dry me and my clothes whenever I sleep, but I still feel the undeniable irritation that comes from soggy hair and clothes as I stride down the street.

Ahead of me in the dim lighting, a man staggers up to his front door, fumbling with the key whilst swearing at it for not magically finding the hole on its own. He trips on nothing and lands in a flowerpot and I laugh.

"A little help," he slurs. "A little fuckin' help. Won't you help your fellow—" I don't know what the end of the sentence would have been because he suddenly vomits into the flowerpot that he has just slid himself out of. The man isn't looking at me, so I cannot be sure he is even aware of my presence and not simply talking into inebriated space, however, telling myself good deeds come in all sizes, I decide to attempt to assist him. There is no fence to his front garden, just a short concrete path which I silently walk down before gently taking him by the right hand as he resumes his struggle to control the wilful door key. His body stills as I grip his clammy hand, but his arm allows me to guide the key safely home and the lock obediently clicks open.

"Whoa...wait, what?" The man attempts to look at his hands, but I get the impression his vision is somewhat wobbly. He chuckles as he flexes his fingers though, so I am not sure if he thinks he has new-found powers or realises that he was helped.

"Lee? Is that you? What the hell have you been doin'?" a voice calls from inside the house.

"Huh? Of course, it is me, your hunsum hubby." He chuckles again, stumbling over the doorstep.

"Are you drunk?" exclaims the woman as she walks into the hallway. "Where's the shopping? Did you get it on the way home at least?"

"Oh, right, well—"

"Oh, for fuck's sake, you useless idiot. I ask for one thing—one thing!" She flaps her arms in exasperation.

"Sorry, honey, don't be angry. I'll go—"

"*I'll* go in the morning." She rolls her eyes. "Will you shut the door? You're letting all the cold air in and you're dripping on the bloody carpet!"

Not waiting for his motor functions to catch up, she storms past him and slams the door. Shaking my head, half grinning, I begin to walk back towards the street when the letter box opens and a slurred voice says, "Thank-ooo, ni-night."

Lee doesn't wait for a reply, instead he instantly removes his fingers from the flap and presumably stumbles around the house under the watchful eye of his vexed wife.

My lack of control is frustrating and lonely, yet I do enjoy the sudden shock of recognition. I wonder if I will ever get used to random encounters. Part of me hopes not, because not knowing who will or will not sense me keeps me on my toes.

There are very few cars moving and even fewer people on the streets now—in fact, a lot of the houses have turned off their lights for the night. Sensible people. Since my death, I don't mind walking in the dark; however, the streetlights are casting more shadows than illumination as they compete with the increasingly thick, wet clouds that have descended into town.

As I turn the corner into Flossy's street, car headlights appear and pull up in front of his house. The front passenger door opens and someone fitting Flossy's stature gets out, but before shutting the door, he leans back inside the vehicle. I am too far away to hear words, yet the tone of conversation is definitely heated.

Flossy shuts the car door and walks straight into the house. Satisfied he is safely inside, the black SUV speeds in my direction and I shudder as I read Leo's personalised number plate. Straining, I try to identify the occupants, but even on a clear day I would struggle to see anything through the tinted glass—however, as the vehicle flashes past, I somehow *sense* Rufus' presence.

With no time to examine this feeling, I run after them, expecting to see Rufus dropped off outside his house, yet as the car reaches the top of the street it abruptly stops.

With the sound of my speeding feet filling my ears, I cannot make out words, but the tone is no less agitated than it was moments earlier as Rufus gets out. He grunts a response, shuts the door, and watches the car disappear down the road. Once the taillights are out of sight, he wraps his left arm around his waist and, heavily limping, makes his way home.

Approaching Rufus, I am struck by a rich, metallic odour. I wish I believed it was copper or iron that I was inhaling, yet thanks to my time in the hospital, I know this is the scent of blood—and probably a lot of it.

Panicking, I look for his colours. They are dancing in a slow, confused pattern encased with muddled red and grey—not the dance of death, but certainly indicating nothing good.

Sprinting to the house, I thump on Kath's front door hoping she or Daniel will hear me. The lights in the living room are on, yet no one answers. Letting myself in, I find Kath asleep on the sofa and Daniel idly watching the television. Running up to him, I scream 'HELP' at the top of my lungs.

Silence.

Nothing—not even a twitch.

A leaf dropping in a forest would get more recognition.

Exasperated, I return to Rufus. Making slow progress, still clutching his waist and groaning, he stumbles on the path. The first time, he catches himself on a neighbour's wall, sighs, and continues, but the second time he has nothing to grab and looks set to face-plant the concrete. Thrusting my arms around his upper body, I force him to stay upright whilst thanking the glitch for granting me access through the realms twice this evening.

Rufus' body freezes for a moment, but in his fear-cum-surprise-cum-confusion, he also regains the use of his legs—which is good, because if he faints I'm screwed. As he turns to me, the whites of his eyes bulge and his Adam's apple bobs up and down, either in attempt to swallow bile or speak—I'm not sure which.

"You okay?" I whisper, slowly releasing my grip of his body.

Rufus nods minimally while his eyes dart from left to right. I think he can only feel, not see me. Maybe the glitch doesn't want him to see the ghost of Hayden's wife—because surely, to Rufus, that is what I would be?

Whether or not I want that, I cannot decide. On one hand I do not want to be known for who or what I was back then; yet on the other hand, the recognition, the connection, between living me and dead me could be interesting. Perhaps I could use that connection to convict the lying, murderous bastard who put me here—but then maybe that pursuit is the very reason the glitch hides me?

Start afresh. Be something new.

If that is the case, then stop tormenting me with old connections!

*Or rise above them.*

While I argue with myself, Rufus stares at his surroundings, searching for earthly explanations for his lack of a fall before turning towards home. It takes him a minute to do a twenty second stroll, but it's a relief to see him make it to the front door without collapsing. The strain is obvious as he stands in front of the closed door, but rather than seeking immediate refuge, he leans on the wall for a what seems like forever before finally reaching into his jeans pocket for a key.

Psyching himself up, Rufus flexes his fingers as though he is testing them out, takes a deep breath, and he opens the door—immediately striding inside, forcing himself not to limp.

"Hello?" calls Daniel.

"Hey? Oh, Rufus, is that you?" Kath mumbles, waking up.

"Yeah, hi, it's just me," Rufus replies as he stands at the bottom of the stairs—grimacing at the thought of climbing them in his condition.

"Where have you been?" asks Kath, her tone barely hiding her anxiety. "Come and see us. Did you eat? Danny cooked, you know?"

Daniel mutters that it doesn't matter, but Kath tuts and repeats her command for Rufus to enter the living room. Probably in her healthier days, she would have met him in the hallway, yet this evening every step is as laboured as Rufus'.

Wincing, Rufus takes his hand off the banister rail and pokes his head around the living room door, making sure that only the right side of his face can be seen by his mother.

"Sorry, Mum," he says lightly, but sincerely. "Time just whipped by, and we had extra work. I'm beat, so I'll go straight to bed. Sorry, Dan, I'll catch you later?" Rufus widens his eyes as he addresses his brother and Daniel immediately reads an extra message in the short, simple sentence.

"Sure, no worries. I'll take Mum up and see you in the morning. We need to discuss moving her bed downstairs."

"Oh…? Right, yeah, of course. Night."

Rufus slowly backs up and forces himself up the stairs, stifling moans as he goes. Feeling like a weird shadow in a rugby match, I follow with my hands out in case he falls again—simultaneously taking care not to unnecessarily touch him on the off-chance he notices.

The second Rufus is behind his bedroom door, he sobs. It could be from the pain of his injuries, but something tells me his tears are equally from the realised implication of Daniel's desire to move his mother's bed downstairs. Whatever is going on in Rufus' world, the foundations of his family are soon to be irrevocably devastated. We all want more time with the ones we love—there is never enough time, but there is undoubtedly too little.

Silently sitting on the edge of Rufus' bed, I cry with him. My tears fall for lost souls while prayers petition for the ability to save those I can.

Together we listen to Kath get ready for bed and wait for the inevitable light knock of the door.

"Enter," says Rufus weakly.

Daniel quietly slips into the room and shuts the door. "Oh shit," he exclaims in a hushed voice the moment he sees Rufus' face. In full light, it is plain to see why Rufus instinctively hid his left-hand side from his mother. "What have you done?" Daniel whispers as he examines the very purple, bloody gash on the side of his brother's eye.

"That's not the worst." Rufus unclutches his side and Daniel carefully lifts his jumper.

Grimacing, Daniel simply says, "I'll get my kit."

I suppose this is one advantage of having a nurse and a paramedic in the family—they are far more likely to have an extensive first aid kit than any other profession (unless you marry a veterinarian, maybe).

"Anywhere else?" Daniel asks as he returns, shutting the door firmly, but almost silently behind him.

"My leg. I haven't seen it, but it hurts."

Reducing Rufus to his pants and socks, Daniel assess' the damage.

"These are not just scratches and I'm not meant to cover crimes, you know? I don't suppose you'll let me take you to the hospital or call the police?"

"I can't."

"Can't?"

"No, *can't*." Rufus raises his eyebrows—well, the right one—as he answers.

"This has to end, before it ends you." Daniel's face and tone are equally serious.

"It's fine, don't stress. Things got a bit messy, but it's okay, they came off worse. We won."

Daniel's entire body shudders. "There is no *winning* in what you're involved in, Rufus. Only today's pursuit of power and tomorrow's next fight to hold onto it. Don't be a pawn in a party that couldn't care less if—"

"They care! We have each other's back, Leo came—"

"Leo is interested in money and self, nothing else."

"We're brothers."

"So are we," Daniel says sadly.

Rufus' face falls apologetically. "I know, I know, and you've got me, I know that."

"Then why can't you—"

"It's okay, Dan, really it is." Rufus scoffs. "If fuckin' Hayden would remember we're brothers, that would be—"

"Did he do this?" The shock and anger on Daniel's face is striking.

"No...not directly."

"But?"

Sighing, Rufus replies, "Let's just say that he and his mates have buddied up on the wrong side."

"What does that mean?"

"It means that—" Rufus cuts himself off. "Never mind Hayden and his bitch of a girlfriend." He laughs. "That daddy's girl is about to get a shock and a half."

*"This is not a joke!"* Daniel's frustration sends waves of invisible energy across the room.

I fear what misery Rufus might bring on himself and his family. Simply helping him down the street is not going to be enough. I reach for Rufus' arm, but my hand glides through him. Possibly touching him now would be useless anyway, but I need to be able to prevent harm, to guide—not stand by watching fools blindly act and self-destruct.

"Yeah, I know," is all that Rufus replies, but it is enough to click Daniel into his calm, professional demeanour as he works on patching up his brother.

Internally Daniel must be chewing over a thousand concerns though because—admission of seriousness or not—it doesn't take a genius to work out that as well as taking a significant beating, Rufus has been stabbed in the side. He is just lucky that neither it, nor the slash across his thigh are as bad as they could have been.

When Daniel has finished, he tidies up his kit and bids Rufus good night but doesn't go immediately to bed himself.

He needs to by the look of him, yet I get the impression his mind is on overdrive, even if his body is not.

Standing in the kitchen with a glass of orange juice, Daniel stares out of the window. Without warning, he downs the drink, leaves the glass in the sink, and walks into the back garden, gazing at the sky—which is now filled with stars after the earlier rain has cleared.

It isn't visible from the living room window, but there is a small wooden bench placed against the wall between the kitchen and living room windows. Whilst dark and soaking wet, it isn't particularly appealing, however on a sunny day I can imagine it being a nice spot to sit. Despite the negatives, Daniel sits on the bench.

Standing by the closed backdoor, I watch him, watching the stars, desperately wishing I could talk to him, comfort him—or at the very least admonish him for not putting on a coat. Some might say I have double standards—after all, I am standing barefoot in a white summer dress in January—but as I am dead and not in the least bit cold, I don't care.

Moments later, I don't know whether to laugh or cry when Daniel begins to shiver. His chills don't distract him from watching the stars though—nor do they detract from the icy lightning bolts he sends under my skin as he confidently says:

"If you sit next to me, I won't be cold."

# 33

Although it takes a minute for the initial shock to dissipate, I slowly make my way to the empty spot on the bench beside Daniel. Closing the gap could take a matter of milliseconds, yet I cannot seem to make myself rush.

Apparently not expecting to see me, Daniel continues to watch the stars, yet his irregular foggy breath contradicts the relaxed tone and posture he is trying to convey. Were I in the same realm and able to feel the cold, my breath would still not betray me because I am holding it so tightly. My heart, however, is thumping as if I were the one being crept up on by a ghost.

Focusing on his breath, I sit on the soggy bench, leaving only inches between our legs. Instantly, the bench dries, and the foggy clouds disappear as an invisible, but unmistakeable warmth surrounds us.

A grin spreads across Daniel's face. "Told you."

Letting out a nervous laugh, I follow his gaze to the stars while my mind dances. I knew that I felt more in his presence, but despite the incident in the street on Christmas Eve, I didn't let myself believe that he was aware of it too. How aware is he? To what degree can he see or sense me? He and Adi said they felt like they were watched over—is that the kind of presence Daniel still feels, or is it now different?

His book collection alone shows that he has a lasting interest in spirits and angels. But does his heart and mind skip at the memory of a fleeting moment on the beach like mine—or is it simply the fascination of the 'other side'? Am I just a curiosity to him?

My brain often races with things I would like to say to Daniel, but I fear not being heard. Maybe it is worse not to try, than to fail?

My words so rarely reach the intended recipient that I often forget to talk. And when I do, my conversations with the in-danger or dying are very different. The words are mine, yet also not. The glitch, an inner voice, something *other*, speaks through me.

I want to speak for myself—when I want to.

I want to be heard.

To listen *and* be listened to.

A simple right and privilege of the living that I forgot to claim—and now I have no given rights at all.

Yet I have this moment and I will take comfort from it, even if all I can have is companionable silence. There is a beauty in comfortable silence, when two souls are at peace with one another. Not all voids need filling—but I would be lying if I said I wouldn't like to fill some.

"Won't you speak to me?" Daniel whispers as he turns towards me, sighing. "Can't I see you?"

"I wish," I reply, but it is clear from his searching eyes that he doesn't hear me any more than he sees me.

Daniel sighs again and I am struck by the worry in his face. He knows how dangerous Rufus' actions are as well as he knows their mother will not live much longer. The burden weighs on him and I wish it were possible to share the load. Were I alive, I would offer him a hug at least—yet, here, so close, I fear the disappointment that would hit me if my hand slipped through him.

"I sense you, you know? Sometimes I think that I'm going mad. Raquel thinks that I've invented you, but I haven't. We're connected, right? You feel it?" He waits for an answer, but the glitch doesn't even provide a breeze on which to send a whisper through time, so my heartfelt affirmation is lost.

Daniel nods, whether to me or himself, I do not know. "You saved me and watch over my family. I don't understand it, but I don't doubt it. I feel like I could touch you..." He raises his hand, hesitantly extending a finger in my direction as though he is waiting for permission. Hoping a ripple in time might occur, I brace myself, but Daniel's finger glides through my arm and he retracts his hand looking disheartened.

Glancing behind him towards the house, Daniel says, "My family...I wish..." He pauses and I see tears welling in his eyes. "I wish you could save her. And Rufus. Lord knows, I don't know what to do with Rufus."

"I know," I reply, unheard. If only the glitch would give me abilities beyond a watchman.

We return to silence, but now I do not feel silent—it is as though our spirits are communicating elsewhere in a language I do not understand.

As fatigue gets the better of Daniel, he yawns. At first, he tries to stifle them, but his body is persistent and the strength of a new wave of yawns betrays him. Feeling bad for keeping him up, I stand, taking two steps away, and observe as a cold chill instantly makes him shudder.

"Don't leave," he says, unwittingly looking through me.

I want nothing more than to sit back down and absorb the serenity of sitting with him forever, but that would be selfish. It is one thing to claim snippets in time, but I can have no more. He needs to sleep, so it must be enough to know that he really does sense me.

Reaching into his pocket, he produces a red rose. *The* red rose. A cynic might say that Daniel just buys a fresh rose every day, but every time I see it, despite it being stored in a shirt or coat pocket, it is always perfect—only the colour has changed, and I witnessed that transformation from yellow to red myself.

Unlike when we stood on the street, I reach for Daniel's cupped palm, not the rose itself, wrapping my hand over his fingers, attempting to fold them over the flower. Gasping, he smiles, laying his free hand over mine.

My skin fires as the rose feels like it is emanating heat. I scan Daniel's face in the dark, hoping a further gateway in time has been granted. His green eyes strain and focus in my direction, desperately searching. I wish I knew what he was thinking, but he looks like he is trying to order dust into a formation by willpower alone. Possibly that would be a more fruitful exercise, for he cannot see me, and we cannot stand holding, yet not holding hands for the rest of his life.

As I let go, he frowns. "Stay—please?"

"I'm never far," I reply with feeling, but still, he doesn't hear me.

Instead, Daniel just holds out his empty hand to me. I take it and pull—fully expecting no more than a warm tickle, if that, but suddenly my muscles tense under the strain and he stands up.

Overwhelmed, I let go, but immediately regret it and reach back for him, only to be left wanting. Daniel's eyes are boggled, but he chuckles—albeit a little nervously. I can't blame him, I'd be freaked out if a ghost touched me, let alone made me stand up.

A cheeky, self-satisfied smile creeps across his face—like he has just won an argument or bet. If the challenge was 'prove other beings exist,' then he has won. Daniel's grin makes my phantom heart skip. I'm not sure what to do with that fact, but it is a fact.

Possibly not a healthy one for either of us.

A light flicks on from upstairs, casting a beam of light onto us. Realising Kath is awake, Daniel's smile drops.

She should be asleep, but then again, so should he.

"I'll need to check on Mum," he says, walking to the backdoor, pausing as he grasps the handle. "Will you come with me?"

Fearing that I'll never want to leave if I stay too close now, I keep still, allowing the cold air to wisp between us.

Daniel waits, then shrugs. "Okay, just don't leave me—or at least come back."

# 34

Rufus woke me as he wandered downstairs this morning. Sleeping on Kath's sofa was the easiest option last night, so after I was certain that Daniel was settled upstairs, I curled up amongst the cushions and drifted off, telling myself I won't make this a habit.

The smell of toast teases my tastebuds as I sit up. As usual, my dress is clean and fresh again, with only a minute ruffle from the way I have been laying. The ring is back. I suppose there is no hope of that leaving me again, even if Daniel and I connect via our magical rose—or whatever force or label you care to attribute to the glitch and its whim.

I expected Rufus to eat and then return upstairs, however, as soon as he has finished, he checks his phone, grabs his coat, and leaves the house before anyone else wakes up. He is slightly less lame than last night, but barely, and the purple bruising by his eye is blooming more than ever.

It is still dark, but there is a man walking his dog down the street. They reach each other under the streetlamp and the man double takes. Neither speaks, but Rufus quickly pulls his hood up, hunches his shoulders, and attempts to move faster. Reading Rufus' less than social body language, the man carries on in the opposite direction and I continue following my charge.

It soon becomes clear that Rufus is heading for Flossy's house, leading me to deduce this can only be another fool's errand. Why nobody else—preferably someone without stitches—cannot visit the old man, I do not know. Why Rufus is only occasionally lent a 'company' car, I also couldn't say, yet as he approaches Flossy's house, I look up and realise there is already an extra car in the driveway. It isn't a vehicle from my disgusting ex-husband's garage, or even his father's showroom, but *my* father's.

This can't be good—Dad should not be here at this time of day; his shifts never start this early. Eager for answers and unwilling to wait for Rufus to hobble up to the door, I run past him.

Inside, Dad is knelt in front of Flossy in the living room while Sophia, still dressed in her pyjamas, anxiously looks on from her wheelchair. "How bad is it?" she asks.

"A scratch, girl, nay more than a scratch!" chuckles Flossy, though his expression is forced.

"Scratches don't bleed like that," Sophia replies grimly. "Please, don't lie, tell me—"

"He'll be fine," Dad replies confidently, and Sophia instantly relaxes her shoulders. "I'm not saying it isn't serious—any such wound is or could be, yet Flossy is fortunate—"

The doorbell rings and everyone anxiously turns towards the front door.

Rufus pops his head around the corner of the window and Flossy snorts. "Get that, will you? The lad had a crappy night too."

Dad raises an eyebrow, but calmly walks to the door, opening it without hesitation.

Although I know he is only here in the capacity of a caregiver, I really hate the fact that my dad is in anyway connected to whatever this mess is. My father is not a drug lord, thug, or bully. Until recently, I didn't realise Flossy was. I thought he was a jolly old guy who sold candyfloss whilst occasionally mocking and swearing at his half-hearted assistants. Everyone's funny, honorary uncle—not someone to fear.

"Oh, hey," says Rufus as the door opens.

"Hello Rufus, fancy seeing you here."

"I could say the same to you—I didn't know you were part of the crew?"

"Get in here, boy, don't talk shit," calls Flossy. "Do you need patching up?"

"Nah, I'm sorted."

"Then why are you here?"

"Leo sent me to check on you, Uncle Flossy."

Flossy snorts again. "You'd think he'd send someone who hadn't had the crap beaten out of them."

"What happened?" Dad asks.

"Nothin'. Nothin' you wanna know. I'm grateful to ye, of course I am, but let's stick to the *need to know*." Flossy narrows his eyes. "Like: how do you know Rufus?"

Rufus shrugs, answering before Dad has a chance. "We've only met a couple of times. My brother married his daughter."

"Hayden?" Rufus nods and anger flashes across Flossy's face. "Fuckin' twat—sorry, if you like your son-in-law, but he is a—"

"He is nothing to me." Dad says coldly.

Even if he cannot know the full truth, Flossy's memory of my demise obviously kicks in because his face twists as he responds, "Ah, yes, sorry." Remembering his more immediate concerns, he sneers adding, "He is mixed in some crap—he and his new girlfriend."

Dad grimaces but doesn't respond.

Sophia is pale and shaking. Dad notices but turns back to Flossy. "Is there anything else I can do?"

Flossy pulls his mobile out of his pocket, unlocking it, but looks up as he replies: "I think we're done. Thank you, I owe you."

"I'm so sorry to call you out at this hour—and on your day off." Sophia stares at Dad in earnest as though she wants to say more.

Nothing changes there then. Their feelings are still as unspoken as the last time I visited. Perhaps that is for the best—but maybe Sophia needs rescuing and Dad is her knight in PPE? All I know is she makes him smile in a way that is otherwise rarely seen—if at all.

"It's all right, I am happy to help. Though I think—"

Rufus' phone rings, stopping all conversation. Peering over his shoulder, I can see it is Daniel calling, but he doesn't answer. I can guess how that voicemail will go.

"We'll have business today," Flossy says watching Rufus put his phone away.

"Yep, a meeting. They're coming here."

Sophia gulps—which is worrying. She seems to have a sweet nature, but having gone through so much already, she doesn't strike me as a woman who rattles particularly easily. Flossy's typical business cannot be a mystery to her either, yet it is clear whatever her grandfather is into now, she is not keen to be party. Thankfully, Flossy doesn't seem too keen to conduct business in front of her either as he quickly replies: "Nope, not here. I'll sort it."

Plainly confused, Rufus replies, "Leo said—"

Flossy grits his teeth. "*I will sort it.*"

Dad packs his things, then rubs his hand across his mouth, like he does sometimes when he is working up to say something. I vaguely remember Mum laughing at him for it—I doubt Sally ever noticed. Dropping his hand, he says, "Sophia, are you busy today?"

Under less stressful circumstances, I think Sophia would laugh at this question, but she simply replies, "No, why?"

"I'm still in between houses, but I plan to spend the day at my new house painting. I had guys doing it, but since Sally and I broke up, I've been happy to do things myself—"

"You broke up?" Sophia's face doesn't hide her shock. "I know you said you are moving, but I didn't realise—"

"Right, yeah, I was waiting until—" Dad scoffs and shakes his head, apparently simultaneously shaking away the rest of the sentence. "If Flossy is busy, and you wouldn't be too bored, you could spend the day with me?"

Totally forgetting her woes for a moment, Sophia's eyes shine. "I'd love to."

Dad smiles, perhaps a little nervously, but genuinely as he replies, "Great."

Flossy seems relieved to have his granddaughter safely taken care of and within twenty minutes Sophia is on the driveway, waiting while Dad shuffles boxes around in his car.

"Sorry, I just need to move stuff off the front seat. I've been half living out of the—"

"I can sit in the back if that's easier?"

"No, no, it's fine. I'll feel like a taxi driver if I put you in the back."

Sophia laughs but stops as Kev pulls up. He sits motionlessly in his car, neither speaking or signalling to anyone while he waits for Flossy and Rufus. The car door is open long enough for me to climb in slowly, and for a moment I believe the seat will hold my form; however, hope quickly turns to predictable disappointment and frustration as I am left standing on the street in all my holographic misery, watching them drive away—taking all their explanations with them.

Once Dad has made space, he gently lifts Sophia onto the front seat. It is a good job that I am small, because I barely fit in between the boxes and Sophia's wheelchair. I could probably sit in the pixelated space where the chair is—if the glitch is sticking to its 'no sitting on unsanctioned forms of transport' rule. In the early days, before I was better aware of the rules and didn't have a sense of caution before committing all my weight to a given surface, I tried sitting in a wheelchair, but all I received was a thump on the backside when I fell to the floor.

The drive to Mrs Crook's is quiet and Dad seems nervously excited as he shows Sophia inside. Leaving her with a cup of tea, he begins to unload the boxes that he has—by his own admission—been dragging around for weeks. Wandering through each room, I check for any changes that have been made since I was last here. The most immediately notable difference is the presence of new kitchen cabinets, but everything else is still very much a work in progress in terms of decoration and furniture. To be fair, all structural changes seem to be complete as the wall between the kitchen and living room now has a wide, attractive archway and all the doorways, although mostly doorless, are wider.

The largest bedroom has a few boxes, and the downstairs bathroom a towel laid out, but Dad clearly isn't sleeping here yet. Nervously, I check Mr Crook's study, hoping that the room has not been gutted, and I sigh with relief when I am greeted by bygones once more. Curling up in the big chair, I absent-mindedly gaze out of the window. For a moment, I just want to sit and leave the world behind.

Sophia and Dad chat happily, providing a background noise to my drifting thoughts, but the pronunciation of my old name shocks my attention back into reality—my reality, anyway. The sound of that name rasps in my ears, scratching the surface as it shoots to my brain. It is only right that Dad uses my old name, I suppose. Why would he call me anything else? Yet he normally avoids it and seems to share my loathing of the shadows that name casts. Hayden smothered her long before he killed her.

'Daughter' is much safer.

Bland, but also benign.

Sophia notices that he trips over the syllables and gently says, "Sorry."

There is a silence, then a chair squeaks as Dad stands up. They are out of sight, but I hear a few footsteps on the tiled floor before the sound of Sophia's chair gently moving reaches me. Without a word, Dad pushes Sophia into the study doorway. She doesn't question or protest, she simply lets him guide her until she can see the room.

"What is all this?"

"The past," Dad says, softly.

"Whose?"

"Family—not by blood, but by all that matters. Until I inherited it, this place was like a time warp. Part of me wanted to leave it as it was so I could be surrounded by the memories, even if I could not have the people."

"You inherited this?"

"Yeah—don't tell Sally, she doesn't know. I even had a fake sold sign put up just in case she saw me come here." Dad chuckles nervously.

Sophia grins. "But how come—who lived here?"

"Gladys Crook. She was a client, but also a dear friend. She had no children, yet doted on mine, so left this place to her and me, but since it is just me..."

I had no idea. There is a certain irony in finding out that twice I was the beneficiary of someone's will. One I received but was too chicken to use—and then got me killed—and the second I died too soon to be in receipt of. It's a shame Hayden doesn't know; I'd like to see him count how many thousands he lost killing me too soon. I'd like to tell him—preferably moments before he died.

Possibly I should let such hatred go. Sometimes I think that I have, but my thoughts anchor to Hayden and he erodes my progress. Knowing that two people cared so much for me that they left me their treasures is humbling, but honestly, poor or not, I'd rather just have life and appreciate it. Neither money nor hatred brings happiness.

"I'm sure they would both want you to make the home yours," Sophia says, reaching out to take my dad's hand.

He gazes down at their entwined fingers, smiling. Perhaps I am wrong. Money does seem to have bought Dad a space for him to find happiness.

No, I'm not so cynical yet—it's not the building, it's the people in it.

The person.

"You're right," he says, "they would. That's why I was extra 'generous' with my old house in the divorce settlement. My sister thinks I'm mad. It is more than Sally is due, but it gives us all a fresh start. We all deserve that, I think." Dad glances around the room. "I want to arrange a few things from days gone by, that's why I kept these things, but—but—"

Suddenly Dad looks like a teenager searching for the words to ask a girl to prom.

*"But...?"* prompts Sophia, willing him on with every drop of positive energy she can muster.

Dad chews his lip, then rubs his free hand across his face. "Maybe now isn't the time." Sophia's shoulders deflate. "I don't want you to think that I've cornered you here to spring ideas on you."

Sophia softly scoffs. "I wish you would."

Dad blushes and I suddenly feel like this isn't a conversation a daughter should hear—dead or alive—yet I desperately want to see him be happy. *Don't clam up now Dad, please.*

"I was leaving—*I am leaving*—this room," Dad says, gulping so hard I'm surprised his Adam's apple can resurface, "for you."

"For me?" Sophia beams.

"If you want it. I'm not assuming anything—we've said nothing, so please, don't think I'm expecting anything, I'm not." Too shy to look for Sophia's response, Dad glances around the room again—possibly seeking moral support from familiar things. For a second his eyes pause on the chair that I am sitting in, making my heart stop. As he smiles, I feel hugged—like he has given me one of his all-embracing hugs that solved everything when I was little—even if it's only in my mind.

"I want it," Sophia whispers.

Grinning, Dad turns back to her, and she giggles sweetly.

Exhaling with a tangible sense of relief, Dad says, "I wanted to wait until my divorce was done, but being the coward that I am, I couldn't bring myself to tell Sally how I felt—or you." He laughs. "Would you believe it took me seeing Sally and her boyfriend—our neighbour—hand in hand in the high-street?"

"When?"

"Christmas Eve."

"Shit! I'm sorry—well, *not* sorry, but still—"

"It's okay, really. I spent Christmas with my sister and her family for the first time in years and it recentred my drifting, procrastinating mind. Here, in this house, I have the memory of those who matter most but have gone, plus the peace to move on."

My eyes overflow hearing Dad with hope in his voice—and more importantly love in his heart that is reciprocated. Sophia tugs on his arm, pulling him low enough she can gently grab his cheeks, smiling from ear to ear.

Dad closes the gap, softly kissing her, and I decide now is a good moment to take my leave.

# 35

Without a specific destination in mind, I head for my default haunting ground—the beach. Finding one of my favourite benches unoccupied, I watch people wander up and down the promenade, making the most of the sunshine. The sand is clear of people except for a few dog walkers in the distance, including a couple of dogs who are splashing through the chilly water as if it were June. Recognising a woman playing with her German Shepherd, I smile—she's the one I scared a few weeks ago. She looks happy and I'm glad to see she wasn't traumatised to the point of not returning to the beach. Afterall, I want to be a good, friendly ghost—*mostly*.

Hoping to keep Adtoft tidy, I tried a similar trick with a kid who dropped a coke can, but my aim was bad, and the boy trotted off with his mates as though the can was meant to be on the floor. Frustrated, I collected the can and put it in the bin myself—which was a waste of time because I turned around to find the can back where I found it. Not surprising maybe, but very annoying, nonetheless. You'd think the glitch would be happy for me to make myself useful, but apparently not.

Observe and occasionally guide, not clean. Cleaning is for the living.

Wearing beige and brown, Oki is almost camouflaged standing by her canvas at the most southern part of the beach. She has a scarf wrapped around her head, obscuring her face, but I know that it is her.

Whilst considering stepping off the promenade to visit her, a chill hits me. It's so rare that I feel cold that I normally enjoy it, but this time my insides feel like they are freezing, and it frightens me.

Searching the area, I try to find who or what could have caused my senses to react this way, but there is no one of note nearby—certainly, no one I know. The pier isn't close enough to see who is bustling in and out of the amusements or the food stands, but whoever is there looks peaceful. No blue lights or sirens are blaring. No one is running or shouting. Maybe I imagined it. Maybe I imagined an old feeling, and tried to convince myself that I can feel?

I don't know if I believe my own conclusions. I do feel. I feel happy for my father. I feel hope for him and Sophia—if they can keep away from any unsavoury connections. With any luck Dad will get the house done, the divorce stamped, and move on without looking back.

The chill hits me again, blasting any doubts of its presence into the sea.

I want to scream at the glitch. If it wants me to see something, why not show me clearly? My eyes are anxiously searching, but I do not understand. With tears of frustration blurring my vision, I stare up at the sky where only dotted clouds and gulls greet me. It seems like they were waiting for an audience because with a single squark the birds break from their peaceful dance, circling above like they are caught in an icy whirlwind. However, as quickly as the performance began, the current changes and a bird darts in land, calling out as it flies.

Directly below, a red Mercedes pulls up on the street seconds after an SUV pulls out of the same spot—almost like the space had been reserved for a VIP. No, not almost, exactly like, as while I watch, a second SUV pulls onto the road as a black Jaguar glides into its place.

The gulls, apparently satisfied with their aerial display, land next to me, animatedly chattering. Their calls increase as a man steps out of the Jaguar. They sound angry—whether at me, or the man, I couldn't say, yet I get the hint: Go follow.

The man is probably somewhere between fifty-five and sixty-five years old, but he has one of those faces that are hard to age. If he has worked hard in his life, it is not on the land or at sea because his skin is smooth and silky—either that or a plastic surgeon is his best friend. His suit is neat and expensive, like his car, his hair is gelled, but not with as much as someone twenty years younger or from the 1990's might use. His aura is as black as his car. I'm not saying other colours are not mixed in, but his overconfident stride and self-important grin make my skin crawl.

Without question he is waiting for the person in the Mercedes to get out. Maybe he is grinning because he thinks they are reluctant to meet him, yet he is quickly proven wrong as she winds down the passenger window, curtly waving her hand as she says, "Oh, don't wait, I must take this call. I'll see you in a moment."

The man nods, smirking, but as he walks away his grin turns to a scowl.

Woman 1 – Man 0.

I say 'woman,' yet now I have seen her, I can name her. Unlike the man, I do know this person, even if I do not know her well—Lianna Garvey is not someone I've ever *wanted* to know well.

Like Maddox Lennox, Lianna's name is spread across town. While 'Lennox' is on half of the cars, 'Garvey' is on half of the lorries—all carrying containers from her ridiculously large cargo ships. As a self-made multi-millionaire, I admire her shrewd business sense, plus her generosity towards various charities and social events in and around her 'beloved' Adtoft, has made her a mini celebrity, but because she's Leo's mother, keeping my distance always seemed wise.

When she finally steps out of the car, wearing a perfectly chosen power suit, Lianna strides towards the restaurant she and the mystery man have parked so expertly in front of. As she opens the restaurant door, the SUV that moved aside for her returns and Lianna nods to the driver. The car pulls into a space down the street, while the other SUV appears and continues down the road—possibly to continue looping until such time as it is released from duty.

Crossing the street between two parked cars, I notice two men, both intently watching the restaurant. Which person they are watching more, I can only guess, but the whole scenario seems bizarre.

How much security can two people need? And why?

Lianna doesn't need to wait to be shown to a table. The concierge is primed and ready to seat her, and as she approaches the man genteelly stands up, offering his hand. She scoffs under her breath, but takes it smiling, making sure to be the one to let go when she is ready, not the other way around.

"Anton," Lianna says without any genuine warmth, sitting down.

"I took the liberty of ordering drinks," says Anton. "I hope you do not mind?"

"Good, good," Lianna smiles.

To begin with, the conversation is routine. Good weather—a bit cold—spring is just around the corner—what would you like to eat?—I love the fish. However, it is clear that they are waiting for their moment. No good businessperson jumps in the deep end without first testing the water and both look like they'd love to throw a weight around the others' neck and watch them drown.

"Thank you for coming, Lianna" says Anton, as the waiter walks away.

"I'd say it's a pleasure, but we both know that isn't true."

Anton raises his eyebrows. "If your son kept his work in check—"

"My son knows how to run a business perfectly well. He has proven that time and again. My town doesn't—"

"This isn't a western, Lianna. You cannot *own* a town, no matter how much you—"

"This town has and always will be mine. You, sir, were nothing here and will be nothing again."

"I was hoping you'd see it differently. We have excellent opportunities here. My daughter is especially keen to remain—"

Lianna scoffs. "Your daughter is the cause of all this mess. Amicable competition is one thing, but poorly planned, poorly made produce, is bad for everyone. It just shifts focuses to all the wrong places. She is a liability, and you know it."

"I'll admit some of her choices have raised a few questions, but she—"

"Should have stuck to her little corner and not tried to wear someone else's boots."

Anton sighs. "We are staying, Lianna. I should make that clear before we continue. This meeting is a courtesy, an attempt to find common ground."

*"Common ground?"* Lianna doesn't try to hide her contempt. "You are mistaken. This meeting is to tell you now, once and for all, that these violent games your pathetic little troops are playing are going to stop. They, and your new 'human enterprises' are endangering all of our businesses."

"There was only one left in the container—"

"Enough." Lianna almost spits across the table. "If you or they remotely attempt to expose me—deliberately or otherwise—I can assure you that I will not go down alone. And you *will* sink a lot faster and harder than I ever could." She manages to sneer whilst smiling sweetly as she pauses. "Clean up your trash and get out—or be put out. The choice is yours but make it now or we'll make it for you."

# 36

Anyone taking Anton and Lianna's photograph as they left the restaurant would not have known anything was wrong. They shook hands, gave a slight bow, smiled, and walked casually to their respective cars—neither remotely glancing at their bodyguards who almost seemed relaxed, yet the second their charges cars pulled away, so did they.

During the meeting, neither party uttered a word of detail, so I am left filling in my own blanks. It would seem that Leo is not the boss of his drug dealing empire as I had assumed. Until recently, I thought it was Flossy, but even he is a rung lower than I realised. As you go down a step the person gets their hands a little dirtier, but regardless of how I see it, the entire ladder is full of scum.

What am I to do with this knowledge? It isn't like I can go to the police or local newspaper and shine a light on how deceived everyone is about Lianna Garvey and all her so-called kind and generous endeavours. Nor can I warn anyone about the new entrepreneur that is selling a lot more than trinkets from China.

Without a warning, people will buy their drugs—quality and otherwise—fall victim to their violence, and if I read in between the lines correctly, be trafficked across the sea in unseaworthy boats.

What use is a guardian angel that just watches that happen?

Disillusioned, I step out onto the sand and wiggle my toes. I can feel the grit under my nails, just not the striking cold that should accompany the current climate. I am numb. A void. A pointless void.

The sound of the sea crashing on the shore normally soothes, or at least centres my anxious thoughts. Sometimes, in my past desperation, I told myself that the sea was calling me, telling me to end it all, but lately I have learnt to translate this as a call to action, not departure. The glitch wants me here, I just don't understand why.

"WHY?" I scream into the wind. "WHAT IS THE POINT?"

A faint female voice calls out to my right as a gull tries to steal fish and chips. I want to scream again—that's hardly a meaningful answer to my woes, is it?

Possibly, when not stealing, those birds do know all, even if they mock more than they talk to me. They pointed me in the direction of a dodgy business meeting, and the real world can see them, so perhaps the glitch should use them as spirit guides, not me.

A quiet voice calls again, but not from the bird lady or her adoring gull. Staring further down the beach, I can only see Oki. She is still standing with her canvas, although she now has someone with her—Nina, I think—who is animatedly waving her arms while Oki steps back a little.

Curious, I cautiously walk towards them, but quickly increase my speed as the gentle call of a distant voice becomes a scream akin to mine moments earlier. Whatever has upset Nina isn't going away, and Oki looks ashen as she pleads with her to calm down.

As I finally get close enough to make out full sentences, Oki freezes with tears rolling down her cheeks, but Nina violently lunges forward, grabs Oki's canvas and throws it into the sand.

"There! Fuckin' paint that!" Nina yells. "Have you nothing to say?"

"Even if I do, you won't listen," Oki says meekly.

"Won't listen? Won't listen? All I do is listen to you! Raquel this, Sean that—oh, and my bloody fuckin' beach hut, isn't it wonderful?!"

"We discussed that—"

"No, *we* didn't! You told me you'd said yes, *after* we agreed no!"

"You said no, not me. I need space—*we* need our space. We can't work like we have been. Surely you see that?"

"You're not leaving me, do you hear?"

Oki looks physically wounded. "Leaving? I said nothing about leaving, but you keep pushing. I want—"

"I know where this goes. There is no need for you and Raquel to be in that hut at all hours."

"She is a friend! She's helping me—perhaps you cou—"

Oki cannot finish as Nina slaps her across the face with all her might, sending her flying on top of her canvas. Oki sobs, but rather than repent of her actions, Nina seems invigorated by them. Venom rises in her expression as her jaw sets and her fists clench. Swinging her right foot back, Nina lands an enormous kick into Oki's side, making her cry out with pain.

"Help you! Is that what you were going to say? *That I don't help you?*" Nina's voice is getting sharper, angrier by the second. If she is drunk, I cannot tell—but either way, she has totally focused her energy into a blind, jealous fit of anger.

Something suddenly clicks in my mind, and I feel sick. That look. I have seen that look before—too many times. Hayden, drunk or sober, it didn't matter, regularly, repeatedly, looked at me that way. Anything I did for myself or not exactly as he wanted, resulted in that expression.

Vomit rises in my mouth. How could I not have seen the signs before? For months—years—I have watched Oki paint. Numerous times I have seen her tired and jumpy. Dressed totally inappropriately for the weather—hiding bruises, just like I used to.

Did I not want to see it? It's not like I can be an active support to Oki, can I? All I am is a witness to greed and disgrace. Seeing Oki's face now is like holding a mirror to living me. I hate that image. I hate what Hayden did to me—what I let him do to me—and that no one else saw in time to help.

But Raquel and her father did. They have given Oki a lifeline. The subtle questions and hints for change make sense more than ever now—they offered an olive branch, hoping Oki would take it.

Right now, Oki cannot take anything as she cowers on the sand. The scene, too familiar, has frozen me, reverting me to the statuesque state of submission that Hayden reduced me to so many times. In my iced state, my heart bleeds for Oki—desperately willing her to save herself and take a full stand before it is too late.

*Do not be me.*

Heaving with adrenaline fuelled anger, embolden by the lack of passersby, Nina grits her teeth, dragging Oki to her feet. "We're going home." No question, just a statement.

The voice might be feminine, but I recognise the tone only too well.

*"Say no, Oki, say, no,"* I whisper.

"You said you'd stop hitting me," Oki splutters.

"And you said you'd not take the hut." Nina sneers. "Let's go."

Oki closes her eyes tightly. When she opens them, there is only sadness. Shaking her head, she says: "I can't."

"What do you mean, *you can't?* Don't talk such—"

Trembling, Oki steps back. "I'm done." Nina closes the gap. "I mean it this time. We can't keep repeating the same mistakes."

Nina's whole-body tenses and her temples bulge. I'm not sure how far into this conversation they have gotten before, but as she lunges forward, Oki braces for impact.

I have seen and lived this scene too many times. Disgust and hatred grasp me, freeing my pathetic limbs from an ice-age of inaction and I grab Nina with both hands. Digging my nails into her shoulders, I yank her backwards, throwing her across the beach like a Scott's man throws a caber.

Now metres apart, the women turn to each other, staring in tear-stained confusion. Nina's mouth opens and shuts without making a sound, and her chest heaves. Her eyes look like black holes as they have dilated further than I've ever seen a person's go before, which is a particularly disturbing sight when the blood has drained from her rosy cheeks. On the other side of me, Oki seems to have gained colour—probably from a mixture of relief and surprise she wasn't beaten again—but she seems no less stunned than Nina does.

Then a new reality hits me.

They are not staring at each other—they are staring at *me*.

# 37

Normally, when I am seen I feel a peace or warmth of some kind, yet not today. Having saved Oki from further attack, I can explain why she can see me, but not Nina. Only those who have been helped in one way or another have seen me, and regardless of me touching them, the glitch has never revealed me to a non-threatened living person. *Until now.* Confusion ripples through me but time seems to have stopped for us all—except for our lungs which are working in double time.

Who is supposed to speak first on such occasions?

Perhaps I do not need to find a voice.

Maybe I just need to be.

Walking over to Oki, unsure whether she will accept my offer, I extend my right hand.

Without hesitation, she wraps her palm around mine and I feel her weight lifted under my grasp in a warm, fresh summer breeze.

Our eyes meet, smiling, despite the sadness. Colours of green, violet, and gold swirl, surrounding a grey-blue cloud around us. Our pain is shared—in silent friendship, we understand one another.

The air of serenity is ruffled by a roar akin to the sort of warrior cry that you hear in films as fighters attack. I never understood why anyone would shout before they attack—surely it gives away the advantage of surprise? Possibly the attacker is too arrogant or too stupid to believe their advance will be thwarted. Nina, it would seem, is that kind of attacker. Her jealous anger, too briefly stunned, causes her to run at me with everything she has.

With the seconds warning I have, seeing that Oki is not the target, I stand my ground, smugly waiting to see Nina fall flat on her face.

As she grabs for my left arm, Nina swings me around, forcing me to face her fully. My senses electrify as euphoric surprise rushes through me. In better circumstances I'd stop to consider, but as Nina's fist approaches my face, I do not have time to marvel at human contact. Instinct makes me duck, and I, rather than feeling pain, hear a swoosh as her fist cuts through the air above me.

Oki screams at Nina to stop, but I know that look—her blood is boiling and no appeals for sense or clemency will stop her advance. Nina's foot swings but misses—no, *glides* through me.

"What the fuck?" shouts Nina angrily, trying to kick me again as her murky red aura spikes and thrashes around her.

My body trembles as my mind speedily replays the countless times that I have been attacked, but a resolute conviction shatters my memories long enough for me to strike out with both hands into Nina's chest, thrusting her backwards.

Screwing up her face, Nina lunges again, putting all her weight into her tackle as she sails through me, face planting the sand.

It's Nina's turn to tremble. Bullies don't like it when victims don't cower or beg. They certainly don't want to be grovelling on all fours.

A voice floats out of me like a harsh winter wind. "Go home, Nina."

Turning white, flight and fright kick in, and Nina jumps up, curses at us, and runs towards town.

Oki and I glance at each other—both clearly afraid, but oddly calm at the same time.

"You deserve much better, Oki. Make the change, now." The voice drifts from within, speaking in unison with me. "Don't go back, only forward."

Suddenly, I am jealous. It is a shameful thing to admit, but such a clear instruction from the glitch can only be envied by one who longs for guidance.

Oki's fingers tighten around mine and I focus again on her gorgeous eyes—is that a little hope I see nestled there amongst the pain? I believe so.

The road will be bumpy, but time and love will heal this beautiful soul.

My heart skips.

The answer to my being: I am to guide—to give a little hope.

Peace and hope.

Internally, I laugh at myself. Didn't Omi tell me that before? And I, in my weakness, still forget and doubt. I crave answers to more questions. Patience might be my lesson today—and to listen for more than words, for I cannot help feeling that I could have somehow helped Oki sooner.

From within her coat pocket, Oki's mobile phone begins ringing and the melancholy tune almost echoes off the water. Holding it at a distance, she doesn't answer but instead looks at me with panic in her eyes. Taking the phone from her hand, I see Nina's name.

Were this living me, I would answer, cry, and accept whatever meagre version of an apology Hayden was offering to make life go swiftly back to a safe, known state. But there is no safe. I am pixelated proof of that. Pressing the red button, I hang up—trying not to giggle with inappropriate glee as I realise I am holding an item in both realms—and begin scrolling through Oki's contacts until I get to R.

Of course, she has more friends. I have no doubt that I could scroll to any number of Oki's contacts, and they would try to help her, but Raquel is the safest bet that I know of for two main reasons. One, I believe she already realises to some degree that Nina is not good for Oki, and two, she is a newer friend, and therefore less connected to them as a couple. For now, Oki needs to start again, not have old friends asking in disbelief whether Nina is really violent.

Tapping on Raquel's name to start the call, I return the phone to Oki. A haze wisps around us, and we marvel as sand dances and glitters like fairy dust in the sunlight. I have never seen such a magical display. It should be blinding us, but the grains do not touch our skin, although we blink repeatably when Raquel answers and the sand flattens.

Glancing down, Oki puts the call on speaker. When she looks up, a disappointed frown upends her smile as her eyes desperately search all around her.

The glitch has faded me once more.

"Hello?" Raquel repeats for the third time. "Oki? Are you okay? Oki?"

The sound of her name centres her and Oki blinks as she snaps into reality. "Yes, sorry, sorry—" Tears choke her words.

"Oh, sweety, what is it?" Raquel's voice crackles sympathetically down the phone. "What happened? Are you all right?"

Oki's body begins to vibrate as she attempts to recall what just happened. "Nina...erm, she..."

Sensing danger, Raquel doesn't wait for Oki to find the right words. "Is she there?"

"No..." Oki's voice quavers. "Not now."

"Where are you?"

"On the beach—near the southern rock face."

"I'll be there in ten minutes. Don't move."

The phone goes dark, and Oki drops to the sand once more. Kneeling behind her, I cross my arms, wrapping them around her body, gently rocking from side to side. After a fight with Hayden, I used to hug myself like this, pretending that someone else was comforting me. Even if she cannot see me, I can only hope that Oki senses my affection.

I should have acted sooner. I should have *realised* sooner.

Raquel's voice calls across the shoreline. It is the third time she has broken my peace in this manner, but at least this time I am ready for her to take my friend away. It is the natural order. The living belongs with the living.

Hearing her voice, Oki stands up as Raquel hastily approaches. Concern is tangible on her face, and it is no less striking when she spots the paint and canvas smashed into the sand. "Nina did this?" There is the inflexion of a question, but no real sense of doubt in her tone. "Did she hurt you?" Oki nods sorrowfully. Horrified, Raquel sucks in her breath, stifling a sob as she struggles not to cry. Dropping her shoulders, she opens her arms towards Oki who gladly sinks into her embrace.

"Have you got anywhere to stay?" Raquel asks into Oki's shoulder.

Oki shakes her head.

"Will you stay with me? I have a spare room."

Oki steps back. "Really? Are you sure? I don't want to impose—"

"Absolutely, I'm sure. As long as you need. Let's get out of here."

Collecting up Oki's damaged goods, the two women set off arm-in-arm towards town. After a dozen steps, Oki pauses, whispering, "Thank you—for everything, you're a true angel."

Raquel replies, "Of course. That's what friends are for."

"To better times," Oki says, trying to smile, glancing back towards me.

Sighing with hope, I reply, "Amen to that."

# 38

Opening Oki's car door, I beam with delight. It would seem that I am right, I can be driven by people I have connected with. This is an exciting discovery and one I hope to investigate—just unfortunately not today.

Oki, too shaken to drive, leaves her things in her boot and then gets into Raquel's car. It is a shame I cannot go with them, but at least Oki is safe, and I will try to find her again another day. Before they left, I was relieved to hear Raquel's suggestion of speaking to her father was not totally rebuffed. Something tells me that Oki will not press charges against Nina, but she might need extra support in the future if Nina continues to take their breakup badly—or if Oki's resolve wanes.

With them gone out of sight, I do not know what to do with myself now. People are moving in the distance around me, carrying on with their lives as the evening pulls in. An ambulance flashes by, too fast for me to follow it. A teenager whizzes past on her bike, while an elderly gentleman gently directs his mobility scooter to the chippy down the street.

The smell of fish and chips hits the back of my throat as I walk past *Off the Hook*. Even when alive, I spent very little time out of Adtoft, but I wonder if fish and chip shops away from the coast smell the same. Probably they do, oil, potatoes, and fish are oil, potatoes, and fish at the end of the day, yet to me this is the familiar scent of hometown comforts—almost like a call to rest—that I like to imagine only being mixed with sea air can produce.

The chip shop has a line of customers and as the gentleman reaches for the door, someone from within opens it, greeting him with the kind of warmth you only get from a close-knit community. Voices rumble with laughter as the man replies. I don't hear the words, but obviously the old man has a sense of humour because the mirth continues as I walk away.

"See ya later!" calls a familiar voice from behind me as the door closes.

Dad has a few flecks of magnolia paint on his shoes, so I think he might have done some work today, yet his face is light and carefree—almost to the point I do not recognise him—as he happily walks down the street swinging a paper bag.

His day might have started dubiously, but I am thrilled that it has turned into a blessing. Of course, his hasty return home could be linked to a preference for warm food, yet I think it is more likely to be his companion he is eager to return to.

Sophia is in the kitchen, and she has been amusing herself by going through some of Dad's books. Smiling, he walks over to her, giving her a brief kiss before unwrapping their meal. Obviously, they have discussed their relationship in my absence as Dad's apology for not taking her with him is brushed off by Sophia with a slightly smutty joke about having a private party. Surely Dad doesn't need to hide from

Sally now, but if he wants to keep his business to himself until the divorce is official, I can see the wisdom in that. If nothing else, it gives these two time to test the waters whilst keeping away from Flossy's dodgy dealings.

*Hopefully.*

After dinner, they chat whilst picking through boxes. Wheeling herself into the living room, Sophia selects a cardboard box on the table marked 'save.' Picking out a doll, she laughs, declaring she didn't pick Dad as a 'doll-kind-of-man.'

Dad wanders over, smiling thoughtfully as he takes the doll.

"I'm not sure my daughter ever played with this. It was just always in the corner of her room," Dad says, turning the doll over in his hand.

Actually, I did play with her for a while. I liked the doll's soft, huggable body and long black hair, but as I aged, I kept her beside me like a comfort blanket. Mum bought her for me to practice styling hair one summer after I declared mine should be braided. She said I could wear it how I liked on the condition that I learnt to do it myself. In hindsight, I think she knew she wouldn't be around to do it for me much longer, so gave me a DIY starter kit instead. For years I would spray the doll's green dress with Mum's old perfume and try to pretend it was her. Eventually the bottle ran out—or maybe Sally used it up, I was never quite sure.

Reaching back into the box, Dad begins to explain that it is full of my old things. My eyes glaze over as I hear Dad lovingly talk about me as a child, recounting silly tales about insignificant items that I once cherished.

"Is this her?" Sophia asks, angling a photo frame towards Dad.

"Mmm-hmm, that's her, at fifteen."

"She was beautiful."

"She was—still is, to me."

Sophia looks up at him sympathetically. "Of course."

"Her birthday is next week—it should be her thirty-first."

Thirty-one? Yes, I suppose that is true. Not that I have any sense of aging or true time now. Has my spirit-self aged? Do I get grey hairs and wrinkles—or am I forever twenty-seven?

"If only I could time travel back to that photo." Dad sighs heavily. "I would make a lot of different choices."

"Wouldn't we all?" Sophia says, tapping the rest of her wheelchair.

Dad gently scoffs, then smiles empathetically.

Sophia dips her hand back into the cardboard box, pulling out a small, poorly decorated wooden jewellery box and Dad laughs. "That was her pride and joy when she was about fourteen. It took her a while to master a hammer, but she was so proud when she brought that box home."

He isn't wrong. I remember shedding more than one tear making that darn thing. Woodwork did not come naturally to me, yet I was determined to finish that box, even if it was the roughest in the class. When it was done, I insisted on painting it, but honestly, I don't think it improved the final piece.

"Ah, I think a ring has fallen out of it," Sophia says, reaching into the bottom of the cardboard box.

I doubt that. The draw was forever getting stuck, so anything I put in there was not expected to come out again any time soon. In hindsight, I should have made a spice rack.

"Oh?" says Dad casually, continuing to gaze at my photograph. "I doubt it is anything valuable if it's in there."

"There's an inscription. Can you read it? I need my glasses...H. L—"

Dropping the photo frame on the table, Dad's eyes bolt upwards. Wordlessly, he leans over, gently taking the ring between his thumb and fingers, carefully studying it as if Sophia has dug up an alien relic.

"What is it?" asks Sophia, watching Dad turn as white as a sheet. "Is something wrong?"

"It's—it's—"

"It's what?"

Dad gulps. "My daughter's wedding ring."

"Oh. Are you sure?"

"Quite." Dad points to the inscription. "This is her wedding date."

"Huh." Sophia seems confused. "Didn't you know that you had it?"

Dad doesn't answer for a moment. His eyes narrow and he swallows repeatably before he says, "No—no, I didn't, because to my knowledge, she was wearing it when she died."

It's Sophia's turn to gulp. "Were you given it later?"

"Her body was never found, remember?"

"Oh. Was she having marital problems? Could she have left it here?" Sophia asks carefully.

"Her marriage was one, *long* problem." Focusing on the ring, Dad furrows his brows further than ever. "But, no, I have no reason to think she would have put it in her old bedroom."

"Then how did her ring get here?"

Dad looks her straight in the eyes. *"Exactly."*

Only now do I check my left hand and see that my ring is snuggly positioned on my finger. Normally I would have thrown it down a drain or into the sea by now, yet I have been so distracted today that I forgot. I remember dropping the ring the last time I slept in Dad's old house, but I thought I was discarding it in a charity box, not a box of keepsakes. Although, honestly, I wouldn't have considered one more dangerous than the other. All I wanted was the ring out of sight and that was the simplest method at the time—I had no idea I was creating a duplicate.

Of all the things that I would like to duplicate, my wedding ring is nowhere near my top one hundred—or one-hundred thousand, come to think of it. I would like to destroy every drop of evidence I was ever that stupid. Even in Dad's box of mementos my late teens and twenties have very little to show. The family album entries got thinner every year—the memories sadder, darker.

No, my wedding day, and all that goes with it, can skip into hell for all I care.

Neither Dad nor Sophia have spoken for a few minutes. Sophia seems to be trying to think of something, but I am sure Dad is having an internal conversation instead. Could he possibly be putting two and two together?

No.

No one is going to think 'ah, right, my son-in-law framed an accident, killed my daughter for money that he didn't get, and she is now trapped in between time, watching the town in the form of a bizarre, lost guardian angel.'

"I hate Hayden," Dad suddenly says passionately.

He watches Sophia, waiting to see how she reacts. I suppose some might jump to attention, excitedly preparing to absorb gossip, whilst others might recoil or even try to preach a path to peace or reconciliation.

Sophia does neither.

Instead, she extends her right hand to his left, linking their fingers, saying, "Then I hate him too."

Clearly moved, Dad smiles and kisses the back of her hand before gently letting go.

The mystery of the ring absorbs him as he stares silently at it. Battling mixed emotions, tears well in his eyes while his jaw clenches. Finally, with a wobbled voice, he says, "I should shove this ring down his throat and choke him with it."

Instantly, I want the ring back. My dad is a passive, peaceful man—even in jest. I feel guilty for driving him to even utter such words, for they are the sort of words that Hayden happily uses, not Dad—certainly not with any degree of seriousness.

"This has to mean something."

Sophia looks concerned. "Like what?"

"I don't know. Do the dead leave signs? Clues to the past?"

"Do you think this is what this is? A sign?"

"I don't know. Possibly. I so often feel like she is still with me. That there is more—" Dad cuts himself off, shaking his head.

"Maybe we should investigate this somehow? Speak to the police, perhaps?"

"Or Hayden."

*No, no, no. Do not go near him!*

I need that ring back.

Jumping up, I rush in front of Dad, swiping at the ring in between his fingers with my right hand. Nothing happens.

I cannot let that hideous band torture him as well as me.

An idea hits me: can I merge the two rings back together?

Slipping the ring off my left hand, mimicking my father's grip, I carefully hold it in front of me. Slowly, I extend my hand to his, delicately lining up one band with the other. As the two meet, a bright-white spark flies, keeping both rings in their different realms, whilst electrocuting my dad. He swears, immediately dropping his ring and we all watch as it settles on the tabletop next to my photograph.

"What happened?" Sophia cries.

"It shocked—burnt me." Dad rubs his fingers. "Look, I have a blister."

A memory of the ring burning me the day I dropped it in the box hits me—that is why I was so keen to get rid of it instead of waiting to pass a drain. A similar sensation had happened before, but I always assumed it was in my head, like a PTSD striking. Yet now I wonder if the glitch has been giving me more opportunities or hints than I realise. I have learnt to pay attention to the wind, why not other sensations?

Of course, the glitch could be merely glitching or teasing me for its amusement at random times—but no, I don't believe that. Random to me is not random to it. Today has proven it has purpose, so I cannot keep pretending to doubt that. How I wish I could tell when the glitch is hinting, guiding, providing opportunities, or just strategically mocking me! I suppose, in my current form, there is no way to truly know.

We all stare at the ring. Still and inanimate as it is.

What is your plan, glitch? Why do you want it in two realms?

"I think that was a sign," whispers Sophia reverently after a long pause.

"Me, too," whispers Dad.

Sophia sighs heavily. "But I wouldn't go near Hayden. If Flossy is right, he is involved in some serious shit."

Dad looks up solemnly. "If *I'm* right, I'm going to kill him."

# 39

The thought of having potentially ruined Dad's newfound peace makes me sick. For a few hours he had made huge steps towards forging a new, exciting chapter for himself. Why did I touch that fucking ring? *Why?*

For over an hour Dad and Sophia have discussed my life and death. It is difficult to listen to, but what is harder still is listening to my father considering how to confront my killer with questions about the state of our marriage.

They throw ideas back and forth, admitting how improbable it is that Hayden would answer honestly—especially given how strained their father and son-in-law relationship was even at the best of times—but like a dog with a new bone, Dad isn't keen on admitting defeat.

Clearly worried, Sophia again suggests the police. Dad says his family liaison officer was okay, but he has no interest in being regarded as the town loon if they do not see any link between a randomly resurfacing ring and a dead girl.

Hoping for a reaction whilst bracing himself for another blister, Dad pokes my wedding ring with a pen. When it moves like any other lifeless, non-possessed object, he sighs heavily, letting his shoulders droop.

"Sometimes I think she isn't dead at all. If the ring hadn't struck me, I might have still believed it is possible she isn't—

but that was a message from beyond. I'm sure of it." Dad says methodically. "I just need to understand it and not be afraid to act."

My skin crawls, but I have a glimmer of relief when Sophia calls for a sense of reason, finally forcing Dad to acknowledge that storming in headfirst is not wise. Like it or not, he cannot deny she knows more about Hayden and his friends' current activities. I know Hayden has an unsettling desire to be powerful, whether that be at home, in business, or just in the general view of town folk. He has a likeminded network of companions, most of whom he has been friends with since childhood, meaning even if their morality is questionable, he has a solid foundation of loyalty. If Hayden has combined that with Mae, getting sucked into her business as Sophia suggests, he is more dangerous now than ever.

Sophia doesn't go into further details beyond Mae's drug dealing and Dad doesn't ask. I take this as his normal, sensible, non-impulsive nature returning—which should only be encouraged, but part of me wishes she would expand more for my own investigations. I try asking, however, as the glitch refuses to give me a voice, I am left gleaning from ploughed fields, not seeded beds—again.

Finally, they decide it is time to take Sophia home. I have barely slept and could easily curl up in Mr Crook's chair, yet I am afraid to miss anything of note, so travel with them. However, the imminent separation renews the joy of their romantic awakening, resulting in the journey being largely filled with soppy chatter. The footnotes are they want Dad's house to be liveable as soon as possible and will spend time together whenever they can—the rest is just lovestruck noise that I am happy for but would prefer not to hear.

As we approach her house, Sophia turns serious, expressing concern that Flossy is not yet home. Dad offers to stay, but she declines, attempting to chuckle away her worry by saying she is being silly.

Unconvinced, but without further argument, Dad tenderly helps Sophia to bed, bids her good night, and then drives back to my aunt's. It's a shame I didn't stay at the house because now I have no ride and no bed. I could crash here, and probably bugs don't travel realms, but my options here are not particularly appealing. The comfiest looking chair has an outline of where Flossy sits, with a new, unappealing crusty, dry pool of blood from this morning and the sofa is covered in his dirty clothes and cat hair. I know, I know, a ghost shouldn't be picky—or maybe I just want an excuse to walk to Kath's—but whatever, I'm only three streets away from a comfy sofa and I am going to find it.

Walking down the empty street, lights switch off in random houses as people turn in for the night. It must be nearly midnight, so I am expecting to find Kath's house in darkness, but the living room is lit as I enter through the front door.

When freshly deceased, angry, and alone, I used to slam doors shut, hoping that my efforts would echo through time and sound barriers, but nothing broke and no one heard me. Now I close the door carefully, like a teen returning home past curfew, afraid of being reprimanded by her parents. I suppose I have just grown more respectful in death—returning to the meek manners I was taught in life.

Scoffing, I think of Hayden. He had ears like a fox when it suited him. There was no sneaking in past him to save myself from a beating if I was late, no matter how benign the reason. 'Being late is just disrespectful,' he said. It didn't take me long to realise that not going out without him was the kind of respect he valued.

Shaking my shoulders to brush away my thoughts, I walk into the living room. Kath turns to me, smiling. "Ah, good, you've come back," she says.

I stand, staring—partly at Kath, but also at the array of colours dancing around her. The rhythm has changed. Her time is coming.

Returning her smile, I remind myself of my role of peace giver. It doesn't change the sadness I feel inside, but it does seem to soothe Kath's weary face.

"Come, sit with me, if you will," she says, patting the sofa cushion next to her. There isn't a great deal of room as Daniel seems to have wrapped his mother in a king size duvet, but I gladly occupy the space she indicates.

"I thought Daniel was going to set you up with a bed down here?" I ask, somehow knowing that I will be heard.

Kath chuckles weakly. "He is—or was. A hospital bed is coming tomorrow, but I honestly don't think I'll need it for long, do you?"

As Kath's colours vibrate, I shake my head. "No, I'm afraid not. I'm so sorry."

"It's all right. It's probably better this way."

"How so?"

"I've seen lengthy deaths as well as quick. Precious few benefit from the lengthy—not when they get to a certain point. I don't want my boys to see that." Kath reaches towards the side table, picking up a frame. "This is how they should remember me."

A hollow feeling hits the base of my stomach as she turns the frame, showing me a collage of happy family pictures. Daniel and Rufus are older, so they will remember their mother in good health better than I do mine. I cling to the happy memories that time hasn't stolen, but I would be lying if I said Mum's latter months don't linger in my mind. We were a happy family though, while it lasted. May Daniel and Rufus be able to hold onto the good memories and love they were clearly raised with when Kath's light passes on.

"Tell me about them," I say. Kath looks at me, still holding the frame. "If you would like to, I mean. If you're tired or—"

Kath chuckles. "I would love to. There is no better subject to tire myself on."

Narrating each photograph, Kath tells stories with such vivid detail that I almost feel like I was there. She asks me to fetch a photo album from the cupboard and I almost protest, but instead decide to try before I declare 'I cannot.' I may need to remember this lesson because my hand grips and lifts the heavy folder, delivering it to Kath without hesitation.

Turning the pages, the stories continue, sometimes with laughter, sometimes with a motherly groan, but all with love. Listening to Kath, I find myself daydreaming—wishing that I was a part of this family—and an image of a life that never was flashes through my mind. Had I lived, Daniel and I could have met and rewritten our futures by falling in love. He could have introduced me to Kath one Sunday afternoon over tea and biscuits and she would have shown me pictures and told stories just like this. I could have added to the family album and retold these stories to my own children, maybe even my grandchildren.

But dreams are for the living—when choice and chance are still available. Hanging onto my regrets and could have beens are of no use to me now.

Once at the end of the album, Kath closes it and strokes the cover. "Will you promise to watch them?" she asks without looking up.

"I already do," I instantly reply.

"I know, but I hope you will keep them both from harm? Daniel is much more sensible, but Rufus—" Kath lets out a mournful moan as a tear rolls down her cheek.

Reaching for her hands, I cup them with my own whilst resting on the family album, causing Kath to gaze intently into my eyes. The colour of her iris' seems to twist and rotate as she waits for me to speak. The intensity of her expression captivates me, momentarily stifling my voice, yet it, as though it wills itself to be released, finally drifts out with honest affection as I say: "I will watch and guide them both as best I can. Whatever is in my power to do, shall be done. My spirit is theirs, should they require it."

"Bless you, dear Angel, bless you," Kath whispers with emotion, then sinks back into the cushions and closes her eyes.

Without speaking, I take the album and put it back in the cupboard. Rather than return to the sofa and risk disturbing her, I sit in the chair opposite when the door opens.

Hearing the click of the handle, Kath opens her eyes. "Oh, Daniel, you should be asleep."

"Sorry, I thought I heard movement, so wanted to check on you." Daniel glances around the room but doesn't see me. "Has Rufus been in?"

Concern strikes across Kath's face. "No. Why, is he okay?"

"Yes, as far as I know." Daniel furrows his brows whilst rubbing his longer than normal beard—I don't think he has shaved for a few days. "I thought I heard voices, that's all."

"Just me and Angel," Kath smiles.

"What?"

I wouldn't like to assume what Daniel is thinking at the moment. As he looks around the room, again his expression could be that of fear, pleasure, or pain—certainly, it is beyond surprise or excitement, but I wouldn't be so brave as to say it is without disbelief.

Whether the dying know that attempting detailed explanations to the living is fruitless, I could not say, yet to my knowledge no one has tried to coherently define my presence to them. Nor has anyone communicating directly with me tried to question how or why I am there. I can only conclude that there is an unwritten, but universally accepted rule that these things *just are*.

Ignoring his question, Kath reminisces about the photos in the frame, repeating much of what she told me, only adding anecdotes as Daniel reacts to her stories. He lets her lead the conversation, but when her voice cracks Daniel realises that her water glass is empty and gets up for a refill. Striding towards the door, he passes me and pauses, like he is considering saying something, but instead wordlessly switches on a table lamp, turns off the main light, and leaves the room.

When he returns, Kath takes the glass with a shaky hand and drinks a third but refuses anything else that Daniel recommends. Having run out of ideas, he quietly sits beside her.

Whilst watching mother and son, exhaustion hits me. Today has been such a roller-coaster and Kath's imminent departure is weighing on me greatly. I want to be clear and focused as she passes, not sleeping on the job, but at the moment the air is warm and stable, so I do not think the breeze is coming for her just yet. With this reassurance, when Kath's eyes peacefully close with slumber, I let mine flutter shut too.

What sounds like the lamp turning off causes me to crack open my eyes, but in the darkness, I see Daniel knelt in front of me, holding out a red rose—my rose.

As my heart roars in my chest, I realise it is becoming a very dangerous little flower.

Can ghosts have heart attacks?

A faint glow from the standby light on the TV shows me Daniel's searching eyes in the darkness. He obviously senses me, even if I have no visible form.

What does he hope to achieve, I wonder?

What do *I* want? To guide and guard? —To be in one of those pictures?

I reach for the rose. I cannot help it.

Immediately, a pink light glows around us. I'd normally doubt if it is seen beyond my realm, but Daniel's face says otherwise. We do not speak any words, but our souls do.

Every time we touch, I feel like my soul is singing—rejoicing at being with its other half. Do soulmates really communicate like this or is it just us? Are we so connected that me being dead doesn't matter?

The word—the reality—hits me.

Dead.

*I am dead.*

The spell cracks.

Wake up, girl.

How many times must I repeat the same thing?

*I cannot claim him.*

I found him too late. This is not my path—and it is certainly not his.

As gut-wrenching anguish hits me, I let go of the rose, throwing the room into darkness as I run outside.

I have no rights here. I am not enough.

With my legs feeling like lead and tears streaming down my face, I open Daniel's car back seat door and lay down, using a discarded jumper as a pillow—reprimanding myself for smelling it.

No one moves inside the house, and I am unaware of movement outside until three hours later when I am awoken by the sound of the refuse lorry on its round. I could easily continue sleeping, but worried for Kath, I wander back inside. She is peacefully sleeping tucked under the duvet, whilst Daniel has covered himself in a blanket on the chair that I was in.

For both our sakes, I must find a way to watch without him knowing that I am here.

Settling myself in the window seat, I watch the sunrise. As the day provides light, a ray bounces off my wedding ring. I suppose it doesn't matter how briefly I sleep, that will still return. Suddenly my eyes catch a new colour—a colour I was not wearing before. For my dress, although still white and crisp like a summer's morning, no longer has yellow roses. They, just like the rose in Daniel's pocket, are now a brilliant, bright red.

# 40

Rufus appears like a teenage homing pigeon—just in time for breakfast. He looks awful, but with a little help from Daniel who doesn't want to stress his mother any further, he manages to hide the worst of it from Kath.

I've seen Daniel glance at the chair he slept in and sigh a couple of times, but I've made a conscious, if not somewhat exhausting, effort to dance out of his way this morning.

Kath hasn't eaten. She tried, but it is painfully obvious that her body is in shut down mode. It no longer requires sustenance and nothing that anyone can do will convince it otherwise. Unable to walk without assistance but wanting to spend every last minute with her sons, the boys eat in the living room, trying their best to pretend this is a happy occasion. Kath isn't dying, Rufus isn't bruised, and Daniel hasn't the burden of worrying about it all.

The doorbell rings.

Rufus seems anxious, Kath curious, while Daniel gets up to answer the door. Following as far as the living room doorway, I lean on the frame as Raquel's smile greets Daniel.

"Hey, Hun, how are you?" Daniel sounds surprised. Obviously, this isn't a planned visit.

"I got your text," she replies, giving him a kiss. "I wanted to support you and come—you know, to see her…"

Daniel nods. "Thank you. Of course, come in, we're in the living room having breakfast. Do you want anything?"

"No, no thanks, I've eaten, and I've got to get to work."

Kath remains seated, but warmly welcomes Raquel. As they all settle, I return to my spot by the rear garden window—fidgeting to find a comfortable position without looking at the red roses that have mushroomed all over my dress. They are like a guilty stain on my spirit, mocking me for my foolish, selfish thoughts. Behind me is the correct family scene, I have no place here beyond guide.

After half an hour or so, with a wobble in her voice, Raquel says she must leave. Kath thanks her for coming and they affectionately hug goodbye—neither saying, although clearly understanding, that in this life it is unlikely they will see each other again. It is a difficult realisation to accept, although possibly a kinder one than living with the pain of 'I should have said...' after someone has gone. Or, in my case, after *I* have gone.

Daniel walks Raquel to her car and Rufus leaves the room, muttering that he needs the toilet. The instant the room has silenced, Kath peacefully closes her weary eyes. Watching a pair of robins on the birdfeeder, I try to absorb myself into the role of twitcher. I almost succeed, yet when a tabby cat stalks the fence line the birds flee, returning my attention and curiosity to the fact that neither brother has returned. Walking to the front window, I immediately regret it as my stomach churns witnessing Raquel and Daniel kiss goodbye.

Groaning at myself for my stupidity, I turn back into the room only to startle when I realise Kath is staring at me.

The peace will very soon come, I can see it all too clearly now, but as I hold her gaze, she softly chuckles, then winks at me—like she has just read a secret on my face. My mouth opens to question her but stalls when the front door closes.

Ruffling his hair with one hand, Daniel returns gripping a large, flat cardboard box.

"Everything okay?" Kath asks, reading his serious expression.

"Mmm?" he says, putting the box behind the sofa. "Ah, yes, sure."

"She loves you, you know?"

Daniel tuts quietly. "Yeah, I know. Raquel and I are just having a few issues, that's all—nothing you need to worry about." He affectionately squeezes her shoulder.

"Hmm?" Kath shakes her head as though she has just awoken from a daydream. "Oh, yes it was very nice of Raquel to visit."

"What's wrong with Raquel?" asks Rufus, re-entering the room.

"Nothing," Daniel says, a little defensively.

"Didn't look like nothin'." Rufus raises his left eyebrow—what's left of it. "I thought she looked annoyed as well as upset when she got in her car—like you had said the wrong thing?"

"Why were you watching?" Daniel asks angrily.

"I didn't mean to—I went for a piss upstairs and caught sight of you both as I passed the landing window."

Looking at his mother, any irritation Daniel feels towards his brother passes. Now is not the time for disputes.

"Whatever," he replies, shrugging. "I just didn't say exactly what she wanted to hear, that's all. We'll sort it out later."

"Do you want some motherly advice?" Kath says weakly.

Daniel tries to smile. "Sure. Always."

"Don't lose what you want for fear of trying." Kath chuckles at her own wisdom. "That goes for all of you."

Daniel answers his mother's words with a kiss on the forehead and Rufus a hug. I know Kath included me in her speech—had I been inclined to misunderstand her, her grin when the boys are not watching confirms it. I won't argue with her, even if I think her advice is too late for me.

\* \* \*

While Kath sleeps, the brothers washup in the kitchen. For a while I stay with Kath, but as a gentle, purple haze rests over her, I decide to check on their progress.

Approaching the kitchen doorway, I hear Daniel again appeal to Rufus to walk away from Flossy. I think Daniel is hoping that sense has prevailed—or their mother's words have finally hit home—but it is woefully clear that his words of warning are falling on stubborn, deaf ears. My only glimmer of hope comes in the form of a nervous scratch of the head, but unfortunately Daniel, with his back turned, misses it. Whether it be sadness from the imminent loss of his mother, or something else, this minute display of doubt could be something to build on as I try to keep my promise to Kath.

Instantly recovering his cool demeanour, and obviously wanting to deflect, Rufus changes the topic: "Raquel seemed okay until you guys went outside—what's up? Is she pissed because you moved out?"

Daniel sighs. "Yeah, basically."

"Surely she gets why?"

"She does, of course she does. She supports that—she always has to be fair."

"Then what's the problem?"

"Erm, a couple of things, but she is upset that I didn't ask her to move in here as well."

"Why would you?"

"That's what I said, more or less." Daniel rolls his eyes. "That was the wrong thing to say, apparently. She doesn't like this area and loves her flat. She can't care for Mum with work, et cetera, so I honestly considered it and dismissed it in one thought."

"But you didn't token ask..." Rufus is surprisingly intuitive.

"Nope." Daniel rolls his eyes as Rufus smirks. "Yeah, okay, smart-arse."

"She'll get over it."

"Eventually—hopefully."

Pinching myself hard on the arm, I remember this is not my place, and return to the living room. Instantly, the air fills with a hot breeze and I rush to Kath's side. She wakes up, smiling warmly, but as I cup her hands, I realise I am seeing her in the centre of the wind, like she is in a tropical departure lounge preparing for her next. Focusing my eyes, I see the earthly Kath as she grows paler and weaker. Calling out, I project my voice towards the kitchen. Somehow, in some way, they hear and race into the room.

Kneeling in front of her, each son takes a hand, telling their mother they love her. She whispers to them as her breathing begins to rattle and both boys simultaneously attempt to stifle sobs.

"Go with love and peace. Eternal joy and rest awaits." The voice—soft and smooth, like a chorus of heavenly beings—sings. It isn't me. As always, I am but the vessel, but they on the other side welcome Kath with open arms as the breeze whips and stills in this realm once more, leaving her sons to openly mourn her passing.

# 41

The hospital bed arrived as Kath's body was taken away. It was a cruel irony, but despite their grief, the brothers privately acknowledged the blessing in her not needing it. She worked so close until her death, but even that was in her nature. She cared for others, that is what made her tick. Not being able to do that effectively meant she could not be herself—at which point, she was ready to go.

The inevitable, essential phone calls and arrangements commenced, with multiple caring and well-meaning messages of condolence flooding in as the news spread throughout the next twenty-four hours. I stayed, telling myself I am watching Rufus—telling myself that I am sticking to my promise to Kath—ignoring the internal voice that whines at me constantly, reminding me I said I would only observe from a distance.

Too tired for more, Daniel eventually switches his mobile off and sits in the living room, looking at the spot his mother made into her final bed. He needs to turn on the TV or radio—not because he shouldn't mourn, of course he should, but I worry that simply staring into the void isn't good for him. Having said that, neither is Rufus' plans to go to the pub with Leo tomorrow.

They eat pizza for tea—or rather they both puddle pizza around in their takeaway boxes for a while, eating half before Rufus declares them done and takes the leftovers into the kitchen.

Returning, Rufus pauses behind the sofa, wiping his eyes. "What's in the flat box?" He half-heartedly kicks the cardboard box with his foot as he speaks. I don't think he is particularly interested in its contents; he just wants something to break the mind-chilling silence.

"A painting, I think." Daniel shrugs. "Raquel dropped it off from Oki."

"Who?"

"Oki, the artist that is staying with us—Raquel. I told you about her."

"Oh, right, yeah, sorry." Rufus sighs. "I suppose you'll be moving back soon?"

Daniel fidgets with the TV remote, slowly spinning it over and over in his hand. "Erm, well, I was thinking not to—or not for a bit—if that's cool with you?"

Rufus stares, then nods. "Of course, I'd like that."

I believe he is genuinely happy to have his older brother around more again. And probably Daniel does want to stick with family now more than ever; however, reading Daniel's hidden expression, a plausible reason for him not moving suddenly dawns on me—and explains why Raquel was annoyed when she left yesterday. It isn't just the fact Daniel didn't ask her to move in with him to help with Kath; Daniel must have told her he wants to stay here longer to watch over Rufus. To be honest, I understand her disappointment, but I also understand the depth of trouble Rufus is dancing around.

Returning to his desire for a distraction, Rufus picks up the brown box. "Can I see?"

"Sure—I haven't opened it yet. Raquel said Oki painted it for me."

"That's a bit weird, isn't it?"

"A little, maybe. Oki painted our portrait back in the summer—it's amazing—but I've no idea why she has anything for me now. Raquel hasn't seen it, but she said that Oki has been working intensely on it since moving in with her. I asked if she wanted to look, but she wasn't exactly in the mood to wait, so shoved it in my hand and left."

Rufus unfolds the lip of the box, revealing the edge of a white canvas. Gently upending the box, he places his left hand ready to catch and the canvas obediently slides out.

Maybe on a normal, less grief-stricken day, Daniel might be more fascinated, but today a present isn't exciting, so his drooping, puffy eyes watch with semi-interest at best. However, when the painting is turned around, his eyes widen, and his body stiffens as though suddenly injected with adrenaline. As Rufus holds the painting, he thoughtfully contemplates the figure in a white dress with intricately depictured yellow roses and jet-black hair that appears to be gently flowing in the wind.

"She's kinda hot. Who is she?" Rufus asks.

Flushing red, Daniel gulps.

"Who is she?"

"Angel," Daniel whispers. "I call her Angel."

"You mean...?" Rufus stops, narrowing his eyes. "You mean *the* angel—from the beach?"

"Yeah." Daniel says, not daring to look away from the painting. "The very same."

"How has Oki painted her?"

Exhaling deeply, Daniel replies, "I've no idea."

They stare at the painting for a few minutes. I'll admit I am staring too. It is weird looking at myself—or this version of myself, for she doesn't look quite how I remember me. Possibly because I do not seem so timid and self-conscious.

"She gives me the feeling of déjà vu," says Rufus, "like I should know her—" I hold my breath, afraid of being named. "But I don't."

I laugh. It would seem that the glitch hides me, has changed me, in more ways than one. I'm not sorry. Signs of past me existing in another form hasn't helped Dad. My ex-half-brother-in-law seeing my spiritual form now isn't going to help.

"I think I met her, though."

Both Daniel and I turn to him in shock. "When?" we ask in unison—although only I know that.

"When I came home in a state. I—I, er, this is gonna sound stupid..."

"Try me." Daniel says encouragingly.

"I was going to hit the deck, but something caught me—someone warm, yet invisible. I tried to tell myself it was just my brain messing with me from the pain. But I felt supported, I felt—"

"Safe?"

"Yeah." Blushing with embarrassment, Rufus picks up the box, peering inside. "Huh, there's a note," he says, slipping his hand inside, pulling a piece of paper out, and passing it to Daniel.

Daniel wryly smiles as he reads aloud. "Maybe more will come to your meetings if you use a better portrait. She saved me, so now I, too, believe in angels."

# 42

When the brothers go to bed, Daniel carries the painting of me upstairs and leans it on top of his bookcase. Sitting on the edge of his bed, he stares at it, while I stare at him.

Probably ten minutes pass in this weird fashion of silent gazing before Daniel reaches across the bed for his jacket, fiddling in the top pocket. For a second, I don't know what he is doing—possibly because he normally wears a shirt with a pocket, not a t-shirt—but he soon pulls out my rose.

He twirls the stem between his fingers, spinning the flower round and round as though he is waiting for it to transform somehow, before finally turning back to the painting.

It is hard for me to look at the portrait. There is no denying the talent of the artist—nor indeed, the accuracy with which she paints. I believe that in those moments of connection, the serenity she has captured, even during the aftermath of a very stressful event, is true. However, it does not stop me wishing for that feeling to be extended. For that feeling of purpose and belonging to unfalteringly remain instead of the self-doubt and lack of clarity or conviction that I keep allowing to creep back into my mind.

Why am I in this room?

The question hits me. I have allowed myself to become too caught in mourning to ask.

Rising to leave, I pause in front of the portrait, telling myself it is the last time I will look at it. I must work to achieve that feeling, not lament it in a painting. Let Daniel use it in a poster—let him try again with his 'touched by an angel' meetings and share life with the living while also dealing with the loss of his mother. But the two of us cannot share a space. Staring at a painting while the subject watches isn't conducive to anyone's happiness. You don't hear rumours about the Mona Lisa haunting her own image, do you?

Daniel slowly rises, standing so I am between him and the painting. His breathing stills as he moves his arms incredibly carefully—like a birdwatcher does in case he frightens a shy bird away—raising his hands with one index finger still curled around the rose.

Watching his hands approach me, I am too mesmerised to move a muscle. It feels like someone has lit a fire as the temperature around us soars, with the furnace reaching its peak as Daniel's fingers gently grasp my jawline. As he realises he has made contact, an awe-struck-cum-victorious smile spreads across his face and he softly exclaims under a chastened breath.

One by one, he tests a fingertip, lightly caressing my cheeks. The finger wrapped around the rose is the only one he doesn't move, yet I feel the rose more vividly than anything else as it seems to be the source of the heat, even if it does not burn. His fingers spread, stroking my skin, brushing over my lips, before returning to my jaw.

My heart races, but as he leans in it stills—like the interim in a song, everything about me waits for the drummer to act. As his eyes search, I am sure the only 'me' he can see is on the canvas behind, yet as his lips meet mine, the drum kicks in, triumphantly igniting the band—playing the anthem of my soul and everything else for a moment disappears.

Not requiring vision, our eyes close and I instinctively reach for his face. Cupping his jaw, my fingers sink into his beard, and I feel electricity ripple through us both—the sensation is euphoric. Neither in life nor death have I felt anything like it. It is tender, yet exhilarating; soothing, yet rousing.

A noise comes from the hallway. It is only very slight, but it is enough to spring open my eyes and break the spell as my hands drop to my sides. Unsure how to read my movement, Daniel releases his grip, but hovers his hands over my cheeks just close enough that the hairs of my skin tingle with the anticipation of being touched.

We stand perfectly still, listening to the night. I don't know if Daniel heard the initial noise, but he certainly hears the bathroom door open and close as Rufus presumably returns to his room.

I keep expecting the sound of his bedroom door closing, but suddenly Rufus mutters to himself saying: "Huh, since when as Dan got a pink night-light? Hmm, must be Raquel's idea, I suppose." His feet then shuffle across the carpet in a sleepy-half awake fashion before his door clicks shut.

The stark reminder that Daniel—neither in life nor death—is mine to kiss, hits me across the face. I hadn't noticed the pink haze, yet as my thoughts rage, the light extinguishes into black mist. This is a woeful misuse of a connection, no matter how much I long for it. I deserve no such thing and neither does Daniel or Raquel.

As I step away, I feel my heart tearing. *Daniel, you may keep it, for I cannot have you.*

He senses my retreat and lunges for where he thinks my arm might be—he isn't wrong, but instead of holding me, his hand glides through the air.

The glitch approves.

With tears streaming, I open the door, run down the stairs, out the front door, and onto the street. Let the girl sleep in the gutter, which is where she belongs.

# 43

I crashed in Flossy's living room, not the gutter; however, having woken up to find my dress is now pink with red roses that are outlined with a thick, black trim I have walked into town seeking a clothes shop. It is high-time that I changed my attire and although the glitch might mock me again in the morning by replacing these clothes, I will not spend the day looking at its idea of humour—or maybe reprimand.

It is winter, so I am finally going to dress appropriately. Black trousers, a thick black jumper, and a heavy, black coat fit my mood perfectly. Leaving my dress in a heap on the changing room floor, I step out onto the street feeling uncharacteristically wrapped up, yet—thanks to my bare feet—still undressed.

The town has several shoe shops, but as I have no preference, the nearest will do. Crossing over the road, I gaze through the glass. In the window are shoes of multiple shapes and sizes, but it is the walking boots that catch my eye. The ones in the window are dark brown with tan laces, but entering the shop, I am greeted by a jet-black pair that are happily my size.

Suited and booted, I return to the street. Colours bounce and float around everyone as they pass me by. Some auras are content, some excited, while others lag and flounder under the weight of one stress or another. I cannot see my own, yet I know only too well which group I belong to today.

I crossed a boundary and it felt glorious for the few moments that I forgot I no longer belong there. Had I not accepted my role? Was I not glad to find some sense of a purpose? Well neither my role nor my purpose involves trespassing or reaching for what is not mine.

A voice in the back of my head asks if I am not interested to know how it was possible to touch—to kiss. But I answer that with a scowl. If I can touch, it should be to protect. To guard or guide.

Nothing more.

A transporter truck drives past the edge of the street with 'Lennox Motoring Group' splashed across it, forcing bile to rise into my mouth. Hayden reduced me to this. If anyone deserves me reaching through the void, it is him. However, a kiss would not be what I was aiming for. I could describe my desired action as providing a service to society because I would be guarding others as well as guiding him to his next. Only he does not deserve the peace of a good death.

And I am not an angel of death—*right?*

As if the truck wasn't enough, I realise the man walking towards me heads the Lennox family tree. Others smile and nod as he passes them, causing me to scoff. Too many see him as the town 'all-round-good-guy,' not the slimy, self-righteous piece of shit that he is. His son has the same airs and graces, the same ability to hide his black heart. His rose wouldn't be outlined, it would be solid black to the core, just with a shiny rim to distract other magpies—or gullible idiots like me.

My plan is to visit the hospital today, then check on Dad, but as Maddox Lennox stops outside a café looking less than relaxed, my curiosity is peaked. He fidgets with his phone, checking the time, then finally walks in, orders a coffee, and sits down in the most dimly lit corner he can find.

Sitting next to him, I peer at his phone for clues; however, unless he is anxious about a recent car order, that isn't what is bothering him.

The antiquated bell above the door rings and both Maddox and I look up. Dropping any anxiety from his face, Maddox smiles, standing up to make the gesture of holding the chair out for his companion. I say companion, because, despite my ability to wildly conject, I cannot imagine Lianna Garvey is here as his date. That ship sailed long ago and although for business purposes I think they tolerate each other; Hayden always told me that Maddox hates her. Probably because she is successful.

Lianna graciously accepts his chivalry, but it's clear she doesn't highly regard its value, nor does she plan on making this a lengthy meeting, because as soon as she has her coffee, she quickly shuts down Maddox's attempt at small talk:

"Yes, yes, it's cold out. What a surprise in winter." She rolls her eyes. "Look, Maddox, I am not here for a social visit."

"I gathered that, Lianna," Maddox replies dryly. "Excuse me for wanting to be polite."

"Hmph, there's a first."

"So, to business. What can I help you with? A new car? Transport?"

Lianna scoffs. "You really are dim, aren't you? I have no need of you for any such thing. I have come here to warn you about your son. Have you any idea who he is dating?"

Maddox cannot hide his surprise as he arches his neck, leaning backwards as he raises his eyebrows. "I didn't know Leo was dating—"

"Not *my* son—*yours*."

"Hayden?"

"Yes, *Hayden*."

"Some girl from the pier, I haven't bothered meeting her yet—"

"*Some girl?*" Lianna exaggerates as she shakes her head. "You really are an idiot. Have you not heard of the issues in town?"

"Yes, of course, the council are concerned about the new gang that seem to have set up camp here. A contact told me there's rumour a man called Anton is the head, but no one can pin anything on him."

Lianna scowls, shaking her head. "And whose daughter do you think I am referring to?" Maddox's face drops its smug mask. "Have you seen Hayden's basement recently? I hear it is *exotic*."

"Oh, fuck."

Lianna reaches into her handbag, pulls out a ten-pound note and pins it to the table with a sugar pot as she gets up. "Get your house in order—*before* it further infringes on mine. Your little shit of a daddy's boy has bitten off more than either of you can chew. I assure you, *I will* spit them all out."

# 44

Before leaving the café, Maddox called Hayden demanding a meeting in the morning. Hayden agreed, trying to match his father's restrained, yet authoritative voice but I could still detect the confused, boyish tone that talking to Maddox has always inspired. I'm not saying he hasn't ever tried standing up to his dad, I could list a couple of minor incidences, but any attempts were usually squashed pretty quickly—either by force or because Hayden truly cannot cope with the idea of being out of his father's favour.

Hayden would probably have dropped everything and met Maddox today had his colleagues and girlfriend not been in the background. I am glad the meeting isn't immediate because it gives me time to get there—*if I decide to go*. If it was at the garage, I know the answer without hesitation: no.

It has been a very long time since I returned to Hayden's garage. For me, that place, along with the cliff top, is haunted. His house is next to the garage—my marital home of misery, deceit, and violence. Possibly I should return. The glitch has pointed me there more than once, but I cannot do it.

I am not ready to cross that threshold.

The few accidental meetings have been traumatic enough—deliberately looking for my husband there is just a step too far.

Vomit threatens at the idea.

For now, I walk to Mrs Crooks' house—Dad's house, as it now is. Two men are returning tools to their truck, while a third shuts the garden gate. Curious, I wander into the back garden and find my magnolia tree standing proudly beside the far fence. It is a large tree and would have taken a lot of skill to move without killing it. Three years ago, I remember Sally questioning why Dad didn't get a sapling. I also distinctly remember his answer as he patiently explained that he had sought out a tree that was planted the year of my birth—one that he hoped that would continue to bloom for me. I cried listening to the explanation and cry now seeing her again. Soon her leaves will flourish ready for another spring while I will remain hidden—bloomless. No bees will visit my flowers. No sun will bless my leaves nor rain feed my roots. I do not even provide shade for the weary.

*"But you can help in other ways, as Adtoft's shadow,"* says the voice from within. *"Stop lamenting the cannots and look to the cans."*

Despite myself, I laugh. I wanted the voice to speak to me, so although a more inspiring peptalk would have been preferable, so be it if it reprimands me—it is right!

Wiping my tears on my sleeve, I go indoors seeking a distraction. The kitchen looks the same, yet Dad has clearly been busy painting. Perhaps the prospect of Sophia visiting more often has helped spur him on. There is even a stairlift installed now. It must have already been on order, but the degree of care that Dad has taken to make this place accessible for Sophia is admirable. There are somethings she will always need help with, but cabinets are lower, doors wider, rails strategically positioned—all with the quiet hope that he would, one day, have the courage to ask her out and she'd say yes.

Searching the cupboards and drawers, I hope to find my wedding ring. I didn't dare touch it again while Dad was present the other day, but now I am very keen to remove it. This would be an excellent time for some more glitch guidance—but nothing comes to me as I root through countless drawers. It would have been better had it been here, because if Dad has it on him, I cannot help worrying about what he might try to do with it.

Tired, I could easily rest here but decide to wander back towards Flossy's house. Maybe no one will visit, but I am as likely to gain information in that direction as anywhere, so I make my way across town via the seafront.

It is relatively busy here today and the pier has a steady bustle of activity around it—including Flossy who is cheerfully sitting at his stall. The hotdog stand is also open, but Mae is nowhere to be seen. Probably because she has embedded herself in more ways than one with Hayden. However, it would seem she has delegated her responsibilities as her replacements occasionally sneer at Flossy.

After sitting on a bench watching the air and general demeanour of people for a while, I continue on my journey—or would, if a couple didn't walk through me muttering about an angel.

Following their line of vision, I look past them to a post where a new poster has been pinned. Whether laughing or crying is the most appropriate response, I couldn't say, but the noise that comes from me could justifiably be described as a hybrid of the two.

Daniel hasn't wasted anytime reprinting his posters. I suppose photographing a painting, uploading it, and adding a headline and caption isn't difficult—neither is stopping at the printers, but it *is* difficult to see people gawping at my portrait. Possibly it was worse when they were my 'missing' posters because then all the negative feelings that went with that were amplified by the fact Hayden couldn't produce a more recent photograph than from our wedding. Not only was I a missing, murdered, potentially washed-up person; I was the sad bride of Adtoft. Or at least that is how I saw it. Always in white. Never pure.

Whatever, I am in black now.

Let Daniel pin me around town. The sooner I learn their positions, the better I can look away.

\* \* \*

Walking through town, the air feels strange—like a weird calm before a storm. Whether it be meteorological or metaphorical, I couldn't say, but as a thick, grey cloud rolls off the sea, adding to the eerie feeling, I am glad to get off the street.

Sophia is home alone reading a book when I find her and the house appears to be strangely ordered—or order*ly*, I should say. Maybe Flossy has finally hired a cleaner. Normally, I don't rummage through random people's cupboards, but I find Flossy's room and start looking—although I couldn't say what for. He has the usual trinkets that people collect over the years, photos, ornaments of varying quality, clothes of varying states of disrepair, and a suitcase filled with an enormous amount of money. Oh, yeah, right, the last one isn't normal, is it?

The money smells vaguely musty, like it has sat around for a long time, waiting for its inevitable exchange for some item or another. Except Flossy doesn't exchange money any more than absolutely necessary and will not buy the flashy car, the hideously expensive suit, the bigger house, or elaborate furniture. He collects and takes comfort in the untouched heap. He works in his line of business because he enjoys it—the power, the respect, the edge—*all of it.*

I cannot help thinking this makes him a difficult nut to crack. He might huff and moan on bad days, but ultimately, he will go down with the ship purely because life on land is dull without the deep water he has sailed all his life.

Continuing my search, I find six more suitcases. The sixth is at the bottom of the wardrobe, but as I put my hand in to pull the case, I jump out of my phantom skin as something hairy moves. Despite the regular reminder of cat hair, I always forget that Flossy has a cat. He doesn't leave the house and is patterned like an angry tiger—with an unfriendly personality to match its ferocious appearance. Sophia told Dad that Flossy bought him for her after her husband left, but seeing as the cat has taken up residence in Flossy's room, something tells me he is not particularly concerned with details such as who he is supposed to belong to.

The cat hisses at me for disturbing his peace—forcing me to realise *I have* disturbed his peace. Swinging his tail methodically, he narrows his eyes in disgust before jumping on the bed and curling up. Apparently, I am not worth wasting any more of his day over.

Remembering the countless spy movies that I have seen, I check lampshades and photo frames, but find nothing. Entering Sophia's bedroom, I feel stupid for even thinking about looking around, but run my fingers around the frame of a wild-sea painting anyway. Spotting the artist's signature, I smile—of course Oki painted it—but as I run my fingers on the far corner, my smile drops as I find a catch.

Clicking it upward, the painting hinges forward, revealing a black safe. Huh. How do I open that? Whose combination do I need to guess? Do I need to guess?

Shrugging, I reach for the handle, and it pops open as easily as a fridge. Apparently there are two options in my realm: open or shut. Accessible or not.

The safe is filled with ledgers, lots and lots of ledgers, all filled with scribbled handwriting. The frame is out of Sophia's reach and the style looks how I imagine Flossy writes, but hoping for proof, I find Sophia's address book. Opening the velvet cover, I am relieved to be greeted by neat, text-like handwriting.

The cat walks in, eyeing me, and for a second, I think it is possessed because I feel judged. He might disapprove of my nosy behaviour, but unperturbed, I continue reading the accounts of Flossy's not-just-candyfloss stall. Opening another book, my eyes bulge as I read details linking Flossy directly to shipments from 'LG.' It is no surprise to me now, but until recently I would have confidently declared the 'L' to be Leo, not Lianna. Lianna is the personification of an ideal, squeaky-clean businesswoman, yet recent meetings have plainly revealed she is the master, everyone else are the pawns—knights at best. She is the King and Queen combined. Only Anton and Mae are on the other side of the board, dancing, daring a dangerous game of skill and luck—biding their time, each hoping the other falls.

The police would have a field day if they saw this book, but I do not see how I can do anything with it. All it does is confirm what I have already seen—it doesn't help me decipher why the glitch keeps circling me around this neighbourhood, nor does it assist me keeping my promise to Kath to watch over her sons.

The cat rubs around my legs, purring as I put the ledgers away and close the painting. It is a contrary creature, but I pet him anyway. He cannot be any more confused than I am, so who am I to judge if he gives mixed messages?

\* \* \*

Flossy returns early evening accompanied by Rufus, so I instantly feel like my stakeout has been justified. When Leo's blacked-out truck arrives thirty minutes later, I feel more so.

Sophia looks anxious when she realises that Flossy is going out again, and gently reaches for his hand when he walks past her. Slowly, he bops next to her chair, kissing the back of her hand with a forced smile.

"Please, stay," Sophia repeats as her grandfather stands up.

"I can't, Soph, not yet." He checks the time on his phone. "Could you call—"

"Maybe, but that's not the point—and you know it." Sophia scowls.

"I know, I know." Flossy sighs. "Will you call him, for me?"

Sophia's eye gives a minuscule twinkle that only I notice. Obviously 'he' is my dad and Flossy is unaware of their affections already being declared. He probably thinks he is playing matchmaker.

"Fine," she says with impressive force. Perhaps she should be an actress.

Rufus fidgets with the door, clicking the lock in and out like an impatient teenager until Flossy is ready, then jumps in the truck behind Leo. While Flossy struggles to hoist himself onto the front seat, I lament not being able to go with them, when a voice inside says, 'why not?'

It would be easy to stop and argue the rational of this question—listing the numerous examples when I have been left with my hand floating through nothing, slumped on the floor, or just standing, refuge-less, and alone when I have yet again been denied access—but for once I do not hesitate, I act. My faith is rewarded as my fingers curl around the handle, pop open the lock, and the door swings back, ready for my admission. As I sit down, I am sure the voice within sniggers.

Let it laugh. I am not going to ask why the rules are changing.

Leo drives away with little more than an "Evenin'" but as he calmly directs the vehicle he does have the decency to express his condolences to Rufus—who gratefully accepts with a wobble in his voice.

I can only hope that wobble of fresh grief is also coupled with the guilt of knowing that his mother would not approve of his plans—whatever they are. Hearing the crack in Rufus' voice, Leo double glances in his rear-view mirror and nods his head before returning his full attention to the road. Watching his eyes, I search for a resemblance between the brothers, but Rufus is more Hudson than Lennox, and Leo more Garvey, so although there could be something in the shape of the nose or curve of the mouth, there isn't a solid brotherly look any more than there is a strong resemblance in strength of character. Leo has some sensitivities, but he has a decade and a half more practice at reigning his emotions under the iron direction of his mother. With him I can imagine Lianna is firm but loving—the two of them against everything else—making a solid bond and formidable team. Suddenly, I feel like I have had an afterlife upgrade as I have a clear vision of them playing in my mind—not unlike a home video streaming at a family reunion or significant birthday party.

Yesterday, Rufus told Daniel he was going out for a drink with Leo, and I assumed it would be at a bar in town, yet the journey is taking longer than I expected. Having lost my bearings, a mild panic hits me as we pull up in front of two enormous metal gates labelled L.G. LOGISTICS. Previous attempts have taught me that if I go too far into the shipping yard the glitch will throw me backwards, meaning I will again be left in the dark.

With no choice but to take my chances, I wriggle against the seat, anxiously watching the electric gates slide backwards, allowing Leo to navigate up the driveway.

It never occurred to me to question exactly where Leo lives, but it seems that he has a rather fancy condo-style house on the edge of the shipping yard. It is too dark to see how it fits in with its surroundings, however, something tells me I will think it is out of place. Why would he not build his house in a more attractive area? —you know, somewhere far away from the side of a noisy, non-stop shipping yard.

The answer comes to me, like so many are this evening: because this way he is on site to control any and every shipment that Lianna doesn't want just anybody sorting. She has literally placed her son in the firing line of activity. He is the overpriced gatekeeper.

As we get out of the car, headlights come up from behind us, but no one seems to be surprised. Two more blacked-out cars pull up, switch off, and people of varying ages pile out, grunting various versions of hello at each other. Every one of them walks into Leo's house with familiarity, positioning themselves around the oversized living room with such ease you would think they had been preassigned seats.

A fancy cooler box ornament-cum table is positioned in the centre of the room. Had I arrived here alone, I probably would have thought it was just a modern art sculpture, but the sides open to reveal fridge and ice compartments. If Leo ever has children, he will probably need to rethink his décor, however, in the meantime the house displays the wealth and persona that he is trying to portray perfectly.

More people arrive until the point that the large house begins to feel small, and conversations become difficult to follow due to noise and number—yet everyone silences the moment Leo raises his voice. He thanks them for coming, makes a joke at Stu's expense—who seems to be scarred but mostly recovered from his fireworks incident—then turns to the room with a serious expression, asking them to raise a glass to Kath.

Rufus obviously wasn't expecting it, but is clearly moved, and for a moment I have hope that this meeting could be nothing more than the collective mourning of a friend's mother. However, my momentary optimism is burst like a spiked balloon as the topic quickly turns to business.

Leo lists the wrongs that have been done to them as a collective. He grits his teeth as he talks, ensuring no one looks away from him, making my spine shiver. I thought Hayden was frightening, I thought his Jekyll and Hyde impression was formidable, but Leo's is perfect. The businessman might shake councillors' hands alongside his mother by day, but by night he does her dark bidding with skill. I wonder how long she held those reins alone before she decided to share? Either way, what a hideous family. They really should consider sterilisation as a national service.

Words like 'retribution,' 'justice,' and 'education' are thrown with venom, quickly stirring the room into a gleeful war cry. Plans for a mass hit on 'Mae and her Merry Men' are received with unsettling delight and I feel sick to my core.

Rufus looks paler and paler as plans are laid out, but when he is given the job of driver, he doesn't balk. He is going to get himself killed and I need much more than the ability to open a car door to help.

# 45

Having overslept, I wasn't sure if I was going to make it to the showroom in time this morning. I considered using this as an excuse not to try, but last nights' meeting proved to me that if I want to rid this town of violence, I need all the information I can get—even if that means deliberately looking for my ex-husband. Although, if the violence were aimed at him alone, I doubt I would be interested in trying to help—unless they needed a cheerleader.

Running across town, I curse the distance between Flossy's and Maddox's showroom, but still manage to arrive (albeit huffing and puffing) five minutes early—wearing my pink summer dress which the glitch so helpfully replaced during the three hours I slept on Flossy's sofa.

Maddox is in his office, typing away on his computer, giving the impression that he is calm and industrious to his employees. He fools me for a moment—until I walk around the desk and see his social media accounts open alongside a word game.

A cold breeze strikes the back of my neck. I was so focused on not being late, I forgot to feel nauseous about meeting my husband. Turning to the icy blast, Hayden walks through the glass door and my stomach knots. He is unaware of my presence, but I instantly regret coming. Being here, on purpose, makes me feel like I have been summoned—controlled—just as I have been by him so many times before.

"Morning, Dad, you wanted to see me?" Hayden's tone suggests he has decided to own or dismiss whatever his father has taken issue with.

"Indeed," replies Maddox, batting Hayden's conviction into the hedge with one irate word. "Do you know what you are doing?"

"Excuse me?"

"With your business. I have heard things." Maddox rolls his eyes, too frustrated to properly construct a sentence.

Hayden obviously understands, yet his resolved expression returns. "Yes, it is fine. I'm expanding. I thought you would be pleased that I'm—"

"*Pleased?*" spits Maddox. "You ignorant child. You have no idea."

Hayden momentarily winces, but stands tall as he says, "It is fine. I have Mae where I—"

"*You have Mae, nothing.* She has you by the balls and you're too thick to see it. What have I taught you all these years?" Hayden looks at him blankly. "For fuck's sake! I should not be receiving lectures from Lianna-fuckin'-Garvey."

"Lianna? What's she—"

"Oh, shit, boy." Maddox rubs his hands across his forehead in despair.

"Do you mean... How do you know?"

Shaking his head, Maddox exclaims, *"How?"*

"I thought you hated her?"

"I do. As she does me."

"Then...?"

"Mutual benefit doesn't require affection. I have learnt to glean for bonuses."

Still attempting to appease his father's favour, Hayden smirks to hide his confusion, yet all he receives in return is a grimace. Dropping the grin, Hayden says: "So you know what she is? What Leo is?"

"Yes, of course."

"For how long?" Obviously, Hayden thought he was ahead in realising the scale of his brother's activities. Idiot.

If he weren't so angry I think Maddox would laugh. "I also know who and what your girlfriend and her father are. Not to mention what you have started at the garage. You—"

"Whatever, Dad, whatever. I have my plans. You'll see." Hayden puffs his chest and chills race all over my body. Now seems like a hideously bad time for Hayden to increase in confidence and attempt to outshine his father.

Unimpressed, Maddox thumps his fist on the table. "There's some business that's not worth going near. I have dabbled, sure, but I keep my fingers clean. You haven't any idea what you're up to. You are weak. You haven't the stomach for what you're—"

"You don't know what I have the stomach for," Hayden snaps. "I have done more than you know. You might think me weak, but I—"

Although Maddox scowls, he simultaneously looks shocked—like he is suddenly seeing something new in his son. "What did you do?"

"Never mind. It's what is coming that's interesting." Hayden's smirk freezes my throat.

The colour drains from Maddox's cheeks. "Shit... You didn't?"

"Didn't what?"

With gritted teeth, Maddox stands up, flushing from white to red in an instant. "I was furious yesterday when Lianna told me. I was ready to gut her for speaking down at me, as well as educate you for your wanton naivety, but now I fear you are just a brainless imbecile. You'll always live in someone else's shadow with your vile deeds and pathetic schemes."

"Dad—"

"Shut up, boy. Just shut up. Sort yourself out, or do not come back. I will not hear of or from you until you have."

Hayden storms out of his father's office in a raging storm with murky reds and dark black tones clashing into each other with every step. Maddox's aura is no less frightening to observe, but neither is the phone call he makes as soon as Hayden has left.

Dialling Lianna, he stoically waits for her to answer.

"Maddox," she says nonchalantly.

"You were right," he replies, hovering his finger over the 'end-call' button. "But you might have to spit harder."

# 46

Kath's funeral was yesterday. I went, but only stayed for the service, making sure that Daniel did not detect me—regardless of how much it hurt. He was by no means alone though and hearing the outpouring of love from friends and family was worth any awkwardness on my part.

It has, however, renewed my observation that people like Kath are more angelic than I am. She made a difference in life—*to life*. I cannot help thinking that if I were an angel of any value, I would not be wandering down the promenade counting corpses, I would be acting. Yet despite certain revelations I still feel like I am in the dark. Knowing the players, and the planned times and locations is useless if I cannot be the log that they trip over.

If it wasn't bad enough that the two gangs are planning on mutilating one another, two more teens died in hospital yesterday after taking Mae's dodgy drugs. Or at least I am assuming they are Mae's as that is what Flossy declared to Sophia this morning whilst moaning that his buyers will be twitchy and the police more vigilant. It is painfully clear that Flossy has no remorse. Aiding and profiting from people's addictions is neither here nor there to him, regardless of the dangers. In his eyes, people dying from someone else's inferior products only vindicates his services, not lessens.

After Flossy left for the pier, I made my way to the beach huts hoping to bump into Oki. When I arrive, her hut is all locked up, but I let myself in and am instantly amazed by the quality and quantity of her work. According to the sign on the door, Oki has already started taking commissions and has people come in to sit for her. I am glad she has something good to focus on because moving on from Nina isn't going to happen overnight. Currently, she is working on a wedding portrait. There is a photograph pinned above a large canvas and although not finished, it has the makings of a stunning replica on it. She obviously needed neither sitting nor photo of me to replicate my image because there is another, slightly smaller version of the painting she gave to Daniel hanging on the wall. I look away sharply as the memory of Daniel's kiss comes flooding back—I do not need help triggering that memory. A way to permanently repress it would be good though.

Having seen enough, I head south for no better reason than I have to go somewhere. Suddenly, my ears feel hot, almost like someone is holding a candle beneath them. It's weird, yet not painful; however, I find myself moving faster, covering my ears as though it might help. After a few more steps my entire body feels flushed as I walk into an invisible, thick, warm cloud.

Stopping dead in my tracks, I try to evaluate my surroundings. It is bizarre. The air is stationary, yet it feels like a swirling bubble of heat—not dissimilar to when you swim into a warm current in the sea, but this has no current, no tide, no wind or breeze moving it nor obviously creating it.

Glancing around me, I search for anyone who might be approaching from either direction on the promenade. Music and voices rumble around. People are spilling in and out from *The Swinging Anchor*, but I cannot see anyone I know or whose colours might indicate a link to me. Stepping forward, my eyes are drawn into the bandstand, and I understand the link—or at least realise what day of the week it is: Wednesday.

Hesitantly, I approach the entrance of the bandstand and find more than a dozen people—all of whom I have met—talking about me.

A strange feeling hits me, and I do not know how to respond. Should I: laugh, cry, run, or sit down? I have tried them all in the past. Angel discussions are not new to me, but previously they were largely generic conversations—or if specific felt more intimate. This club has too many members for privacy, even if the means of entry is somewhat unique.

"I think it is wonderful that Adtoft has its very own angel!" Ammi says enthusiastically.

"How do you know she only lives in Adtoft?" asks Adi, stretching his arm around her shoulders casually. Having not seen them for a few weeks, I am again struck by how sweet they are together.

"Well..." Ammi pauses, tucking a few stray hairs under her colourful beanie hat. "I don't, but why not?"

Adi smiles, scoffing lightly. "Fair point."

"All I know," continues Ammi, "is you all seem to recognise the same woman in the painting. That's why you all came today, right?"

Voices of agreement combine as Daniel laughs. "It's a shame Angel didn't visit an artist sooner. I might have found you all a lot quicker."

A ripple of chuckles and soft sniggers respond to Daniel before conversation moves on. They decide to introduce themselves by recounting their stories, comparing how, when, and why I appeared, mimicking an AA meeting—only they are sharing their experiences with a spirit, not *spirits*. Volunteered by Ammi, Adi goes first. I still get goosebumps hearing him recount that day and I would love to add my narrative, for he will always be my first encounter, my first save—even if I cannot take any credit for it.

Encouraged by Adi's experience, a man in his twenties tells his story of being guided home when drunk, then a woman in her fifties speaks of a 'healing presence' reassuring her before heart surgery. Although I didn't think much of either occasion, I remember them both. I knew the lady had seen me, she was pale and frightened and gripped my hand with force when I offered it; but I thought the man was too drunk to reliably recall anything when he sobered up.

Daniel pauses halfway through his story when Oki gingerly appears next to me in the entrance. Sensing her reluctance, he encourages her to sit down and only continues once satisfied she is settled.

Despite having heard Daniel's story before, I hang on every word. Unlike when he told Adi and Ammi the first time, he doesn't mention or reach for the rose that I am certain is in his pocket. Whether he is keeping his trump card until later or he doesn't want to share, I do not know, but as Adi catches his eye, pointing to his jacket pocket,

Daniel hastily concludes by signalling to Oki, praising her for 'the beautiful portrait that brought them together.'

Everyone dutifully claps, then a woman stands up, coyly smiling at Oki. An image of a person choking comes to me, clicking my memory into place: Elana. Her name is Elana.

Instantly recognising Elana, Oki enthusiastically hugs her, exclaiming she cannot believe they are meeting under such unusual circumstances.

Elana laughs, "I'd expect nothing less from us!"

The group politely listen while they explain that they were school friends, but Elana moved away when she went to university.

Ammi, obviously remembering her earlier ideal of me being for Adtoft alone, looks a little disappointed as she asks: "Ah, did you meet our angel out of town?"

"Er, no, here—just over there actually." Elana points in the direction of the café. "I was visiting Mum and choked on a peanut. Mum was freaking out, I felt myself blacking out, then an almighty, all-compassing peace embraced me. The peanut flew and, as oxygen rushed through my veins once more, there she serenely stood beside me."

A hush comes over the group each time someone describes me. It is strange to be revered when I am nothing— although I am enjoying Ammi's relieved smile. I am guessing she is pleased her theory hasn't been disproven.

Oki gently breaks the silence. "She has a tranquil aura, despite the circumstance, doesn't she?"

"Absolutely." Elana tilts her head towards Oki. "So, you've seen her, too? To know that, you must have—plus you have painted her perfectly."

Oki shifts in her seat, pulling at her sleeves anxiously. Too often, I have seen her do that and not truly seen. The evidence, the writing on the wall—the reflection in the mirror.

"If you don't want to share, or not yet, there is no pressure." Daniel says reassuringly. "I'd love this to be a safe space to share, but only if you want to. I am just so grateful you all came."

The group mutter in agreement as I feel something brush against my lower leg. Looking down, I am greeted by the soulful eyes of Dougal, the Cairn Terrier, who must have been quietly sat by Jaiden's feet. He wags his tail, sniffing the air whilst making an excited noise that is somewhere between a squeal and a bark.

Jaiden gently pulls on Dougal's extending lead. "I hope it is okay that I brought my dog? It was the only way I could get out of the house without explaining to my wife."

"Of course." Daniel says, patting Dougal who has walked in the opposite direction to Jaiden.

"Great," Jaiden replies, "because, to be fair, Dougal was saved by Angel as much as I was."

"Really?" Ammi says, leaning forward. Gauging from everyone's expressions, I have just become a whole lot more interesting because I save dogs as well as people. Why wouldn't I?

Jaiden explains about the house fire while everyone listens in awe. By the end of the evening, they have all concluded that I am an angel of all trades, appearing at the very moment I am needed the most—whether that be on land, in the sea, in traffic, in a fire, or whilst dining in inappropriate fashions.

They are not wrong, and I am glad that I help—but I again find myself wishing that I controlled it.

As the meeting looks set to disburse, Oki fidgets when Elana questions if she wants to tell her story. Daniel again jumps to the rescue, repeating that no one has to share. Raquel obviously filled him in on the essentials regarding Nina and Oki's breakup, so even if he is secretly intrigued to hear how Oki met me, he is too gentlemanly to probe now.

It would be easy for Oki to bow away from the topic now, but instead she straightens her posture, saying, "It's okay, I want to talk about it. I think it will be good for me to speak openly without people thinking I have lost the plot like my mum does. She believes me about, well, the more *human* aspect of that day, just not the rest. To be fair, you probably need to have seen her—felt her, to really believe it is possible. But, Daniel, when I wrote you that note, I wasn't joking when I said that Angel saved my life."

A hushed silence falls as everyone waits for Oki to speak again. Blushing, she pulls up her sleeves and the silence is broken by stifled gasps as hideous bruises and old scars come into view. They are the kind of scars that can easily be missed on a normal day—either hidden by clothing, jewellery or maybe even healing time—but the bruising highlights the unnatural order of her skin that only prolonged abuse produces.

"Who did that?" asks Jaiden.

"I don't want to go into that," Oki replies, "but suffice to say that I trapped myself into a toxic home for too long. I thought I might die there, actually, because every time I tried to break free, I ran back." She sighs. "Until now."

Elana reaches for Oki's hand, gulping back her tears.

"Angel broke the cycle. Her intervention was literally a matter of life and death for me. Whether that moment or one in the future would have been the final blow, I do not know, but it was coming—yet I now feel, however painful my path to recovery, that I have a future to build on."

"That's amazing," says Daniel.

Oki bows her head a little. "I felt like she understood, like she had empathy—lived empathy."

"Like a kindred spirit?" Elana asks.

"Sort of, but it was more than that."

"What do you mean?"

"Her face was serene and peaceful. Her ambience, her aura, her soul, spoke and comforted me like a friend, but her eyes told me more—they held, mirrored, the empty pain that I have felt in such a way that I believe she has experienced it herself."

"Maybe that kind of empathy is just part of being an angel?" Elana says thoughtfully.

"You're probably right," Oki says, scuffing the toe of her shoe into the ground.

"But?" asks Daniel, dipping his back to look up at her face.

"I wondered—I wondered if she was once alive."

"Alive?" Elana's eyebrows furrow. "Like, before becoming an angel, not just *born* an angel?"

"Yeah."

Wiping my brow, I feel beads of sweat smear into my skin. I cannot remember the last time I sweated at all, let alone enough to perspire. The collective heat from those I have touched, mixed with the lingering white haze of their auras swooshes around me, whipping up emotions my body long forgot to express. Oki questions if I once lived, but in this moment, I question if I truly died.

But I did—although I am glad a part of me lives in them all.

No one speaks. Even Dougal isn't sure what to do with the confounded ambience that has befallen the group, but after a moment's reflection, he signals towards the exit. At least someone is decisive.

Taking the hint from his dog, Jaiden glances around the group, saying, "I should get going. Maybe we could all meet again? Elana, are you in Adtoft for long?"

Elana chuckles. "When I met Angel, I was only here for the weekend, but I moved back permanently last week. I'd been considering it for a while, then decided that maybe that was a divine sign or something."

"Nearly dying was a sign *to come* here?" Adi asks incredulously.

"No," Elana replies seriously. "Being saved was."

# 47

I will not pretend that my mind isn't conflicted as I walk away from the bandstand, but I also cannot *not* admit to feeling recharged like a solar panel on a clear summer's day.

As Elana and Oki walk into *The Swinging Anchor* for a drink, I suddenly catch a glimpse of their auras and smile as hints of pink dance around yellow. Maybe there was something in their past that Nina squashed, I do not know, and maybe it is too soon for Oki's pink to flourish fully, but a friend with potential—a true, honest, caring friend—is exactly the kind of hope she needs. Beyond wishing them well, I will not get involved though—after all, I'm hardly qualified to be a matchmaker, am I?

To stop myself from following Daniel home, I walk to the end of the pier and sit down, swinging my feet back and forth as I watch the sea roll in and out. The sound soothes me and although I would prefer a bed or at least a blanket, I could happily sleep here. Since Dad moved and I got too attached to Daniel, I haven't found a regular bed for myself. History tells me I need one because with no routine it is too easy to spiral into unhealthy patterns of greater-than-normal self-pity.

Mr Crook's armchair is the nearest, least controversial place I can think of, so I get up and turn towards the southern shoreline. As I straighten up, the glitch slaps my cheeks with a warm breeze, startling my senses.

*There is no one here—what is wrong?* I ask into the void, but nothing and no one answers.

Gauging by the moon and the semi-lit promenade, it is past midnight. Pubs and restaurants are closed, no blue lights flash signalling an accident, even the hardier teens are tucked in bed or at least somewhere warmer, and my comedic seagulls who love to mock me are perched out of sight until morning.

A pink haze out in the water catches my eye, chilling my heart. Not another dinghy, please. I do not want a repeat of that night, crashing against the rocks while people drown. But no, as I stare, I realise the haze is neither large nor mobile enough to be a boat. Whatever it is, it is stationary in the water about twenty-five metres from the shoreline.

Racing down the beach, sand grinds under my nails as I speed towards the increasingly bright haze. Pausing on the edge of the sea, my eyes widen in disbelief as I see the outline of a person's head and shoulders with one outstretched hand holding the glowing object above the chopping water.

My heart instantly tells me who it is. I feel like it could burst through my chest and drop to the floor in the same instant. What have I done to him that he feels like this is the answer?

"DANIEL!" I scream, immediately running into the water. He doesn't answer.

Swimming up to him in seconds, I grasp his body with both hands, igniting our now all-too-familiar furnace of heat, snapping his attention to me. He attempts to grin, but being half frozen and fatigued, his teeth and lips just tremble instead. How the current hasn't swept him away, I have no clue, but I wrap my left arm around his torso, and he flops into my embrace without any resistance as I escort us back to shore.

Facing the sand, Daniel splutters, but it only takes him a few seconds to fully absorb the heat that we have created and stop shaking. Sitting next to him, cupping his hand with mine, too dumbfounded to speak or move, a thousand questions echo inside my mind.

Focusing on my hand, Daniel laces his fingers with mine before looking up. Our eyes meet and rather than seeing through me, he holds my gaze precisely and his body shudders, letting out a sigh. Lifting his free hand, he runs his fingers through my hair, illuminating me with the pink glow of the red rose—the beacon that called me.

He beams and, despite my confusion and laboured breathing, I return his joyful smile. Leaning forward, our foreheads meet, forcing our eyes to readjust so they can continue communicating without words.

My heart dances as our noses touch. Daniel twists his head gently, but it is me who closes the gap, brushing my lips against his. Fully embracing me, he pulls my body to his, and the kiss intensifies as our beings melt together.

Teetering on the edge of blissful oblivion, we pause to take in the wonder of the moment; keeping our foreheads connected whilst allowing the night air a small channel between our lips.

"I knew if I waited long enough, you'd come," Daniel whispers.

The words are spoken lovingly, but they cut me like broken glass. Dropping my hold of him, I quickly stand up and Daniel instantly looks confused.

"What is it?" he asks, scrambling to his feet.

I do not give myself time to consider if it is justified, but anger and frustration rise in me along with sheer terror as I realise that while others are reinvigorated by meeting me, Daniel is not. Only a few hours ago I felt the blessing of having helped people—giving them hope for their futures, in whatever form that might be. But Daniel nearly killed himself summoning me. *Yes, summoning.*

"I'm not a genie," I reply, angrily. "You can't just rub my lamp and I'll come running."

As Daniel screws up his face, I feel sick realising the first words of mine that he has heard are in anger.

"Of course not," he replies. His eyebrows furrow with sorrow. "I'm sorry, I—"

"Don't you realise how dangerous that was?" I ask, pointing at the sea.

"I knew you'd save me."

"It doesn't work like that! I don't get to choose! What would have happened if—" My voice breaks. "I cannot have that on me, I couldn't bear it." I sob.

"I'm sorry," Daniel repeats. "It's just I've been talking to others who have met you—actually seen you—and the common theme is times of need. I feel you with me sometimes, especially when with my mum, but since she's gone—" He stares at the sky as though he is looking for Kath before turning back to me. "But I feared you were done with us after she left and began to doubt if you felt the same after we kissed in front of the painting. Surely that wasn't one sided?" He again pauses, his eyes searching mine for an answer.

My heart answers although my head screams for silence. "It wasn't."

Encouraged, Daniel steps towards me again and I do not move. "I've been desperate to see you, so I thought if I—"

"Nearly drown yourself, I'd feel it?" I say, my tone somewhere between sarcasm and sadness.

"Precisely," he says sheepishly. "When you put it like that, it does seem a little—"

"Crazy? Stupid? Reckless?"

"Yeah, okay, okay." Daniel grins. "I was hoping you'd think it romantic. A kind of new-age *Romeo and Juliet*."

"*Romeo and Juliet* is *not* romantic. They both die!"

"For love—that is romantic."

I feel my face grimace. "If they had communicated a little better, they could have *romantically lived*."

"Can't we?" Daniel says, lifting our rose between us once more.

"No."

"Why not?"

"Because you already have a girlfriend, and I am already dead." I sigh. This is not how I imagined our first conversation would go.

"Raquel and I broke up."

"What? When? Why?"

"We want different things, and it was time to acknowledge that. I hope we will be friends again in the future, but—"

"Take it back. Tell her you're confused, you made a mistake, you're just grieving." I am not fulfilling my promise to Kath at all well right now. I said I would watch over his life, not destroy it.

Daniel looks hurt. "No, I'm not." He reaches for my hand. "Want me or not, I love *you*. I cannot be with one person when my heart is so connected to another."

I want nothing more than to wrap my arms around him and spend the rest of our days watching the sun rise and set together. My soul tells me he is the one I should have found, but my head reminds me it is all too late. The glitch may torment me with snippets of what might have been, but it is not my purpose anymore.

"Don't you think we are meant to be?" he asks. It is like he is reading my mind—or parts of it.

"In another life, maybe, but not this one."

Suddenly, I realise what I must do. Juliet must save Romeo.

"Promise me you'll never do anything like this again." Daniel looks at me suspiciously. "Promise me, because I promise you, another time I will not come."

I feel the pain of my words ripping through both of us, but neither speaks, we just stare at each other, searching for words in each other's eyes.

"I love you," Daniel whispers. A knife for a knife. Past me balks—she has never had such tender words whispered to her. She heard the words, but they always came with a dark agenda. The speaker wanted something, some control, to summon for some selfish whim, or for meaningless forgiveness for an act that would be repeated all-too soon.

These words are different, but as such they also cut deeper, purer. I hope that makes my following act all the more selfless and that one day he will thank me.

Stepping forward, I gulp as a single tear betrays me, spilling down my cheek. In the glow of our rose, Daniel notices and gently wipes it away, then leans in to tenderly kiss me. Wrapping my arms around his neck, I sink into his embrace. Daniel shudders with delight with each move as I let my hand wander down his back and slowly trace his arm—feeling the muscled tension as he firmly holds my waist. Reaching his hand, I cover it with mine before pulling back, whispering, "I love you, too, but this is goodbye, Daniel."

His eyes widen as the meaning of my sentence sinks in. I do not—*I cannot*—give myself time to think. Wrapping my hand around the rose, I crush it with all my might, sending it in pieces into the breeze.

"NO!" cries Daniel, grasping for the petals as their light extinguishes. Crestfallen, Daniel turns back to me, but I have gone—spiralling back into my realm, invisible, miserable, and alone.

# 48

Leaving Daniel shouting 'Angel' across the beach, I run through the grassy dunes, only briefly stopping to vomit bile before continuing my meaningless hike. My heart feels like it is bleeding out and when I wipe my mouth or nose, I expect to see blood, not mucus.

Inside my head, I scream at the glitch. *Why? Why be so cruel? Is my death and service not enough, you have to torment me as well?*

Wandering the paths, I find myself at the top of the cliff. It has been four years since I have been able to come here. The last time was about a week after I died. Having spent days screaming at Hayden, the police, my dad, and everyone else I passed, I finally wormed my way back to 'the scene of the crime.' For hours, I stared over the abyss watching the salty water thrust itself against the rocks below.

The glitch boundaries were unknown to me then. It was later that I learnt I cannot swim out to sea until exhaustion takes me or lay on train tracks until a cargo train rolls over me. At that point I thought I had the option of slipping myself off the edge like a discarded pebble and contemplated how long and how painful the fall would be until I met my maker.

Perhaps my initiation with the glitch would have been less bruising on my pride if I had chosen that route, but I couldn't bring myself to shuffle off the edge. I told myself it would be more effective, more certain, if I took a running jump from a speed that I could not easily break from.

I walked back to the point that I am currently standing on. The road was tarmacked but poorly maintained by the council because it was 'just one of those roads motorists expected to be crappy.' Probably fearing another lawsuit, they quickly resurfaced after Hayden took a settlement from them. Had he not been hiding his murderous activity and seeking my money from Dad at the time, he would almost certainly have pushed for a full court case.

Anyway, I stood here and ran, putting every ounce of effort into my legs and arms, pumping my heart with everything I could. Devoid of all hope, I didn't falter at the last step and channelling my inner athlete, I leapt off that edge like an Olympic long jumper.

There was no sandpit, but neither was there a watery nor rocky grave for me—instead, I found the springboard of pain. The invisible jelly-like wall that throws me backwards, hastily landed my sorry arse in the dirt and left me to again cry out my sorrow. I've since learnt walking, not running into the Adtoft perimeter wall doesn't hurt.

If it were not for this vivid memory, and perhaps the notion—however deep-down—that I have a purpose beyond my heartache, I might attempt a long jump now.

No, despite my misery, I am not yet done trying. Walking to the edge of the cliff, I sit down, dangle my feet and wait for sunrise.

*Alexia Muelle-Rushbrook*

\* \* \*

Waking up, I find myself wearing a pure white summer dress with a seagull perched on a rock next to me while its friends circle above. Funny, real fucking funny, glitch. Today I do not want guidance, comfort, or direction. I cannot jump into the void, but I can give the one inside of me time to process.

"Let me absorb my loss in my way, please," I say to the bird.

It tilts its head, listening to my words, but makes no attempt to move. I could flap my arms and encourage it to fly, but if, as I suspect, my time-space-continuum makes no difference to the gull, it will only add to my foul mood. Better to not find out and assume benevolence.

With the exception of a handful of hikers, dog walkers, and cars seeking the picnic spot, my peace is largely undisturbed all day. Possibly the heavy blanket of clouds and potentially cool temperature has dissuaded most people from wandering up here today, but about half an hour before the sun sets the clouds clear, making way for a beautiful dusk sky.

By now, my body should be crying out with cramp, but I think my general being is so numb that it cannot be bothered to appeal to my senses. I hear a car pass, then another one, causing my back to prickle, but I refuse to acknowledge them by turning around.

Silence resumes—minus the wind and sound of the water, but those sounds have become part of me, so I do not count them as a disturbance—until two voices approach. My skin stings with irritation and I glare in the direction of muttered speech. Why can't they look at the sunset from somewhere else?

As they edge around the corner, my heart flips and groans simultaneously. Daniel, wearing black trousers, a dark green jacket and beanie hat that matches his eyes, is a little way ahead of Rufus who is respectfully carrying a small silver container. It only takes me a second to realise it is an urn. The seagull next to me squarks and I instantly flack my arm at it. It doesn't move. I knew it—I just knew it.

"Where are you going?" Rufus asks, wandering to the cliff edge, cautiously looking down. "We used to stay at the picnic site with Mum to watch the sunset, right?"

"Yeah, Mum didn't like stopping here as the road bends badly and she was always worried about us getting hit," Daniel replies.

"She wasn't wrong."

"Pardon?"

"This is where Hayden and his missus had their car accident the other year, remember?"

"Oh, yeah, right." Daniel rubs his face. "I was there, actually."

I stare at Daniel.

"What? What do you mean you were there?" asks Rufus.

"After, I mean after. I was working that night. I was called to attend."

How do I not remember that? *Er—you'd just been murdered. Faces of paramedics weren't high on your list of things to notice.*

"Oh right. You didn't need to do much though—I mean Hayden was okay, wasn't he?"

"Yeah, just minimal bruising. He was lucky."

Rufus rolls his eyes. "Yeah."

"That luck may run out, you know." Daniel looks serious.

"I don't doubt it. Karma *is* going to be his bitch."

"What does that even mean? You sound like Leo." Worry spreads across Daniel's face. "You don't want to be in the crossfire. Please—"

"Dan, we're not up here for you to give me a lecture on working with Leo. I'm not the only one with crap to sort—but not today, okay?"

Daniel shakes his head. "Fine." Distracted, he wanders towards the point where I died.

"What are you doing?" asks Rufus impatiently.

Daniel shrugs. "Sorry, I just thought I sensed something when I drove past."

"Sensed or saw?" Rufus sneers in confusion.

"Oh, forget it. Shall we go back to the picnic spot Mum liked?"

"Sure, makes sense to go to her favourite spot—quick though, the sun is about to set, and we promised we'd let her go at exactly sunset."

I follow. I know I shouldn't, but I still have my promise to Kath to uphold and if they came in separate vehicles, I might be able to get a ride into town with Rufus—I won't go with Daniel, even if I can.

The brothers rest against the safety rail that surrounds the picnic site as the sun drops below the horizon. A beautiful hue of purple and pink fills the sky, outlining the few clouds that remain with glorious colours as though nature is defiantly calling out to the world before everything turns black.

Somehow, it manages to invigorate my weary soul.

Saying my own private prayer, I turn to leave the brothers to their final moment but pause as Daniel speaks.

"To a love that never dies and a mother who could give no more. May we be the sons you deserve and live on in a manner that makes you proud." His voice is strong, but gentle. As Rufus lets the ashes fly out across the sea, Daniel adds, "Until we meet again."

"Until we meet again," echoes Rufus. "Love you, Mum."

# 49

There are only three cars to choose from in the car park: Daniel's which I know only too well, an MPV with dog cages all over the seats, and a black 4x4. It doesn't take a genius to work out which is Rufus'. The door opens for me without delay or denial, so I sit on the passenger seat, waiting for my chauffeur.

As Rufus gets into the car, I reprimand myself for observing Daniel so intently and force myself not to watch him drive away. Passion turning into stalker-style obsession is not a crutch I wish to add to my list of reasons to hate myself.

Rufus puts the key into the ignition but pauses when a beep comes from within the glove compartment. Tutting, he reaches for his phone, and as he reads the message I am frightened by the significant change in his expression.

"Shit…shit, shit, shit!" Rufus throws his phone into the tray between our seats, starting the engine. He reverses at speed and flies out of the car park and past my point of death in such a manner that I wonder if he hasn't been commanded by some higher power to finish the job that Hayden started. But he carries on, only slowing when the increased volume of traffic of town forces him to.

"Shit," he repeats, sounding the word through gritted teeth. "Come the fuck on!" he shouts at the queue of cars in front of him.

Picking up his mobile, I am surprised when the screen responds to my touch and nervously check that Rufus cannot see what I am doing. Tapping his fingers impatiently on the steering wheel, it is clear he has no idea I am here. Good. Now isn't the time for a Casper the Ghost moment.

The open message is from an unknown phone number, but I don't need to know the sender to understand the context: 'VALENTINE SPECIAL: ROSES ARE RED, THERE'S NO NEED TO BE BLUE, CANDYFLOSS CAN SPILL BLOOD AND SO WILL YOU.'

My blood feels heavy as my heart attempts to pump it around my body. Gauging from the state of Rufus, he is having the same problem. I read the next messages. They are from Kev, Leo, and a few others from Flossy's crew. Some are in the same group chat that the poem was sent to, but realising they have been infiltrated, most are being sent via a new group or individually—but either way, the same angry, half panicked tone is pinged across the airwaves as they scramble around town in an attempt to find Flossy.

Never have I wanted wings or the ability to teleport more.

Leo's last message instructs Rufus to immediately drive to his house, but we are not heading the right way—we're going to Flossy's. It is so unlike Rufus to act unguided, and I cannot help wishing that today weren't the day he'd chosen to listen to independent thought.

Screeching to a halt outside Flossy's house, Rufus doesn't bother to slow down enough to pull up the drive, instead choosing to leave the car slightly angled on the pavement, taking the keys as an automatic gesture, rather than conscious decision. His haste encourages mine as we run up the driveway. There is no need to knock, the door isn't shut, yet there is nothing welcoming about this scene as the previously neat, royal blue door is now displaying a rather large hole that was probably made by an axe.

"Flossy?" shouts Rufus, running inside. "Uncle Flossy? Are you here?"

He freezes in the living room doorway, letting out a stifled curse. As I wait for him to move, I sense what we are going to see as a metallic stench hits the back of my nose. Suddenly Rufus turns back, runs through me and out the front door, only just making it to a flowerbed before he vomits profusely, coughing up yellow and orange chunks until his stomach runs out of food.

I've always considered myself to have a strong constitution. I am not saying that I like vomit or blood, but I always figured it was part of being a nurse—part of caring for others that you may need to see some low points in order to pick people up again. In my career as an angel, in particular at the hospital, I have seen some cuts to challenge my sensitivities, yet I have not shied away from any of them. Walking into Flossy's living room, with the aura of darkness and death increasing with every step, all I can do is gasp in horror.

The axe, which was so masterfully used to open the front door, is lodged in Flossy's chest, but not on its first swing.

Parts of him hang and lay on the floor as he sits, slumped in his favourite chair with a candy cane perched between his lips. The room is turned over and inside out, much like his guts, and it is only sheer terror clogging my throat that is preventing me from screaming.

Whether I thought him a good or bad person, whether the peace would—or indeed has—welcomed him the same as the other Adtoft residents I have seen pass over, I cannot say. All I know is, I am too late, Flossy's soul has gone, and a heinous crime has been committed.

Adtoft, my Adtoft, has a villain, a despicable villain, worse than it has ever seen before and I, their servant, must find and stop them.

Outside, Rufus is talking on the phone. Not wanting to miss out, I rush to his side.

"Why are you there? Morten and Jack are on route," says a strong, masculine voice. Leo.

"Those lazy fuckers would just see his car gone and keep driving." Rufus sneers.

"Where's his car? It's not by the pier like we thought."

"How the fuck should I know? Probably halfway to being a cube by now." Rufus is shaking all over. "Flossy's a mess, Leo, a complete mess."

"Shit," says Leo, momentarily softening his tone.

"What do I do?" Rufus' voice trembles. "Call the cops?"

"Fuck, no," Leo replies coldly. "Get out of there. If Floss is as bad as you say, there's nothing to do. Is Sophia home?"

"I don't know—I didn't look for her. Shit, do you think she's dead too?"

"Go—check now, while I'm on the phone."

Rufus dutifully runs indoors, avoiding looking at Flossy as he darts in and out of each room. "I can't see her. Her chair isn't here."

"Good, she must be out with her carer or someone. Get out."

"Then what?"

"Go home and stay there until you hear otherwise. Sophia will call it in, she's okay, let her deal with it like it's a psycho-burglary. No need for any of us to get involved, not via the police. War was coming, now it is here. No more eye for eye, we'll take them all." The venom that comes through the phone makes us both shudder.

"But—"

"Rufus. Enough. I'll call later. Get out. Go home. NOW." Leo hangs up.

Returning to his typical behaviour, Rufus obeys his brother's order without even glancing backwards—while dread rises within me as Kath's promise weighs on me more than ever.

# 50

Leo told Rufus to let Sophia call the police, but she'll have nightmares for life if she sees her grandad in this state—yet regrettably I doubt if I can stop her.

Not wanting to inhale any more blood, I walk outside and sit on the doorstep, trembling from head to toe, feeling increasingly sick. It's a shame I still feel. Don't get me wrong, I am glad I am not absolutely numb in my current state, but angel PTSD is something I could do without.

My wait for Sophia is thankfully short, but something deep inside of me groans when Dad's car pulls up. I know someone earthly has to find Flossy, but I would rather it wasn't him.

Wasting no time, he gets out of the car, walking to the back to get Sophia's wheelchair. Jumping up, I slam my hands on the boot, hoping, if not believing, that I will hold it down. For a moment, the boot resists and Dad curses under his breath, pulling harder on the stubborn metal frame. Just as I dare to believe that I might win, my realm reclaims me, allowing the boot to defy my will as it effortlessly glides open.

"Dammit!" I scream.

"What's that, Soph?" Dad asks.

"Huh?" she says from within the car.

"Did you say something?"

"No?"

"Oh, never mind, must have been the wind. It sounded distant."

Hope rises in me. I scream has loud and long as I can. "DON'T GO IN THE HOUSE!"

Dad pauses, furrowing his eyebrows as though a scrambled thought has come to him, and he is willing it to translate into an intelligent sentence. I shout again, but he brushes away his confusion with a simple shake of the head, simultaneously triggering the security light.

Looking up at the house, Dad gulps as he notices the axe mark in the door.

"What is it?" Sophia asks, trying to twist in her seat to see what is causing his delay. "Are you okay?"

Dad clears his throat. "Something is wrong. Wait here, I'll go check."

"What do you mean?" Panic spreads across her face. "No, we'll go together."

"Look at the door, Soph, I'm not taking you in there until I know it is safe."

"I can wheel my chair myself, you know? I'm not going to sit here while you—"

"I'll just take a quick peek, then come straight back, I promise."

Sophia protests, but Dad doesn't wait to hear her out. Gingerly, he walks inside, calling out to Flossy as he steps over the threshold, grabbing a hold of a makeshift weapon in the form of a 'helping hand' disability aid.

When the cat appears, miaowing strangely, Dad jumps. The poor thing knows what has happened. Normally Dad would pat the cat, but he cautiously moves forward, all the while holding the disability aid like a bat. He must be able to smell the air too. I doubt slaughterhouses smell any less disgusting. Entering the living room, Dad immediately sees Flossy's body. Without stopping to examine Flossy for signs of life—honestly, only a fool would consider it—Dad runs to the car, pulls out his mobile phone, and dials 999.

"What is it?" Sophia asks as tears stream down her face. She already knows the answer.

Pausing with his fingers hovering over the call button, Dad walks around the car, bopping in front of Sophia's open door. "I'm so sorry, honey."

"What's happened?"

"Flossy has been attacked; he is—"

"Dead?" her voice breaks saying the word.

"Yes. I'm so sorry." Dad rubs her hands and arms sympathetically. "I need to call the police, okay?"

Sophia nods, then breaks down, sobbing.

\* \* \*

Blue lights quickly fill the street. The police refuse to let Sophia or my dad back into the house, declaring it a major crime scene. Copious amounts of yellow and black tape surround the house while the driveway gets treated with blue and white strips declaring: 'POLICE LINE DO NOT CROSS.'

"We'll need you to come to the station to make statements," a young policeman says to my dad.

"Of course," Dad replies. "Can we come now? If possible, I don't want to keep Sophia outside any longer, it's not good for her circulation."

"Yes, yes, that's fine." The officer turns to Sophia. "Do you have somewhere to stay for a while?"

Sophia pauses. "Erm, I'm hoping—"

"Yes, she's going to live with me." Dad says confidently, laying a hand on her shoulder.

"Are you sure?" she says, smiling through her tears. "I know we spoke about it, but—"

"I'm certain."

"What about the cat?"

Dad shrugs, wryly smiling. "An inherited furbaby?"

"Excellent," says the officer. "I'll just sign off site with my colleagues and then we'll get going."

"You know you probably saved my life?" Sophia says as soon as they are alone.

"I'd never leave you on the street! I want us to be a couple, you know that—"

"I don't mean now." Sophia grimaces. "Earlier, had you not taken me to the cinema, I would have been in the house. Do you think they would have left me as a witness?" She shakes her head. "No. No, they wouldn't."

Silently gulping, Dad's face drains of colour. There are no words of comfort. His eyes say all that Sophia needs to hear as he bends to kiss her forehead.

The quicker they get out of here the better.

\* \* \*

We ride silently in the car to the police station. Once there, a female officer takes Sophia in one direction while the male officer from the house takes Dad in another. I alternate between rooms while they give their statements. It is fairly straightforward for Dad—not living with the murder victim certainly helps. Listening to the officers, I don't think they doubt Sophia, but they seem genuinely baffled to why anyone would want to kill a candyfloss seller.

Sophia's answers are measured without sounding measured. If I knew nothing, I would say she is clueless. Yet I do know, so I can only conclude that Flossy kept her on the right side of the dark in many aspects of his life, and what he couldn't hide, he trained for in the hope she remains blameless in the eyes of the law—and two violent gangs.

Finished with his statement, Dad is sitting in reception, looking anything but relaxed as he runs his fingers around his chain necklace, jigging his knee at a hundred miles an hour. Why does he seem more nervous now than earlier? Is he having a delayed reaction to trauma? That would be perfectly understandable—but he keeps eyeing the woman on the desk like he wants to say something to her.

A door from behind the desk opens and Chief Constable Rogers, Raquel's father, walks in. Dad spots him and jumps up, still clinging to his necklace with one hand as he waves with the other.

Since when did Dad even wear a necklace?

"Er, hello, Chief Constable," Dad splutters as Sean takes in his face. "I'm—"

Sean extends his hand, smiling sympathetically. "Yes, sir, I know who you are, we met three years ago when your daughter—"

"Four, actually—"

"Four, already? I'm sorry, time, it—"

"It's okay, I wouldn't expect you to recall dates perfectly, the pain is mine, not yours. But, if I may, it's actually something to do with my daughter that I wanted to talk to you about."

"Oh?" Sean doesn't hide his surprise but recollects himself quickly. "Of course, how can I help?"

Dad fidgets. "Would it be possible to speak privately?"

Sean nods and gestures for my dad to walk to the side of the desk where he opens a section of the counter and ushers my father inside. I can feel my cheeks flushing with confusion—fear and confusion—as they walk into the Chief Constable's office.

It isn't a small room, but it is plainly decorated. A few photographs and awards line the walls, but the furniture is otherwise for function, not adornment. Dad sits, slightly bent forward in one of the chairs in front of the desk as Sean rolls his chair—which is probably the most expensive thing in the room—up to his side of the desk.

"So, what was it you wanted to say?" Sean asks kindly.

Dad shuffles in his seat, rolling his finger through the chain around his neck. Suddenly, I glimpse what is hanging on that chain. *Please don't, Dad, just don't, I beg you.*

"This is going to sound weird. I should say that from the start." Dad says in earnest.

"Okay, well, I've heard a few weird things in my time. So, try me."

"You remember my daughter's disappearance, right? You said you do?"

Sean narrows his eyes. "Yes, she died in an accident on the cliff top."

Dad sighs, rubbing his forehead.

"What don't I know?"

Dad bobs his head, willing words to rise from his mouth while I pray they stay down, and Sean puts this whole conversation down to PTSD and stress.

"Okay, put it another way," says Sean. "What do you know that I don't?"

"It's less what I know," Dad says, pulling the chain from under his shirt, undoing the clasp, "and more what I suspect." He lays his necklace, complete with my wedding ring, on the table on top of today's local newspaper. The headline celebrates a large budget being announced by the council for Adtoft's development. Tomorrow's headline is set to be significantly bleaker.

My insides weep seeing the ring. It is no wonder that I couldn't find it in the house, Dad has been carrying it around his neck like a bad omen. Petrified of making more replicas, I haven't discarded mine since that day. Fiddling with it now, I repeatedly curse the day I said, 'I do.'

"What am I looking at?" Sean asks, trying not to sound exasperated.

"My daughter's wedding ring."

"Right...?"

"I've just moved house. I found it recently when I packed up her things."

Sean curls his lip. "You've lost me. Why—"

"My daughter hadn't lived with me for over ten years when I lost her. All her things in my house were from before that time. There is no reason why she would have left her wedding ring there—especially not if her marriage was as happy as that waste of space said."

Sean rearranges his pens as they stand in an old mug. "You mean Mr Lennox?"

"Hayden, yes." Sean doesn't reply, so my dad continues. "I told your colleagues then that he was no good, but no one believed me. They absorbed his crocodile tears like it was some sort of magical fairy dust and took me as a grieving, angry father looking for someone to blame for the loss of his only daughter."

Sean sits back, weighing up my dad's words, but I am sure as the cogs turn within his mind, he is still considering whether his colleagues were not right.

Dad sighs. "You don't believe me."

"It's not that I do or don't believe you, but I do not have any evidence. A ring is not clear evidence. It is curious, but it is not evidence of—well, let me be clear: what exactly are you accusing your son-in-law of?"

"Murder."

Sean's eyes widen. "Is it possible your daughter fled, perhaps? There was no body, after all?"

"My girl wouldn't leave me—nor him. She made her bed, and she was too loyal, too sweet, to do anything about it." *Too stupid, too worthless, more like.* "In a way, I don't think she has left."

"Pardon?"

No, Dad, no. Don't say it—

"She sent me a sign from the other side."

*Shit.* Now Sean is going to think you're truly mad.

"Don't look at me like that. The ring, it electrocuted me. That was her, telling me she isn't gone, not completely. I'm sure she wants me to seek justice for her." No, no I do not. I want you to live a long, happy, and free life.

Sean's face is a picture of pity and compassion. He has a daughter, he understands, but he also doesn't believe. He pulls out his phone and begins searching for counsellors on the force payroll.

"We have some excellent resources for people such as yourself—people who have suffered a great loss and need guidance to—"

"I'm not mad," Dad says irritably. "I want this town cleaned of scum. If you lot looked a little harder, you'd see where the root of that is."

Dad is right. It isn't just Hayden, but he is the root of so much evil. All of my pain loops back to and through him.

Maybe I cannot leave it—not if I or anyone I love is to ever live or rest in peace.

Frustrated, Dad stands up to leave, slowly reaching for the ring as though he is hoping that Sean will change his mind. He doesn't, but I do.

Milliseconds before Dad reclaims the ring, I pull mine off my finger, briskly swiping it into the replica. Sparks fly as the ring separates from the chain necklace, forcing both men backwards. Stunned, Sean remains against the wall, but Dad quickly recovers, grinning from ear to ear.

"I told you!" Dad declares jubilantly. "Sweetie, are you still here?" His voice crackles. "I miss you so much. I failed you. I cannot do that again. What have you to say? We're listening."

My heart yearns to hug my father and ease his pain. I desperately wanted to avoid causing him any more anguish, but my inner voice tells me we have been joined for a cause—one that requires our pain to push us forward, not linger in the past.

Sean is whiter than a sheet, but my father's cheeks are flushed as he intensely stares at the golden band, waiting for me to do something.

Normally I mourn my inability to communicate. Last time the rings clashed, I still didn't see a way, but poking the ring I see the spark was powerful enough to etch a brown circle on the newspaper. I cannot help chuckling—the glitch has literally laid a prop before me. Never has *The Daily Adtoft* been so interesting!

I can only hope that I understand enough to transmit a meaningful message.

Where do I start?—I'm trapped? I'm dead? Hayden killed me?

No, I know that is not why I am here. I need to be more up to date, less selfish.

Keeping my ring in my right hand, I use my left to slide the ring in their realm across the newspaper. The ring covers four lines of text, fitting eight to ten letters in the centre, depending on the sentence. Desperately reading the article,

I search for words that convey my message and quickly find myself lamenting the headline story being relatively happy—the one day a murder or tragic illness would be useful, I get a government grant!

The index column suggests a more fitting story on the next page—a car accident. Lifting the corner, I turn it over, but only in my world. I groan. How do I get them to turn their page?

Pushing the ring to the bottom right corner, I wait, hoping they understand. At first, they are too awe struck, only seeing the ring moving and seek to control it rather than watch it. So much for 'we're listening.' Typical.

Annoyed, I spin the ring to the far edge of the desk out of their reach before returning it to the newspaper, circling on the corner.

"Does she want us to turn the page?" Sean asks, staring so intently I think he might pass out.

"Maybe..." Dad says, flicking the page over, gently sliding their ring onto the desk.

"Woohoo!" I shout as the ecstasy of being understood fills me with hope.

This page has details of a drink-drug-drive accident, an advert for a garden centre, plus stories about a rescued cat, a new cake shop, and the number of children in understaffed schools. If I want to stay on topic, I should only need the former.

"How do you know this is your daughter?" asks Sean, recovering some of his usual astuteness.

"Pardon?" Dad looks confused, although to be fair, it is a perfectly reasonable question.

"I'm trying to take this at face value—ignoring the part of my brain that is screaming this is a trick of some kind—but how do you know? Has she told you?"

"I just *know*."

Sean doesn't seem convinced. I scan the page for something Dad will understand—a word that will have meaning, but it is a picture, not a word that catches my eye. On the bottom right of the page is a rectangular advert for *All Roots Great and Small,* Adtoft's major garden centre. Their logo has always depicted the glorious purple magnolia tree that stands outside the shop. Mum used to love taking me there as a child and I'm sure that's why the magnolia tree became my favourite at a very young age—and why Dad chose a purple one to represent my life.

Taking both rings, I circle the tree and Dad chokes on his tears.

"Does that mean something to you?" Sean gently asks.

Dad smiles. "It means my daughter is with us." Sean raises his eyebrows, wordlessly questioning Dad as he pulls out his mobile phone. Turning the screen to Sean, he says. "Please visit my home to verify its location and species, but this *is* my daughter's memorial tree."

Astonished, Sean's eyebrows rise further than I thought possible, but rather than asking anymore, he stares at the ring.

I'll take that as my cue.

Laying their ring with the word 'drug' in the centre, I place the ring in my realm over the top of it, causing another spark. Despite expecting it, my eyes flutter as they react to the sudden brightness while both men shield their faces like the sun has just risen in front of them.

Putting his hands down, Dad peers at the newspaper, then chuckles. "Can I have some paper, please?" he says, helping himself to a pen from the mug.

With a slightly shaky hand, Sean produces a notebook from his drawer and slides it over to my dad. Continuing to push the ring over the paper, I patiently wait for them to make note of the word in the middle of each scorched circle. By the third word, they learn to anticipate the flash and turn away until the realms clash. The room quickly smells of burnt paper, but they soon have a sentence to begin questioning me on.

"Drug war in Adtoft," Sean reads. "We're aware of our gang problem—we've been mopping up after them for months. The promenade, a wasteland beyond the shipping yard, and an old farm unit have been their haunting grounds to date—plus a few nightclub brawls. Only two nights ago we were called to an incident, but they were gone before we arrived. They are highly organised and keep moving before we can track them. They must have a base, somewhere they can consistently come back to." Sean sighs. "It's tough, but we are working on it."

"Too slow." Dad reads out my reply. "Things escalated."
"When?"
I move the ring again. "Now."
"You mean Flossy's murder?" Dad asks.
"Yes."
"He was murdered by a gang?"
"Yes."

"For drugs?"

"Yes." An orange glow flickers around the ring. I need to find a new 'yes' because after three uses this one is ready to ignite.

"What about Hayden?" Dad asks, remembering his original mission while Sean uses the base of his mug to suppress any residual heat in the paper.

There's no 'kill' or 'murder' on the open pages. So, I make do with 'fatal,' making sure I miss out the following word 'accident.'

Dad covers his mouth with his hand and stifles a sob.

"Shit," whispers Sean, running his hand through his hair.

"You have to arrest him!" Dad cries.

"On what charge?"

"Murder, of course!"

Sean scratches his forehead as he thinks, then drops his hand, saying, "Where is our evidence? What is our source? If I present *this* to the court," he says lifting the newspaper briefly, "you and I will both be in a psych ward."

Sorrow flashes across my father's face. "If it were your daughter, you'd be willing to take that risk." Sean softly inclines his head but doesn't answer. "So, you're willing to let him get away with murder?"

"No, I'm not, of course not."

"But?"

Sean repeatably rubs his face while Dad impatiently jigs his leg with increasing speed.

"Is he part of this drug war?" Sean asks, looking around the room—presumably for me.

Finding a new 'yes,' I run their ring over to it and chip it with my ring.

"Is he the leader?"

I wish I could pin that on Hayden, but I want to catch him for the truth, not lies. "No."

Disappointment spreads across their faces.

"Girlfriend," I indicate.

"Girlfriend?" Sean says.

"Shit," Dad mutters. "Flossy himself told me Hayden and his girlfriend were mixed up in something. I didn't ask details at the time—I didn't want to know."

Just like I didn't want to know. Just like I have gone around town looking for clues, but avoiding the one place that I know I will find them.

Not anymore.

Sticking my finger inside my wedding ring, I coast it across the newspaper to the bottom right corner, circling it so Dad turns the page and repeat the manoeuvre until he flicks to the classifieds at the back. There, in all its familiar, ghostly glory is the advert that I knew would be there. It always is—because many years ago I set up a standing order.

Laying the ring over my old surname, I connect the two rings, holding them in place with the tip of my finger. The page momentarily ignites as the rings merge, but they do not burn me. Both men gasp as the golden band disappears, leaving a glowing paper ring in its place.

"H. Lennox Auto Repairs and Sales," reads Sean, seconds before the advert turns into scorched dust.

"The garage!" Dad semi-yells. "You need to search Hayden's garage."

"Hmm," Sean says, thinking intently. "Indeed." He smiles—almost grins—with satisfaction. "I propose that if we cannot pin him for the heinous crime we know he committed, then we convict him for another."

# 51

Making him promise to stay there, Sean told my dad to take Sophia home. I wasn't convinced that Dad was going to do as he was told, but thankfully, neither was Sean because he instructed an officer to watch Dad's house.

I'm not sorry. Dad had a rarely seen, but undeniably determined glint in his eye and I do not want him to summon a misplaced sense of untouchable righteousness and put himself in danger by approaching Hayden. Not to mention the fact that Mae is more dangerous than Hayden. Who knows how safe Sophia is with Mae and her crazed crew running around with axes? If they are willing to hack up an eighty-year-old man, I'm pretty sure a middle-aged woman in a wheelchair wouldn't bother them.

Wasting no time, Sean has used Dad's false witness statement to plan an immediate raid on Hayden's garage. On another occasion you might call this behaviour 'bent,' but I choose to see this as 'thinking outside the box for the greater good.'

Someone else can argue the merits and morals of that another day. I'm not too concerned what method they use; I just want justice. Peace and justice for this town, for Kath, for the one's I love, and ultimately for myself, too.

It is true that I haven't searched every house, every outbuilding, or factory for signs of Mae and her men. In fact, I am pretty certain she does have a secondary store somewhere, but I also know that the glitch has pointed me to Hayden so many times that his garage has to be a hive.

*It has to be.*

Now isn't the time for doubt. I must believe in myself as much as others. I have come too far to let my own insecurities hamper exposing what I feel is the iceberg polluting this town. Excitement rises in me. Is it really possible that Hayden and the gangs could be swooped up thanks to me?

Having heard the particulars of Sean's plan to strike predawn before the gangs have time to regroup, I seek fresh air, aiming to flush the smell of blood and burnt newspaper that has taken up residence at the back of my nose.

Outside the police station, the ground sparkles with glorious frozen jewels and the sky mimics it as thousands of stars twinkle way up high. Breathing deeply, I attempt to settle the butterflies in my stomach. For so long I have waited to feel hope, yet now I sense it at the tips of my fingers, waiting for me to reach out and claim my share.

Softly chuckling, I shake my head. Who would have thought I'd ever *want* to visit that blasted garage again? It calls to me—the glitch calls to me.

It is time.

A breeze rushes across the carpark—I can almost see it coming for me, like white horses breaking from the tide as they race to the shore. Whirling furiously, the breeze envelopes and lifts me an inch off the ground, blurring my vision with hundreds of speeding colours. Images flash, but none stay long enough for my eyes to register objects. In an instant, the whirlwind twists as though it is tying a knot—tying me back together—resting me back on the ground as it races away down the street.

The street?

I wasn't on a street.

Shit—oh my—shit.

Do I laugh or cry?

"Neither," says the voice within. "Get to work, girl. *It is time.*"

# 52

I know this street only too well. For years it was where I lived, but it was never my home and certainly never a sanctuary. The 'family' business stands next to the house of horror. It too holds painful memories, yet I am certain that it also holds the path to Adtoft's peace.

The lights are out in the workshop, but a security light beams across the sales forecourt. It is a miniature, largely less expensive version of his father's forecourt, but it is by no means little or insignificant—much like the basement that Hayden gleefully had installed the year after we married. The signing-off inspector is a friend of Maddox's and absolutely open to 'bonus' payments, meaning the basement and underground carpark are much larger than originally approved—although, ironically, it was openly praised for its space saving, eco-friendly design.

Standing on the street, I feel somewhat confused. I wanted to come here. I felt ready to come here—or as ready as I'll ever be. However, my plan was to watch the police do their thing and cheerlead from my phantom front row seat, not turn up early or see Hayden any sooner than absolutely necessary. Yet the glitch has brought me here now—why?

Another breeze rattles down the street, but this time it is accompanied by a car. The driver pulls up at the end of the road, immediately turns off their engine, opens the door, and walks in my direction.

When he has stepped no more than twenty paces, a second car turns into the road, and a warm wind hits me again. I don't need to be closer to know it is Daniel—the wind torments me with his scent, even though he doesn't really wear a cologne.

Daniel abruptly parks his car. There is no sound, but the bumpers are obviously very close as the first man runs back, shouting:

"What the fuck?" Of course, it is Rufus. "You nearly hit my car! Leo will—"

"Fuck Leo," replies Daniel's familiar voice in an unfamiliar tone, slamming his car door closed. "What the hell are you doing here?"

"Are you following me?" Rufus says, ignoring the question.

"After what just happened? Of course I'm bloody following you!"

"I shouldn't have told you—I was in shock."

"You're still in shock—rightly so." Daniel softens his tone but speaks no less firmly.

"Go home, Dan, go home."

"I will not. I promised Mum. You need to get out. For me, for Mum, but mostly for yourself. This is beyond work, friends, loyalty—this is potentially fatal madness."

"I know," whispers Rufus through gritted teeth, as tears rise in his eyes, "I know."

"Then come home! You're all the family I have, and I will not lose you to this stupid idea of revenge."

"*Honour,*" says Rufus, holding onto the notion that he is somehow in the right.

"Revenge," Daniel corrects.

"Look, once this is done, I'm out." Daniel narrows his eyes, grimacing as though he is absorbing pain. He clearly doesn't believe Rufus. "Truly. I agree, all this is too much, but Flossy was good to me, and I cannot let it pass. He needs justice—after what I just saw, *I* need to see justice."

Daniel winces. "Not like this, please—"

"I need to talk to Hayden."

"Why?" Daniel drops his shoulders, sighing with his entire body.

"Mae must pay for what she did. It's up to Hayden if he pays with her."

Although I destroyed Daniel's talisman rose, I have kept my distance during this conversation—forcing myself to stay on mission and not lament the fact he *isn't* reacting to my presence. However, a wave suddenly emanates from him, like a sorrowful call, a cry for help to a higher power, and it soaks into my most inner being just as powerfully as if we were holding the rose between us. I may not consider myself to be a 'higher-anything,' but I am certain our souls connect and instantly vow that I will not leave this place until both Daniel and Rufus are safe.

A door opens down the road, blasting an icy chill into the already frosty night.

The glitch is not subtle, is it?

Hayden steps out into the street, leaving the light from his house shining into the road. Despite it being somewhere in the small hours of the night and logic saying he should be asleep, Hayden is warmly dressed, like he is expecting to go out. He quickly spots Rufus and produces a grin that curdles my blood as it cuts through the darkness.

Why does Daniel have to be here? Rufus would be bad enough. Kath's voice echoes in my mind: *Get them out of here.*

"Hey," Hayden says casually. "Why are you hanging out down here?"

"I was just seeing Dan off, we bumped into each other on the way over," Rufus replies, trying to hold onto his composure.

Hayden eyes up Daniel, waiting to see if he is going to confirm or deny Rufus' lie.

"I was on my way home from work and we crossed paths." Daniel sounds convincing, but his aura mixes with red and grey-blue. Normally his leading colours are green and indigo—caring and gentle, not anxious or sad. Hayden's—well, let's just say Hayden's colours are 'heavy' and not dwell on him any longer than necessary for me to see them. "This can wait," Daniel says with a measured sense of authority. "Come on, Rufus, you can chat in the daytime—right, Hayden?"

Hayden cocks his head. That arrogant tilt sends my heart thudding through my chest. "No, it's cool, let's do it now. I was up anyway."

"It's late," Daniel says limply.

"Or early, depending on how you look at it." Hayden shrugs. "Come, too, Daniel. I don't think you've ever been to my garage before?"

Sure of the answer, Hayden doesn't wait for a reply. Instead, he ushers the brothers forward, walking them towards his house. Forgoing my ideal to keep away, I scream, trying to tug on their arms, but my voice chokes and my hands grip nothing but air.

Briefly skipping in front, Hayden shuts his front door before wandering across the garage forecourt, making insignificant remarks about the cars he has parked there.

As though under a spell, my body switches to autopilot, but as I walk into the garage, my mind struggles to repress the memories that flood in. If memory lane was a happy place, this video replay might be enjoyable, but my skin crawls and burns with every step and the part of my brain that forgets I am already dead screams at me to run.

There is a small showroom to one side of the office and a large workshop at the rear of the building. In between is a breakroom that doubles up as a waiting area for customers while their cars are serviced. Hayden and his mates have always used the breakroom like a social club, so it is no surprise that he escorts Daniel and Rufus there now, casually tapping on the staircase handrail as he walks past. The metallic echo makes me shudder. To most people, those stairs simply lead to a boring storage area, but they also link to Hayden's house, and I've been pushed down those stairs numerous times.

"Beer?" Hayden says, opening the fridge.

"No, thanks," says Daniel. "I'm driving."

"Right," Hayden replies sarcastically, throwing a can at Rufus. "So, what's up?"

Rufus fidgets with the top of the can, making no attempt to open it. If he isn't careful, he never will because he is going to twist the ring pull off in the wrong direction.

"Surely you didn't get me up at this time for shits and giggles?"

"No, of course not." Rufus too easily sounds like a child.

A thud comes from downstairs and lights appear in the rear carpark. "Do you work during the night?" asks Daniel.

"Business never stops," grins Hayden. "It's pretty boomin' actually—thanks to Mae."

Rufus sneers at the mention of her name.

"Something to say, little brother?"

"Your business was fine before."

"Before Mae, you mean?" Hayden smirks.

Rufus nods.

"Small chips—different potatoes."

"You need to get out. Now." Rufus stands himself straight like a little colt trying to prove to a stallion he also has balls.

Hayden sees his brother's stance and flares his nostrils. "Or what?"

Another thud comes from downstairs. What is going on down there?

Daniel looks panicked. "We don't want—"

"What? Trouble?" Hayden smirks. "What trouble could there be between brothers?"

Daniel turns to Rufus, silently pleading for him to see sense and leave.

"Why would there be trouble? The half-brother of my half-brother can be counted as my brother—isn't that right, Rufus?" Hayden scoffs. "Even if Leo might be about to redefine those bounds."

"It's Leo I've come to talk to you about," Rufus says, sensing an opportunity instead of walking away as Daniel indicates. "And Flossy."

Daniel grimaces and momentarily Hayden pauses before his scornful sneer returns. Is it possible that a line has been crossed, even for him?

"There's nothing to say about either of them," calls Mae from the storage gallery. If I was feeling kind, I'd say she's standing like a supermodel in a short, low-cut dress as her hair flows over her shoulders—but I'm not.

"Quite right, my love," Hayden replies, his words prickling my already frozen skin.

"I was hoping to talk without Mae," Rufus says boldly.

"Really?" Mae tosses her hair behind her back, exposing a little more chest than she was before.

Subtle, bitch, real subtle.

It works though because Hayden laughs. At what point she revealed her true character, I have no idea, but Hayden, despite his previous preference for weak, easily led women, obviously thinks his new business venture and partner are worth it all. Perhaps if his father really will not give him the validation he has been dancing like a proverbial monkey for since he was in nappies, he has decided this beautiful, toxic woman is the power-hungry substitute he has been waiting for.

After all, poisons and toxins will always be happy to mix, no matter how lethal the results.

"A fight is coming, you know?" Rufus asks Hayden, ignoring Mae.

"Of course it is—we've been waging it long enough." Hayden groans.

"I'm trying to give you a way out," Rufus says through gritted teeth.

"A way out, where?" Hayden laughs. "We provoked Leo. That was always going to happen, one way or another. We can't coexist, he and I. I'd hoped you'd come with me, but it seems like you've picked a side." He shrugs, turning up his nose. "So be it."

"Why was it always going to happen?" Daniel is desperately trying to keep lines of communication open, but I do not need Hayden to answer to know the truth. Suddenly it is all too clear to me. I was right about Mae being a substitute for his father, but it is more than that. Despite everything, he thinks he is in control of her, because she has blinded him by providing an even greater gift than power and recognition—the downfall of Leo's reign over the shadows in this town. He couldn't care less if Lianna is the real kingpin, without her minions she is vulnerable to exposure so he can destroy or repurpose her at a later date.

No. Mae has stoked a fire that already burned and nothing—absolutely nothing—would please him more than taking out the brother that has overshadowed him all his life.

"Destiny." Hayden says, standing straight, glancing up at Mae.

For a second the downtrodden voice of Hayden's wife whispers in my ears. 'He never looked that way at me,' she says. 'I was never enough.'

I want to shake her and choke out every drop of self-deprecation. 'No. *He* is not enough,' I reply—for once I do not need the voice within to correct me.

Mae triumphantly laughs, declaring, "Hook, line, and *sinker*!"

"They're at the yard?" Hayden asks, smiling.

"Yep." The glee on Mae's face is frightening. Slipping on a designer jacket, she slowly struts down the staircase like an overconfident, randy peacock. "See?" Turning up the volume, she spins her phone around, showing multiple live feeds of a fight. To them, Leo's element of surprise is wholly unsurprising. She has been preparing for this since the day she arrived in Adtoft.

"People will die—on both sides!" Daniel cries.

"Not the ones who matter. It's funny how easily people can be paid for a little time inside. Our main guys are working downstairs, and we're happily tucked up in our beds, far-far away from any 'nasty' business." Mae's sweet sarcasm makes me want to commit a crime of my own.

"They'll track you." Rufus sniggers.

Mae scowls. "No, they won't. I can hack security feed without leaving a trace to me."

"Signals all go somewhere."

"Very true, and this one will go to Leo's." Mae curls her lip. "Or maybe even your house."

"Look, Rufus. You came to warn me. I let you come to warn *you*. You thought you had two hours, well, I am telling you now, you have none." Hayden's tone is hard but has a minuscule sense of an apology.

Daniel's face tells me he understands, but Rufus asks: "What do you mean?"

"You're either an extra alibi, or another victim." Mae has zero apology in her tone as she pulls a knife from her jacket.

Daniel immediately steps backwards, pulling Rufus with him.

"Des recommended an axe," Mae says, turning the immaculate nine-inch blade over in her hand. "But I told him that I've had such fun times with this knife that I am reluctant to change now. Daddy had a beautiful sheath made for it—see, it tucks in almost any jacket unseen, but it is there, ready for action."

"You fucking bitch!" Rufus mutters, backing away, but Hayden, who was always disturbingly fast, flies at him, slamming his right fist into Rufus' cheek, crunching his nose before he pulls his hand away. It will be a miracle if that isn't broken.

So many feelings race in and around me—love and hate; hope and fear; panic and despair—causing my insecure heart to roar.

Daniel clenches his fist, swinging for Hayden, wobbling him just as he shifts his weight to punch Rufus again. Knocked back, rage flashes through Hayden's eyes. Bellowing, he charges forward, rugby tackling Daniel into a table before throwing him to the floor. Rufus jumps to Daniel's defence, but Hayden is bigger, stronger, and has years of practice defending himself—sending Rufus through the breakroom doorway and into a parked car with little more than a grunt.

Hayden grins. He is enjoying this. Such violence really is child's play to him and if he cannot personally fight Leo tonight, this will do while his minions do the groundwork. After all, beating one disloyal brother is almost as good as another.

My body trembles as the look that has frozen my entire being sets into Hayden. He becomes a new beast when his adrenaline truly fires. This is the look that I knew would one day kill me—and the same one that leant over the cliff four years ago and laughed.

*Well, the joke is on him,* says my voice within.

Hayden storms after Rufus, ready to pummel him where he lays, but Daniel jumps him from behind. Tussling, they stagger around the workshop until Daniel trips, giving Hayden the opening he was waiting for to launch a frenzied attack while Mae cheers him on. Suddenly, I feel the cloak of control that Hayden has smothered me in break into a million pieces and I grab his shoulders, spinning him round to face me and don't let go.

We stand, eyes fixed, while the rest of the world melts away. His pupils dilate as he tries to make sense of what he is seeing, while in their reflection I see my eyes burn with a fire that was longing to be set free.

Grinning, my hand effortlessly slips to his throat, and I mimic the cold, heartless smirk that he bestowed on me so many times. "Hi, honey, did you miss me?" I ask.

"Who the fuck is she?" Mae shouts but doesn't dare move.

Frozen in painful heaps on the floor, Daniel and Rufus stare while Hayden trembles from head to toe, gulping repeatedly, but saying nothing.

An icy wind whips from behind me, encapsulating us in hues of brown, grey, murky red, and black. Power surges through every ounce of my body. In this moment I know that I could kill him. With just my will, my hands could crush his throat and I am sure the world would be better off.

Omi's words come to me. *"You are a plethora of colour within, you must banish negative energy and shine, my angel, shine."*

If I give into the darkness, it will consume me, and Hayden will still have won. He is the lasting anchor of my darkness.

Yet the power is mine.

He cannot take it.

Let the glitch be his judge and executioner, not me.

I will banish the darkness and cut the chain.

*It is my time to shine.*

Shifting my weight whilst grinning, I prepare to push him away when a stream of white and blue lights shines through the back windows.

Mae is the first to react, running to the office door to peer through the glass windows. "Shit!" she shouts, instantly returning. "The little fuckers called the cops! So much for a fuckin' brotherly warning!"

"No, we didn't," mutters Rufus, picking himself up off the floor. "But it serves you right, you murderous piece of shit."

Had I more time, I might lament Rufus' lack of sense, but the bear, with her foot in a trap, sensing her downfall, settles on taking a victim with her. Not wasting a second,

Mae throws herself in his direction, knife in hand, ready to plunge.

Panic is replaced by determination as I fling Hayden into his office with such force that the door cracks as he bounces off it. With no time to revel or run, I transport through the air, delivering myself in front of Rufus a second before Mae reaches him, thrusting her away before our bodies meet.

The speed of impact topples me backwards onto the floor and, unable to control myself, I take Rufus down with me, semi using him to break my fall—but not enough as I suddenly feel pain for the first time in years.

Mae stares at me, shocked, but not totally stunned as she shouts, *"What the fuck are you?"*

The knife has gone, or I think it has until I look down and see it lodged in my side as red spreads across my white dress. Cold inches over my body, but I don't have time to appreciate the feeling as Hayden springs out of his office, gun in hand.

"Enough!" he shouts, aiming the gun at me. "I won't fuckin' miss this time!"

A shot fires, whisking through the air. Time slows as I watch the bullet hurtle across the garage, cutting a path through atoms and auras as it lands in its target's chest.

Hayden drops to the ground and Mae screams, but rather than running to his aid, she heads for the back door—and straight into the cuffs of the police as they fill the room. With his gun still drawn, Sean runs to Hayden, standing over him as blood bubbles out of his mouth.

"Your father-in-law was right. If it were my daughter, I'd not let it go either," Sean whispers through gritted teeth.

"There's enough shit in my prisons without putting you there."

Choking, Hayden shudders, and I see his chest deflate as his soul leaves him. If the warm breeze takes him, I do not feel it. Perhaps the glitch doesn't want me to know the location of Hayden's next—possibly I do not need to know anymore.

Daniel rushes to my side, heaving from pain and distress as he links his fingers with mine. Our eyes meet in the same realm for the first time while our souls rejoice like two lost travellers finally uniting.

Daniel's voice crackles. "You came back."

I softly chuckle. "I never left."

His body deflates, yet instantly rises as something flickers behind his eyes, and he snaps into practical mode, assessing the damage. As Daniel shouts for help, the next flicker in his eyes tells me what I need to know without asking.

Already approaching, Sean immediately stops, calling for an ETA on an ambulance.

"Two minutes," the voice on the radio says.

"Hold on," commands Daniel, bending to softly kiss me. Leaning his forehead against mine, like he did at the beach, our laboured breath combines. "Do you hear me?" he says, struggling to maintain his composure. "Hold on, you *can* survive this. I'll not lose you now—*just hold on.*"

As waves of white and purple dance all around, a golden beam envelops me. Suddenly, a warm breeze soothes my pain and I smile, realising that one way or another, all will be well.

I want to live. For so long I felt like I was nothing and so had nothing to lose. Now I know I am something—someone—and have everything to lose, but I am also willing to give my all in the defence of another. Finally, I am the person I want to be, but if the breeze has come to take me, then I will go with a sense of purpose—with both a fulfilled past and a hopeful future.

"Guide me home and lead me onwards," I whisper serenely to the breeze.

Footsteps hurriedly approach and Daniel sits back although doesn't loosen his grip on my hand.

"Honey, can you hear me?" a lady in green asks as she swiftly kneels beside me.

"Yes," I say. "Yes, I can."

"Excellent, let's get you to the hospital." She smiles and my senses flush with more life than I have ever felt before. The simple joy of being seen and heard is truly invigorating.

"What's your name, sweetie?" she asks.

My tongue rolls back, ready to answer, but I pause.

I'll not use my name of old.

She died long ago, and I'll only look forward, not back.

I take a deep breath.

"Call me Angel."

If you liked *They Call Me Angel*, please consider leaving a review on Amazon, Goodreads, or any other social media that you use. Honest reviews are invaluable to any author, but especially independent ones like Alexia.

If you would like to join Alexia's newsletter and be the first to receive updates on forthcoming novels as well as read exclusive short stories, please visit www.alexiamuellerushbrook.co.uk

Utopia surrounded by dystopia, the balance of self, nature, machine, secrets, and society has never been so delicate

THE MINORITY RULE TRILOGY
by Alexia Muelle-Rushbrook
IS AVAILABLE TO READ NOW

# ACKNOWLEDGEMENTS

To all who have encouraged me, championed me, and helped along the way—THANK YOU!

My husband, Sergio, must top the list of appreciation because he listens to me witter on for hours, reads the first draft before anyone else, and keeps me going on days when I threaten to quit. I cannot forget my wonderful beta readers—I am eternally grateful that you were willing to take the time to read Angel's story and provide such great feedback—and my brilliant editors, Belle Manuel and Jessica Netzke. Working with you both is such a positive experience and my manuscript is certainly the better for your care. Last, but by no means least, my readers. A million thank yous for taking a chance on a shy, indie author. It means the world.

# AUTHOR BIO

Alexia Muelle-Rushbrook is a sci-fi and fantasy author who lives with her family in rural Suffolk, UK. Having spent her life surrounded by animals, she has a passion for the natural world and an interest in genetics—both of which feature in her debut work, *The Minority Rule trilogy*, alongside a dystopian tale of difficult families, morally grey areas, and artificial intelligence.

A self-confessed geek, Alexia has always found solace in books and her own storytelling—although it wasn't until she received positive feedback for her terrier poetry that she reached for her dream of being an author. Having found the courage to put pen to paper, Alexia now has no plans to stop, and she hopes to write across sci-fi and fantasy subgenres—keeping both herself and the voices in her head happy!

Printed in Great Britain
by Amazon